Javelin Man

By Gerald Rainey

Self-Published

June 30, 2022

Introduction

One Sunday morning my wife, Rikki, and I were in church listening to a sermon about the trial of Jesus of Nazareth. The pastor briefly discussed how Pontius Pilate, Governor of Judea, conducted the trial and unsuccessfully attempted to free Jesus. Our pastor moved on to the crucifixion with little discussion about Pilate. I wondered why Pilate tried to release Jesus rather than just execute him as a troublemaker if nothing else. I wondered whatever happened to Pilate. I began to research and what I discovered was nothing short of remarkable!

This book is a historical fiction. It's a series of historical, documented facts combined with conjecture to paint a picture of Pilate's life and how it led to one of the most significant events of human history: the culmination of the trial, crucifixion and resurrection of Jesus the Christ. The research I conducted incorporated hundreds of websites, papers, documents, and commentaries of the period. I researched the Christian gospels, the Apocrypha, the writings of historian Josephus, Roman documents from the Vatican, and so much more. Very little is known of Marcus Levilius Pontius Pilate before or after the trial of Jesus. What I have attempted to create is a plausible tale of how Pilate's life developed and why he tried to free Jesus rather than execute him. You will be the judge if I have succeeded.

I've incorporated footnotes through the book to explain various words, titles, military structures and so forth. I did so to eliminate an appendix. The links in the bibliography are those of websites I researched and used in this writing, so kudos to those who posted this information on the internet.

We know that much of the information on the internet is false, unproven, fictitious or misrepresented. Yet, in the midst of that, there is truth. I validated the information as much as I could

Gerald Rainey   Javelin Man

through cross references, research and supporting documentation. My goal is to present a factual novel interspersed with conjecture to tie elements together.

I would like to thank the following people for their support and assistance with this project:

- Doctor Larry Burke – a good friend and professor for reviewing the timeline and events of the trial, crucifixion and resurrection for accuracy.
- Gregg and Mary – my dear neighbors and avid readers who proofed it for flow and content.
- My wife Rikki – For encouraging and supporting me through this challenging project.

I hope you enjoy reading this account as much as I did researching and writing it.

Thank you

Gerald (Jerry) Rainey
Javelin-man@comcast.net

Other books by the author

- *Wuhan* – Fiction/Novel – Virus outbreak and coverup by China

- *The Memory Project* – Fiction/Novel – When a mutated virus cures Alzheimer's Disease – sequel to 19Q

- *19Q* – Fiction/Novel – Story of genetics gone bad

- *The Fiduciary Guide* – Explanation of fiduciaries for the layman

- *The Professional Fiduciary Guide* – Considerations and case studies of a professional fiduciary

Table of Contents

Chapter		Year	Pages
1	The End of the Republic	44 BC	1-6
2	The Praetorian Guard	27 BC	7-15
3	Sejanus and Pilate	21-20 BC	16-21
4	The Friendship	3 AD	22-32
5	Brothers in Battle	14 AD	33-46
6	Introducing Caligula	19 AD	47-51
7	Struggle for Power	23-26 AD	52-65
8	Pilate in Judea	27 AD	66-82
9	The Protests	28-29 AD	83-101
10	The End of Sejanus	30-31 AD	102-128
11	The Betrayal	31 AD	129-154
12	The Trial	31 AD	155-172
13	The Crucifixion	31 AD	173-184
14	The Resurrection	31 AD	185-197
15	The Letters	32 AD	198-207
16	Transfer of Power	34 AD	208-212

Chapter		Year	Pages
17	Mount Gerizim	36 AD	213-229
18	Pilate called to Account	37 AD	230-264
	Epilogue		264-266
	Author's Comments		266-269
	Reference		270-276

Cast of Characters – In order of appearance

- *Julius Caesar* – Last emperor of the Roman Republic
- *Marc Antony* – General of Roman military
- *Caesar Augustus* (Gaius Octavius) – First emperor of the Roman Empire
- *Albus Antoninus* – Secretary of Senate under Caesar Augustus
- *Lucius Seius Strabo* - Commander of the Praetorian Guard under Caesar Augustus – Father of Lucius Sejanus
- *Lucius Aelius Sejanus* – Commander Praetorian Guard under Caesar Tiberius
- *Marcus Levilius Pontius Pilate* - Governor of Judea
- *Livia* – Wife of Caesar Augustus
- *Tiberius Caesar Augustus* – Stepson of Caesar Augustus and second emperor of the Roman Empire
- *Drusus Julius Caesar* – Biological son of Caesar Tiberius
- *Claudia Procula* – Pilate's wife
- *General Germanicus* – Nephew of Caesar Tiberius adopted as a son
- *Caligula* – Born as Gaius Caesar Augustus Germanicus – Adopted grandson of Caesar Tiberius, son of General Germanicus and Agrippina the Elder, third emperor of the Roman Empire
- *Apicata* – Ex-wife of Sejanus
- *Junilla* – Four year-old daughter of Sejanus
- *Livilla* – Wife of Drusus Julius Caesar
- *Joseph Ben Caiaphas* – Head priest of Jewish Sanhedrin
- *Herod Antipas* – Tetrarch or 'king' of the Jewish nation – son of Herod the Great
- *Manlius* – Pilate's secretary in Judea
- *John the Baptist* – Jewish Prophet near Jerusalem
- *Gaius Asinius Gallus* – Senator accused of being a public enemy to Rome

Cast of Characters – In order of appearance (continued)

- *Jesus of Nazareth* – Jewish Messiah
- *Antonia Minor* – Sister-in-law of Tiberius, daughter of General Marc Antony
- *Marcus Antonius Pallas* – Freedman of Antonia Minor
- *Naevius Sutorius Macro* – Commander of the police in Rome, successor to Sejanus of the Praetorian Guard
- *Lucius Bracchus* – Senior Senator and Secretary of the senate under Caesars Tiberius and Caligula
- *Joseph of Arimathea* – Pharisee and senior member of the Jewish Sanhedrin
- *Nicodemus* – Pharisee and member of the Jewish Sanhedrin
- *Mary, Martha and Lazarus* – Friends of Jesus of Nazareth – Lazarus was raised from the dead
- *Annas* – father-in-law to Caiaphas and prior head priest of the Sanhedrin
- *Judas Iscariot* – Disciple of Jesus of Nazareth
- *Barabbas* – Prisoner freed on Passover
- *Longinus* – Senior centurion who conducted the crucifixion
- *Gistas and Dysmas* – Two criminals crucified with Jesus of Nazareth
- *Dositheus* – Samaritan leader who led the ascent of Mount Gerizim
- *Janus Mitius* – Commander who engaged Dositheus and the Samaritans at Mount Gerizim
- *Lucius Vitellius* – Legate of Syria
- *Linus Marcellus* – Successor governor of Judea to Pontius Pilate
- *Tiberius Gemellus* – Co-Caesar with Caligula and his cousin
- *Incitatus* – Caligula's horse

"If you declare with your mouth, "Jesus is Lord," and believe in your heart that God raised him from the dead, you will be saved."

Romans 10:19

Chapter 1   The End of the Republic
44 BC

Rome. The great city, just thirty kilometers[1] from the Mediterranean Sea, is hailed as the center of the Roman Republic and arguably the world power at the time. It boasts the largest, most sophisticated port in the world able to process thousands of merchant vessels from every known country. Rome rules the Mediterranean without question. Their quest to militarily conquer the Mediterranean countries and ultimately the known world is well known and feared, yet the internal political factions undermine the future of the republic.

The Roman progressive democratic republic sets the standard for a free society to operate as a democracy. In years past a body of 900 senators established law and policies through democratic vote. The emperor was a figurehead and ultimate authority appointed and confirmed by the senate to operate in unison with the senate and carry out their wishes. It was an effective government until emperors past began to rule as dictators neglecting the democratic process and the Senate. The governing senate dropped from 900 senators to a meager 200 over the years. It was a validation of a fact: whoever had the support of the military led the country with or without democratic support. Julius Caesar had that support.

On this particular evening, the streets of this mighty city were cold, dark and empty. The March air was chilling as it blew in from the Mediterranean Sea. Emperor Julius Caesar hurried past the marble columns in the Theater of Pompey toward the curia[2], a chamber designed for the Roman Senate to meet and debate issues. It was the center of the Republic where the democratic process unfolded. Tonight, it was the place for a special meeting called by the senate.

---

[1] 30 kilometers – 19 miles
[2] Curia – Latin for court. A place of assembly, court, or council particularly of the senate

Gerald Rainey   Javelin Man

    Caesar's footsteps echoed off the stone walls and walkway as he briskly made his way along the corridor, through the courtyards, past ponds and ornate statues of emperors past that lined the approach to the curia. As he entered the chamber, he noticed that only about a third of the senators were there to greet him rather than the full senate of two hundred plus. A handful of senators said, "Hail, Caesar," in unison as Caesar entered and passed by them and stepped onto the stage to face the group.

    Julius Caesar was a middle-aged man of normal stature. He was slightly balding and had the air of a leader by the way he took command presence even though he had been emperor less than a year. Wearing his white toga with purple trim that was draped over his shoulder, he settled into his seat in the center of the stage eyeing the senators before him with curiosity. His chair faced rows of seats encircling the platform in a half-moon shape, each row slightly higher than the first, creating a theater like setting. It was designed to maximize acoustics so anyone could be heard from any location, and at the center of the stage where the emperor sat everything could be heard. Most of the senators took their seats while some stood close to the stage.

    "What is so important as to call this special session at this hour?" Caesar asked in disgust. He was obviously irritated that he had been called to a special session of the senate at such a late hour, interrupting his evening festivities.

    Senator Tillius Cimber glanced at the other senators, cleared his throat, and approached the emperor. He was a middle-aged man and known among the senators as being a bit wild. He lowered his head and gaze as he knelt before Caesar, slowly extended his hand and presented the emperor with a document. "Mighty Caesar. I petition you to recall my brother, Publius, from exile."

    "Publius?" Caesar laughed. "This is the important matter that called for a special session of the senate!?" he said showing his agitation toward the group. "That would explain why less than half of the senate is here!" he said scoffing. Several senators started to encircle the two men on the platform to show their support[3] for

Cimber's petition as others left their seats and walked toward the stage.

"I plead with Caesar to consider my request," Cimber added as he extended the document closer to the emperor. Caesar dismissively waived the petition away in disgust. In one, swift motion Cimber reached out and grabbed the emperor's arm and yanked him close. With his free hand he grabbed Caesar's toga and pulled it down around his shoulders, thus disabling the emperor and restricting his movements. The toga acted like a straitjacket, pinning Caesar's arms against his side.

"Why this violence?" Caesar yelled as he struggled to free himself from Cimber's grasp.

---****---

Torches dimly illuminated the walkway to the Theater of Pompey as Roman General Mark Antony hurried toward the curia to intercept Emperor Julius Caesar before he met with the senate in a specially called meeting. He could hear his footsteps echo off the marble walls and empty walkways. His heart was pounding as his pace quickened. Unaware that he was but moments behind the emperor, Antony walked quickly along the walkway toward the curia. His eyes darted back and forth searching the dark corners where opposition could hide.

He had recently met with Senator Maximus Dysius who vaguely informed him of a plot by some senators to assassinate the new emperor. In less than a year, Caesar had cast aside the structure of the Roman Republic and installed himself as a dictator with absolute rule and complete disregard for the senate or its authority, thus infuriating many of the senators. Antony believed Senator Dysius was telling the truth about the plot because he could see the fear in Dysius's eyes and hear the trembling in his voice when he told him. What they were about to do was murder

---

[3] Senate voting – the voting process for the senate was indicated by senators gathering around those they supported or voted for.

the emperor and Dysius was scared. General Antony was determined to stop it.

As General Antony approached the theater, Consul Gaius Trebonius stepped from the shadows and intercepted him. The assassins suspected General Antony would try to warn Caesar of the plot and planned to intercept him if he tried.

"Hail, General," Trebonius said as Mark Antony approached.

Antony was startled and immediately began to draw his sword when he recognized the man. "Trebonius! What are you doing here?"

"Antony. This is not the time nor the place for you to be," he replied. He looked at Antony's hand still on his sword. "It is best if you return from where you came, my friend," he said calmly.

Suddenly, the two men could hear someone yelling from the curia. They looked at each other and realized the plot was unfolding. Antony knew there was nothing he could do to save the emperor. He was too late. He had a choice to make; either fight Trebonius on the spot and attempt to stop the assassination alone or flee. Being a general in the Roman military he knew how to calculate strength, opposition, and the likely outcome for every battle. This battle was already lost. He believed Trebonius would prefer not to fight but would if challenged. Antony nodded to Trebonius and took his hand off his sword. "It appears I am too late," he said.

"For Rome," Trebonius said as he watched Antony turn and flee leaving him in the shadows of the theater.

---****---

Caesar struggled to free himself from Cimber's grasp. As the two fought, Senator Servillius Casca thrust a dagger toward Caesar's neck, which narrowly missed. Caesar grabbed Casca's arm and held fast yelling, "Casca! What are you doing, you villain?"

Senator Casca was surprised at the strength Caesar had and feared both he and Cimber would be overtaken. "Help, brothers," Casca yelled as the two struggled with the emperor. Twelve senators quickly surrounded the three struggling men at the throne and joined in the murder, each producing a dagger, and began blindly stabbing at the emperor as the other senators crept in to watch the assassination. Caesar struggled and tried to get away from the bloody assault pulling Casca and Cimber with him. Most of the thrusts were superficial and only injured the emperor, who was blinded by his own blood. As he fought to break free and out of the curia, he slipped on the bloody steps of the portico and fell to the floor. The mob continued to surround him, jabbing and yelling "For Rome" as the defenseless Caesar tried to crawl away, bloodied and confused. Each thrust resulted in a cry by the fallen emperor that echoed through the empty theater. As the life blood flowed from Caesar's body, he stopped crawling and rolled onto his back.

    The mob stopped momentarily and gazed at their fallen emperor. Caesar lay on the floor in pools of blood still seeping from his mutilated body. He tried to wipe the blood from his eyes to see. His toga was stained crimson from the bloody assault. He was gasping for air as he faced his murderers and saw his friend and benefactor, Marcus Junius Brutus, standing above him holding a dagger in his hand. The dagger was dripping blood. "You, too, Brutus?" the emperor whispered in a faint, weak voice. Without reply, Brutus thrust the dagger into his friend one more time.

    When the deed was done, the senators stepped back, encircling the body as they gazed upon their fallen emperor as the other senators moved closer to see. Caesar's white toga was stained red with blood from the twenty-three stab wounds he received. Even so, only one wound was fatal. Blood was splattered on the men's clothing, the emperor's seat, the floor, the walls. The lifeless corpse of the emperor lay on the cold, marble floor in front of them. The emperor's dead eyes stared upwards as each assailant leaned forward and used the emperor's toga to wipe the blood off his dagger. Brutus was last and, instead of cleaning his bloodstained dagger and hand, he raised it high above his head in victory. "Rome is free!" he yelled.

Gerald Rainey   Javelin Man

    The other senators failed to join in the celebration and, instead, quickly fled the room leaving Brutus alone with his dead friend.
    It was March 15, 44BC. Emperor Julius Caesar was dead. It was the end of the Roman Republic and the beginning of the Roman Empire.

Chapter 2   Creation of the Empire
27 BC

The splendor of Rome was evident by the engineering marvels visible everywhere, none more so than on the main roads leading to the center of the city. Expansive boulevards were lined with buildings of stone and marble standing a hundred feet high. Giant marble columns and facias[4] were adorned with eagles, wreaths and decorative emblems made of gold and brass. In the center of the city stood the palace with marbled walkways leading to marbled steps, which led to the balconies of the senate and emperor affording them the best view down the main road of the city.

    Today, the boulevard was filled with thousands of infantry soldiers in military attire with swords, javelins and spears. The soldiers were in a checkerboard formation by cohort[5] in rows of three cohorts across and six deep holding their weapons. They faced the palace and stood at attention in front of the 100 ballistae[6], followed by the 1,000 cavalry and 2,000 archers. Tens of thousands of citizens lined the roadways behind them and beyond. They had all come to the palace with great anticipation to see the new emperor.

    Rome had been in civil wars for seventeen years following the assassination of Julius Caesar. The Roman government, in particular the senate, was so dysfunctional they preferred to not have an emperor installed until the dust settled on the civil wars being fought on multiple fronts. The main successor to the throne would be Gaius Octavius, the great nephew of Julius Caesar and a member of the Julian family. Only those who followed the imperial family line, known as 'Julians', could be emperor. None of the rebel

---

[4] Facia – A flat surface where the wall and roofline meet
[5] Cohort – 480 men
[6] Ballistae – Plural for ballista, which is a wooden type of field crossbow capable of shooting large projectiles of 45 kilos (100 pounds) up to 457 meters (500 yards).

factions waging civil war in their quest for power were of the Julian family.

The assailants of Julius Caesar's assassination dispersed into opposing factions who collaborated with regions to conduct war against Rome. General Marc Antony collaborated with Cleopatra of Egypt and were the last faction to be hunted down and defeated. Though General Antony was not a conspirator against Julius Caesar, he joined with Cleopatra and opposed the new emperor in an attempt to use his military acumen and power to become emperor of Rome. Their defeat closed the final chapter of the civil wars and resulted in a time of celebration. After seventeen years, the Senate was ready to install and support their new emperor before the citizens of Rome.

Inside the senate chamber, nearly 200 men dressed in purple with gold trimmed togas, rather than their everyday white, sat in their assigned seats facing the throne where Gaius Octavius sat wearing a white toga with gold trim. It was the same seat where Julius Caesar was assassinated seventeen years prior. Gaius was just twenty when the assassination occurred. Now, at thirty-seven he was in the prime of his life, strong and fit, the epitome of a Roman commander[7]. His hair was short and cropped across his brow making him look even younger. Standing next to him was the senior senator Albus Antoninus, an older, wise, well-respected senator and secretary of the senate. Senator Antoninus unraveled a scroll, held it up, and began to read with a strong voice.

"We the senate, hereby declare that all of the regions under dispute by factions who opposed Rome and who waged civil war against Rome are, once again, under Roman rule."

Several senators clapped but were quickly hushed.

"We the senate, hereby acknowledge Gaius Octavius as the commander of the Roman armies who, under his leadership, was

---

[7] Commander – The ranks of the Roman army can be confusing. In this book, we will use Commander to represent various ranks associated with leading a contingent of military units, similar to a general or field commander.

triumphant in the civil wars waged against Rome for seventeen years.

We the senate herby acknowledge that the testamentary documents of the estate of Julius Caesar adopted Gaius Octavius as his son and beneficiary of his estate, name, and title.

Therefore, we, the senate, herby convey to Gaius Octavius the title and name of Imperator Caesar Augustus, princeps[8]."

The senator rolled the scroll up, turned to Augustus, knelt and bowed his head as he said, "Hail, Caesar Augustus."

The other senators in the chamber stood and said in unison, "Hail Caesar Augustus," several times. Then, everyone broke out in clapping and cheers.

Julius Caesar was assassinated because of his determination to install a dictatorship over Rome in less than a year. With the defeat of the last rebel faction and culmination of the civil wars, the Senate finally acted upon the testamentary documents of Julius Caesar and confirmed his relative as successor emperor to his great uncle, Julius Caesar.

Today, the Roman Empire had begun.

Roman Standards

The exit from the senate chambers to the balcony was framed with large, black marble columns trimmed with white lace blowing gently in the breeze. Rows of flowering roses and geraniums lined the walkways along with statues and busts of prior emperors. Ten guards in full armament stood on each side of the exit and fanned out into the balcony where the standards[9] were displayed

---

[8] Princeps – the first in line or order, chief
[9] Standards - Imperial Standards – Bronze or brass symbols representing Rome mounted on poles or buildings, typically circular or an eagle with a lightening bolt.

across the railing and above the emperor's seat. Caesar Augustus exited the curia first, followed by thirty of the prominent senators who surrounded the throne. The remaining senators stood around the back of the balcony and spilled out onto the steps to the courtyard below. The crowd made a thunderous roar as the group appeared on the balcony and waved to the throng.

"Gaius, Gaius," was heard as thousands of people chanted their approval of their new leader and with great anticipation waited for the announcement. Gaius Octavius raised his hands to silence the crowd. Within seconds, it was completely still. He stepped aside as senator Albus Antoninus stepped up to the front of the balcony. Senator Antoninus unfurled the scroll and held it high for everyone to see.

"Citizens of Rome," he began with a loud, strong voice. The acoustics were superb. His voice bounced off the tall buildings framing the long entryway to the palace and down the boulevard to the joy and excitement of every listener. "Today, our civil wars have come to an end." The crowd roared with approval. Antoninus allowed them to continue for almost a full minute, then motioned for quiet. "Rome is strong. Rome is great. Today, we, the senate, herby install our new emperor of Rome; Imperator Caesar Augustus!"

The crowd roared with approval as trumpets blared on the sides of the platform and soldiers snapped to attention and saluted in unison. Pigeons were let out of cages and flew over the delighted crowds. Caesar Augustus smiled as he approached the railing at the front of the balcony and took in the sight. He raised his hands and the crowd got louder. At first, he welcomed the roar, but soon motioned for the crowds to be silent.

"My fellow Romans. Rome is, and will be, the greatest power the world has ever known." It was completely silent. He had their complete attention as he spoke in a quiet, but strong voice. "We are strong. We are loyal. We are compassionate and yes, we are full of fury." The crowd started to cheer, but Augustus continued, increasing his volume as he progressed. "No one shall ever defeat Rome. We will only be defeated by ourselves or by the gods. I commit my blood to you, to the gods, to Rome unto death." He raised his hands and the crowd exploded with excitement chanting, "Augustus, Augustus. Hail Caesar."

Caesar Augustus smiled broadly and opened his arms as if to welcome every person there. "Let the games begin!!" he ordered.

---****---

"And why are we here?" senator Antoninus asked from his seated position in the chamber while most of the other senators took their seats. A handful of senators were standing near the door ready to leave to watch the Ludi Romani[10].

The Ludi were competitive games similar to the Greek Olympic games of skill, strength and stamina and were a major source of entertainment for the citizenry. The games were often a celebration of a military victory in a battle or campaign. It was a means whereby leaders in a region, such as governors, could show off their strength with pomp and splendor. They were created exclusively for the military to participate in and demonstrate their skills such as archery, javelin, discus, weightlifting and hopscotch. Competition at the highest levels. The games were so popular amongst the Romans that the city of Rome had more than 165 games in a year.

Over the centuries the Roman government used barbaric and ruthless competitions of hand-to-hand combat in the games to administer capital punishment on criminals. Those condemned to die for a capital crime sometimes had the opportunity to obtain freedom if they fought well in the arena against a gladiator; a warrior trained to fight. Often, one would hear the voices of the condemned yell, "Those who are about to die salute you, Great Caesar." It was a last-ditch effort hoping that if they provided a high enough level of 'entertainment' to the emperor, their lives just might be spared. If not, then they would be killed by the gladiators in the arena in front of a rabid crowd of spectators as their criminal

---

[10] Ludi Romani – Roman Games

punishment. This form of justice created a perverse appetite for the gladiatorial events in the games thereby satisfying the blood lust of the citizens.

Today's games would offer the very best entertainment because they were to be conducted in honor of the newly installed emperor. Caesar Augustus knew the senators were anxious to get to the games, so this afforded him the perfect time to present his new ideas and plans with little resistance or objection to a captive audience.

Caesar Augustus was seated on his throne as he answered senator Antoninus. "There are four issues of the empire that I plan to address quickly, so I thought best to inform you of my intentions and start gaining your support…..early," he said as he seated himself.

"Are these military in nature?" one senator asked.

"Yes, in a sense. First, I believe Rome needs a standing army."

"What? Do you mean mandatory service of…..?" a senator asked but was cut off by Augustus.

"Yes, senator Cassius." Augustus chose his words carefully. "Rome has been in civil wars for seventeen years. If we require mandatory service of our men, they will know who Rome is and develop an allegiance to her through military discipline."

"You sound sure of yourself, Caesar," someone commented.

"I am. I have seen boys forged into men in minutes…in battle." Caesar stood to his feet as he continued. "Their devotion to each other and Rome is in their blood. I want every Roman male to know what that feels like, to know the honor of serving Rome to the extent you would lay down your life for her."

"Here, here," someone said.

"Starting age then, Caesar?" Antoninus asked.

"Young. Maybe sixteen."

"Prime of their life," someone called. "I can't remember when I was sixteen," another said as laughter erupted.

Caesar laughed with them. "Yes, senator. The prime of their lives. Full of vigor, energy, eager to learn, eager to apply, eager to rule."

"Eager to go to the games," someone called to a loud "Here, here."

"And how long shall they serve?" Antoninus asked.

"Twenty years," Augustus replied without hesitation.

The senators mumbled. "Twenty? That seems a bit much, Caesar."

Caesar Augustus stepped off the platform and stood before the senators. "A standing military will enable us to respond to any threat immediately. They will be well trained and well equipped. We will have Duxes[11] ready for battle, any battle, at any time. Rome will be strong and stay strong. These men will become Rome."

The senators began clapping as Caesar Augustus moved amongst the senators and continued. "Rome also needs roads that enable us to trade freely with the countries to the east. And on those roads, we need a communication network of couriers."

"Couriers?" a senator asked.

"Yes. Couriers who will deliver messages between regions, commanders, governors and senators. Our outermost strongholds must stay strong and in communication with Rome at all times."

"Here, here," came a reply.

"And your fourth item?" someone called.

Augustus smiled. "The creation of structured fire and police services."

"We have the military. Why would we need police?" someone asked.

Augustus returned to his throne and sat. "The military is for the protection and expansion of the empire. Fire services are self-explanatory. The police service, however, will be for the protection of the citizens of Rome. They will conduct arrests and detain criminals to be processed through our judicial system. But they will do more, much more than that."

---

[11] Dux – General of more than one provincial military unit.

"For example?" Someone asked.

"They will protect us; you and me."

"Bodyguards?" Antoninus asked

"Yes. Julius Caesar was assassinated right here, in this seat." Augustus stood and walked through the assembly again as he spoke. "It is not difficult to imagine there could be more assassination plots in the future against any of us. The police force will protect us and the citizens of Rome. That will be their only purpose," he said as he patted a senator on the shoulder. "They will be the Praetorian[12] Guard. We…" Augustus opened his arms to encompass the audience and continued "….will not fall victim to nefarious plots."

"And just how will you pay for the increased military, roads, courier service and police?" Senator Cassius asked.

Augustus smiled broadly. "Taxes." Several senators started to voice their objection when Augustus raised his hands to quiet them. "Not on Roman citizens, but on the people of the countries we occupy."

"Will that not create conflict and unrest when you attempt to collect those taxes?" someone asked from the crowd.

"Possibly, but I believe if we have strong governors in place to maintain peace with a show of strength, the foreigners will pay taxes as requested…..or suffer the consequences," Augustus replied.

"Very well, then, Caesar Augustus," Senator Cassius said as he stood and bowed to him. He continued with sweeping arms. "I believe _we_ are all in agreement with the direction you are going in….provided it is out the door to the games!!!!" he said to the sound of boisterous laughter and applause.

"So be it," Caesar Augustus said as he returned to his throne and watched the senators crowd out the exit and empty the chamber. He was in no hurry to attend the games; however, he knew he had to make an appearance. Once the curia was empty, he

---

[12] Praetorian – derived from praetor or high ranking Roman Civil Servant

slowly rose and proceeded to the balcony where he looked out on the city with the Circus Maximus arena in clear view. "Rome."

Gerald Rainey					Javelin Man

# Chapter 3	Sejanus and Pilate
21-20 BC

The assassination of Julius Caesar made Caesar Augustus well aware of the threat to his personal safety. Government leaders, particularly the emperor, were susceptible to conspiracies, assassinations, or removal from their position for a variety of reasons, some worthy; some not. His concern for his safety compelled him to establish the Praetorian Guard; a devout special military unit that acted as a bodyguard primarily for the emperor. Augustus sold the idea to the senate by implying the Guard would protect them as well. However, Caesar Augustus was first concerned with his own safety, not the senators. The Guard quickly evolved into a personal protection service for the emperor and reported directly to him.

Caesar was appointed the supreme military commander of the Roman military, which included the police force and the Praetorian Guard, tribune[13] and censor[14] for life. He alone controlled the power of Rome. To keep the Guard as a special military unit separate from the police force, many members of the Guard wore togas and civilian attire rather than the stiff, recognizable Roman military or police uniforms. This enabled them to blend in with civilians at all events. Each soldier hid their daggers and swords under their togas and tunics and were quick to use them should anyone be considered a threat to the emperor. Their actions were never questioned.

The Guard was a formidable source. It consisted of nine cohorts with three cohorts stationed around Rome and the rest spread amongst various cities and regions.

---

[13] Tribune – in this instance, the title of an elected official that acted as a check on the authority of the senate. A military tribune was equivalent to the rank of a colonel and was from the equestrian class commanding up to 1,000 soldiers
[14] Censor – a magistrate who conducted a census, supervising public morality, and overseeing aspects of the empire's finances.

Caesar Augustus appointed Lucius Seius Strabo as commander of the Praetorian Guard. Strabo was of the equestrian class[15] and was well connected to the Julian family, which provided him opportunities to serve Caesar at the highest level. That, combined with his military career as a field commander, made him a perfect fit for such an elevated, trusted position.

Commander Strabo had absolute authority over the entire guard. He also had the emperor's ear and complete trust since he reported directly to him. His duties consisted of primarily protecting the emperor, but also to conduct many of the administrative functions of the emperor. Caesar Augustus had such confidence in Strabo's abilities that he also delegated several of his ambitious plans to him to execute. The expansions of roads into various new territories of the Roman Empire were one such task. He was also responsible for collecting taxes for the empire and establishing a courier system. He quickly became the most powerful person in Rome next to Caesar, and the most trusted by him.

---****---

The sun was beginning to crest the hillsides warming the spring air causing the leaves of the vineyards and pomegranate groves to explode with green shoots. The sound of a woman screaming, and pleading could be heard in the streets of the small village near Rome. The agony of childbirth was not well hidden in ancient times, particularly in the quaint village of Volsinii nestled in the hills on the outskirts of Rome.

"You are almost there," an old woman said as she watched the head of the baby appear between the mother's legs. The wrinkles on the woman's face attested to her longevity and wisdom. "All right. Now, push!" she said as she held her hands ready to catch the birthing child. The mother let out one last scream as the baby's head popped out and the rest of the body slid

---

[15] Equestrian class – Highest civilian level below a senator or royalty.

into the old woman's hands. "There!" the old woman yelled as she caught the baby. A huge smile crossed her face as she looked intently at the newborn and said, "Welcome to the world, little one."

Another, younger woman was standing by with water and cloths observing the birth. "You did it!" she exclaimed with a joyous fling. "Lydia. You did it!"

The older woman handed the baby off to the standing woman, then snipped the umbilical cord and quickly tied it. The once pregnant woman sighed in relief and struggled to see the baby. "I don't hear it," she said with concern.

"Hear *him*," the young woman corrected her. She cleaned out the inside of the baby's mouth and turned the baby onto its stomach. She began to gently rub and pat his back. With a cough and sputter, the baby began to breath …. and soon wail. "Hear *him*," she said again with a smile as she laid the baby at its mother's breast.

The mother smiled as she softly stroked her son's head and back. "It's a boy," she said with delight. "A boy."

The old woman laughed. "Yes, it is. Good of you to notice," she said with another laugh as she cleaned up the birthing area.

A military commander in full uniform entered the room and looked at the old woman as if waiting for a report. "Did I hear a baby?" he asked.

"Yes, Lucius," the new mother replied softly. "It's a boy."

The man walked to the bedside of the new mother and gently kissed her on the forehead. "We have a son?" he whispered. The woman smiled as they both looked at the child. Then, the man took the child in his large hands and looked at him intently for a moment, deep into his eyes. The baby stopped crying and opened his eyes to see his father. The man walked out of the room without a word carrying the newborn in both hands. He passed through another room, out the door and into the street in front of the house. An old man walking by stopped and watched as the commander stepped into the middle of the street and held the baby high above his head with both hands.

"I thank you, oh Jupiter, for this, my son. I Lucius Seius Strabo, Commander of the Praetorian Guard of Rome, give to you Lucius Aelius Sejanus. May he be a warrior for you and a leader of Rome."

The baby wailed and squirmed in the warrior's large hands as the old man looked on with wonder.

---****---

One year after the birth of Lucius Aelius Sejanus, a young boy ran excitedly through the streets of another small village near Rome. "Papa! Papa!" It was mid-morning, and the streets of the village were crowded with merchants selling their wares. The boy rounded a corner and ran into a small fruit cart that an elderly man was tending nearly tipping it over. Several pieces of produce rolled off the cart and onto the ground.

"Watch where you are going," the old man yelled as he picked up the spilled fruit and brushed it clean. "This is my life!" he said as he held up two lemons, then repositioned them onto the cart.

The boy ran excitedly past goats who bayed at him. He startled some chickens who flew into the air cackling as he continued weaving his way through the throng of people. "Watch where you're going!" someone yelled as he ran by. He dashed to the front of a small house and burst through the door, only to be met by a tall, elderly man wearing a toga. The man reached out his hand and grabbed the back of the boy's shirt as he started to run by, lifting him off his feet, which were still running.

"Why the hurry, my grandson?" he laughed as he held the boy up with one hand. The strength of the gray-haired man startled the boy.

"Let me go!" he yelled as he kicked and squirmed while in the air.

The man dropped the boy and knelt to look him in the eye. "Again, I ask, what is the hurry?"

"My uncle, Commander Pontius has a son!" the boy declared trying to catch his breath. "I have a cousin!"

The old man rose to his feet and smiled. "I have a new grandson? You must take me to commander Pontius and this new addition to our family and your new cousin."

Commander Savius Pontius was well known in the small village of Bisenti, Italy. He was from the equestrian class of society; one who was considered a knight and one level under a senator. His elevated social status was the result of his father's connections both politically and socially. The Pontius family was from the Samnite territory well known for the powerful and elite families that originated from there.

The boy and his grandfather worked their way through the crowded street lined with artists, animals and vendors.

"Red wine, white wine here. A delightful brew for your evenings," someone yelled.

"Bread." "Figs." "Olives," other merchants called.

The pair made it down the small street and past the cart that the boy had previously upset. "So, I see you have brought this little villain back to pay for the damage he did to my produce," the old man said with a scowl as the two approached his cart.

The grandfather stopped and looked down on the child. "Damage?"

"It was an accident," the boy said as he lowered his head in embarrassment.

The grandfather pulled a coin out of a small pouch and handed it to the merchant. "Here. This should cover his damages," he said as he took an apple from the cart.

"Thank you, sir," the old man said as he smiled and placed the coin in a box.

The two continued down the street to the edge of the village where a long pathway led to a house sitting on a hill overlooking a small vineyard. The pair passed the gardens and animal pens as they made their way to the courtyard in front of the house. They approached the door where a woman stood nearby and greeted them.

"To what do we owe this honor?" she asked.

"We came to see the baby," the boy blurted out.

The man looked down to his grandson and smiled. "Yes, we did come to see the new addition to your family," he said with a broad smile.

The woman directed them to a back room where they both stood at the door and looked in. The room was lit by candles and somewhat smoky. They saw a woman filing a basket with bloody rags at the end of the bed. As they moved closer, they saw a woman lying on a mat with a baby on her chest. A man was standing next to her with his hand on her shoulder and noticed the two at the doorway. "Father," he said. "Say hello to Marcus Levilius Pontius."

Marcus Pontius and Lucius Sejanus, born just one year apart from the same social class, would cross paths and develop a friendship that would ultimately lead to one of the most profound events in human history; the trial and crucifixion of Jesus of Nazareth.

Chapter 4   The Friendship
3 AD

Ancient Rome had a long history of providing social entertainment to the citizens of Rome through the presentation of the Ludi Romani. The ludi were the primary entertainment for Romans and were free to attend. They were usually sponsored by a military leader, government entity, or wealthy businessman with significant political connections. There were up to 165 ludi a year in Rome during the reign of Augustus. Some were far better than others in terms of skill levels and the breadth of entertainment. One such Ludi occurred at the installation of Caesar Augustus and was considered to be one of the greatest events ever. Today's games some thirty years later were expected to be significant, but not nearly as great, considering they were only celebrating the installation of several senators. Regardless, the citizens of Rome anxiously awaited the celebration and entertainment of the games.

The long road leading through Rome to the Circus Maximus was lined with thousands of Roman citizens and military personnel cheering wildly. At the front of the procession several Roman soldiers carried the imperial standards high and proud. The circular, gold symbols of eagles holding lightning bolts were carried on poles followed by rows of chariots anxious to participate in the Ludi. Ornately decorated horses pranced as they pulled their chariots behind them through the cheering crowds, past the large marble columns of the tall government buildings lining the road to the Circus Maximus. People threw rose petals from the rooftops making the scene look like colored snowflakes showering onto the procession below. The chariots were followed by competitors, gladiators, horses and musicians with trumpets and drums. At the rear of the parade were the condemned who would fight the gladiators as their criminal punishment. They were crowded into a jail wagon pulled by several chained prisoners. The procession entered the main gates of the Circus Maximus to a thunderous roar of Rome's citizens.

This was a season when the gladiators ruled the games of life and death. They would do an exhibition today as well, but after the more mundane exhibitions of wrestling, archery, running, and javelin. It would also be a limited 'exhibition' consisting of only those condemned to die by the judicial system of Rome. A way to have the citizens of Rome witness capital punishment if they so choose – in an 'entertaining' way.

Twenty-four chariots proceeded into the entrance of the Circus Maximus and circled the track two chariots wide resulting in a frenzy of excitement and anticipation from the crowd of 150,000 Roman citizens. The entire procession paraded past the center balcony where Emperor Augustus was seated to observe the festivities in the same manner he did at his inauguration thirty years prior. Clouds of dust slowly followed the procession as the horses jumped and stutter stepped, excited to run, muscles tense and glistening. The horses were paired two to a chariot with each chariot decorated with streamers and fabric of their represented color and trimmed in brass. The drivers stood erect on platforms behind low profile shields wearing full armor. A large spear that was normally mounted to the side of the chariot shield for use in combat was replaced with a flag flying the team color. The procession, all but two of the chariots, circled the arena and exited through a side corridor into the bowels of the arena. The remaining two chariots, one each from the red and blue teams, approached a line across the track at midfield and stopped.

The chariots were divided into four groups of different colors (red, white, green and blue) and would compete in each event in pairs in a round robin format[16]. They were, by far, the highest attended event of the games, even more than the gladiator battles. Today, one race would be conducted at the beginning of the ludi to draw the people into the games. It was to set the stage for the remainder of the events to follow.

The crowded audience pressed forward anxious to see the opening race. "It would appear our emperor is about to provide a

---

[16] Round robin – process of single elimination until a winner.

preliminary race to whet our appetite for the games," a man in the crowd said as he watched the spectacle.

The chariot drivers nodded to each other and saluted the emperor by extending their right arms parallel to the ground, hands open, palms down. The emperor rose and walked to the front of his balcony trimmed with gold and red streams of material bordered with roses and hyacinth. A large gold seal hung from the rail identifying the balcony as the emperor's. Augustus nodded his approval with a return salute and returned to his seat, leaning forward with anticipation. The drivers with reigns in hand and standing tall turned and faced the starter. A man stood between the chariots and held a cloth high above his head and then let it drop. The cloth floated to the ground and as it touched, the chariot drivers yelled, whipped their horses, and bolted from the starting line in unison. The arena exploded with thunderous excitement.

"This is the way to begin the games," a soldier yelled. "Go, blue!" he cheered as the crowd roared.

"Blue?" a soldier next to him asked. "You should cheer for a winner – Red!"

The two soldiers were about the same height and age; six foot plus and twenty years old. They could have passed as brothers had anyone asked.

"Care to wager a small bet?" asked the first soldier.

"Of course. Shall we say…. A denarius[17]?"

The other soldier laughed. "Where is your confidence, tribune?" he said, mocking his rank.

The soldier smiled as he reached into his pocket and withdrew three denarii. "Here is my confidence," he said as he smiled and extended his hand.

The other soldier looked at the coins. "Agreed," he said as he stuck out his hand and the soldiers sealed their agreement with a shake. "I am Lucius Aelius Sejanus," he said.

"And I am Marcus Levilius Pontius," came the reply. He paused for a moment. "Sejanus? Lucius Strabo's son?"

---

[17] Denarius– A coin worth nearly a day's wage for a Roman soldier.

"Yes," came the reply. "Yes, the son of the Praetorian Guard commander."

Pontius smiled. "Then I best lose, I suppose…." he said with a smile, "…or I may have to face your father."

Sejanus leaned in and whispered, "It will be *me* you face if you win, tribune," Sejanus replied with a wink.

The two men looked up to see the chariots rounding the third turn in a huge cloud of dust on their way to finishing the first lap. Chariot races were for seven laps with, basically, no rules. These were the races of warriors and competitors, not gladiators. There were no weapons, no spears, no instruments of any type to influence the outcome of the race. It was sheer horsepower and skill that was utilized to drive the chariots at breakneck speeds inches apart. The contestants were allowed to bump their opponent and even try to cause them to flip, but that only happened occasionally.

"Faster, Blue! Faster," yelled Pontius. "He's pulling ahead," he said as he slapped his opponent on the chest.

"We have six laps left, my new friend," Sejanus said stoically. "The battle is far from finished."

The chariots continued to battle each other around the track. The crowd roared with each attempted maneuver of one to pass the other. Dust clouds followed the chariots as they circled the track, each time roars of satisfaction coming from the spectators as the drivers bumped the chariots together or pulled slightly ahead.

"I have never seen such a close race," Sejanus yelled as the chariots entered the last lap.

"Nor have I," replied Pontius.

The chariots battled back and forth, bumping into each other in the hopes one would force out the other, or at least slow him down. It was pointless. They would battle to the very end, crossing the finish line with the crowd cheering wildly. Two men stood on each side of the finish line holding a small flag. The man standing on the blue side of the track raised his flag first, indicating the win.

"Ha-ha! I won!" Pontius yelled. He turned to Sejanus and, with a broad victory smile, extended his hand to receive his reward.

Sejanus reached into his pocket to withdraw the coins and reluctantly dropped them into Pontius's open palm, one coin at a time. Pontius held up one of the coins as if to examine it. "To the victor goes the spoils," he said gleefully.

Sejanus laughed. "I believe it is military custom for the victor to buy the loser a drink," he said with a smile.

Pontius seemed confused at first, then realized Sejanus was making that up. "Oh, yes. I believe it is custom…or should be." He slapped Sejanus on the arm. "We can do so right after my event."

"What event are you in?" Sejanus asked.

"Javelin."

"Well. Then we shall meet again, Marcus Pontius."

The Circus Maximus was sectioned off after the first chariot race to provide for varying competitive venues. One end of the arena housed the archery competition. Archers in full armor stood side by side flinging arrows to their targets 50 meters[18] away. Observers stood behind wooden barriers to the side of the target to score the shot. An observer would raise a red flag to indicate a miss and yell, "Sin[19]!," or a white flag and yell "Kill!" One after another eliminated archers were required to stand along the sidelines and watch the competition whittle down.

Next to the archers was the slingshot competition. Soldiers and commoners stood 25 meters[20] away from their respective target: melons resting on a pole. The sound of the slings whirling through the air over their heads made a strange, almost melodic whistling tune. Melons exploded with a 'thump' as the projectiles burst them to pieces. Children emerged from behind wooden barriers in between competitors to gather the broken pieces and

---

[18] 50 meters – 164 feet
[19] Sin – Greek based - missing the mark
[20] 25 meters – 82 feet

haul them off in baskets. Soldiers placed new melons on the poles for each volley.

Next were the wrestlers. Near naked men wrestling in a circular ring, grappling, grunting, and yelling as they attempted to throw and pin their opponent. It was a show of sheer strength as muscular men yelled and groaned as they pushed and shoved each other. Several men were carried off on stretchers because of the broken bones or pulled muscles they received in the match immobilizing them.

One long side of the arena housed the runners. Men dressed in a loin wrap raced barefoot four at a time. The losers would line the race lanes while the victors circled back to the starting line for the next race. This continued until a single victor in a race was carried the length of the race on the shoulders of the second and third place contestants.

Next to the races was the hopscotch competition. Large, complicated diagrams were drawn in the dirt for the competitors to maneuver the course by hopping on one leg without going outside the lines. A favorite of the soldiers, this game was originally created in China almost 3,000 years before. Six soldiers would compete at each diagram, tossing an object into a location and then attempt to maneuver through the course without going outside the lines. Failure to do so resulted in ridicule and laughter from the competitors, sometimes evolving into a scuffle. It was a highly competitive game of skill and balance that anyone could partake.

Next to the hopscotch was the weightlifting competition. Muscular men would lift progressively large boulders above their heads. If finalists lifted the same weight, they would rotate until only one could lift the boulder one last time.

The arena was full of continuous competitions that held the attention of the thousands of observers. The favored event beside the chariot races and the gladiators was the javelin.

The autumn sun was high in the sky warming the air making it difficult for competitors to hold their weapons in the competitions because of their sweaty hands. Marcus Pontius could feel the sweat rolling down his back and arms as he felt the weight of the javelin in his hand. Known as a pilum, the weapon was two meters[21] long and weighed around 2.2 kilos[22]. The wooden shaft was attached to an iron shank just over a centimeter[23] in diameter and just over a half meter[24] long. It had a pyramid tip with a barb on it. It was specifically designed to penetrate a target and get stuck. If the enemy tried to withdraw the javelin from their body, armor or shield, the shank would bend, making the weapon useless to the enemy. It was an effective way to disable the enemy's shield, forcing them to discard it and become defenseless against an attack.

The effective range of the javelin was from 15-20 meters[25]. However, in competitive events like the ludi, the range and accuracy were tested to their limits by each contestant.

"So, you think you can hit that shield, Pontius?" a voice called from a group of competitors.

Pontius looked over to see Sejanus approaching with three javelins in hand. "So, *you* are my competition?" Sejanus just smiled. Pontius continued. "I know I can hit it at this range, but can you?" he asked with a wry smile.

Sejanus set two javelins aside and felt the weight of the remaining weapon in his hand. "We shall see," he said with a smile. "We shall see."

"Lucius Sejanus," came the call.

Sejanus stepped forward and looked downfield at the shield placed in front of a straw soldier. It was 20 meters[26] away. He took a couple of steps back and felt the weight of the javelin balanced in his fingertips of his right hand. His muscles rippled as he adjusted his grip around the shaft. He took a few steps forward, leaned into the throw, and grunted as he released the projectile. The javelin

---

[21] Two meters – 6 feet 7 inches
[22] 2.2 kilos - Five pounds
[23] Centimeter – less than ½ inch
[24] Half Meter – approximately two feet
[25] 15-20 meters = 50-70 feet
[26] 20 meters – 70 feet

flew through the air effortlessly and found its mark, penetrating the center of the shield and straw warrior behind it. An older, tubby man stepped from behind a side barrier to inspect the strike. "Kill," he yelled and waived a white flag. Sejanus turned toward Pontius and with a wink and a smile said, "Your turn."

Pontius stepped forward and, with little mental preparation, let the weapon fly.

"Kill," yelled the observer. Another perfect toss. Another white flag. Pontius bowed to Sejanus as he returned to his mark to await the next throw.

The two men battled with each other and other contestants as the contestants were positioned further away from the targets after each throw. The targets were now at 35[27] meters. Spectators started to gather around the final few men as they demonstrated their skills. One competitor stepped up, felt the javelin in his hand and took a deep breath as he looked around, trying to steady his nerves. He took a few steps forward and let the weapon fly with a mighty yell. The javelin missed the center completely and pierced the barrier below the target. The observer stepped out from a side barrier, raised a red flag, and yelled, "Sin!"

The next competitor stepped forward and repeated the process, also missing the target to the jeers and laughter of several soldiers in the crowd. The battle continued as the fault line[28] was moved back in five-meter increments until Pontius and Sejanus were the final two competitors.

"Lucius Sejanus," came the call.

"Looks like I just need to hit the target to win," he said.

"First, hit the target. We can talk about winning after that," Pontius said smiling.

Sejanus stepped forward and focused on the target. He took a few steps and let the javelin fly, watching it as it penetrated the upper quadrant of the shield. "Kill," yelled the observer raising the white flag. "Your turn," he said to Pontius almost laughing.

---

[27] 35 meters – 115 feet
[28] Fault line – the line where competitors threw from

Pontius stepped forward and closed his eyes as he felt the javelin's weight. He remembered when he was a young boy of thirteen and his father telling him to extend his body as he threw. "Flow with the throw. Smooth. Follow through," he would say. He took the other hand and slid it along the sleek shaft, feeling the smoothness of the weapon. He opened his eyes and focused on the target. A few steps, release, and the weapon sailed through the air and into the center of the shield. "Kill," came the call with a white flag. The spectators let out a roar of approval. Pontius smiled at Sejanus, who appeared to be surprised and perturbed at his competitor's throw.

"Fifty meters," came the call from the judge. The contestants were moved back to a distance of 50 meters[29] from the targets. Spectators in the crowd mumbled how no one can hit a target at that range consistently. If they did, it would just be dumb luck.

"Lucius Sejanus," came the call. Sejanus stepped forward and, this time, looked uneasy. He studied the target, feeling the weight of the javelin, over and over. It was warm, his hands were sweaty. He wiped his palms and again felt the weight of the spear in his hands. The spectators were eerily quiet. Sejanus took a deep breath and advanced. With a mighty yell, he released the weapon. "Sin!" came the call with a red flag. He turned away in disgust.

"Marcus Pontius," came the call.

Pontius looked at the spectators gathered around watching his every move as he took his position. Some whispered that he might get lucky. Pontius reached down and took a handful of dirt and rubbed it into his hands and onto the shaft of the projectile. He stood, took a deep breath, a few steps and with a yell hurled the weapon toward the target. People were straining to see if it hit. The observer stepped out and raised a white flag. "Kill," came the call.

The crowd of spectators roared with approval. "Lucky throw," someone yelled from the crowd.

---

[29] 50 meters – 164 feet

"Lucky?" Pontius replied. He grabbed another javelin from a competitor's hand and stepped to the line. The observer down field was gathering his personal items from the side barrier and was unaware that Pontius was going to throw again. Pontius felt the weapon in his hand and, with three steps, let it fly. The observer standing by the target jumped as the javelin pierced the target next to the prior throw, almost splitting the previous javelin as it hit and penetrated the target and the stuffed warrior behind it. The observer looked at the javelin next to him and fainted, falling backwards into his protective barrier. It was a perfect throw.

The crowd let out a roar of approval. Marcus Pontius was the winner of the event.

"Well, you proved yourself, tribune," Sejanus said. "From here on, I shall call you Pilate[30]; Marcus Pontius Pilate," and with an exaggerated gesture, bowed to him in honor.

Pilate and Sejanus sat at a small table on the side of the street drinking their wine. They were watching the people make their way along the thoroughfare going to and from the various events of the ludi. Many vendors positioned themselves along the walkway to sell food, wine, and other products during the games. The games afforded them one of the many opportunities to display their wares before thousands of people.

"This is fairly good swill, Sejanus," Pilate said as he held up his goblet and laughed.

"In this heat, anything liquid seems good, as long as it isn't boiled," Sejanus replied. He watched as a woman passed by carrying some bread and fruit followed by two young boys. "Did you hear what the Jewish king did?" he asked Pilate.

Pilate placed his goblet on the table with a thud. "Yes. I did," he said angrily.

"He heard a new king of the Jews was born, their Messiah. So, he had all of the boys under two years old in a small village executed," Sejanus added.

---

[30] Pilate – 'skilled with a javelin'.

"He is a paranoid coward. No king of any worth will kill innocent children purposefully," Pilate said disgustedly.

Sejanus replied, "Difficult to believe anyone would see a two-year old boy as a threat." He paused. "Messiah. The Jews have been talking about their 'Messiah' for centuries. Yet, they are still our subjects."

"We could make them slaves overnight, except for the good graces of our emperor," Pilate replied. "We should make their 'king' a slave. Make him an example."

Sejanus took another sip. "You know. It doesn't matter if it's true or not, or if they kill each other off completely. That will make governing them much easier," he replied.

"It would," Pilate agreed as he finished his drink. "Let's go watch the discus finals."

Sejanus gulped down the last of his brew. "Let's," he said as he rose from the table.

Chapter 5   Brothers in Battle
14 AD

The friendship between Pilate and Sejanus grew as the years went on. They were so much alike. Both were from the equestrian class of Roman society. Both were from the same region, were the same age and were called to join the military at the same time. Both were skilled with their weapons of choice. They served together in the battle Bellum Batonianum in 7 AD and battle of the Breuci of Sava Valley in 8 AD. They both received recognition for their valor, courage, skill and leadership. They proceeded to advance through the ranks, each obtaining a command of their own. Pilate advanced to become a tribunus millitum[31] commanding more than 1,000 men near Rome while Sejanus advanced to the rank of Tribunus Angusticlavii[32] and shared the command of the Praetorian Guard in Rome with his father, Lucius Strabo.

---****---

An older woman walked through the hallway of the palace carrying a small bowl of figs. She was dressed in a long, flowing purple gown with a sheer white wrap. The summer air was thick and heavy. It was well after sunset yet still quite warm. She rounded a corner where two guards stood erect at the open doorway to the emperor's bed chamber. A hazy smoke wafted through the doorway from the incense burning in the room. The room smelled like lavender covering the odor of urine. "Caesar, Lady Livia," a guard announced as she approached the door.

    "How is he?" Livia asked as she approached the bed where Caesar Augustus lay and placed the bowl of figs on a side table. His eyes were closed.

---

[31] Tribunus Millitum – Military tribune commanding 800 infantry and 240 cavalry.
[32] Tribunus Angusticlavii – Second highest equestrian rank commanding Legionaires

"He is dying," Caesar replied as he opened his eyes and continued. "A slow, lingering death." He coughed and smacked his lips, then smiled.

"Oh, my dear, dear Augustus," Livia said as she leaned over and brushed the hair away from his brow. "You look as handsome now as the day I married you."

"The gods will strike you for lying so," Augustus replied with a chuckle, then a wheeze. "Did you bring them?"

Livia eased herself onto the side of the bed and took his hand. "Yes. I did."

"Good." Caesar smiled at her as he tried to sit up. Livia and an attendant helped him adjust himself with pillows until he was partially sitting up in bed. "There. That was …. more effort ….. than………"

"Than defeating Marc Antony?" Livia asked.

Caesar chuckled and coughed. "I would say not." Cough. "He was difficult. Dying is easy."

"Watching is not," Livia replied. She turned to the attendant and nodded to the door. The woman bowed and left immediately. "We must all pass," she added.

Caesar spoke slowly and clearly between breaths. "We must. Our life is a play that always ends the same way. Dead."

"In the fields of Elysium[33]," Livia replied as she moved the bowl of figs within his reach. "You asked that I prepare these figs for you. Have one, dear. It will help ease your discomfort."

Augustus took a fig and held it up. "Livia. I have always loved your figs. Today is no exception, even more so. Thank you," he said as he eyed the fruit. He took a bite and tilted his head back. He savored the flavor of the sweet fruit. The sweetness covered the bitterness of the poison making it quite palatable. Livia held his free hand as he finished one fig and ate another, coughing in-between. Livia watched as tears started to roll down her cheeks. After

---

[33] Fields of Elysium – A place where Romans believed a Roman would go after death if they were undeserving of punishment

Augustus finished two figs, he laid back on his pillows and closed his eyes.

"Guard," Livia called. "Please send in Tiberius and Strabo." The guard nodded and left. Within moments, Lucius Strabo, Commander of the Praetorian Guard, entered the room without announcement. "Hail........" He noticed Caesar was laying with his eyes closed and stopped his salutation. "Is he....?"

"No." Livia replied.

Strabo could see she had been crying. "This is difficult, my lady," Strabo said. "He is a great man, a true leader. I wish there was something....."

"There is nothing we can do, Lucius," Livia interrupted. "We are doing what is best for him and for Rome."

Augustus coughed and rolled his eyes as if he was trying to look around. "I cannot see very well," he said. "Is that Lucius?"

"It is, Caesar," Strabo said as he moved closer to the bed. "I am at your command."

Tiberius entered the room behind Strabo without announcement. He saw his mother and Commander Strabo standing over his adopted stepfather. "Caesar," he said as he approached.

Augustus opened his eyes. "Ah, Tiberius," he said and closed his eyes.

Tiberius knelt at the bedside as Caesar laid his hand on his head, coughing and wheezing. "I have planned my exit. You are to ... be ... emperor," he said as he struggled. The poison was starting to affect his nerves and speech.

"I am your servant," Tiberius replied.

Strabo saw that both Pilate and Sejanus came to the door and started to enter when he motioned for them to stop. They stood at the doorway and watched as Caesar's eyes rolled back into his head and he coughed. He struggled to look at the people near his bedside. "Have I played the part well?" he asked as he tried to look around the room.

Livia held his hand. "Yes, mighty Caesar."

Augustus laid his head back and closed his eyes. He whispered, "Then, applaud as I exit." He took a deep breath, slowly exhaled, and died. The three standing over Augustus quietly applauded.

Strabo turned to Tiberius and saluted him. "Hail, Caesar Tiberius. Emperor of Rome."

---****---

To assure a smooth transition of power, Caesar Augustus had planned his exit well in advance. He would leave Rome in the hands of Tiberius Caesar Augustus, his stepson, and Lucius Strabo, commander of the Praetorian Guard.

Emperor Tiberius was quick to assume the duties and power of the emperor. For his loyalty to Emperor Augustus, and to set an expectation that he would have that same loyalty to the new emperor, Tiberius retained Lucius Strabo as the Praetorian Guard commander. Strabo had regular meetings with his son Sejanus, Augustus and now with the new emperor Tiberius to prepare Sejanus as his successor as commander of the Guard. Tiberius had complete confidence in Strabo and Sejanus. He knew that they could handle anything he threw at them. They were true Romans devoted to the empire and their emperor.

---****---

Rome continued to expand its empire and found opposition as they entered the region of Pannonia, a northern most province of Rome. A revolt broke out in the region that needed to be addressed by the emperor before it escalated out of control and the region broke away. Rome must show its strength quickly and decisively to deter other provinces from revolting. Tiberius sent his biological son, Drusus Julius Caesar, and Sejanus to quell the revolt. Sejanus, realizing the limited combat leadership experience of Drusus, needed a commander with field experience and asked Pilate to join them with Tiberius's approval. Tiberius hoped some of the military acumen of Sejanus and Pilate would rub off on his young son, Drusus. Pilate would command a small cavalry unit while Drusus would command the frontal assault with Sejanus.

The Pannonians were pushed back by the Roman military into the northside of a small valley nestled in the hillsides in the lower Pannonia region where the ragtag soldiers chose to make a stand against the advancing Roman army. The Pannonians believed they had an advantage, at least number wise, against the Romans. The battle lines were drawn. On one side stood almost two thousand angry Pannonians armed with arrows, spears, swords, hatchets, farm tools, scythes; anything that could kill their oppressive enemy. On the other side stood two cohorts of Roman soldiers standing at attention holding their weapons of choice. They were arranged in two rows of shield bearers followed by two rows of archers and 20 giant ballista each with a three meter[34], 45 kilo[35] spear ready to load. Behind them stood the remaining soldiers and a cavalry 50 horses strong. Everyone was prepared for battle though the Romans were outnumbered two to one.

Sejanus rode his horse to the front of the line and dismounted. As the tribune of the contingent, he was the senior commanding officer coordinating the attack. He walked in front of the hundreds of soldiers as he spoke. "Today, the rebels of Pannonia will feel the cold, Roman steel of our swords and arrows as they pierce their armor, their bodies and their very souls!" Sejanus yelled to the delight of his troops. "Today, Rome will be feared by all nations." The troops yelled and banged their shields in agreement and a show of power.

Pilate and Drusus rode up to Sejanus and stopped. Pilate dismounted and walked with Sejanus. "We are Roman soldiers. We fear nothing!" The troops banged and yelled as Pilate continued. "If you find yourself lying in the grass with the sunshine on your face,

---

[34] Three meters – almost ten feet
[35] 45 kilos – approx. 100 pounds

then the battle is already over for you because you have gone to the Fields of Elysium!" Many of the soldiers laughed and cheered. "The battle will not be over for those of us left behind until the enemy is completely destroyed!" More cheers and more banging.

Drusus watched from his horse as the two soldiers whipped the troops into a battle frenzy. He tried to think of something to say to show he was a commander as well. "We fight for my father, Caesar Tiberius, and Rome!" A few soldiers cheered and yelled, but not nearly as enthusiastically as with the other two commanders, leaving a bitter taste in Drusus's mouth. "For Rome," he yelled again raising his sword.

Pilate agreed. "For Caesar Tiberius and Rome!" he said as he raised his sword with Drusus. The troops cheered, banged, yelled, and raised their weapons in unison. Drusus looked displeasingly toward Pilate.

Sejanus pointed to an area on the side hills. "Pilate. You take the cavalry. Wait for my signal. Flank them from the right when we open the weak center."

"Yes, commander," Pilate replied as he mounted his horse and galloped away.

"Drusus. Double line defense, weak center[36]. Begin with the ballistae. Unleash hell on them," Sejanus ordered.

Drusus nodded, turned his horse, and rode to the middle of the battle line, stopped, and faced the troops. "Double line defense, weak center. Ballistae to the ready," he ordered. A line of ballistae rolled forward and positioned themselves behind the shields in the center of the defense line. The winches ground and clanked as each ballista was loaded with a spear. The opposing army continued to chant, yell and bang their shields as the soldiers prepared for engagement. "Ready," Drusus ordered. Each ballista had a flagger standing to the side. The flaggers raised their flags one at a time, indicating their devices were loaded. Once all the ballistae were ready, Drusus gave the order. "Open!" The line of

---

[36] Double line defense weak center – Roman military strategy that draws the enemy into a trap and surrounds them

shields creating the center defense separated like a sliding door, exposing the loaded ballistae. Drusus raised his sword and yelled, "For Rome! Fire!"

The enemy continued to yell and chant as they slowly advanced toward the Roman battle line, ready to engage. Their faces were painted with wild colors and markings, attempting to make them look more menacing, distracting their enemy should they be in hand-to-hand combat. In an instant, they could hear the whistle of the projectiles flying through the air and penetrating deep into their battle lines. Each projectile would penetrate several men, spearing them like a kabob and pushing them back into their fellow soldiers, creating chaos and panic. Horses were impaled and thrust back onto unsuspecting soldiers nearby. Several leaders shouted as they started running toward the Romans, followed by a now hesitant rag-tag army. The ballistae succeeded with instilling terror and confusion into their enemy.

"Archers, to the ready," Sejanus ordered. A line of archers stood behind the shield bearers and drew their bows. Before they could fire the Pannonians launched a volley of arrows that flew into the Roman soldiers, striking some down. The Roman archers that were struck released their arrows as they fell, shooting their nearby comrades. "Fire," Sejanus ordered. The remaining archers released their arrows in unison, creating a cloud with the sound similar to a swarm of bees as the arrows flew over the small valley and penetrated the enemy lines killing hundreds.

Pilate sat on his horse and watched as the battle unfolded ready to lead the charge from the side to cover the flank of the enemy. "On me," he yelled, directing them to form a line. "Hold the line." The horses galloped in a line that swept around the side of the battle lines and down the hill toward the rear of the battle. Pilate could see that a defense line had been created to attempt to stop them. "Separate," he ordered as the horses split into two advancing lines and attacked each side of the enemy resistance. The battle was brutal. The Romans slaughtered the poorly manned defense line with few casualties. Pilate led his troops killing as many of the enemy as any soldier. At one point, he saw several enemy combatants try to flee over the hillside. He followed them, soon catching up to each of them, slaying them with ease and without hesitation.

At the main battle, the enemy lines were rapidly advancing toward the Romans. Sejanus watched as a line of combatants advanced on horseback toward the front line. "Spears front and ready," he ordered. The 'doors' of shield bearers at the weak center closed as the ballistae rolled back allowing a line of 50 men with long, sturdy spears to advance to a position behind the weak center. Each man had an assistant who quickly dug a hole for the spearman to anchor his spear. It was precision teamwork. Everyone had a place and a purpose. The shield bearers concealed the spearmen from the advancing cavalry, which was quickly approaching. As the enemy cavalry reached the battle line, Sejanus ordered, "Open!"

The shield bearers quickly moved behind the spearmen in the weak center making it appear that they were fleeing and the battle line had broken, thus drawing the enemy into their trap. The horses instinctively veered into the broken center where the spear-bearers had their anchored spears at the ready. Horses screamed as they rode into the spears and were impaled. Riders flew off their mounts and onto Roman swords. The center clogged as horses and men piled up causing the advancing army to stop.

In an instant, the double defense line split like sliding doors and covered three sides of the enemy. The remaining cavalry advanced on the flank surrounding the enemy. The sides collapsed into a slaughtering battle. It was a brilliant move for the Romans. It was a devastating blow to the Pannonians.

Drusus rode his horse through his advancing army yelling, "Advance. Advance," as he made his way to the rear of the battle. No one noticed him moving to a safer area away from the fray. Pilate and Sejanus advanced into the midst of the raging battle while Drusus watched from a side hill, afraid to join the melee. *I must stay alive to rule Rome*, he thought. It was his excuse formed in reason. *For Rome*.

Pilate and Sejanus eventually ended up at midfield amongst their troops fighting hand-to-hand with the enemy. Pilate was in a fierce battle with a man much larger than him. Their swords clanged as they fought until Pilate gained the advantage and thrust his sword through his opponent. He looked around to see Sejanus in battle across the creek about 50 meters[37] away. He watched as Sejanus stumbled backwards over a body and fell to the ground. Pilate quickly grabbed a javelin from the ground and, as Sejanus was about to be slain, he launched the projectile. It pierced Sejanus's opponent in the chest and drove him backwards a couple of steps. The man looked down at the javelin handle protruding from his chest, dropped his sword and tried to pull it out bending the shaft. He screamed as he dropped to his knees and tried to reach around to his back. He looked at Sejanus and slumped backwards dead. The javelin was protruding from his back, causing him to be half propped up on his knees with his head slumped backwards as though he was looking up to the sky. Pilate ran to Sejanus, killing a combatant on the way. Sejanus struggled to get to his feet as Pilate approached.

"Sejanus. Are you ok?" Pilate yelled.

Sejanus's arm was bleeding from a wound he received in battle. "Yes, thanks to you, my brother."

The two continued to fight as the battle raged on, at times fighting back-to-back. Soon, the battle was over. The remaining Pannonians fled the scene, pursued by the cavalry who slew them as they ran.

It was a horrific slaughter. It was an open graveyard with bodies everywhere. Pilate and Sejanus stood in the middle of the field surrounded by the dead. They were both covered in the enemy's blood.

"You fared well, Roman," Sejanus said as Pilate approached him. An enemy soldier groaned as Pilate passed by, who quickly thrust a sword into him without a thought. It was instinct.

---

[37] 50 meters – 165 feet

"As did you, commander," Pilate replied as he wiped the spattered blood from his face. "It looks like someone got the best of you," Pilate said as he pointed to Sejanus's bleeding arm. "The gods must have favored you, so it wasn't cut off!" Pilate reached down and cut a piece of cloth off a body. He split it and wrapped Sejanus's arm. "That should stop the bleeding."

"It will heal," Sejanus said. "I owe you my life, Pilate."

"You owe me nothing, Sejanus. We are now brothers, born in battle, forged by blood."

Sejanus looked around at the slaughter. "The taste of victory, my brother."

Pilate laughed and looked at Sejanus with a wild eye as he licked the blood from around his lips and smiled. "*That* is the taste of victory!" he replied with a laugh. "To drink the enemy's blood!"

Drusus saw the two bloodied men meet at midfield and realized he had almost no blood on his clothing. He jumped off his horse and crouched near a body reaching out as if he was trying to grab something, thus laying his body across a bloodied body. The man moved and startled Drusus, who jumped up and thrust his sword into him. He realized it was a Roman soldier who lost his helmet and slowly withdrew his sword, mounted his horse and left.

"Have you seen Drusus?" Sejanus asked. The two men looked around the area watching soldiers strip their enemy of clothing, weapons, and all the spoils of war they could carry.

"There," Pilate said as they watched Drusus pull the sword out of a man. They watched as he mounted his horse and rode toward them.

"It appears you have fought well, Drusus," Pilate said as Drusus rode up on his steed. His uniform was covered in blood, Roman blood.

"We all fought well, tribune," Drusus replied.

Sejanus looked closely at Drusus's clothing. The blood was on his torso and legs, but there was no blood on his arms, face, or hands. It would be impossible to be in a battle like this and not have some blood everywhere on their person. Rather than confront him, he chose to keep quiet. It was not wise to insult a future emperor. Not at all. "You fought well, Drusus," he said with a wry smile.

Drusus looked away and onto the field. "Today, we won this battle for Rome," he said as if he had contributed to the win.

"For Rome," Pilate replied as he held up his bloody sword.

"For Rome," Sejanus said quietly as he looked toward Drusus and his clothing.

Drusus glared back at Sejanus.

---****---

Lucius Strabo was sitting in the Praetorian Guard command room in the palace in Rome. He was reviewing several documents as Sejanus walked into the room. "You called for me, father?"

"Commander of the Praetorian Guard, if you please," Strabo loudly corrected him.

Sejanus was taken aback by the reply and stopped. He knew not to challenge his father at all. "Commander of the Praetorian Guard," he said as he saluted him.

"As *you* are," Strabo replied.

Sejanus was obviously confused by the reply. "I...I don't understand, commander."

Strabo stood to his feet and approached Sejanus. His graying hair showed his age giving him an air of wisdom as he laid his hand on Sejanus's shoulder. "Commander.... Of the Praetorian Guard," Strabo said as he shook his son's shoulder.

Sejanus lowered his head in reverence. "As you wish. For Rome."

"For Rome indeed," Strabo said as he returned to his seat. "Emperor Tiberius has appointed me as Prefect[38] of Egypt."

"Egypt!" Sejanus said. "Egypt. That's the highest rank an equestrian class can achieve, is it not?"

---

[38] Prefect – Any of various high officials or magistrates having different functions

"It is," Strabo replied. "One level below the emperor or senator."

"What a great honor, father."

Strabo smiled. "For me and for you, Commander of the Praetorian Guard. You have been selected to take my post here, in Rome."

"I am honored and humbled that our emperor has such trust in me," Sejanus replied.

"You proved yourself at the battle of Pannonia. You proved yourself with the assignments I have given you over the years. You proved yourself to be worthy of this appointment, and emperor Tiberius agrees. It is a position that you have shown you are worthy and able to hold."

"May the gods allow me to prove myself once again, then, as the Commander of the Guard," Sejanus replied.

Strabo laughed. "I am certain you will have opportunities to prove yourself worthy of this appointment." Strabo positioned himself in front of his son to gain his attention and to stress the importance of his next sentence. "You will be the most powerful person in Rome next to the emperor. How you use that power will determine how you serve Rome and how you will be remembered."

"I will use it only to make Rome better, stronger, and more powerful than any country in history," Sejanus replied.

Strabo placed his hands on Sejanus's shoulders. He looked deep into his eyes. He saw his son, a little boy, grown into a Roman soldier and leader. He also saw the ambition in Sejanus's eyes. "Power corrupts. Stay true to Rome."

"I shall, father. On my honor as a Roman."

---****---

"More grapes! We need more grapes!" said a young woman standing in a large tub that reached her waist. Her feet and ankles were stained purple from the sweet juice of the grapes she was stomping.

"Here." Pilate lifted the basket off his shoulder and dumped it into the tub. "Your order, Queen Cleopatra."

"You better address me properly, slave, or you shall suffer the consequences!" the woman said flashing her beautiful smile at him.

Pontius laid the basket on the ground and leaned over the edge of the tub. He noticed how beautiful the young lady was with her dark, curly hair put into a bun with the curly stragglers hanging down around her ears and onto her shoulders framing her rounded face. Her tan tunic had crimson stains around the bottom even though she was holding it tight around her hips in a vain attempt to keep it from dragging in the juice. Pontius admired her legs and figure. "I will be your slave, my queen, if you will but spare me a walk with you."

The woman laughed so hard she had to stop stomping grapes. "Do you think I want to go for a walk after stomping grapes all day?" She started back into the stomping motion as an older man dumped a basket of grapes into the tub.

"Then I shall carry you," Pilate replied. The man that dumped the grapes overheard Pilate and stopped to look questioningly at him. "You doubt me, Roman?" Pilate asked as he seemed to grow about four inches. The man bowed, turned, and walked off.

"You scared poor Cassius away," the woman said. "Aren't you the brave one. Who are you?" she asked without stopping.

"I am Marcus Pontius Pilate, at your service my queen," he said with a bow.

The woman extended her hand and held her tunic. "Then please help me exit this swill, Pontius Pilate" she said with a laugh.

"Only if I know your name," Pilate insisted.

"No. I think…."

Before she could finish, Pilate grabbed her extended arm and swiftly, but gently, pulled her toward him and over his shoulder.

"Put me down. Why the…." The woman began struggling and could feel Pilate's sheer strength as he held her fast.

Gerald Rainey   Javelin Man

"I said I wanted to go for a walk, so……" Pilate started to walk down a path with her slung over his shoulder and several people looking on laughing.

"You can't carry me very far," Claudia scolded.

Pilate stopped. "Are you saying you are fat?"

"No! You…….."

Pilate laughed and continued walking while carrying her as if she was no weight at all. The years of service in the military conditioned him to be exceptionally strong. Any good Roman soldier could carry a 34 kilos[39] pack at a brisk walk for 40 kilometers[40]. In fact, it was required.

"You need not struggle," Pilate assured her in a calming voice. "Relax. Enjoy the ride. The scenery is beautiful," he said as he swept his free arm across the grape vineyards filled with workers picking grapes.

The woman pushed herself up on Pilate's shoulder and looked around. She scooted some and held around his strong neck for support as she got a better look. Pilate stopped walking and scooted her onto his shoulder into more of a sitting position. She was a petite woman and Pilate took every advantage he could to demonstrate his strength. "There," he said as he continued walking. "You still have not told me your name."

The woman chuckled. "I...I suppose I have not."

Pilate waited. "And……?"

"Claudia. Claudia Procula."

Pilate stopped walking and gently lowered Claudia to the ground. She stood bashfully in front of him, towering over her by a foot. "It is a pleasure to meet you, Claudia Procula," he said as he bowed and kissed her hand, making her blush.

---

[39] 34 kilos – 75 pounds
[40] 40 kilometers – 25 miles

Chapter 6   **Introducing Caligula**
19AD

Sejanus walked briskly along the corridor toward the emperor's chamber. It was the middle of October, and the air had a chill. His footsteps echoed as he hurried past several banquet rooms and down the hall toward two large wooden doors framed by two guards. "Guards. Is the emperor alone?" he asked.

"No, commander," one of the guards answered. "Drusus is with him."

Sejanus opened the door and walked in without announcement, startling Tiberius and Drusus. "What are you……..?" Drusus asked, but Sejanus cut him off.

"I just received a report from Antioch, mighty Caesar." He said with a bow.

"Antioch?" Tiberius asked as he lowered himself into his chair.

Sejanus cleared his throat. "Germanicus is dead."

The room went eerily silent. Tiberius stared at the floor. "How did my son die?"

"He fell ill while in Antioch," Sejanus replied.

"Ill?" Tiberius asked as he stood to his feet. "Ill?" he said even louder.

"The report I have is….."

Tiberius cut him off. "Is that he was murdered by Syria's governor, Piso!" Tiberius stormed toward the door and stopped. He turned back to the pair who were intently watching their emperor's moves. Tiberius continued. "He had a feud with Piso about.. about something….. Germanicus told me Piso was furious with him. He must have killed him!"

Drusus spoke first. "Is it not possible that he just became ill and died?"

Tiberius turned to face Drusus. "He was a legion commander of a third of our armies in excellent health," Tiberius said loudly. He paused as he carefully studied Drusus's face. "You are now my successor. Did *you* know about this?" Tiberius asked as he leaned in closer to Drusus.

Drusus was shocked by the accusation. "No! I didn't! How could you..."

"Mighty Caesar," Sejanus interrupted hoping to quell the upheaval. "I will investigate this death and punish anyone responsible."

Tiberius turned and looked at Sejanus with angry eyes. "You have been jealous of Germanicus and how Rome loves him! He is the greatest commander Rome ever had!" He walked closer to Sejanus. "Did *you* have anything to do with this?"

Sejanus was stunned. He quickly drew his sword and handed it to Caesar as he knelt. "I give my life to you, here and now, to show my innocence and my honor."

Tiberius took the sword in both hands and looked down on Sejanus. "Arggggghhh," he yelled as his anger peaked and he flung the sword onto the marble floor. "Germanicus," Tiberius lamented as he moved to his chair. "Germanicus. My dear son."

Sejanus raised his head slowly and looked around, verifying it was safe to rise. Drusus looked at Sejanus, terrified to move or make any noise. They exchanged looks of relief. Each was accused of conspiracy to commit murder. Neither was charged.

"I take leave of you, great Caesar," Sejanus said as he bowed and exited the room, leaving his sword lying on the floor.

Tiberius looked up and saw Drusus standing alone. "Go!" he said.

Drusus could hear Tiberius weeping as he left the emperor's chamber.

---****---

The Ludi funebres[41] for Germanicus at Circus Maximus in Rome was significant. His high, military rank almost demanded that the games would be performed in his honor a month after his burial. The

---

[41] Ludi Funebres – funeral games

family had sufficient time to mourn their loss, as did the citizens of Rome. Many people wailed as they walked the streets during the mourning period lamenting the death of their supreme general. Tiberius agonized over his loss. He expected his son, Germanicus, to be his successor to the throne. Now, those hopes were dashed. He questioned how he died and became paranoid regarding his own safety. The only person he felt he could trust was Sejanus who was willing to die rather than be accused of dishonor. Anyone who would offer their lives on the spot to prove their loyalty was above scrutiny.

It took some time for Tiberius to mourn and accept the death of his son. He withdrew from public life and his responsibilities as emperor during his mourning period and neglected to meet with the government leaders until today. The Ludi Funebres was the perfect way for him to close this chapter and start the business of Rome again.

Sejanus and Pilate were not participating in the games this time. Instead, they were meeting with Tiberius to discuss the road expansion into the Rhine. It was Sejanus's idea that they meet during the games as a kind of honor to Germanicus and Rome and discuss the continued expansion of the empire. He could see that Tiberius needed something to focus on other than Germanicus's death. Tiberius had withdrawn significantly from public view but agreed to meet Sejanus and Pilate during a break in the games.

"Great Caesar," Sejanus said as he saluted and knelt. Caesar and his six-year-old grandson, Caligula, both saluted. Caligula was wearing a little Roman uniform complete with boots, breastplate and a helmet with a red fan tail across the top. His mother, Agrippina, would dress him up with the anticipation that he would, someday, become emperor. "I see you have an emperor in training."

Tiberius smiled as the boy answered. "I am Gaius Caesar Augustus Germanicus," he said as he stood tall and proud. "General Germanicus was my father."

"Well, Gaius Caesar Augustus Germanicus……or how shall I address you?" Pilate asked.

"Caligula," Tiberius added.

Sejanus and Pilate held back their laughter. "Caligula? *Little soldier boots*?" Pilate asked.

"He received the name from some soldiers in the field because of how he was dressed. It has stayed with him," Tiberius said. "His mother Agrippina likes it."

"Someday, you will bow when my name is spoken," Caligula said as if he was emperor now.

"Great Caligula, I bow now, and humbly apologize if I have offended you," Pilate replied.

Sejanus interrupted. "Would you like me to show Caesar Caligula a few things about being a Roman Soldier?"

"And what would you show *me*?" Caligula asked defiantly.

"Well, Pilate could show you how to throw a javelin," Sejanus answered as he nodded toward his friend. "He was champion at the Ludi in Rome. We call him the 'javelin man'."

"I remember that," Tiberius added. "He hit his target at, what, 100 meters[42]?"

Sejanus laughed. "It is amazing that, as time goes on, the distance of the target grows."

"I believe this young soldier will need a little more meat on his bones before he can heft a javelin," Pilate said as he patted the boy on the shoulder.

"You dare to touch the emperor's grandson?" Caligula said in challenge.

Pilate and Sejanus bowed, both with smiles. "We meant no harm to the great Caesar," Sejanus said.

Caligula glared at Pilate. "You *will* regret……….," he started, but was interrupted by Tiberius.

"Well, you wanted to discuss the expansion of the road into the Rhine. Over here, if you will," he said as he pointed to a large table with a map on it.

---

[42] 100 meters = 109 yards

Caligula just watched Sejanus and Pilate ignore him and follow the emperor across the room. Drusus watched from the side hall where no one could see him.

The door flung open as Drusus walked into the chamber where Sejanus was resting by the fire. He was obviously upset about something and glared at Sejanus as he approached him. "You!"

Sejanus stood to his feet and bowed. "To what do I owe this honor?" he asked.

Drusus walked up to a chair and stood behind it, firmly gripping it with his hands as he leaned on the back and spoke. "You! A stranger who was invited to assist in the government while the emperor's son is alive." The tone in Drusus's voice was menacing. "You should be in the field with the troops and horses eating slop, not here in the palace dining with the gods."

"I serve at the pleasure of Caesar," Sejanus said as he bowed to Drusus. "I go where he tells me."

Drusus stepped from behind the chair and stood in front of Sejanus. He was challenging the commander. "I will expose your treachery. Somehow, something will surface to show your true desire; to overthrow the emperor."

"I have no desire to ……" Before Sejanus could finish, Drusus slapped him in the face.

"You dare to lie to the emperor's son?" Drusus questioned.

Sejanus recoiled and slowly turned back to face Drusus. He smiled, turned and started to walk away. Drusus grabbed his toga and stopped him. Sejanus turned back to face Drusus. "If you please, lord…." He said as he pulled his garment from Drusus's hand and continued. "… At Pannonia, there was no blood on your sleeves." He bowed slightly, smiled, and walked out the door, closing it behind him.

Drusus stood staring at the door. He slammed his hand on the table and yelled, "Curse you, Sejanus!"

Chapter 7   Struggle for Power
23 - 26 AD

The villa at the end of town was bustling with people this evening wearing their very best for the occasion. Pontius Pilate was dressed in a purple toga with a yellow hairnet as he greeted guests in the courtyard. It was a fine celebration of marriage. The courtyard was decorated with cut flowers and vines twisted between columns leading to the garden. The smell of lilac and hyacinth was strong. Torches illuminated the courtyard wall with flickering, amber light. Dignitaries and military leaders, some with wives, shared stories of battles, hobbies, and grandkids. With Pilate being the groom and of the equestrian class, many of his acquaintances over the years attended. Since he was friends with Sejanus, the very elite of Rome attended.

"Pilate!" Sejanus entered the courtyard and sought out his friend. "There you are!" He walked briskly across the courtyard to greet him.

"Sejanus!" Pilate grabbed Sejanus's forearm in a mighty embrace. "It is good to see you, commander. I was not sure you would attend."

"And why, pray tell would I not attend the wedding of my friend?" Sejanus asked.

"I did not see Tiberius here, so I thought you might be.....busy. Busy doing the work of the empire."

Sejanus laughed. "I am always busy doing the work of the empire, but never too busy to watch my friend make the biggest mistake of his life!"

"How can marrying my lover and friend be a mistake?" Pilate asked. He realized Sejanus was mostly kidding, so he punched him in the arm.

"Only if she holds you back from your full potential," Sejanus replied.

"Did your wife, Apicata, hold you back from your potential?" Pilate asked.

Sejanus smiled. "And why do you think I divorced her?"

"I see."

Sejanus moved closer to Pilate. "Now, I am free...free to rule Rome," he said with a smile and whispered, "And rule, I shall."

Pilate leaned in close to his friend. "And Tiberius?"

Sejanus pulled Pilate close and continued to whisper. "He is getting old. I am concerned for him. His mind is failing. He is doing things that..... that an emperor should avoid," Sejanus replied.

"What is that, may I ask?"

"Pontius," a man called, interrupting the two. "It is time."

Sejanus rolled his eyes as Pilate followed the man to a stage at the end of the courtyard where the wedding party was positioned. A tall archway covered with roses framed the beautiful bride who was ornately dressed in a white, streaming toga with a veil covering her shoulders. Her hair had little spears through it to symbolize power to the Romans. She had small flowers interspersed in her hair with a wreath on top covered with a yellow hairnet. It was a work of art. She wore selected jewelry and a necklace. She was beautiful by any measure.

"Claudia," Pilate said as he stepped onto the stage. "You are so beautiful."

Claudia blushed as her father took her hand and joined it with Pilate's. "This is a day of celebration. This is a day of marriage. I give my daughter, Claudia Procula, to the hand of Marcus Pontius Pilate, to place her under his authority and care." As he raised their hands, the attendees cheered and raised goblets as the couple was united in marriage. "Let us celebrate!" her father cheered as he pointed to the line of servants bringing out food and drink and placing them on long tables.

Sejanus watched as the festivities unfolded. He thought about his prior marriage and the hinderance his wife, Apicata, created. She was always telling him he was going too far. One time Sejanus sought to solidify his connection with the imperial family by betrothing his daughter Junilla to Tiberius's great nephew, the son of Claudius, Claudius Drusus. At the time the girl was only four years old, but the marriage never happened. The boy mysteriously died of asphyxiation a few days after the betrothal. Another mysterious death of an imperial family member. That was the final straw for his ex-wife, Apicata. It was more than she could handle. Sejanus wondered if she had anything to do with the boy's death.

Sejanus knew that he could not become emperor unless he was a part of the imperial family. He had to find a way to insert himself into the Julian line to be accepted by the senate as a viable successor to Tiberius.

It was late into the evening and many in the wedding party, attendees and guests were showing signs of fatigue from the ever-flowing river of wine and food. It was time to conclude the marriage celebration, so Claudia's mother, father, and siblings pulled her onto the stage and gathered around her. They pretended to dote on her as their helpless, little girl, saying such things as, "We'll protect you," and "Poor helpless little girl."

Several men stood across the room and began slowly clapping their hands in unison, increasing the tempo and volume with each strike. As they reached near applause, Pilate stepped from the group and advanced toward Claudia in a determined, crouching manner as though he was sneaking up on his prey. He stepped onto the stage and grabbed Claudia from her family's grasp. A mock struggle ensued as he pulled her away and tossed her over his shoulder with her pleading and crying. It was like the time he swooped her out of a grape vat and carried her through the vineyard. They both laughed as he quickly left the stage and headed toward the exit, followed by Claudia's family as well as most of the wedding guests, applauding and cheering him on as Claudia pretended to be abducted.

"You brute," someone yelled as they laughed and cheered.

"Don't drop her," Sejanus yelled.

Pilate adjusted Claudia into a sitting position on his shoulder like he did at the vineyard, and maneuvered his way through the crowd, out the courtyard, and down the street to his house. The wedding party followed them carrying a spina alba, or a whitehorn torch, honoring the goddess Ceres[43]. They were singing the Hymanaeus, or song of marriage, as they followed them to Pilate's house playing their stringed instruments and drums. People along the route opened their shutters and doors and sang along as the procession went by. They were waiving, throwing flowers, and burning incense in their honor.

When they arrived at Pilate's house, several people were at the door waiting for them. Pilate lowered Claudia to the ground and peered inside. The entry room was decorated with flowers, candles, some bread and fruit, some wine, and a sofa with pillows. Pilate turned to the guests, smiled, and walked into the house.

One of the bridesmaids handed Claudia a bag. She pulled out some sheep's wool soaked in oil and fat. She smeared the doorposts with the mixture to symbolize protection from the gods. After she finished, Pilate stepped to the doorway and broke a loaf of bread over Claudia's head. The wedding party broke into cheers and applause as the newly married couple entered Pilate's house and closed the door.

Claudia and Pilate were married. Pilate was forty-three years old and becoming well established in his military career. They had their whole lives ahead of them.

It was early in the morning following Pilate's wedding. Sejanus returned to the palace, tired and half drunk. He walked into his quarters to find Livilla, Drusus's wife, waiting for him.

"Livilla! What are you doing here?" he asked.

"I came to see you, to be with you," she replied seductively.

"Where is Drusus?" Sejanus asked as he looked over his shoulder half expecting him to be standing there.

"Away on some business of the emperor," she said as she ran her fingers along the smooth edge of a table as she approached Sejanus. "My husband is always away, doing something, with someone. He neglects me so much."

---

[43] Ceres – Goddess of agriculture, grain crops and fertility

Sejanus could smell the lavender in her hair as she leaned in close. "He is a fool, then," he said, "to leave such a beautiful woman alone."

"And in need," she replied. She leaned in and kissed him passionately. Sejanus could feel his heartbeat increase, his hands became sweaty as they kissed.

Sejanus pulled back to look at her beauty. "I fear we will be caught. We must use discretion," he said.

"Hah," Livilla replied. "Discretion. I prefer we make it so no one will question our 'friendship'."

"And just what do you suggest?" Sejanus asked.

Livilla laid on her back across the bed and looked up toward the ceiling. She smiled. "Patience."

---****---

Sejanus followed his father as head of the Praetorian Guard, a relatively new entity formed to protect the emperor and assist him with the administration of the empire. Lucius Strabo had developed the guard into a military powerhouse with nearly 12,000 soldiers stationed in and around the city of almost two million people. They were the elite force that everyone feared, and Sejanus was in charge.

Sejanus knew the power he had, and he wanted more. He transferred almost all of the administrative functions of the empire to himself, making many of the decisions and initiating plans that only the emperor would normally consider. Tiberius was aging and it was easy for Sejanus to show he needed his help. The death of Germanicus had a profound impact on the emperor and his health. Sejanus could see he had an opportunity to position himself in such a way as to become the only Roman citizen to ever be emperor. All he needed was to install himself into the Julian family in some way for the senate to confirm his appointment as emperor. His failure to do so through the betrothal of his daughter, Junilla, was a devastating setback, but was not the final blow to his quest. He already had the full trust and support of the military.

---****---

Three years ago, Sejanus attended the wedding of Pontius Pilate and Claudia Procula. Today, he stood at the bedside of Drusus Julius Caesar who was extremely ill. Drusus laid in his bed, eyes closed, barely breathing. His life was slowly leaving his body. He had been sick for days and getting worse. Some said he was being poisoned. Others that he had an incurable illness, possibly an infection. No one knew why he was dying. Only that he was.

Livilla, his wife, was sitting on the side of the bed wiping Drusus's forehead with a cloth. "Poor dear," she said. "If only they knew what was wrong. I pray that the gods will heal you and make you strong again, my love." She leaned forward as she kissed him on the forehead.

Drusus barely opened his eyes and looked at her. He could see Sejanus standing behind her with his hand on her shoulder. "....Sej.. you did…." Drusus was so weak, he could hardly speak.

Livilla leaned closer, turning her ear to his mouth. "…You……you…." He coughed.

Livilla looked to Sejanus. There was no one else in the room. She smiled and said, "He's trying to tell me something."

Sejanus stepped forward and leaned over Drusus. "What is it, my friend?" he said with a smirk.

Drusus tried to spit in Sejanus's face, but the saliva ran down his chin instead, making him look even more of an invalid and totally helpless.

Livilla wiped up the spittle. "There, dear. Just rest."

Sejanus leaned in close to Drusus's ear. He whispered, "There was no blood on your sleeves."

"What was that?" Livilla asked.

Sejanus ignored her question. "Call me when it's over," he said as he headed for the door. Tiberius burst through the door, startling Sejanus. "Caesar," he said and bowed. "I was coming to get you."

Tiberius approached the bed and looked at his son. Drusus's eyes were closed and drool was seeping from the corner of his mouth. He struggled to open his eyes to see Tiberius. He tried to move, but his arms were like lead. He tried to speak, but nothing came out. Tiberius moved closer to his lips to hear him. Drusus whispered something, closed his eyes and let out a sigh.

Tiberius leaned down to listen to his heart. Nothing.

"What did he say?" Sejanus asked.

Tiberius looked at him intently. "Beware."

"Beware?" Sejanus asked. "He must know of a plot against you, Caesar."

Livilla glanced briefly at Sejanus, who was still standing near the opened door. She laid her head on her husband's chest and began to wail. Her despair was quite convincing.

Tiberius brushed Drusus's hair back from his forehead and kissed him. "It will go with him to his grave, I fear." He turned and walked out of the room.

Livilla continued to cry as the attendants came in to prepare the body. Livilla walked to Sejanus, who offered his shoulder in support. As Livilla laid her head on his shoulder crying, Sejanus whispered, "For Rome," as he rubbed her back and comforted her.

---****---

The command center for the Praetorian Guard was situated in the Castra Praetoria, a large building on the outer edge of the Roman government complex. The center room of the Castra was where Sejanus conducted his business of running the empire.

Much had happened in the last few years. Tiberius's son, Drusus, unexpectedly died leaving a void for succession. Many thought Drusus had been poisoned, possibly by his wife, but no one would speak out about it.

Tiberius's nephew, Claudius, was a possible successor. However, his speech impediment and shuffling gate left many to believe he was not fit for the position. Instead, Tiberius looked to one of his grandsons as successor. He saw Caligula as a viable successor even though he was much younger than his older brothers. At thirteen years old he had a lot to learn, particularly since his father, General Germanicus, died when he was at a young age. Caligula spent much of his time with his grandfather Tiberius, who filled the fatherless void.

Tiberius's mental health continued to decline as he aged becoming more paranoid each day after Drusus's death. Drusus's parting warning struck deep into Tiberius's soul. He seldom went to the imperial throne room, the senate or in public because of his growing paranoia. His involvement with actively running the empire had trickled down to almost nothing. The death of Drusus left Tiberius with an administrative void, too. Tiberius had been transferring some of his administrative powers to his son in the anticipation of him becoming emperor. Instead, he now needed to transfer the same responsibilities and powers to Sejanus, the one person he felt he could trust.

Sejanus felt that Tiberius might now be ready to embrace him as a son through marriage. He decided it was time to approach the emperor about something very important to him.

The corridor was dark and musty. The room at the end of the hall was where Tiberius spent most of his time now. He would meet with guests in his chamber rather than a public space because it felt safer. It would be more difficult for someone to assassinate him there, except by poison, so everything he ate and drank was tested by his cupbearer.

"Sejanus," Tiberius said as he watched him enter the room. "Come. Sit," he added as he patted the seat next to him. Sejanus walked across the room and, after bowing, sat next to the emperor. "To what do I owe this visit?" Tiberius asked.

Sejanus glanced around the room to see two guards standing nearby. He nonchalantly motioned for them to exit. Tiberius was so engrossed fiddling with a piece of papyrus that he was unaware the guards had left. "Great Tiberius," Sejanus started. "I would like to ask your permission for something."

Tiberius pushed the papyrus aside. "It sounds serious, my friend," he said as he looked up. "What is it?"

Sejanus cleared his throat. "I ask for the hand of Drusus's widow, Livilla, in marriage."

Tiberius glared at Sejanus. "You want to marry the widow of my dead son?"

As soon as Sejanus heard those words, he knew he had made a mistake. His hands began to sweat, his heart raced. "Great Tiberius. She is a lonely woman for whom I feel compassion for…"

"Compassion?" Tiberius asked as he raised his voice. "Compassion or lust?"

"Great Emperor……."

"Yes," Tiberius said as he cut Sejanus off. "Emperor. Don't you forget that, Sejanus," Tiberius said as he rose to his feet and looked down on his visitor. It was one of the few times Sejanus saw the power and anger of the emperor. He knew that Tiberius could order his execution at any time, even if it likely would not be carried out because of his own control over the Praetorian Guard. It was a demonstration of the power between the two men, and Sejanus relented.

"I will always be your subject, great Tiberius," Sejanus said meekly as he bowed.

Tiberius took a few steps away and whirled back to face Sejanus. "You would do well, Sejanus, to not overstep your boundaries or fall victim to your ambitions." He moved a little closer, sat next to him, and looked him in the eyes as he continued. "Do I have your complete and total loyalty?"

Sejanus didn't hesitate. "To the death, Great Caesar," he said as he bowed.

Tiberius paused. "To the death?" He looked intently at Sejanus. "I hope it never comes to that."

"Great Caesar. I have known Livilla many years. I meant no disrespect." Sejanus rose, bowed before the emperor. "My life is yours, Caesar." He saluted, turned and quickly left the room. He did not want to give Tiberius enough time to change his mind.

Pilate walked briskly down the corridor of the Castra Praetorium toward Sejanus's office. His armor rattled as the sound of his footsteps echoed off the stone walkway and walls. *Why does he want to meet with me? What's so important to rouse someone from sleep?* It was well before sunrise when Sejanus called Pilate out of his slumber to an important meeting. Pilate could only speculate what could possibly be happening. He wondered if Tiberius died and Sejanus was now the emperor.

Pilate rounded the corner and past the guards at the door. He saluted Sejanus as he entered. "Commander."

Sejanus looked up as Pilate entered. "You must be wondering why I called you here at this hour," he replied.

"I do wonder, Sejanus. Is it Tiberius?"

Sejanus laughed. "No. Our esteemed emperor is still alive and playing with little boys," he said disgustedly. "I have called you here because I have an appointment as governor for you that must be filled right away."

"Governor?" Pilate was surprised by the statement. He had no intentions of becoming governor of any region. It wasn't a thought that he even entertained. "Of where?"

"Judea."

"The Jews?" Pilate walked over to a chair and seated himself.

"Is that a problem?" Sejanus asked. "I know you think poorly of them, but will your personal feelings interfere with your ability to govern?"

"No," Pilate said emphatically. "I may not like them, and consider them cowards, but I will govern as needed," he replied. "They are just a bunch of stubborn, short-sighted fanatics."

"They are, but they are easily controlled," Sejanus added. "They operate under a religious hierarchy under a king. Herod Antipas: Herod the Great's son. He's a puppet for Rome but we need him to govern the people in concert with the religious leaders. The end result is they can deal with their own issues with little to no involvement from Rome. You will be responsible for collecting taxes and maintaining order in the region."

"That sounds good," Pilate replied, "but we know how much they oppose Rome and are awaiting their messiah – their 'king' – to arrive and free them."

Sejanus laughed. "A king, yet they have no military to speak of. We could crush them in a day. No. They will be a people who will remain as subjects to the empire."

"And how can you be so sure?" Pilate asked.

"First, do you fear a king whose father murdered babies to protect his kingdom?" Sejanus asked.

"Of course not. I fear no one."

"Good," Sejanus replied. "The leader of the religious government is a high priest named Joseph Ben Caiaphas. He has been their religious leader for years. I suggest you retain him as a show of his acceptance by Rome and our partnership with the Jews. He should be able to control the religious fanatics."

"And the governor of Syria? Does he agree with my appointment and retention of Caiaphas?" Pilate asked. As governor of Judea Pilate would report directly to the legate[44] of Syria and require his approval of his appointments.

"He is absent. Senator Lucius Lamia is legate of Syria, but he has yet to go. His duties in Rome are prohibiting him from leaving."

"And the current governor of Judea?"

"Valerius Gratus. He died unexpectedly," Sejanus answered. "That is why I called you here at this hour. I need to make sure we have Judea under control until Senator Lamia arrives at his post. We do not want them to try and amass an army or institute a rebellion because Rome has no presence."

Pilate thought for a few moments. With the legate of Syria absent, he would be free to rule Judea the way he saw fit. There would be no oversight except for Sejanus, his brother in battle, until Senator Lamia arrives in Syria. Pilate stood to his feet. "I am your servant, Sejanus."

---

[44] Legate - similar to a deputy general commanding the legions in a region controlled by Rome. The provincial governors reported to the regional legate who reported to the emperor.

"Good. Good," Sejanus said as he slapped Pilate on the shoulder. "You will make a good governor, Pilate. Now, sit. Please. I have a lot of information about the Jews to share with you before you leave."

---****---

Tiberius was often found wandering the grounds of the government complex, from the praetorium to the senate and beyond. Sometimes he was seen walking with little boys and Caligula, playing and holding hands. Rumors had begun to spread of the perversion Tiberius and Caligula were involved with. It was an abomination that revolted many, but no one would openly speak out against it. Instead, secret conversations about their misdeeds were held in the dark hallways and alleys of the empire.

Sejanus had failed to insert himself into the Julian family by marriage of his daughter, Junilla, or himself. His last option would be to isolate Tiberius away from Rome and show the senate that Tiberius was getting too old and unable to rule because of his 'incapacity.' This would enable him to continue to consolidate his power and eventually seek the agreement and appointment as emperor by the senate. It would be the first time a citizen from the equestrian class became emperor of Rome.

Sejanus stood at the door of the emperor's chambers, waiting. Soon, the door opened slightly and a guard exited, followed by Tiberius who closed the door behind him. Sejanus could hear the sound of giggling from inside the room. .

"What is it, Sejanus?" Tiberius asked. He was obviously annoyed by the interruption.

"Mighty Caesar. As commander of the Praetorian Guard, my first duty is to your protection."

"I know that," Tiberius retorted.

"I believe you should consider moving to a safe location where you can be free to live out your life as you please unhindered, and be safe from any nefarious plot against you that could arise," Sejanus answered.

"Explain."

Sejanus paused. "As you age, great Caesar, we know that factions for power can surface and be embolden to try to gain control of the empire. Your predecessors encountered challenges to their position during their reigns. Some have fallen victim to the quest for power from others. I humbly implore you, oh great Caesar, to consider a temporary move for your safety."

"What are you not telling me, Sejanus? Spit it out!" he demanded.

Sejanus had Tiberius exactly where he wanted him. "Great Caesar. Agrippina, the wife of Germanicus, is gathering support from the senate by convincing them Germanicus was poisoned."

"How do you know this? What is my daughter-in-law trying to do?" Tiberius asked.

"I don't know."

Tiberius was obviously upset at the thought that a plot against him could be brewing. "I should have her executed on the spot!" Tiberius yelled.

"I would caution against that, great Caesar."

"Why?" Tiberius asked, confused.

"If she is executed, the revolt could break open and the conspirators could gain power and remove you. If she is watched, the traitors will be revealed and I can capture them. I can watch her every move, who she meets with," Sejanus said as he moved closer to Tiberius. "There could be conspirators in the senate," he whispered.

"And where would I move to? The villa on Capris is not finished."

"The countryside in Campania."

"Campania? I'd be in the shadows of Vesuvius," Tiberius replied.

"Yes, with the rich soils, the grapes, the ocean air…it will do you well, great Caesar," Sejanus replied and bowed slightly. "We have a secure location where you will be safe with the protection of the Praetorian Guard. You will also be relatively close to Rome for communications."

"Campania." Tiberius whispered. "Yes, safe. I have grave concerns that I will also fall victim to someone's ambition for power. My sons are gone," he said with a sigh, "and now you tell me my daughter-in-law is conspiring against me! She must be plotting for one of her sons to be my successor. Yes, I believe it would be good to temporarily relocate to a safe area and allow you to 'clean up.'"

"Very well, great Caesar. I will arrange the move and assure we stay in constant communications regarding the affairs of the empire. You will be under the constant protection of the Praetorian Guard." Sejanus bowed, turned and walked down the hallway.

Sejanus was successful with playing on Tiberius's paranoia and was able to easily isolate him from Rome and the senate. Now he could move forward with his plan to become emperor.

Chapter 8   Pilate in Judea
27 AD

Caesarea Maritima was the largest city in Judea with a population of more than 125,000 people when Pontius Pilate and his wife, Claudia, arrived. The magnificently engineered harbor was a major center for shipping and commerce. The city was situated along the coastline with the palace, a theater capable of seating 5,000 people, a library and cemetery.

    Pilate took in the sights while Claudia admired her jewelry box on her lap as their carriage, known as a carpentum, rattled slowly down the road from the harbor through the city. The leather seats were soft and cool as the couple swayed to the rhythm of the rocking carriage. "This is going to be quite the experience," he said.

    "Why do you say that?" Claudia asked as she pulled a necklace from her box and held it to the light to see the jewels sparkle.

    "These Jews," Pilate said as he pointed to the people along the roadside watching their carriage rattle by. "They are quite an odd group. They believe in one god and that he is going to deliver them from Rome by sending a 'savior' for them."

    "I don't see anything odd about that. Many countries have odd beliefs and want to be freed from Rome's grasp," Claudia replied still admiring her jewelry. "You know there are Jews in Rome."

    Pilate turned to her. "Of course I know there are Jews there," he said in an irritated tone. "I just don't understand their dogmatism toward their beliefs. They have no compromise and demand that everyone obey their religious laws without exception."

    "Everyone that is a Jew," Claudia replied.

    "Oh. So you know a few things about these Jews?"

    Claudia smiled. "I have met with Jews in Rome and had many questions for them," she replied.

"Why would you have questions?" Pilate asked.

"Marcus. You have heard the stories of the Jews and their escape from Egypt, how their god parted the Red Sea so they could cross on dry land......"

"..... and drowned the Egyptians when they tried to follow by closing the sea," Pilate interrupted. "Yes, I've heard the stories, and so has every Roman and most all peoples in this region."

"What if it was true?" Claudia asked. "You would have to at least believe in the miracles."

"What?"

"What type of people are they who say their god is the only one, true god, and then have miracles like that occur?" Claudia asked. "What if it was true?"

"It wasn't. It couldn't have happened," Pilate replied and gazed out the window again. "You haven't become a secret Jew, have you?"

"No. Not hardly," Claudia replied. "Just curious and intrigued," she said as she returned to admiring her jewelry.

"You know, their military is made up of mostly Romans," he said changing the subject to something he felt more comfortable with after his indoctrination with Sejanus. He was repeating what he had learned more for his benefit than Claudia's. "Herod the Great was appointed King of the Jews when Marc Antony was governor of Egypt, which included Judea. Antony didn't protect them from the Parthians, so Rome sent Herod back to Judea with an army, a Roman army. We've been established there for years. The only people opposing Rome are the religious leaders and fanatics, and they have no one to lead them."

"Don't they have a Jewish king?" Claudia asked as she exchanged the necklace for a ring.

"Herod the Great's son; Herod Antipas. A puppet. He has no real power." Pilate turned to her. "Did you know his father had babies murdered because he thought a newborn was their Messiah and was going to become the new king?"

Claudia returned the ring and closed the box on her lap, folding her hands on top. "Yes, I had heard that and I think it was a horrible thing to do. Killing defenseless children," she replied.

"I'm not worried about him."

Claudia could tell something was bothering Pilate. "Then, what *are* you worried about, my love?"

Pilate looked up. "I don't know. I have a feeling...."

"Feeling!" Claudia snickered. "I have a feeling, too," she said as she leaned across the carriage and kissed him. "That you will be an excellent governor."

The carriage came to a stop and the door opened. Pilate stepped out and looked around as a soldier helped Claudia out of the wagon. The line of wagons behind them came to a halt in a cloud of dust. A bustle of people started to unload the cargo of personal property and supplies of the governor.

"This is beautiful," Claudia said as she took in the view. The city was magnificent by any standard. Perched along the shore, it looked out on the blue Mediterranean Sea lined with sandy beaches. The enclosed port was an engineering marvel of the Romans. A large palace was situated on the shore near the theater, which faced the sea. Long, stone and marble hallways linked the various buildings together. The warm breeze smelled of salt and sea.

A soldier walked up to the couple and saluted. He was in his mid-forties with greying hair at the brow and a big smile. "Governor Marcus Pontius Pilate. I am Manlius, your secretary. Welcome to Caesarea Maritima – your new home," he said with a bright smile as his hand swept across the expanse.

Claudia held Pilate's arm and smiled. "This looks like a rather pleasant place to stay," she said with a broad smile.

Pilate smiled and patted her hand. "It does."

"This way, governor," Manlius said as he led the procession up the steps into the place, followed by a line of slaves carrying their belongings from the wagons.

The palace was ornate with large rooms, stone and marble hallways, a small theater where one could orate a thought or present a defense before the governor, pools, cooking areas, a library, and more. Guards were placed around and in the palace at strategic points to assure safety and privacy of the governor and his wife.

As the new governor of Judea, it was important that Pontius Pilate make his presence and power known to the people. Though he was a military commander, the primary duties of his position were to act as head of the judicial system and to collect the all important taxes. He was responsible for maintaining civil peace. Any unrest would not be tolerated since it would likely be reported to Rome by Herod or the legate of Syria. Fortunately, the legate of Syria was absent for the first few years of Pilate's appointment, so he was free to rule as he saw fit. His rule was absolute. Regardless, he could not afford to have any bad news reach Rome about his governing of Judea, particularly since this was his first regional command. It was his intent to keep the Jews on a tight leash.

Pilate's troops were meant more as a police force than a military force in an attempt to appear less controlling. He had the power to impose sentences for any crime based on Roman law up to and including **capital punishment, which he often did**. Herod also had the authority to inflict capital punishment as king with the governor's approval, but seldom administered that punishment, except when he was insulted or acted impetuously. The priests had the authority under their religious laws and, on occasion when stoning was expected, the fervor of the mob would take over and execute punishment. Since it did not involve Roman law or was a military threat, Pilate could care less if they killed each other off.

Pilate was also responsible for collecting tributes and taxes, for disbursing funds and for the minting of coins. Because the Romans allowed a certain degree of local control, Pilate shared a limited amount of civil and religious power with the **Sanhedrin**[45]. If

---

[45] An assembly of seventy-one Jewish elders that sat as a tribunal regarding spiritual and cultural matters of the Jewish people.

Pilate believed he could benefit from using the local leaders whatever their capacity, he would do so without hesitation.

One of his first acts was to appoint the chief priest of the Sanhedrin. Being a Roman, he knew the importance of gods in a culture and was willing to expedite their selection to keep continuity with their leadership. To do so, Pilate would have to travel to Jerusalem, 110 kilometers[46] away. It would take him a month to make the round trip, stopping in several cities along the way to make himself known and administer trials or judgment in the region as needed. Claudia chose to stay in Caesarea Maritima rather than travel to Jerusalem, though she had every right to accompany her husband on such trips and be well cared for. She was content settling in and had no desire to go with him this time. Besides, she had no interest in riding in a cramped carriage for weeks. Without Claudia he could pack much less and be ready to go in the morning. But before he could leave for Jerusalem, there was something he had to do.

Pilate knew that his appointment and arrival could be suspect by many people considering he had no prior experience with leading such a post. He pondered the best way to show his authority and to squelch any possible opposition from the Jews or otherwise. He wanted them to know he was the absolute ruler in this region.

"Bring him in," Pilate ordered to the guards. The guards escorted a man into the room and before Pilate. The man's hands were chained, his clothes torn and dirty. He was bleeding in several spots on his body. His face was beaten. He looked down at the floor as he stood before the governor.

"Linus Dio. Theft of some bread and food from a vendor, assault, escape," a guard read from a small scroll.

"My family was starving, governor, and I….." the man started to say.

"Stop!" Pilate ordered as he raised his hand. "Thieves will not be tolerated in my kingdom."

---

[46] 110 kilometers = 62 miles

"Kingdom?" the man asked. Pilate stood to his feet. The man immediately realized his words were not welcomed.

"Yes," Pilate said as he slowly approached the man. "Kingdom. And for your crimes, you are to suffer ten lashes."

The man looked up and with a slight smile and said humbly, "Thank you, sir."

"…….. and crucified," Pilate added.

The man froze with a look of disbelief. "Why? I have…."

"Because you are a thief. I will not have thieves in my province. Take him away." The guards started to drag the man off who did not resist. He knew his fate was sealed. "Wait," Pilate ordered. The guards stopped and looked back to the governor. "Make sure he has a loaf of bread stuffed in his mouth when he is crucified," Pilate said with a smile. "You wanted bread, you shall have it. My gift to you."

The man went limp as the guards drug him from the room. Pilate returned to his seat. "Next."

The parade of prisoners lasted almost an hour. One after another Pilate listened to the charges and sentenced each one, either to prison, lashes, or crucifixion. No one was exonerated. He was merciless with his judgement. Word traveled quickly of his brutal nature to the surrounding areas. Pilate accomplished exactly what he wanted; for everyone to fear him, civilian and soldiers alike.

Now he could leave for Jerusalem.

---****---

The palace of Herod the Great was situated on the western side of Jerusalem and overlooked the city and temple. The compound was of such size that it easily accommodated Pilate while visiting Jerusalem and was near the Praetorium where Pilate conducted his administrative tasks. It was constructed of marble and stone with main structures built on raised foundations. The buildings were complete with banquet halls capable of seating a hundred guests. The palace had ponds with bronze fountains, walkways of marble, gardens and porticoes decorated with flowers of all types, courtyards and main quarters for the royal family and special guests.

Pilate was in the Praetorium standing near a window looking out across the city toward the hills when a soldier entered the room and saluted. "Joseph Ben Caiaphas is here to see you," the soldier announced.

Pilate turned to see the soldier standing alone at the doorway. "Where is he?" he asked.

"Waiting in the courtyard, commander."

"Why is that?" Pilate asked.

"He said it is against their laws for them to come into the Praetorium where a Roman was because they would be defiled," the guard replied.

"Defiled?" Pilate asked as he turned to face the guard obviously irritated. "He wants me to come to him?"

Manlius was seated at a table across the room reading some

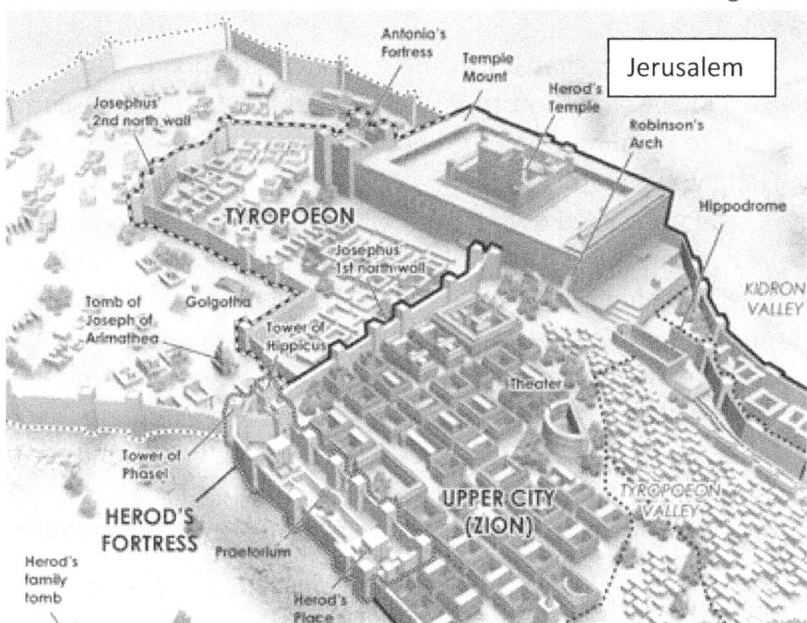

documents. "It is a small request for now, Pontius," he said as he looked up. "We must gain the support of the Sanhedrin to keep these people under control, governor."

"Very well," Pilate said as he took a deep breath and walked out the archway into the courtyard.

"Esteemed Governor," Caiaphas said as he and the two priests with him bowed while Pilate approached. He spread out his arms in welcome. "We welcome you to Jerusalem." The long, flowing black robes of the high priest of the Jews was decorated with gold embroidery, special designs and precious stones. He wore a turban on his head with a long veil over the top draped over his shoulders and along the side of his arms. On his chest he wore a large breastplate with precious stones aligned in rows forming a square. In his right hand he carried a large, wooden staff. Standing before Pilate in his priestly dress with his long, grey beard he looked like a man to be respected. "I trust your trip was comfortable?"

Pilate composed himself. He wanted to slap the priest for making him come to them, but instead was subdued. "Comfortable?" Pilate replied. "If you like riding in a tumbling barrel, it was fine."

"I must try that sometime," Caiaphas quipped. "I am pleased I have this opportunity, esteemed governor, to welcome you and to learn how we, the spiritual leaders of the Jewish people, can help you govern."

Pilate walked over to the rail along the courtyard and looked out on the city again. He could see thousands of tents erected outside the city walls. Smoke from campfires filled the air. Throngs of people filled the streets and marketplaces. The temple was ornate and crowded and stood majestically overlooking the city. Hundreds of vendors around and in the temple offered animals for sacrifices. The air was filled with the hustle and bustle of city life.

"Why are so many people here in this city?" Pilate asked.

"Tomorrow is the 'Day of Atonement[47],' one of the most important Jewish celebrations of the year. It refers…." Caiaphas began, only to be cut off.

---

[47] Day of Atonement – When the high priest would offer a sacrifice in the temple

"I don't care what the day represents." He turned back to Caiaphas. "My only concern is to make sure your people do not step out of line and cause me any trouble."

"What trouble could we possibly cause, esteemed governor? We have no military."

Pilate walked up to Caiaphas and stood before him, looking down on the priest to intimidate him. "So, are you saying there is nothing I should be concerned about?" Pilate asked.

Caiaphas cleared his throat. "There are very small groups of zealots that we, the Jewish leaders, have addressed and imprisoned with the support of Herod. Other than that, we have a few people who proclaim a 'king of the Jews' is coming, but we have had that proclamation for centuries. It remains a wish, esteemed governor, an empty hope of the people."

"And who is proclaiming this?" Pilate asked as he turned back to the window and looked out on the city.

Caiaphas chuckled. "One is a wild man at the Jordan River."

"A wild man? What do you mean, 'wild'?"

"He stays in the wilderness eating off the land. He never comes into Jerusalem. He has very few followers, maybe fifty. They have no weapons, no uniforms, no military background. They are nothing, governor."

Pilate looked at Caiaphas. "There is always something, priest."

"He stands by the river proclaiming a king is coming, one who will rule the Jewish nation, with justice and....."

"Enough already," Pilate said cutting Caiaphas off. The two stood quietly for a few seconds before Pilate continued. "What other 'festivals' do you Jews celebrate that brings all of these.....people here?"

Caiaphas chose his words carefully. "The Passover[48] is one of the most significant of our celebrations."

---

on behalf of the Jewish nation for the forgiveness of sins.

[48] Passover – A major Jewish holiday that celebrates the exodus of the Jewish people from slavery in Egypt. The celebration lasts seven days.

"How many people come here?"

"Maybe…..100,000."

"What?" Pilate briskly walked toward Caiaphas. "Are you telling me 100,000 Jews, plus the 100,000 that live here, are not a threat to my rule?"

"I assure you, they are not," Caiaphas replied.

"How can you be so sure, priest?"

"They are here for religious purposes, to offer sacrifices and worship. Not to battle Romans."

Pilate paced in front of Caiaphas, unsettled that so many people would be in one place at one time. "It would seem that your knowledge of your people, traditions, and purposes is of significant value to me and Rome. Prefect Valerius Gratus was pleased with the work you did to represent your people. Therefore, I am going to retain you as the high priest of your people."

"Thank you, esteemed governor," Caiaphas replied as he bowed.

"But make no mistake, priest," Pilate added as he stopped in front of Caiaphas. "I expect you will keep your people under control, or the streets will flow with their blood."

Pilate watched as Caiaphas nodded, turned and exited the room. "I believe I need to see this wild man for myself," he whispered.

----****----

The Jordan river was a beautiful sight meandering through the lush valley just 32 kilometers[49] east of Jerusalem. The water was green and calm. The river was lined with trees, grasses and bushes that framed the gently flowing stream. It was quite a beautiful sight to Pilate as he crested a small hill on horseback, followed by four Roman soldiers. They stopped at the summit and observed the activity in the little valley below. A man was standing in the river about mid-thigh deep in the water. A few people were sitting along

---

[49] 32 kilometers – 20 miles

the banks listening to him. Pilate and his troops were just close enough to hear.

"Repent and be baptized for the forgiveness of your sins," the man yelled. "The kingdom of God is near. There is one coming after me that I am not worthy of untying his sandal. I baptize you with water; but He will baptize you with the Holy Spirit and fire."

The soldiers could see that there were no weapons, no military, no horses. Several of the people appeared to be lame. A man stepped forward and waded into the water as the others watched. Pilate and his soldiers watched from the hill as the wild man in the river yelled, "Heavenly father, forgive this man of his sins." With that, he dunked the man under the water and pulled him up. The man raised his arms triumphantly and yelled. Several people on the bank clapped as the soaked man returned to the bank.

"That's it?" Pilate asked. "Some crazy man dunking people in a river? That is my opposition?" Pilate whirled on his horse. "I've seen enough."

"What would you like us to do, governor?" one of the soldiers asked.

"Nothing right now. We will keep a wary eye on him. Tell me if you see or hear anything developing. Otherwise," Pilate chuckled and continued, "...go take a bath with him if you want." Pilate kicked the horse in its shanks and galloped off, followed closely by his soldiers.

The wild man in the river watched as they rode over the horizon.

----****----

Pilate didn't care much for Herod Antipas, the current ruler of the Jews. The idea that any leader could kill children because they perceived them as a threat to his rule was as bad as the Caesars who slew their family members or friends to gain power. Pilate felt that Herod was a nuisance and came from a cowardly line. He would prefer to not meet him at all.

The feelings were mutual for Herod who considered Pilate an 'interference' to his rule rather than a superior. Herod liked to live like a king. His palace boasted several banquet halls with ornate decorations and long hallways with statues and sculptures. A large throne sat facing the entrance where he liked the pomp and splendor of people formally addressing him. Herod was careful not to call himself 'king' because of the potential conflict with the emperor. Therefore, he resigned himself to be the tetrarch[50] to avoid any misconceptions by Rome. However, he did not want to share his rule with anyone, particularly a Roman governor. He disliked Rome's oppression as much as the next Jew, maybe more, because it undermined his own rule as king. The reality though was he had to acquiesce to the power of Rome or suffer the consequences. And Herod was not one to suffer.

Pilate was reclining on some pillows next to a long table covered with food and drink. It was Herod's way to try and impress the new governor and win his favor. Some musicians played their instruments as a woman danced nearby, attempting to arouse the manhood of the guests, to no avail. Pilate ignored her and continued speaking.

"I rode out to the Jordan this morning and saw a man standing in the river dunking people."

Herod finished his gulp of wine and sighed. "Yes. That would be John," he said disgustedly.

"John? A friend of yours?"

"Oh, no. No. Not a friend." Herod shifted in his seat.

"Is he a threat to the peace and safety of the region?" Pilate asked. Herod laughed irritating the governor. "I don't see this as being funny at all."

"No. Governor. I apologize. I was struck to think John the Baptist could be a threat to anyone...other than the locusts he eats," he said as he laughed again.

"John the Baptist?"

---

[50] Tetrarch – 'ruler of a quarter'

"Yes. He has been standing in that river for some time now, trying to get the Jews to repent of their sins and be baptized," Herod replied. "I assure you, Pilate, he is quite harm......"

Pilate slammed his fist on the table causing Herod to spill his goblet of wine. The musicians and dancer stopped. "You *will* address me as governor, Herod," Pilate said menacingly.

"I apologize, esteemed governor," Herod said as he choked out the bitter words. "I meant no disrespect." He motioned for the entertainers to continue.

"Very well." Pilate quickly settled down and returned to the conversation. He knew Herod was scared of him, and he liked it. "Then, this John the … the… what? Baptist?"

"Yes. Baptist." Herod could see the puzzlement on Pilate's face and continued as he pushed some grapes into his mouth. "It's symbolic. He submerses people as a symbol of them washing their sins away and becoming pure through the forgiveness of God."

"Does he have an army?"

Herod choked on the grapes. "I'm sorry," he said as he tried to gather himself. "Army!" The entertainers stopped again.

"I should have you drawn and quartered right now!" Pilate yelled as he stood to his feet and looked down on Herod, still choking.

Herod continued to compose himself as he tried to explain. He motioned for the entertainers to leave the room. "No, Governor…" he held up his hand to stop Pilate. …*cough*… "The idea of John…."_ *cough* "… with an army.." *cough*… Herod motioned to Pilate's seat. "Please…." *cough*

Pilate returned to his seat and waited. Herod gathered himself and continued. "Mighty governor, I meant no disrespect. It was just the thought of John having an army. He doesn't even have clothes to wear or food to eat. He is completely harmless, I assure you."

"Then why are people following him?"

Herod took a large gulp of wine to clear his throat. "Our people believe God can forgive sins and give us eternal life with Him. They seek Him," he said as he pointed upwards

"The Fields of Elysium," Pilate replied.

Herod ignored Pilate's comment and continued. "I assure you, governor. Neither John nor his followers are any threat. In fact, us Jews as a nation are not a threat to Rome."

"Until someone comes and leads them," Pilate said sternly.

"*I* am leading them, and they are not a threat," Herod replied.

Pilate stood to his feet and wiped off his uniform. "Then, it appears we will have a good working relationship, Herod Antipas."

"We will," Herod said as he rose to escort Pilate to the door with a full goblet of wine in his hand.

Pilate stopped at the door and turned to look Herod eye to eye. "We better," he said, and walked out.

Herod watched Pilate leave, then slowly turned back to view the elaborate spread of food and drink he laid out for the new governor. He walked over to the table and began kicking the food and drink onto the floor like a child having a tantrum. "Damn him," he yelled as he trashed the banquet with his goblet in hand spilling the wine. When finished, he raised his goblet in a mock toast to Pilate. "To our relationship, governor," he said with a sinister smile as he took a gulp of wine. When he realized the goblet was empty because he spilled its contents during his tantrum, he threw it across the room in anger. "Damn him," he yelled.

---****---

"As you go," the captain said as the ship sailed toward the island of Capris. Tiberius was standing on the deck watching the island approach as the ship neared. It was a short trip across the sound from the Sorrento Peninsula to the secluded island. Normally the

Villa Jovis

trip crossed treacherous waves and currents, making the journey most uncomfortable to those prone to motion sickness, as Tiberius usually was. Today, however, the seas were calm and serene. Tiberius could feel the ocean breeze blowing through his hair as he watched the waves gently lap against the side of the ship as it glided through the deep, blue water. The salt air was refreshing.

"Your home, Caesar," Sejanus said as he walked up to the rail and stood next to Tiberius. They could see a magnificent structure sitting on a clifftop. Sejanus worked with Tiberius over the last three years to build an opulent palace on a clifftop overlooking the deep blue sea. He called it *Villa Jovis* – "Villa of Jupiter." A single steep, winding road along the cliffs made the location very difficult to reach. The villa was built into the rock face with the first two floors of significant length feathered into the cliffside. The remaining two floors were the main centers of activity. The villa covered eight levels of 40 meters[51] from one end to the other. The south wing was used for administrative purposes. The north wing housed the living quarters where Tiberius's personal quarters resided. The east wing contained the kitchen, reception areas, banquets and such. The west wing had an open hall for meetings with a breathtaking view of the valley of Anacapri. The villa was heavily guarded for protection and privacy.

"Just as I envisioned it, Sejanus," Tiberius sighed. "I have been planning this since Drusus died. A palace where I will rule and be safe."

"It is stunning, Caesar. A perfect place for an emperor."

The two men walked through the villa inspecting the work that had been completed. There were a few issues that needed to be addressed, but considering the location, size and magnitude of the villa, the engineering feat was remarkable. The villa stood 100 meters[52] above the Mediterranean on a sheer cliff and was spread over 7,000 square meters[53]. There was only one way to the villa and that was on foot for two kilometers[54]. A tall watchtower stood at the south end of the complex and could easily see someone approaching. It was used as a lookout and to message the mainland by using smoke or fire.

The island had little fresh water to use. The engineers designed the eight levels of the buildings as a rainwater collection system. The building rooflines cascaded to the end of the villa where giant cisterns were located to collect and store the rainwater. From there it was gravity fed into the villa. It was engineering brilliance.

Inside the compound there were ponds, fountains, flowers, walkways, birds and pools. Statues of bronze and marble sculptures were scattered throughout the grounds.

---

[51] 40 meters = 131 feet
[52] 100 meters = 333 feet
[53] 7,000 square meters = 75,000 square feet
[54] 2 kilometers = 1.25 miles

Sejanus and Tiberius were walking through the villa when Tiberius stopped at a rail overlooking the sea. "Sejanus," Tiberius said as he leaned on the rail and looked out. "Do you know why I trust you so?"

"Caesar?"

He turned to look at him. "You are the only person I can trust because your sole responsibility is to protect *me*."

Sejanus was taken aback for a moment. "It…is, great Caesar."

"That was why the Praetorian Guard was created; to protect the emperor," Tiberius said, as though he was trying to convince himself. He turned to look out to sea again and continued. "You are a Roman Commander. I know you would never break your oath of loyalty to serve me."

"*Never*. But, I sense you are greatly troubled, Caesar."

"I am."

"Ask of me, then, what you will," Sejanus said. "My life is yours."

Tiberius continued to look out at the blue water. "I believe there is a plot under way to remove me from power."

"Great Caesar. I have looked into the accusations of Agrippina but have found little. I will continue to investigate. If there is a plot, I will find who the factions are, and I assure you we will capture them."

Tiberius turned to look at Sejanus questioningly. "Capture? You misunderstand, Sejanus. I want them dealt with decisively, quickly. I want them eliminated." Tiberius pulled a small scroll from his toga and handed it to Sejanus. "Take care of this," he said as he handed the scroll to Sejanus who opened it.

Sejanus looked at the list of names. "I see."

"These are people I have never trusted," Tiberius explained. "They have my suspicions."

"I understand, great Caesar. I will take care of this," Sejanus said as he held up the scroll. "And anyone else that I discover will be dealt with……. appropriately."

"You have my approval to administer the harshest judgment against any conspirators you uncover," Tiberius said.

Sejanus nodded. "I will, Great Caesar."

Chapter 9
28-29 AD

The Protests

"Joseph ben Caiaphas and members of the Jewish council of the Sanhedrin are here to see you," the guard announced as he entered the room.

"Where are they?" Manlius asked as he stood next to Pilate, who was reading something.

"They are waiting in the courtyard."

"Oh, yes. Defiled," Pilate quipped.

Pilate and Manlius walked out the archway to the courtyard where Caiaphas and two members of the Sanhedrin stood, patiently waiting. "Honorable governor," Caiaphas said as he bowed.

"It's about time, priest," Pilate barked as he approached the group.

"It is a long trip, governor," Caiaphas said as he stood before Pilate. Pilate pointed to some benches lining the courtyard near them. "Thank you," Caiaphas said as he and the two priests with him eased onto the bench. "It *is* like riding in a tumbling barrel," he said with a smile.

Pilate ignored his comment. He got right to the point. "Did you see that mob outside?"

"I did, governor." Caiaphas paused to gather his thoughts. "I am not sure they would be considered a mob."

"Then what would you call them?"

"Protesters, governor," one of the priests replied.

"Protesters? They have surrounded my palace for five days now," Pilate retorted. "They started with a few people and now they are emboldened. Look at the size of the protest. That is why I called you, to break them up or I will."

"I understand, governor," Caiaphas replied. "We spoke with them about their protest when we first arrived. They are angry about the imperial standards you placed in Jerusalem."

"Standards? They represent Rome," Pilate replied. "Where Rome rules, the standards are displayed."

"I understand, governor. But us Jews....when you use words like 'divine' and place them on symbols in or near our temple, it is offensive to us and our God," Caiaphas explained.

Pilate stood and looked down on Caiaphas. "Your god?" He walked over to the railing to see the people who had surrounded his palace at Caesarea Maritima for the last five days. He watched as they milled about and occasionally knelt to pray. He could feel the anger welling up inside. "Do your people not realize that I can have them punished for their disrespect to me and to Rome?"

"They do, mighty governor," Caiaphas replied.

"Then why are they continuing?"

Caiaphas walked over to the railing and stood by Pilate leaving the other priests on the bench. He looked out on the people and answered. "Their belief in their god is strong."

Pilate looked at Caiaphas curiously. "Stronger than their desire to live?"

Caiaphas chose his words carefully. "It is a protest, Governor. Not a revolt," Caiaphas replied. "They have not hindered anyone, us included, from entering or leaving your palace. They have done nothing worthy of punishment based on Roman law."

"Roman law! You dare to lecture me on Roman law?" Pilate asked angrily.

"I did not mean to offend nor imply anything governor. They merely want to make a statement of their disapproval," Caiaphas replied without changing expressions or tone.

Pilate looked back to the mob standing around the entrance to his palace. "Guard!"

A soldier entered the room. "Yes, commander."

Pilate continued to stare at the people. "Tell the Jews I will listen to their petition. Have them meet us in the arena." The guard bowed and exited the room. Caiaphas looked at Pilate curiously. "They will have their opportunity, priest."

Gerald Rainey   Javelin Man

The amphitheater of Caesarea Maritima was a magnificent structure with tiered seating for several thousand people. Located adjacent to the palace, the venue faced the blue Mediterranean Sea creating a picturesque backdrop for any activity.

The seventy protesting Jews were escorted into the theater by four guards and directed to the center of the area in front of the governor's balcony rather than the seats surrounding it. They were mostly men and some women with children interspersed. When they were directed to the center of the theater, they suspected they would summarily be punished, but no more guards appeared.

Pilate and the priests entered the arena and sat in the Governor's box facing the crowd of protesters. "State your petition," Pilate ordered.

A man stepped forward and bowed. "Mighty Governor Pontius Pilate. The imperial standards that have been placed in Jerusalem and near the Temple Mount have inscriptions referring to Caesar as divine, a god. We find this to be highly offensive to us Jews and our God. Our laws require that we worship no other gods and allowing the placement of such emblems in our holy temple amounts to the worship of other gods. We ask that the emblems be removed, great governor." The man bowed with reverence.

"Offensive to your god? Do you not think that your statues and plaques are not offensive to *my* gods?" Pilate replied.

"Jerusalem is holy to our people," the man replied. "We have worshipped there for many centuries, mighty governor. We believe it is the city of David; not Rome. We humbly ask that the standards be removed."

"You have made a mockery of my rule by surrounding my palace for five days now," Pilate said as he stood, becoming angrier by the moment. Caiaphas leaned forward in his seat as Pilate motioned to the side of the arena. A stream of thirty guards entered the arena in two columns at double time march and surrounded the people. It was a show of force. The crowd collapsed into a smaller group huddled together in the middle of the arena as the guards surrounded them. Women pulled their children close and held them, covering their eyes.

"What are you doing?" Caiaphas yelled as he stood. "You cannot slaughter innocent, unarmed people?"

Pilate ignored Caiaphas's protest and continued speaking with the man at the center of the arena never lifting his gaze. "Do you not realize that merely by provoking my anger, you risk your very lives?"

The man looked at Pilate and Caiaphas standing together on the balcony. He spoke in the same tone as when he presented the petition; humble and respectful. "It is not our intent to anger nor mock your greatness, mighty governor. It is only our intent to honor our God and petition to have the standards removed."

"Guards, to the ready," Pilate ordered. The guards drew their swords in unison and held them ready to slay the group.

"If you desire to execute someone for this protest…." The man slowly knelt before them and lowered his head and continued. "….then let it be me, great governor. Not my people."

Instantly, without direction, each person in the group slowly fell to their knees. Women wept as they held their children close to their breast so they would not see the slaughter.

"You can't possibly…" Caiaphas pleaded before he was interrupted.

"Quiet priest or you will be joining them!" Pilate yelled. He turned back to the group kneeling in the arena. "Your defiance and refusal to disperse can be considered treasonous!" Everyone knew what Pilate meant; he was building a case to slaughter them. No one raised their head. No one moved. Children were crying and the women were weeping quietly. Guards stood ready to kill indiscriminately, knees slightly bent with swords pointed at their target.

"Please," Caiaphas begged as he fell to his knees beside Pilate. The two priests with him followed suit.

Pilate ignored Caiaphas and stared at the kneeling crowd before him. It was a tense few seconds as Pilate thought. He could show his power and execute everyone. His brutality could backfire and create a revolt amongst the people making his governorship extremely difficult to manage and his ability to rule questioned by

Rome. He knew he would have the support of Sejanus, but what of Tiberius or the senate? Finding the right balance between power and reason was not as easy as he had thought, not with these obstinate people. Pilate realized if he went ahead, he would be no better than Herod the Great when he slaughtered the children thirty years ago, and he despised that.

"Return!" Pilate ordered. The soldiers sheathed their swords in unison without hesitation and returned to attention, still surrounding the people.

"Thank you," Caiaphas whispered.

Pilate ignored him. "Your petition has been heard," he told the group who were still kneeling. "I will remove the standards from the Temple Mount."

The man leading the group rose. "Thank you, mighty governor, for hearing our petition," he said as he bowed. The people remained on their knees surrounded by the soldiers.

Pilate stepped out of the balcony and down some stairs to the arena. He walked up to the man leading the group who rose to meet him. No one had left. No one moved. "This is the only time I will relent, as a show of my good nature. Next time, the blood of you, your women and your children will flow from this arena into the sea. Their blood will be on your hands."

The man bowed again.

"Guards," Pilate yelled. "Fall out." The guards quickly exited the arena in single file double time, leaving Pilate and the group in the middle. "Go!" Pilate ordered.

The remaining people rose from their knees one at a time and exited the arena, leaving Pilate alone. He looked up to see Caiaphas standing at the railing with the other priests looking down, stunned at what he had just witnessed. Pilate's reputation as a butcher rang true. Caiaphas knew Pilate could kill innocent people indiscriminately if it meant making Rome, or his governance, stronger. "Do not expect me to be so benevolent next time, priest," Pilate yelled as he pointed to Caiaphas, who sighed and hung his head.

----****----

The senate chamber in the curia of the Theater of Pompey in Rome was full with more than 300 senators who were called to a special assembly by Sejanus. They mumbled and questioned what the purpose of the meeting would be. Was it for a special request of funds, to review another project for Rome or maybe to review some outstanding issues before the senate and begin the voting? It was an unusual situation that they were trying to figure out when Sejanus entered the chamber flanked by four guards, walked up to the chair, the same chair where Julius Caesar was assassinated, and stood. He opened a scroll and the chamber immediately quieted. The scroll was blank, but no one knew that except Sejanus. "I, Caesar Tiberius, do hereby declare that senator Gaius Asinius Gallus is a public enemy of the state....."

"What?" Gallus interrupted as he stood to protest. He was a prominent senator in his mid-sixties who had questioned some of the actions taken by Sejanus since Tiberius moved to Capris. "This can't be!" Other senators quickly joined in with the protest.

"Silence!" Sejanus yelled. "Guards!" Two guards broke away and seized senator Gallus. They roughly escorted him to the platform where Sejanus stood still holding the scroll. Sejanus rolled the scroll up and put it in his pocket.

"Sejanus, this can't be........."

"Quiet!" Sejanus ordered. The other senators mumbled and whispered amongst themselves questioning the accuracy of the charges. Being a public enemy was vague and could apply to anyone. Why a senator would be so charged was disconcerting. Some senators remained standing in protest as Sejanus continued. "You have been charged with being a public enemy of Rome and of Emperor Caesar Tiberius," Sejanus said. "What say you, senator?" Sejanus asked.

Senator Gallus looked around at the other senators staring at him and Sejanus on the platform. He suspected his defense would be futile. "Senators, and esteemed Commander of the

Praetorian Guard, Lucius Sejanus. I stand here trying to understand why these charges have been brought against me. I believe I am a victim of a personal offense that occurred many years ago, not as an enemy of Rome." The chamber fell silent.

"What do you mean?" Sejanus asked.

"When Caesar Tiberius was installed after Caesar Augustus's death, I made a comment to him that was not well taken. It was meant to be a joke but went very wrong."

"What 'joke' would you make to a new Caesar?" Sejanus asked.

"Caesar Tiberius said he would take charge of any department he was assigned by the senate. I merely asked him which one he wanted to oversee. He was offended. I know not why. I attempted to quell the situation but was unsuccessful. I believe that offense has grown into bitterness and anger for our emperor resulting in these false charges," Gallus said contritely.

Sejanus laughed. "You want us to believe this charge by Caesar Tiberius is related to a misplaced joke fourteen years ago?" The senate started to laugh. "Silence!" Sejanus yelled. The senate immediately quieted down and Sejanus continued. "I believe it is more, much more than that, senator Gallus. Caesar Tiberius has charged you to be a public enemy of Rome. Therefore, you will be sentenced to imprisonment and isolation. Guards!"

"Isolation? I....." Gallus tried to protest but was quickly seized and removed from the chamber to the protest and objections of the senate.

"Senators," Sejanus yelled. "Quiet!" The chamber quieted down as Sejanus spoke. "It is with great remorse that I execute judgment on someone as well respected and noble as senator Gallus. However, I have a duty to Caesar and Rome, and I will execute my orders as directed."

"If Gallus is suspect by Tiberius as an enemy, I fear any of us can be as well," a senator said.

"Here, here," someone concurred.

Sejanus stood and faced the senators. "It is not my desire to harm anyone. The charge against senator Gallus came from Caesar

Tiberius alone. If the validity of the charge is in question, then it is Caesar Tiberius that is in question. I suggest you tread lightly," Sejanus cautioned as he exited the chamber leaving the senators to discuss the capacity of Caesar Tiberius.

Sejanus was successful with planting a seed of doubt about Tiberius's capacity with the senate. His personal purge of opposition was underway clearing the way for him to eventually become emperor.

---****---

It was another Jewish festival that Pontius Pilate needed to attend to ensure that peace and Roman power were present. It seemed like every few months he was needed to make a trip to Jerusalem. This trip, however, included a meeting with the leaders of the Sanhedrin to discuss allocating temple funds to a citywide project. Pilate was staying at Herod's palace, as usual, when a commotion outside his quarters developed early in the morning. "Get back. Get Back or….." Pilate woke to the sound of people shouting outside in the street. "I said get back!"

As a Roman soldier, Pilate was trained to awaken quickly and ready for battle. He jumped out of bed and stormed to the window, angry that someone would wake him just after daybreak. He looked out to see a mob of about fifty people standing outside the portion of Herod's Palace where he was staying in Jerusalem arguing with the guards. He could see that the four guards were trying to control the crowd which was rapidly growing in size. Pilate grabbed his uniform, quickly dressed and went to investigate

"You cannot use the temple funds to build your aqueduct," someone yelled. "That is blasphemy before God to have you use our temple funds."

"I don't care what you say," a soldier responded. "You need to leave." A centurion[55] walked up holding his vine staff[56] and

---

[55] Centurion – commander of a military unit of 100 (infantrymen/soldiers).
[56] Vine staff – a three-foot-long wooden stick that the centurion used as a symbol

raised it above the man's head. "Break this up or you will feel the wrath of Rome!" he shouted as Pilate approached with about twenty guards.

"What is this?" Pilate yelled to the centurion.

"Governor, these Jews say their temple funds were used to build the aqueduct. They are angry," the guard replied.

"I can see they're angry," Pilate yelled as he slapped the centurion. He pointed to the two sides of the protesters. The guards quickly moved to hem the protesters in on the sides. Only their flank was exposed providing them one route to escape. A simple battle tactic.

The crowd ignored the soldiers and continued to be vocal and angry. "You can't use our funds for your water," someone yelled.

"It's *your* water, not mine. It comes from the pools of Solomon," Pilate retorted.

An elderly man dressed in temple garments indicating he was a an elder stepped forward from the group to face Pilate. He raised his hand and the group immediately quieted. "Mighty Governor. We understand our temple's treasury was used to pay for the Aruub Aqueduct." Pilate just stared at the man as he continued. "We have sanctified and designated our funds to be used for God's purposes; not Rome's."

"That's right," someone yelled. "It's holy to God," someone else yelled.

The man held his hand up to silence the group.

Pilate stared at the elder and said nothing, confusing him by his silence. "Mighty Governor, we……." He was cut off by the sound of several horses approaching from the rear. They stopped and formed a line across the flank of the protesters, now hemming them in on all sides. There was no escape. The elder looked around at the soldiers and horses and continued. "We are not here to fight, mighty governor. We merely protest the use of our temple funds for your work."

---

of his position and as a tool to beat wayward or laggard soldiers into submission.

"You woke me up," Pilate said through clenched teeth. He was seething with anger. "You shouldn't have done that. Disperse, or I will disperse you," Pilate said fixing his gaze on the elder. Pilate knew how to read a man, particularly in battle. He could see the fear in his opponents' eyes and knew he had already won.

The man looked at his followers. They were a mixture of young and elderly men and a few women. No one had weapons. No one spoke. He looked back at Pilate. "We are unarmed, mighty governor. We simply protest the use......"

"I've had enough of you Jews and your protests. Guards!" Pilate yelled as he turned on his heals and walked away from the man. "Disperse them!!" He said with a wave of his hand.

The soldiers on the sides pulled out small, handheld clubs and began beating the people, pushing them backwards toward the horses. The protesters began yelling and crying as the soldiers continued to beat and push the group away from the building and into the horses. The horses began rearing up and wailing as the two groups met. Chaos quickly developed as the horses began trampling some of the protesters while the guards beat them down with clubs. The protesters collapsed into a small group surrounded by soldiers swinging clubs and horses trampling them as they tried to flee. Pilate watched as some protesters broke from the pack and fled through the ranks of the Romans. It was total chaos. In a few minutes, it was over. Bodies lay on the ground, beaten, bloodied, some dead. Women were crying. Pilate watched.

The leader of the group slowly stood up. He had been beaten down by a guard and was bleeding profusely from a gash on his forehead. He looked around at the bodies surrounding him. Some dead, some groaning in pain and calling out. Pilate watched from the steps above the scene as the leader slowly climbed one step at a time, each step seeming to be more difficult than the last to ascend. A guard started to stop the man and Pilate held out his hand to not intervene. The guard stepped back and watched as the bloodied man slowly climbed toward the governor.

When he reached the top, he stood before Pilate. His face was covered in blood, so much so that when he spoke, it sprayed from his lips. "It's *God's* money," the man said, spraying small droplets of blood from his lips.

Pilate moved closer to the man, face to face. The blood didn't disturb him at all. In fact, it invited him into the man's presence. Pilate reached out with his index finger and scooped some blood from the man's face and licked it off his finger. With a sinister smile, he said, "I will do as I please," and pushed the man backwards. Pilate watched as the man tumbled down the stairs backwards, hitting his head on the stone steps, killing him instantly. Pilate looked around at the bloody scene. "Release those that are alive...... and clean this up!" he ordered as he turned and started back to the palace entrance.

"Yes, commander," the centurion replied.

"I'm going back to bed," Pilate said without looking back.

----****----

Four months had passed since the conflict with the Jews over the aqueduct took place in Jerusalem. More than twenty people were killed in the melee, but the losses were a necessary cost according to Pilate's thinking. It was a small skirmish, relatively speaking, and did not require any notification to Rome or the legate of Syria. The aqueduct was a major accomplishment for the Jewish people and for Pilate. It displayed the engineering ability of the Roman empire, which was far beyond the Jewish people's abilities or resources.

It was evening as the Roman centurion who was instructed to keep an eye on John the Baptist arrived on horseback to Pontius Pilate's palace at Caesarea Maritima. He dismounted from the horse and handed the reigns to two soldiers standing guard by the steps. "Here," he ordered as he walked briskly past the guards and up the steps to Pilate's palace. He was in his late-thirties and in peak physical condition. The day's ride from Capernaum had no effect on his stamina or determination to inform Pilate of the news.

Pilate was finishing dinner with Claudia as the centurion was announced. "Centurion Casius Quinnius from Capernaum," a guard said as the young man entered the room, stopped and saluted.

"Capernaum. That's a hundred kilometers[57]," Claudia said. "You must want some food or drink," she said as she motioned to a servant to get some for the soldier.

"I came to report a.....a development in Capernaum that the governor should know about," the soldier said, still standing at attention.

"Report, then!" Pilate ordered.

The servants placed food and drink in front of the soldier who ignored it. "A man called Jesus of Nazareth has.... is....."

"Is what?" Pilate asked, becoming impatient and raising his voice.

"This Jesus has been healing people miraculously," The centurion declared.

"How do you know he is doing this?" Claudia asked.

The centurion hesitated for a moment. "He...he healed my slave from palsy."

"What do you mean?" Pilate asked.

"My slave was sick, paralyzed, unable to move and failing fast. He was sick to the edge of death. I heard of this Jesus and went to see him."

"Why would you go see this man?" Pilate asked. "Are you a Jew?"

"I am a Roman!" the centurion declared. "My slave is important to me, and if anyone could heal him, I wanted him healed. It would not matter if it was a donkey who could heal him."

"Continue," Pilate ordered as he took a sip of his wine.

"When I met this Jesus, he told me to return to my house and I would find my servant healed. I did, and he was."

"He was what?" Pilate asked.

"Healed. *Completely*," the centurion said.

"So? He is a good physician, then," Pilate said with a laugh as he held up his goblet of wine and took another drink. "Or a soothsayer."

---

[57] 100 kilometers = 62 miles

"Commander. It is more than that," the centurion said. "He also healed a royal official's daughter in Capernaum."

Pilate placed his goblet on the table as Claudia listened intently. "Go on."

"He is gaining a following, mighty governor."

Pilate adjusted his seat. "Following?"

"Yes. People are following him around to see what he does. Sometimes hundreds of people," the centurion said.

"Weapons?" Pilate asked.

"None."

Pilate was taken aback. "None? Then who is following this Jesus?"

"Mostly the elderly and women. Many are lame or sick seeking healing," the centurion replied.

"Then what threat is he to Rome?" Pilate asked.

"None yet that I know of mighty governor."

"Keep a wary eye on him. If anything develops, squash it like a bug under your boot," Pilate replied.

The centurion bowed and remained at attention. "Please, we have food and drink for you after your long journey," Claudia said pointing to the table.

The centurion looked at the table and back at Pilate. "Is there something else, centurion?" Pilate asked.

"Yes, governor," the centurion said apprehensively. "Herod executed the Baptist."

"Who?" Pilate asked.

"The man they called John the Baptist. We were watching him as ordered. He was baptizing near Jerusa......."

Pilate interrupted. "Herod executed him? Why?"

"Apparently, it was to fulfill a request from... from a dancer that was entertaining Herod and his guests at...."

"Dancer?" Pilate yelled. "By whose authority did he execute this man?"

"His own, mighty governor," the centurion replied.

Pilate stood to his feet obviously angry. "He doesn't have authority to administer capital punishment without my approval!"

Pilate paced across the room and continued. "What has happened to this Baptist's followers?"

"They are now following this Jesus. The Baptist told his followers Jesus was the 'Lamb of God who takes away the sins of the world,' and they were to follow Him."

"What does that mean?" Pilate asked.

"I do not know, commander."

Pilate thought for a moment. "What is their strength?"

"About fifty men."

"Are they planning a revolt?" Pilate asked.

"No, governor. Not that we are aware, and we are watching them. They are unarmed," the centurion replied.

"Continue to observe. Tell me immediately if they begin to amass weapons or organize militarily. Dismissed! Unless you have another surprise?" Pilate asked.

The centurion bowed and left the room. Pilate looked at Claudia. "So, what do you think of this....report?"

"I am not sure what to think. Healing people miraculously. Maybe one of the gods has found favor with him. Or he is a magician and has blinded the people to his tricks," Claudia replied.

"Not him. He's no threat," Pilate replied. "I mean about Herod. He threatens to undermine my authority and spark a revolt. I need to deal with him swiftly and decisively."

Claudia knew Pilate was not asking her opinion, but rather venting. "I am sure you will," Claudia confirmed.

---****---

"Where's Herod!?" Pilate yelled as he stormed into Herod's palace unannounced. "Where is that fool!?"

"What is going on here?" Herod asked as he rounded the corner into his throne room. "What is this shouting.....?"

"Are you completely mad?" Pilate asked.

"Governor. I didn't expect to see ...."

Pilate cut Herod off. "I don't like making this trip just to clean up your mess!" Pilate yelled.

Herod could see Pilate was furious about something. "Governor, please," he said as he gestured to a chair nearby. "May I get something for you to calm…."

"I heard you executed that Baptist guy from the river," Pilate said refusing to sit.

Herod stood and was flanked by two palace guards. "Leave us," he said dismissing them. "Mighty governor. John the Baptist was a nuisance. I feared he would amass a larger group of followers, so I took control of the situation and ……."

"*Situation*? I know what happened, Herod," Pilate said, still standing. "Nothing escapes me. You promised something beyond your authority and had to fulfill that promise."

"I have the authority to do with my Jews as I please," Herod argued.

"You do <u>not</u> have authority for capital punishment unless I give it to you," Pilate retorted. "Especially if it involves a promise to a dancer!"

"She was more than just a dancer!" Herod argued, raising his voice and facing Pilate.

"Well. Look at the mighty 'king'." Pilate smiled as he moved closer to him to intimidate him. "Challenging a Roman governor."

Herod realized he had overstepped. "Honorable governor. I challenge no one except those that would disrupt my rule over Judea."

"*Your* rule," Pilate replied. "*Your* rule. You would do well to remember who is really in charge here, Herod. The one with power is always in charge," he said as he leaned in close enough to smell his breath.

"Mighty governor. I dispatched John the Baptist to eliminate any possibility of him amassing a group of rebels that would challenge your rule," Herod replied.

"You better hope his execution doesn't result in a revolt."

Herod bowed slightly. "I assure you John's followers are nothing. They are the old, lame, and weak."

"You keep your Jews under control, Herod," Pilate said. "Keep them on a tight leash, or I will."

"I am always willing and ready to partner with Rome to assure safety for the Jews."

"You *better* partner with me, Herod, or so help me I will chain your ankles to a chariot and drag you through the streets until nothing is left but your feet." Herod bowed slightly as Pilate continued. "You may not have capital punishment authority, but I most certainly do."

Pilate turned and walked out of the room without waiting for an acknowledgement from Herod, who slumped onto his throne.

----****----

The temple in Jerusalem was central to Jewish life. Jews from all over Israel would venture to the temple to worship or offer sacrifices to their god. Vendors displayed their wares around and in the temple, selling sacrificial animals, clothes, food and services. It was the center of Jewish culture in Jerusalem in every way.

At one end of the temple stood the Hall of Hewn Stones. The long building had entrances on each end with interior access to the temple sanctuary. It was called the Hall of Hewn Stones to differentiate it's construction with the temple. Hewn stones were not allowed to be used in the temple construction to keep in alignment with God's instruction to the Jews that no hewn stone be used to build the temple complex. Using hewn stones would imply carving the stones with iron, which is associated with war. Hewn stones are also associated with the carving of images resulting in idolatry and, therefore, could not be used in the construction of the temple, but could for other buildings around the temple, such as the Hall of Hewn Stones that connected to the temple.

The hall was built specifically for the convening of the Sanhedrin, a council established to rule the Jewish people from both a civil and religious perspective. King Herod was merely a figurehead over the Jews and a connection to Roman rule. The real authority over the Jews was the Sanhedrin.

The council consisted of seventy-one members who would meet daily to review criminal charges and civil issues, assign public fasts and holidays, collect local taxes, discuss spiritual matters, and administer justice over the Jewish people. They were the supreme court of the land for the Jews. Joseph ben Caiaphas was the chief priest of the Sanhedrin.

"State your name for the record," Caiaphas ordered the man standing before the intimidating assembly. Each member of the Sanhedrin was dressed in their priestly robes and seated in the chamber theater looking onto a stage facing them. It was similar to the curia used by the Romans; acoustically perfect.

"Jairus Kohen," the man replied. He was in his mid-fifties with a potbelly. "I arrange the temple for worship services," he added.

"Yes, Jairus," Caiaphas replied. "We know you well and know you to be a devout Jew and one who honors God." Jairus humbly bowed as Caiaphas continued. "We have a report that is……quite troubling. We heard this Jesus of Nazareth has raised your daughter from the dead." Jairus said nothing. "You choose to remain silent, yet your servants and neighbors have not. What do you say?"

"I was instructed to tell no one."

A member of the Sanhedrin stood. "It has already been reported to us. We only ask if this is true or not?"

Jairus looked down to the floor, then back to the council. "It is true."

The chamber erupted into shouts disputing facts, challenging the authenticity of the event, dissenting views everywhere. "Silence," Caiaphas ordered. The assembly quickly quieted as the members returned to their seats as Caiaphas continued the questioning. "Then, you believe she was raised from the dead, as you say?"

"I know this, honorable Caiaphas. She was dead. Now, she is not."

The chamber erupted again. "How can that be?" someone yelled. "You must be mistaken," someone else chimed in. "She wasn't dead," another called out.

Caiaphas raised his hands to quiet them down. "How is that possible? No one has ever raised anyone from the dead. You must be mistaken. She was only asleep."

"She was not asleep. She was dead," Jairus replied. "It was truly a miracle."

The Sanhedrin erupted again. Caiaphas sat back in his seat and allowed the turmoil to continue as he thought about the implications of such an event. He could see the Sanhedrin was in absolute chaos. They had never dealt with anything like this. He didn't know what to do. He finally stood and motioned for silence. "You are dismissed," he said.

Jairus nodded and quickly left.

A member of the council stood and addressed the assembly. "Brothers, this event must be in error. No one can raise anyone from the dead except God Almighty."

"Here, here," someone called out.

Caiaphas stood and faced the assembly. "We must not perpetuate this event through gossip or rumor. The people are in error. She was only asleep," he said. "Our people are being led astray by this man Jesus. We must find a way to stop him."

"Here, here," someone called out.

"I believe we need to discredit his teaching, catch him in a lie or inaccuracy of our laws. If we can expose him for the charlatan he is, the people will reject him and his teaching," Caiaphas said.

The assembly majority agreed. From here on, they would attend his sermons and teaching and attempt to expose him as a fraud. It was for the benefit of the people that he not lead them astray. They believed it was their job to protect the Jewish people from the false teachings of Jesus.

Caiaphas knew he needed to get control of the situation before it got out of hand.

Chapter 10   The End of Sejanus
30-31 AD

Sejanus sat in the chair facing the small portico looking at the woman standing before him. Her hair was unkept. Her clothes dirty. The circles under her eyes revealed the lack of sleep she endured last night. Sejanus had guards retrieve Agrippina from her home the night before and drag her to the Imperial Palace to meet with him. They sequestered her in a room without explanation. She sat awake all night wondering if she was going to be executed in the morning. With Tiberius safely removed and now living on the island of Capris, she realized she was standing before the most powerful person in Rome; Lucius Sejanus with no one to advocate for her.

"Bring them in," Sejanus ordered the guards. Two young men in chains were brought in flanked by guards. Nero and Drusus (nephew of deceased Drusus) saw their mother across the room. They had been held in the jail away from her until their appearance before Sejanus.

"Nero!" Agrippina yelled. She started toward the men only to be held back by two guards. The guards escorted Drusus and Nero to their mother's side where the three of them stood facing Sejanus. They were surrounded by guards.

"Nero Julius Caesar, Drusus Julius Caesar and Agrippina." Sejanus began. "You have been charged with treason to the emperor and high crimes against the empire."

"By whom?" Agrippina demanded.

"By the senate and the emperor," Sejanus answered.

"That is impossible," Agrippina replied. "Tiberius would never do that. I am the wife of General Germanicus and……"

"*Was* the wife," Sejanus interrupted. "Germanicus is dead, his brother Drusus is dead, and you have been found, along with your sons, to be guilty of treason by conspiracy."

"I am guilty of nothing but serving Rome and my grandfather," Nero claimed. Drusus stood silent.

"Have you executed Caligula?" Agrippina asked. "Where is he?"

"Gone. He went to Capris before I was able to arrest him," Sejanus said. "A little coward in little soldier boots," he mocked. Sejanus stood to his feet and slowly approached the trio. He could see the sweat forming on their brows as the tension of the moment escalated. They were waiting for the execution order. "You will be exiled to the island of Ponza," he said in a near whisper. "You will live out the rest of your days there, away from the empire, away from Rome. When you die from starvation, the dogs and birds shall pick at your corpses until there is nothing left of you. Not even a memory."

Drusus hung his head. Agrippina and Nero stood staring at Sejanus. They knew there was nothing they could do. If they fought, they would be killed on the spot. If they complied, they could possibly be freed from exile when Caligula became emperor, if he ever did. Agrippina spoke first. "And Caligula?"

"Yes. 'Little soldier boots'," Sejanus said with a laugh as he turned away from them and returned to his seat. "He will be allowed to play with his grandfather on Capris. The senate charged you and only you. Caligula is not a concern right now." Sejanus looked to the guards. "Remove them from my sight."

The guards grabbed the arms of the prisoners and removed them from the room with no resistance.

The ancient historian Cassius Dio wrote:

Sejanus was so great a person by reason both of his excessive haughtiness and of his vast power, that, to put it briefly, he himself seemed to be the emperor and Tiberius a kind of island potentate, inasmuch as the latter spent his time on the island of Capreae.

To secure his authority, Sejanus had anyone that he considered a threat to his rule charged with treason, tried, and either executed or exiled. Senators, commanders, tribunes, and civilians all bore the wrath of Sejanus. No one dared cross him. No one dared challenge him.

The purge of resistance was underway.

---****---

Caesar Tiberius was alone in the bath. The thick, steamy air made it difficult to see for the Roman guard who entered the bath chamber hesitantly. "Caesar?" he called, hearing his voice echo through the marble room.

"Here," came the reply. The guard maneuvered his way through the steam to the spot where Tiberius sat at the edge of a pool wrapped in a towel. Caligula was sitting in the pool drinking some wine. The guard was relieved no one else was present, particularly the children. "What is it?"

"There is a messenger from Rome here to see you," the guard said as he stood before the emperor.

"Who?"

"A freedman[58] of Antonia Minor. Marcus Antonios Pallas," the guard replied.

"Very well. Make him comfortable while I dress," Tiberius said. "You may go."

Pallas had not been waiting long when Tiberius walked into the banquet hall and seated himself across from him near the end of a table. He was an older man with a pot belly and balding. He was enjoying a plate of food and some wine as reward for the long trip from Rome. "Mighty Caesar," Pallas said as he rose and bowed. "I am Antonia Minor's freedman, Marcus Antonius Pallas."

"As I have heard," Tiberius said with a smirk. "To what do I owe the honor of my sister-in-law's freedman making such a long trip?"

---

[58] Freedman – Historically, a person who has been released from slavery, typically by legal means

Pallas pulled a document from his satchel and handed it to Caesar. "This is for you and you alone, Caesar. Antonia Minor instructed me to deliver this to no one else, even if facing death."

Tiberius examined the document and noticed the seal. "This is the seal of Antonia Minor, my sister-in-law. What does the great daughter of Marc Antony have to say that is so urgent?" Tiberius wondered aloud. Pallas didn't hesitate. He bowed and exited the room, grabbing some figs on the way out. Tiberius opened the document as Caligula entered from the side shadows.

"Who is that from, grandfather?" Caligula asked. At eighteen years old, he was fully grown, yet still had a childlike appearance.

"Oh. There you are. It's from your grandmother, Antonia Minor." Caligula had drawn close to his adoptive grandfather and was seldom excluded from anything, particularly regarding running the empire. Tiberius believed he had an obligation to involve his grandson in everything since he very well could be his successor.

Great Caesar Tiberius
Greetings in the name of the goddess Veritas[59].
It is with a heavy heart that I write to you about the death of your son, Drusus Julius Caesar. Apicata, the ex-wife of Lucius Sejanus, informed me personally that Sejanus conspired with Livilla, to kill Drusus by poison.

"He killed my uncle?" Caligula asked as he moved closer to his grandfather.

"Sejanus!" Tiberius seethed as he continued to read the letter.

Sejanus is betrothed to Livilla, bringing him into the Julian family. He has imprisoned Agrippina and her sons Drusus and Nero to remove all opposition.

"My mother and brothers are in prison?" Caligula yelled. Tiberius did not stop reading.

---

[59] Veritas – Goddess of the personification of the Roman virtue of truth.

Now, Sejanus is conspiring to assassinate you and Caligula and place himself as Caesar through the senate.

I implore you dear Tiberius to beware. Please protect yourself and Caligula from harm. Choose allies wisely.
Antonia Minor

"Sejanus!" Tiberius could feel the rage welling up inside as he closed the document. "And Livilla." Tiberius turned to Caligula who was still trying to understand what had happened. "Sejanus wanted to marry her to become a Julian!"

"He is evil, Caesar," Caligula said as he moved close to him. "He murdered my father and now has my mother and brothers in prison. For what?"

"Power," Tiberius replied. "We need to have him removed immediately."

"We need to expose the traitors," Caligula added.

Tiberius looked puzzled. "How?"

The two men thought for several moments. "'Choose your allies wisely,'" Caligula said. "We need someone we can trust to take over the Praetorian Guard and uncover who is involved with the plot," Caligula replied. "Maybe a general or someone in power. Someone close to Sejanus who is not his ally."

Tiberius thought for a moment. "Macro. Naevius Sutorius Macro, prefect of the vigiles[60]. He is faithful to the empire."

"He is. I believe we can trust him grandfather," Caligula confirmed. "He has been a good friend to me."

"We can trust him to work with us to remove Sejanus," Tiberius replied without hesitation. "He has control of the police force in Rome."

"Then I have a plan to diminish the support for Sejanus," Caligula said.

Tiberius looked at his young grandson. He could see the ambition in his eyes and was curious. "How?"

---

[60] Commander of The Police and fire departments of Rome.

"We cannot remove him outright for he may decide to invoke a revolt. We need to decrease his support by creating confusion, doubt and uncertainty among the senate about your support for him," Caligula replied.

"But how?" Tiberius asked.

"If you send a series of contradictory letters to the senate both praising and denouncing Sejanus, they will be at a loss of your true position for him."

"Confuse the enemy."

"Exactly. Then, you step down as consul[61]. As the second appointed consul Sejanus will have to follow and also step down," Caligula said.

"I see," Tiberius replied with a smile.

"Once he steps down as consul, confer a special priesthood upon me," Caligula added. "As priest of Rome and from the house of Germanicus, I will be in a position welcomed by the senate."

"Then have Macro intervene and arrest Sejanus," Tiberius concluded.

"Yes," Caligula confirmed. "At a specially called meeting of the senate," Caligula added with a broad smile. "What better way to make a statement of your authority and power than to remove a powerful traitor in the midst of a senate meeting," Caligula replied.

"Brilliant!" Tiberius exclaimed. "You will make a great Caesar, no doubt."

The next morning, Marcus Pallas was outside the palace preparing for his return trip to Rome. Tiberius approached him as Caligula stayed back and watched from afar. "Pallas," Tiberius called. Pallas quickly stood and bowed. "Sit. Please," Tiberius said and motioned to the seat near them. Tiberius sat next to him and spoke quietly. "I know Antonia trusts you implicitly."

"Yes, Caesar. I believe so, as do I her."

"Meaning?"

---

[61] Consul – The highest elected office of the Roman Empire. Two consuls were appointed each year.

"She said you were an emperor of reason, one whom I can trust with my life. So, I do, great Caesar," he said as he bowed.

"Good. I want you to take this letter to Naevius Macro, prefect vigiles, immediately. Stop for no one. Talk with no one," Tiberius said as he handed a document to Pallas.

"I understand, Caesar," Pallas said as he noticed the emperor's seal on the document. He carefully placed it in his satchel.

"No one," reiterated Tiberius.

Pallas stood and bowed. "For Rome, Mighty Caesar."

As Tiberius started back to the palace, Caligula stepped from the side entrance and joined lockstep with him as he passed by. "Sejanus will pay for his treachery, grandfather," Caligula assured Tiberius.

"He will," Tiberius agreed.

---****---

It was a beautiful spring day. The surrounding hills near Bethsaida on the northern shore of the Sea of Galilee were covered with lush, green grass where thousands of people sat, listening. The hills surrounding a small area near the water created a natural amphitheater where Jesus of Nazareth was able to speak to the multitudes. People sat quietly for hours listening to his teachings about the god of the Jews. Many came to see him perform another miracle of healing. Others out of curiosity. Jesus spoke in a manner no one had heard before. The Jewish people had many prophets of past, but none spoke like this man. He spoke in parables that demonstrated his understanding of God and heaven. He spoke as one with authority and personal knowledge of a loving god. He spoke as a friend and answered their questions.

The news of his teachings and healings spread rapidly throughout the region. Today, thousands of people were scattered on a hillside listening intently to Jesus's teachings and stories. It was getting late and several men accompanying Jesus, called his disciples, were concerned for the welfare of the people. They knew the people were getting hungry and approached Jesus to voice their concern.

"Jesus. This is a remote place, and it is already very late," one man said as he pointed to the size of the crowd. There were more than 7,000[62] people covering the hillsides. "Send the people away so they can go to the surrounding countryside and villages and buy themselves something to eat."

Jesus smiled at his disciple and looked out to the crowd that had gathered. He felt compassion on them as though they were sheep without a shepherd, lost, vulnerable. "You give them something to eat," he said to his disciple.

Another disciple was surprised at his answer. It seemed ludicrous to think they would have enough to feed the multitude. "That would take more than a half-year's wages! Are we to go spend that much on bread and give it to them to eat?" He laughed at the absurdity of the directive.

"How many loaves do you have?" Jesus asked. No one answered. "Go and see."

Each disciple took a basket and split up, walking through the crowd asking if anyone had some food. "Do you have any food that you can spare?" they asked. A young boy approached them with two fish that he recently caught by the shore. Other people had a little bread here and there that they had brought. After canvassing the crowd, the disciples returned to Jesus and showed him what they had gathered. Their disappointment was obvious as they approached him with mostly empty baskets. "We found five small loaves of bread and two fish," one of them said as they reluctantly showed Jesus the baskets.

Jesus looked at the baskets and back to the crowd. "Have the people sit in groups on the grass," he directed them.

The disciples were puzzled. They mumbled amongst themselves that there was no way they could feed a crowd this size with almost no food. "Is he expecting to feed all of these people with this?" one asked.

---

[62] 7,000 – Scripture indicates the number of men to be 5,000. (Mathew 14:21)

"Do what the teacher says," one of them replied.

The disciples walked through the crowd and directed the people to sit in large groups of fifty to a hundred. Jesus watched as the people maneuvered into circles scattered over the hillside. The hills looked like giant flowers had sprung up with varying colors of people's attire interspersed in the circles. Jesus smiled as the disciples returned and waited for further orders.

Jesus stood and faced the crowd who immediately became quiet and watched with great anticipation. "Heavenly father," he said as he grabbed a loaf of bread and held it up. "You are the one who feeds the sparrows of the air. You alone provide the rains to water the crops that produce the wheat for our bread. You made the fish that fills our seas and our stomachs. I ask that you bless this food of which we are about to partake for your glory." Jesus broke the loaves of bread into pieces and placed the pieces in the twelve baskets that surrounded him. Then he divided fish in the same way and gave the baskets to the disciples to distribute.

The disciples looked at the few pieces of bread and part of a small fish in each of their baskets. They looked at each other in disbelief and back to Jesus. Jesus just smiled and motioned for them to go into the crowd with the baskets.

"I'm sorry but this is all we have," one of the disciples apologized as he held the basket out for someone to take some food. As the person reached in, the basket immediately became quite heavy, so much so that the disciple had difficulty holding it. "What?" he exclaimed as people reached in and took their fill as he passed by. "What is happening?" he yelled.

Another disciple yelled as well, and soon all twelve disciples were shouting their amazement and laughing loudly as the baskets filled themselves. They looked back to Jesus who was watching their reactions. Then Jesus looked up to the sky, raised his arms and smiled.

As the baskets passed through the crowd, people began to shout and yell. "Glory to God," someone yelled. "It's a miracle," others shouted. The volume of the praises and shouts increased as the baskets made their way through the crowd. People were taking hands full of fish and bread. Many were laughing, others crying for joy. "God has visited us!" someone yelled.

As the baskets made their way up the hillsides, people would jump to their feet and yell or wave. As they did, the hillsides looked like giant flowers blossoming as the joy spread through the groups and up the hill.

After everyone had their fill, the disciples gathered the extra food together and returned to Jesus. They had twelve baskets full of bread and fish.

"This is amazing," one of the disciples said. "How can this be?" another questioned. Jesus simply laughed with them as they praised God for providing for the masses.

Two Pharisees were standing near the summit of one of the hills observing the scene. They were dressed in civilian clothes as to not be noticed by the crowd. They were Nicodemus and Joseph of Arimathea.

---****---

"Macro!" Caligula ran to greet the guest as he approached the palace steps in Capris. "It is so good to see you," he said as they embraced. "It has been a long time," Caligula added.

Quintus Naevius Cordus Sutorius Macro was the head of the police and fire brigade in Rome. He was in his mid-fifties and well built. He towered over other people being over six feet tall. His grey hair gave him an air of authority and wisdom. His experience gave him power and confidence. He was one of the most powerful people next to Lucius Sejanus, commander of the Praetorian Guard, to whom he reported. "Gaius. Good to see you, young Caesar," Macro replied.

"Macro!" Tiberius said as he approached.

Macro bowed low. "Great Caesar Tiberius. I am here at your command."

"I am pleased you came so quickly," Tiberius added.

"When Caesar calls, I run," he said jokingly. "It is good to see you and young Gaius, too."

"Gaius?" Tiberius questioned.

"Yes, grandfather. Macro has always called me Gaius instead of that horrid nickname my mother gave me," Caligula replied.

"It is with great respect I do," Macro added as he bowed to Caligula.

"Well, be that as it may, welcome to Capris," Tiberius added. "This way, if you will," as he directed Macro and Caligula to the palace. The trio entered the banquet hall where food and drink lay on a long table. "Please," Tiberius said. "Partake of our meal with us."

"I am honored, great Caesar," Macro said as he sat at the table. "But before I partake, I trust you have called me here for something more important than to enjoy good food and fine wine," he said as he refused to take any food or drink offered by the servants.

"To the point, then," Caligula said as he waved the servants away. "We require your assistance with a delicate matter that involves Rome's future." Macro sat stoically as Caligula continued. "Lucius Sejanus is positioning himself to become Caesar."

"I am not surprised. I have questioned some of his recent actions," Macro said.

"We have knowledge that Sejanus murdered Germanicus and Drusus in order to become emperor," Tiberius said almost seething.

"How can that be?" Macro asked.

"He conspired with Livilla, Drusus's wife, to poison him. Now, he is betrothed to Livilla," Caligula added.

"I thought that to be rumor," Macro replied.

"It is not," Tiberius replied. "We have trusted sources."

"He has also imprisoned my mother and brothers," Caligula added.

"I was told that was an order from you, great Tiberius," Macro replied. "He imprisoned senator Gallus under that same order."

"Gallus! He was not on my list of suspects!" Tiberius proclaimed.

Tiberius and Caligula went over the list of names that they had given to Sejanus, with Macro looking on, only to find out none of them had been charged or sequestered by Sejanus. Instead, Macro informed them of the people that Sejanus *had* removed or executed for treason.

"None of those people were suspect," Tiberius proclaimed.

"He is using our list as a pretense to remove people that oppose *him*, not you, grandfather," Caligula surmised.

"That viper!" Tiberius yelled as he threw his goblet of wine. "I want him dead! I want...."

"Great Caesar," Caligula interrupted, placing his hand on Tiberius's shoulder to calm him down. "We *will* remove him, with Macro's help."

Macro quickly stood and bowed. "I am your servant, great Caesar."

"Good," Tiberius said as he calmed down. "Good. I knew we could trust you with our plan," he said.

Macro returned to his seat and poured himself a goblet of wine. "How will you remove him? He has the entire Praetorian Guard and most of the senate supporting him." He began to pick at the food on the table.

"We will send a series of contradicting letters to the senate, some praising Sejanus, others questioning his actions," Caligula explained. "This will create confusion and uncertainty whether Tiberius truly supports Sejanus or not."

"Why not just remove him?" Macro asked.

"He might decide to invoke a revolt using his authority to control the Guard," Tiberius replied.

"We need to discredit him and arrest him in front of the senate with their support," Caligula added.

"And the contradictory letters will discredit him," Macro commented.

Tiberius continued. "I will announce that I am coming to Rome to bestow military tribunician[63] powers on him. That is when you will read my final letter to the senate and arrest him upon my order."

Macro was quiet as he thought. "Why me?"

"We can trust you, Macro," Caligula said. "*I* can trust you. Since I was but a child you have shown respect and honor towards me and Rome."

"And you have served me and Rome faithfully for many years," Tiberius added. "You have the manpower with the police to arrest Sejanus. No one else does."

"I see," Macro commented.

"We also need someone to replace Sejanus as the commander of the Praetorian Guard," Caligula added. "You."

Macro smiled. "Well, to a plan well thought," he said as he raised his goblet of wine. "For Rome!"

Both Caligula and Tiberius joined in the toast. "For Rome!"

Three months passed since the meeting between Tiberius, Macro and Caligula in Capris. Tiberius sent a volley of letters to the senate both praising and denouncing Sejanus for his actions as commander of the Praetorian Guard. He also informed the senate that his health was failing fast. The ensuing confusion among the senate and Tiberius's pending death emboldened Sejanus to continue his purge of resistance based on the manufactured conspiracy against Tiberius. Sejanus used the confusing letters to question the emperor's capacity. Sometimes the letters would ramble into nonsense, thus proving Sejanus's case of incapacity.

One of the last letters Tiberius sent stated he was very near death and would need to step down as consul, the highest elected office of the Roman Empire and mostly symbolic of the Roman Republic heritage. Sejanus was forced to step down as second consul following in Tiberius's footsteps, thus diminishing the appearance of his power and authority and raising concerns amongst the senate.

---

[63] Military Tribunician – a position of authority over the military

In the same letter Tiberius conferred an honorary priesthood on Caligula, reestablishing support for the house of Germanicus. Sejanus did not see this as a threat for his quest for power considering he would soon be emperor after Tiberius died. He believed he would be able to petition the senate for appointment as Emperor, particularly since he was betrothed to Livilla and planned to join the Julian family line.

Then, he would deal with Caligula. Or so he thought.

"Senators. Please. If you will take your seats," Sejanus ordered from the curia stage. As the room fell quiet, Naevius Macro entered the chamber. "Senators. Prefect Naevius Macro has a letter from our emperor in Capris regarding matters of the empire." He motioned for Macro to begin.

Macro stood beside Sejanus, pulled a document from his satchel and handed it to him. "Would you please inspect the seal, commander?" He asked.

Sejanus glanced at the seal and nodded. "It is Caesar's seal," he said as he handed the document back to Macro to be read to the senate. Sejanus assumed Caligula placed the seal and expected it was a notice of Tiberius's death. Otherwise, why would Macro be reading such a notice unless he expected some type of unrest from the announcement?

Macro opened the document and began.

To the senate in Rome
Greetings from Caesar Tiberius

As I draw near to the end of my life, I reflect on the accomplishments we have made to grow and expand the empire's boundaries.

The senators listened intently as Macro read the letter. Tiberius detailed several accomplishments of his reign to the nods and affirmation of the senators.

These accomplishments would not have been successful if not for the dedication and fortitude of Lucius Sejanus.

Sejanus smiled and nodded as Macro continued.

My death draws near. My successor is prepared. Rome is prepared.

Sejanus sat up straight as he listened and waited for Tiberius to support his appointment as Caesar. That, plus marrying Livilla, would seal his ascent to become emperor. This was the moment he had waited for.

Lucius Sejanus has demonstrated that he is a leader worthy of the highest position in Rome. However, his trustworthiness is like that of a viper.

Macro nonchalantly nodded to a police guard near the door and continued. The senators began mumbling amongst themselves. *A viper? What is he talking about?* Sejanus shifted in his seat wondering what just happened.

Sejanus has attempted to become emperor by inserting himself into the Julian line by murdering my son Drusus Julius Caesar ….

The senators became vocal as the letter was read. Sejanus stood and attempted to stop Macro. "Wait," he yelled, but Macro continued, raising his voice above the protests of both the senate and Sejanus as a line of policemen marched into the curia. "What is going on?" Sejanus demanded.

The policemen surrounded Sejanus as Macro read louder and louder, drowning out Sejanus and the senators who were yelling and becoming more animated and vocal with their protests and disbelief.

Therefore, for the crimes of high treason and the murder of my son, Drusus Julius Caesar, I hereby remove Lucius Aelius Sejanus from the position of prefect of the Praetorian Guard…

Sejanus looked as though he was in a panic. "What? How can….? GUARDS! Arrest him!" Sejanus yelled as he pointed to Macro, who continued to read unaffected and over the growing uproar. The Praetorian Guards hesitated because they just heard Sejanus being removed by the emperor.

…..and appoint Quintus Naevius Cordus Sutorius Macro as prefect of the Praetorian Guard and order him to arrest Lucius Aelius Sejanus…..

The order appointing Macro as Prefect of the Praetorian Guard resolved the question of who was in charge. The Praetorian Guards near Sejanus quickly stepped back and allowed the police guards to surround him without incident. The curia was in near chaos and erupted as Macro finished the letter by yelling over the growing volume of the irate senators and Sejanus, who tried in vain to protest.

"……..and charge Lucius Aelis Sejanus with high treason, sedition, murder and conspiracy to overthrow the emperor and sentence him to death!"

The curia exploded with shouts and confusion. "Guards! Arrest him!" Macro ordered as he pointed to Sejanus, who was standing in front of the throne objecting and yelling. Sejanus tried to command his guards to arrest Macro instead, but he was drowned out by the shouts and jeers of the senators. Tiberius's removal of Sejanus as commander of the Praetorian Guard was absolute. It was read from a letter confirmed to be from Tiberius and properly sealed. There was no debate. Sejanus was out. Macro was in.

Sejanus struggled mightily as the guards apprehended him and placed chains on his wrists. The attitude of the senators immediately changed and they began to yell and spit on Sejanus, letting their pent-up anger, frustration and fury that was built up over the years control the moment. Most of them hated and feared Sejanus because of his belittling manner and constant threats toward them. They were terrified by him. Now, it was their turn to have Sejanus fear them. "Traitor! Kill him!" they yelled. Those senators associated with Sejanus quickly left the curia unnoticed.

"Take him to the Tullianum[64]," Macro ordered.

Sejanus resisted and objected in vain as the guards drug him from the curia yelling. Senators continued to shout their approval or question the action just taken. The chamber was in absolute chaos.

Macro closed the document and handed it to senator Lucius Bracchus, secretary of the senate, for confirmation. Senator Bracchus quickly scanned the letter and handed it back to Macro. He bowed slightly. "For Rome," he said.

Macro smiled. "For Rome!"

It was evening. The senate convened in the Temple of Concord near the curia to review the case against Sejanus and determine the appropriate sentence. Sejanus was sentenced to death by Tiberius and summarily removed from prison and brought to stand before the senate to affirm the sentence. Once the epitome of Roman strength, Sejanus stood before the senate, dirty, beaten, bloodied. He had been in prison less than eight hours yet looked like he had been there for weeks. His hands were chained. His head bowed.

"Unchain him," Macro ordered.

Senator Bracchus stood and read the charges against Sejanus. "You have been found guilty of sedition, treason, conspiracy against Caesar and Rome and the murder of Drusus Julius Caesar." Sejanus knew there was nothing he could do in

---

[64] **Tullianum** - A prison near the palace facing the curia.

defense of the charges. He was a dead man standing quietly as senator Bracchus continued. "It is the order of this senate and our great Caesar Tiberius that you be sentenced to death."

As soon as the sentence was read, Macro nodded to the two guards standing on each side of Sejanus. Senators began rising from their seats and approached the platform where the prisoner stood. They encircled Sejanus showing their support of the sentence[65] and stood quietly, staring at him with disdain. Sejanus turned to a guard standing by him. "Cassius," Sejanus whispered. "Do what you must."

The guard grabbed Sejanus around the throat and began strangling him. The second guard quickly joined in as Sejanus fought and kicked for a minute, then slumped being held up by the two guards. In seconds, many of the senators on the stage joined in, kicking, hitting and beating Sejanus as the guards continued to strangle him. The guards stopped and released their grips on Sejanus causing his limp body to fall to the floor. He was dead, but the senators continued to kick the lifeless body.

"Cast him down the Gemonian Stairs[66]," Macro ordered.

The guards grabbed Sejanus by his ankles and drug him out of the curia and to the stairs as the senators continued to kick him, leaving a trail of smeared blood along the way. When they reached the stairs, Macro stood stoically and held up a document. "Lucius Aelis Sejanus, Prefect of the Praetorian Guard," he declared, "Guilty of treason, murder, conspiracy….." As Macro read the charges to the people gathered at both the top and bottom of the stairs, the guards threw Sejanus's mangled body down the stairs where a crowd was anxiously waiting at the bottom. The lifeless body tumbled down the stairs into the waiting crowd who swarmed on it and tore it to pieces. In a few moments, they stopped and left the

---

[65] Voting in the Roman senate was displayed by senators casting an affirming vote by standing next to the subject or person or remaining in their seats as a vote against.

[66] Gemonian Stairs – a stairway in Rome where executed criminals were cast down for the crowds to dispose of.

body parts scattered at the bottom of the stairs. Macro stood at the top of the stairs and looked down on the mutilated body with satisfaction.

The mutilated body of Sejanus lay on the stairs for several days, rotting. Once the stench became bad enough, Macro ordered that the body be tossed into the Tiber River.

The rule of Sejanus was over. His faulty error of not proofing the letter from Tiberius before it was read to the senate resulted in his demise and ended his quest to become the first civilian emperor of the Roman Empire.

Soon after Sejanus's death, riots ensued in the city. Mobs of citizens hunted down anyone they believed was tied to Sejanus and summarily murdered them and cast them into the Tiber River. Praetorian Guards began looting. Chaos was rampant.

When news of the death of Sejanus reached Tiberius and Caligula, they were elated. They received a letter from Apicata, Sejanus's ex-wife confirming Livilla conspired with Sejanus to murder Drusus Julius Caesar. Two days later, Apicata committed suicide.

Tiberius ordered Livilla's slaves to be interrogated. They confirmed they administered the poison to Drusus when they were questioned under torture. Tiberius became furious and ordered the executions of all of Sejanus's family and anyone associated with him. Their bodies were also cast down the Gemonian Stairs.

No one escaped the wrath of Tiberius and Caligula. Senators, family members, and other perceived conspirators were arrested and summarily executed, often without a trial.

A noted historian writes:

Executions were now a stimulus to his (Tiberius) fury, and he ordered the death of all who were lying in prison under accusation of complicity with Sejanus. There lay, singly or in heaps, the unnumbered dead, of every age and sex, the illustrious with the obscure. Kinsfolk and friends were not allowed to be near them, to weep over them, or even to gaze on them too long. Spies were set round them, who noted the sorrow of each mourner and followed the rotting corpses, till they were dragged to the Tiber, where, floating or driven on the bank, no one dared to burn or to touch them.[67]

News of the execution of Sejanus and the purge of Tiberius spread across the empire. No one was safe from the wrath of Tiberius….and Caligula.

---****---

"Bang, bang, bang."

Herod was awakened by the loud banging that was occurring outside his bedroom chamber. He was still half drunk from the banquet the night before and slow to wake. "What is that noise?" he yelled. "Where is that coming from?" He stumbled to his feet and went to the window to see where the noise was coming from. He could see several Roman guards affixing something to the outside columns of his palace. "You! What are you doing there?" he yelled. The guards never looked up as they continued their work.

Herod hurried down the stairs to the portico, stumbling along the way and nearly falling had he not regained his balance. "What is this?" he asked as he approached two guards hanging a brass emblem on the column outside his chamber. The item was a circular brass wreath with the likeness of Tiberius sculpted in the middle and some words inscribed around the edge.

Divi Augusti Filius (son of divine Augustus)

"Take that down!" Herod ordered. The Roman guards ignored him and continued their work. When they finished mounting the emblem, they moved to the next column to hang another. "You can't do this," Herod protested. "This is a Jewish palace; not Roman!"

One of the guards, a centurion, stopped to face Herod as several palace guards approached. Two Roman guards stood by

---

[67] Tacitus Annals V1.19

waiting for their orders to resume. "We have been ordered by Governor Pontius Pilate to display these standards around your palace," the guard said.

"I don't care who told you. You need to....."

The centurion interrupted. "I need to obey my orders from my commander; not you!" he yelled as he raised his vine staff in opposition. The Roman guards standing by placed the remaining emblems on the ground and waited with their hands on their swords.

"Guards!" Herod ordered. The palace guards, six in total, drew their swords. "If you...."

The centurion drew his sword. "To the ready!" he ordered as he placed the tip of the sword just six inches from Herod's chin. The two Roman guards drew their swords and took a 'ready' position; knees bent, slightly leaning forward in a crouch with the swords pointed at their opponents. "You better reconsider, Jew," the centurion said.

Herod looked at the Roman guards. It was six against three. The odds were in his favor, but the reality was that the centurion could have fought all six of the palace guards and likely won after dispatching Herod. The Roman soldier's battle skills were far superior to the palace guards. Herod motioned to his guards to sheath their swords.

"Wise move, Herod," the centurion said as he sheathed his sword. His guards followed suit.

"Pilate will hear from me about this," Herod warned. He turned and walked back into the palace followed by his palace guards.

"I'm sure he will," the centurion said as he picked up an emblem from the ground and handed it to one of his guards. "Here. Mount this over his doorway," he said with a laugh.

The sons of Herod petitioned Pilate to remove the standards from Herod's palace. Pilate refused. Herod's sons then threatened to petition emperor Tiberius, to which Pilate ignored their threat. Pilate was unaware that Sejanus had just been executed and had no consideration or concern about Rome's oversight of his governance. The legate of Syria received the petition and angrily reprimanded Pilate for unnecessarily stirring up the Jewish people and threaten peace in the region. It was a small situation that was unnecessary, and he wanted it corrected. It was imperative that Pilate work with the tetrarch to maintain peace in the region. Pilate was ordered to take the standards down immediately, to which he reluctantly complied.

The legate neglected to involve Tiberius because it was such an insignificant matter. Instead of having Pilate's name brought before Tiberius and possibly associated with Sejanus, it went unnoticed. For whatever reasons, Pilate escaped the purge of Tiberius for now.

---****---

It was late in the afternoon. The evening shadows were beginning to stretch across the temple grounds. Priests continued to file into the Hall of Hewn Stones to attend a special meeting of the Sanhedrin to discuss the man named Jesus, who was causing quite a stir among the people. As the hall filled, they began talking and soon shouting amongst themselves about Jesus and his miracles.

"Silence!" Caiaphas yelled. The hall quickly quieted down as the final few men took their seats. "We have another report of this.... Jesus of Nazareth causing a near riot among the people in Bethsaida," he said.

Joseph of Arimathea stood and addressed the council. He was a respected member of the Sanhedrin and quite rich. He was in his late fifties, nearly six foot tall and well-built for his age. "I must object!"

"Object?" Caiaphas asked. "Object to what, Joseph?"

"Object to the report that a riot was developing," Joseph replied.

"Then what would you call thousands of people following this man and neglecting the laws of the Sabbath... the basic laws of our beliefs laid down by God Almighty?" Caiaphas asked, nearly yelling.

"They were not rioting, great Caiaphas," he answered. "They were listening."

"And just how would you know that?" another member of the Sanhedrin asked.

"Because I was there," Joseph replied.

Several members of the audience gasped in disbelief that Joseph would attend such a gathering. They began to whisper and mumble that he might be a secret disciple.

"As was I," another member said as he stood. He was an older man in his sixties and was just over five foot tall. The members of the Sanhedrin looked to see who spoke. It was Nicodemus who continued to address the council. "I saw what happened at Bethsaida," he said.

"Are you both secret followers of this false prophet?" Caiaphas asked?

"I went to see what he was teaching, to confirm he was leading our people astray as the council had recommended," Joseph replied.

"As did I," said Nicodemus.

"Then tell me, Joseph, what was your observation?" Caiaphas asked.

Joseph looked at Nicodemus, took a deep breath, and began. "I saw this Jesus feed thousands people with……….nothing."

The council members began yelling and shouting their disbelief as Joseph finished his sentence.

"Stop!" Caiaphas ordered. Once the council quieted down, Caiaphas continued. "How can any one man feed so many with no provisions? How can that be possible?"

"I do not know," Joseph calmly replied. "What I saw was Jesus blessing some loaves of bread and a couple of fish and had his disciples distribute them among the people. They ate until they were satisfied," Joseph replied. The council erupted in shouts and jeers. Joseph held up his hands to quiet them down and continued. "I do not know how this happened. What I do know is… the people were fed and there were twelve baskets full of bread and fish when they finished."

"It's witchcraft!" someone yelled. "He is possessed by a demon," someone else yelled.

Nicodemus stood and asked for silence. "I do not know how this happened either, but I concur with brother Joseph. It happened as he said."

Joseph and Nicodemus took their seats as the council exploded.

Caiaphas saw that the council was out of control. He watched quietly as the members yelled at each other sometimes with accusations of treachery or conspiring with Jesus and his disciples. First the report from Jairus about his daughter's healing. There were other reports of miracles performed by Jesus as well. Now he has two notable members of the Sanhedrin professing they saw a miracle occur with the feeding of several thousand people. He could see Jesus's teachings and 'miracles' were tearing the Sanhedrin apart. He feared they would do the same to the nation of Israel. He had to find a way to stop Jesus.

---****---

The afternoon sun was warming the veranda at Caesarea Maritima where Pilate and Claudia were enjoying some food and drink when Pilate noticed a ship pulling into the harbor. "A Roman ship," he said as he pointed.

"I wonder what they are bringing us?" Claudia asked.

Pilate smiled. "I hope it is *good* wine," he said with a laugh. "We could certainly use some."

Claudia smiled. "Like the wine I made with my feet when we first met?" she asked with a giggle.

"Most definitely," Pilate replied. He watched as a Roman soldier disembarked the boat, grabbed a nearby horse from another soldier, and galloped toward the palace. "Must be something more important than wine, I fear," Pilate said as he watched the horseman make his way through the streets. "If you will excuse me, my dear, as I greet our guest."

The soldier approached the palace and dismounted as Pilate was walking out onto the steps to greet him. "Mighty Governor," the soldier said as he approached Pilate and saluted. "I have news from Rome."

"What could be so important? Has the emperor died?" Pilate asked.

The soldier opened his satchel and handed Pilate a document. He noticed the seal of the Praetorian Guard. "Oh. From Sejanus," he said as he opened the document.

Governor Pontius Pilate
Greetings in the name of Jupiter

Lucius Aelius Sejanus, prefect of the Praetorian Guard, has been charged with treason, conspiracy, sedition, and the murder of Drusus Julius Caesar and has been executed. Quintus Naevius Cordus Sutorius Macro has been appointed as Prefect of the Praetorian Guard

Pilate stopped reading and slowly lowered the document as he looked out to the sea, ignoring the courier standing before him. He turned and walked quickly into the palace, leaving the courier standing alone on the palace steps.

"Go!" Pilate ordered the guards as he approached the veranda where Claudia had been patiently waiting. Once they were alone, he began. "Sejanus has been executed."

"What? Sejanus?" Claudia asked. "There must be some mistake."

"There is no mistake," Pilate replied tersely as he handed Claudia the document. "Macro is the new prefect of the Praetorian Guard."

"Sejanus was charged with the murder of Drusus?" Claudia asked as she read the notice.

"The fool!" Pilate exclaimed. "How could he think he would get away with that?"

"Did you know about that?" Claudia asked in surprise.

"No. Of course not," Pilate replied almost indignantly. "It was obvious he was serious about becoming emperor when he attempted to betroth his four-year-old daughter to a Julian. That was when I started to distance myself from him."

"Do you think he killed Drusus?" Claudia asked.

"I don't know. I've seen him kill many men...in battle," Pilate replied.

"Someone who knew must have told Tiberius," Claudia surmised as Pilate paced around the veranda.

Pilate ignored her comment. "Sejanus! Damn him!" he yelled as he pounded the railing with his fist. "I thought Tiberius was near death."

"Obviously not," Claudia retorted. "Isn't he in Capris?"

"Yes. With Caligula," Pilate answered as he gazed out to the blue Mediterranean Sea. "I suspect he will return to Rome to clean house."

"You mean....."

Pilate turned to Claudia. He was never one to show fear of any type. He was a Roman soldier, a commander of men, a governor. He relished the adrenaline rush of battle, savored the taste of victory and basked in the glory of his accomplishments. Yet, the thought of Tiberius on a purging rampage shook him. "Rome's Caesars tend to eliminate any threat or perceived threat to their reign. Tiberius will be no exception, I'm sure." He sat back in his seat across from Claudia and leaned in close. "He will purge Rome of anyone he believes opposes him," he said softly as if he feared someone was listening to their conversation.

"But you don't oppose him," Claudia assured him.

"Anyone *he* believes opposes him," Pilate said. "It doesn't matter if it is accurate or not. Anyone associated with Sejanus will be suspect."

"But you haven't seen or heard from Sejanus in a long time."

"Doesn't matter," Pilate replied. "I was close to Sejanus, and Tiberius knows that."

"You have been friends with Sejanus since…"

"Since the ludi twenty-five years ago," Pilate replied. "Sejanus appointed me to this position. We fought the battle of Pannonia together."

Claudia had forgotten that Sejanus appointed Pilate as Governor of Judea, and it shocked her. "Marcus!" Claudia reached across the table and grabbed Pilate's hands. "What are we to do?"

Pilate thought for a moment. "Nothing. We do nothing." Pilate stood and started to pace as he thought out loud. "Herod's sons petitioned the legate of Syria about the standards I placed at their palace a few months ago. The legate ordered me to remove them, so I did. I do not know if Tiberius was ever informed of the situation, but we must avoid all scrutiny from him until…… until he dies."

"Dies?" Claudia asked. "You're not planning…."

Pilate stopped her before she said it. "No! Not that. Tiberius is old. He must be seventy years old or more," Pilate replied. "His days are few. We need to wait him out and not bring his scrutiny upon ourselves. I cannot have another questionable altercation with the Jews until he dies. I must keep them under control." He stopped at the railing and gazed out to the sea again. "My name must not cross Tiberius's lips. Otherwise, he might remember my friendship with Sejanus and perceive me to be a threat to his reign."

"Marcus," Claudia called as she walked toward him. "I'm scared." She fell into his arms.

Pilate took a deep breath as he held Claudia. "As am I," he whispered. "Damn you, Sejanus!"

Chapter 11   The Betrayal
31 AD

Four Roman soldiers galloped across the hills toward Bethany. A cloud of dust followed them as they searched for the crowds following Jesus. They heard he was headed to Bethany, and they wanted to observe him from a distance. It seemed that many people wanted to see him yet not be associated with him. They were following orders to keep an eye on him to see if he was amassing an army to rebel against Rome. As they summited a hill near the village, they saw a throng of people, probably several hundred, following Jesus on the road to the village.

"What shall we do now?" one of the soldiers asked the centurion. It was the same centurion whose slave was healed by Jesus.

"Wait here. I will go see what is happening," he said as he dismounted. He pulled some clothes from his pack and quickly changed. He set off on foot leaving his troops waiting behind.

"Jesus," a woman yelled as she ran toward the man followed by a large crowd of people. They were a short distance outside the village of Bethany, which was a mere three kilometers[68] from Jerusalem. Jesus was informed two days prior that a close friend of his named Lazarus had fallen ill. Lazarus had two sisters, Mary and Martha, both of whom had met Jesus before and drew close to him. They sent messengers asking Jesus to come heal their brother. However, Jesus delayed two days before arriving at the village. Now, Martha ran to greet him as he approached the village. She was a woman in her mid-thirties with brown eyes and long, black hair that flew behind her as she ran.

The centurion watched from a distance as Martha stopped Jesus and the crowd in the street. He maneuvered closer to hear what they were talking about.

---

[68] 3 kilometers = 2 miles

"Lord, if you had only been here sooner, my brother would not have died," Martha said as she wept at Jesus's feet. "But I know that even now God will give you whatever you ask."

Jesus gently helped her to her feet and looked her in the eyes. "Your brother will rise again," he assured her.

"I know he will rise in the resurrection on the last day," she replied.

"I am the resurrection and the life," Jesus declared. "The one who believes in me will live, even though they die; and whoever lives by believing in me will never die," he said. "Do you believe this?"

Martha looked into Jesus's eyes. "Yes, Lord. I believe that you are the Messiah, the Son of God, who is to come into the world."

Jesus smiled at her. "Please, go get Mary," he said.

Martha quickly ran back to the house where many people had gathered to mourn Lazarus's death. Women stood in front of the house wailing and pacing. "Where's Mary?" Martha asked. She ran into the house and pulled Mary aside. "The Teacher wants to see you," she said.

The two sisters quickly left the house and ran toward the edge of the village. Many of the mourners thought they were going to the tomb, so they followed the couple. When Mary reached Jesus, she fell at his feet, weeping. "Lord. If you had been here, my brother would not have died," she said.

Jesus looked down on her with compassion. She was more petite and younger than Martha. He could see the despair and sadness that engulfed her. "Where have you laid him?" he asked.

Mary rose to her feet. "Come, and see," she said as she led him toward the tomb. Jesus wept as he walked with Mary and Martha to the tomb of his friend followed by hundreds of people, including the centurion. People mumbled amongst themselves. One man said, "See how he loved him." Another said, "Couldn't he who opened the eyes of a blind man not have kept this man from dying?"

The tomb area was along a cliffside outside the village. Several tombs had large stones either sealing them or leaned up against the mountain wall beside the tomb waiting for their occupant. The tomb Lazarus was in was sealed with a very large stone. Jesus looked around at the crowd who were watching his every move. "Remove the stone," he ordered.

Onlookers were shocked. Martha took the arm of Jesus. "Lord, by this time there will be a bad odor because he has been dead four days," she warned him.

Jesus looked her in the eyes. "Did I not tell you that if you believe, you will see the glory of God?" Martha nodded and released his arm.

With great effort, two men rolled the stone away from the entrance of the tomb and stepped back, covering their mouths and noses to protect them from the stench. Once the stone was rolled away, Jesus raised his arms to the sky and said, "Father, I thank you that you have heard me. I know that you always hear me, but I said this for the benefit of the people standing here, that they may believe that you sent me."

Martha and Mary embraced as they watched. The crowd edged closer to see and hear what was happening, anticipating another miracle. The centurion gently pushed through the crowd to get a better look.

Jesus pointed to the tomb and yelled, "Lazarus, come out!"

The crowd was completely silent as they watched the entrance to the tomb with great anticipation. Suddenly, a man wrapped in burial linens stumbled to the doorway and stopped. He pulled the linen from his face and looked around, dazed. The crowd exploded with amazement, yelling and cheering. Pandemonius joy!

"Take off the grave clothes and let him go," Jesus ordered as several people approached the once dead man and helped him out. They quickly removed the linens and wrapped him in a robe.

The centurion couldn't believe what he had seen. Neither could several of the Pharisees observing from afar.

----***----

Claudia was packing some clothes and other personal items for their trip to Jerusalem when Pilate walked into the room. "Must we go to Jerusalem again?" she asked.

"Unfortunately, yes," he replied. "It is their Passover celebration. I need to show Rome's benevolence by releasing a prisoner for them," he said as he gathered a few personal items and handed them to Claudia. "There will be thousands of Jews traveling to Jerusalem to visit the temple. The benevolence and power of Rome need to be displayed."

"If they are going to a 'temple', I would think there would not be any problems."

"One would think. But these are an obstinate people. I don't need a report of an uprising getting to Tiberius," Pilate replied. Claudia looked at him with concern as he continued. "We don't need *any* reports getting to Tiberius. Not now."

"Maybe we will have an opportunity to meet this Jesus of Nazareth," Claudia said changing the subject. "His fame and notoriety are spreading."

"As long as he doesn't become a problem to Rome, he can do whatever 'miracles' he chooses."

---****---

Caiaphas was finishing his evening meal when it was interrupted by two pharisees who had demanded they see him immediately. They were dressed in civilian attire instead of their priestly robes, which most pharisees always wore. One of the men was Joseph of Arimathea.

"Joseph! What are you doing here at this hour?" Caiaphas asked?

"Honorable Caiaphas," Joseph replied as he bowed. "We...we have just witnessed something extraordinary," he replied.

"And what might that be?" Caiaphas asked obviously perturbed at the interruption.

Joseph looked around to make sure they were alone. He nodded to the servant standing nearby. Caiaphas excused the servant and Joseph continued. "Yesterday, we saw Jesus of Nazareth….." Joseph paused.

"What? What did he do? Spit it out!" Caiaphas demanded.

"…..raise a man from the dead!" Joseph finished.

"You saw what?"

The other man, Abner, confirmed Joseph's statement. "We did. A man called Lazarus of Bethany was dead four days and buried in a tomb, and Jesus called him out!"

"Impossible!" Caiaphas yelled as he approached the men. "No one has ever been raised from the dead."

"What of Jairus's daughter?" Abner asked. Caiaphas ignored Abner's question.

"It happened, Caiaphas," Joseph replied.

"It must have been a trick," Caiaphas replied. "They were both tricks of some type. No one can bring a person back to life except God himself," he said as he opened his arms wide and looked upwards toward heaven.

The two men looked at each other as Joseph continued. "It happened. We saw it," Joseph insisted.

"He came out wrapped in burial clothes," Abner added.

"Then they must have planted the man inside and wrapped him in burial clothes and then had this Jesus call him out," Caiaphas replied. "It was planned! You have been deceived!"

"And if it was not a trick?" Joseph asked.

Caiaphas ignored the question. "We must stop this man!" Caiaphas announced as he started to pace. "He is leading our people astray and threatens the peace of our nation."

"But Caiaphas…"

Abner was cut off by Caiaphas, whose anger was growing. "I am calling a meeting of the Sanhedrin immediately," he said. "This man must be stopped!" he yelled as he stormed out.

The Hall of Hewn Stones was full as members of the Sanhedrin questioned why they were there at such a late hour. Many of them were complaining about the interruption to their festivities or sleep. It had to be something significant. Rumors were shared as Caiaphas stood before the assembly. "Brothers, we have a report that this Jesus of Nazareth is stirring up trouble amongst our people."

"How so?" someone asked.

"He has used trickery or witchcraft or some other unholy means to lead our people astray by appearing to have raised a man from the dead!" Caiaphas declared.

"Raised from the dead?" someone shouted. "Impossible," someone else yelled. The men began talking and shouting, overtaking the meeting from Caiaphas, who had to stand and order them to remain quiet.

"I also believe this is impossible, but the greater issue is the threat that this Jesus of Nazareth is to the sovereignty of our nation and the sanctity of our beliefs!" Caiaphas declared.

"How so?" Nicodemus asked. "He has done miracles that we cannot explain, such as this."

"It is not a miracle when it is a trick," Caiaphas said.

"But he has done other miracles of healing….," someone said.

"…and feeding the thousands….," another added.

"Stop!" Caiaphas ordered. "What are we accomplishing? Can you not see that he is dividing our nation just like he is dividing us? We are allowing this man to continue to deceive our people and teach the scriptures as though he was educated in our scriptures."

"But what of the miracles that we have seen?" Joseph asked. "I saw that man walk out of the tomb."

Another member stood. "Brothers. Here is this man, Jesus, performing many signs and miracles. If we let him go on like this, everyone will believe in him, and the Romans will come and take both our temple and our nation away."

"But he must be from God, otherwise how could he do such things?" Joseph asked.

"Stop!" Caiaphas ordered. "You know nothing! Do you not realize that it is better for you that one man die than a whole nation perish?"

"Are you saying he needs to die?" someone yelled.

"We have no authority to administer capital punishment," Joseph added. "Only Rome has that authority."

"He has blasphemed God Almighty," Caiaphas declared. "He teaches of the kingdom of God as though he has been there and seen it. People believe he is the Messiah, and he has not rebuked nor corrected them. In fact, he continues to lead them into believing he is the Messiah. He is not going to free us from Rome's grasp! Our law requires that such an imposter be put to death," Caiaphas declared.

"What then are we to do?" Abner asked.

"We must arrest him. If anyone knows where he is, they must tell us so that we can arrest him," Caiaphas ordered.

"We are about to celebrate the Passover, Caiaphas. If we arrest him now, the people may riot," another man said.

"Then we wait," Caiaphas ordered. "Someone knows where he is. We will arrest him and deal with him swiftly....before we lose our temple and our nation."

"And what of this Lazarus that many believed he raised from the dead?" someone yelled. "Many people are believing in Jesus because of his testimony."

"Then he, too, should be put to death," Caiaphas declared. "But we have no law that will allow us to do so."

The men continued to debate the need to kill Jesus right away lest he turn the entire Jewish religion on its head. Several of the members voiced their opposition to deaf ears. Caiaphas needed to figure out how they could capture Jesus without creating a revolt.

---****---

The warm, spring air was filled with the fragrance of the blooming wildflowers that covered the hillsides nearby as the caravan crested the hill overlooking the plateau where Jerusalem lay. The city was surrounded by a stone wall seven and a half meters[69] high, almost seven meters[70] wide and stretched more than five kilometers[71] around the city. It contained thirty-four watchtowers and seven gates. In the center of the city was the temple; a massive structure with secondary walls surrounding a central, rectangular building and courtyards. Outside the city walls was a sea of sojourners with thousands of tents and camps. The smoke from the fires both inside and outside the city could be seen for miles.

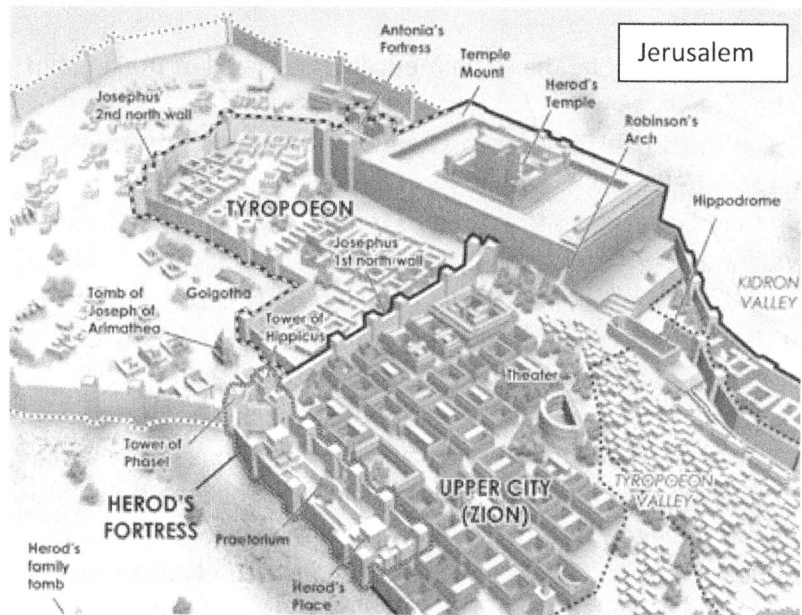

"I have never seen so many tents," Claudia said as their caravan continued toward the great city.

"It's their Passover celebration. Jews from all over come here to worship and offer sacrifices," a centurion replied, riding his horse alongside the wagon where Claudia and Pilate rose comfortably.

---

[69] 7 1/2 meters = 25 feet
[70] 7 meters = 22 feet
[71] 5 kilometers = 3 miles

"There must be 100,000 travelers here," Pilate said.

"Or more, governor," the centurion replied.

"Ride ahead. Make sure the road is clear and that we have no one trying to stop us," Pilate ordered.

"Yes, governor," the centurion said as he rode off at a gallop.

"Oh, look," Claudia exclaimed. "What are all of these palm branches for?"

"It must have been some type of celebration or something," Pilate replied.

Claudia turned and smiled. "Or maybe your Jewish friends are welcoming us," she said with a giggle.

"I think not." Pilate wasn't amused. He was concerned about the sheer number of people in the city for the Passover celebration and how he was going to maintain control should unrest arise. "I'm going to have to double the patrols."

The caravan made its way through the throngs of tents and camps to the exterior wall of the city. The smell of bread, roasted meats and sewage was strong. At times, smoke from the campfires was almost choking. Children playing along the roadway waved as the caravan passed by. They continued on to Herod's palace where they would stay during the Passover celebration. It was imperative that Pilate maintain order. He believed his presence would assure that.

Claudia was looking out the window at the sea of tents surrounding the city. "There are thousands of people here," she said. "Did you see the children?"

Pilate sat at a table with a goblet of wine and some fruit as he looked over some papers. It was a long ride to Jerusalem, and he was tired, tired of dealing with the Jews. Tired of having to watch his back fearing Tiberius might have him arrested anytime for conspiracy with Sejanus. The stress weighed on him. "Yes," Pilate replied. "I saw the children. They looked like dirty little rats," he answered.

Claudia started to say something when a centurion entered the room and saluted. "Report," Pilate ordered barely glancing at the soldier standing before him at attention. The centurion hesitated as he looked toward Claudia, watching them. "I said report, centurion!"

"Mighty Governor. We have reports of a Jesus of Nazareth causing an…… an uprising of sorts with the Jewish people."

"Uprising? Explain!" Pilate ordered.

"There have been reports of miracles and healings," the centurion answered.

"So? What is that to me?" Pilate asked.

"Some reports are……… that he brought a man back to life," the centurion said almost timidly.

"What?" Claudia said surprised.

"Hah. Impossible," Pilate exclaimed. He brushed off the comment and continued. "I have heard of him before. Does he have an army?"

"No, governor. Just a lot of people who follow him to hear his teachings."

"The old and crippled still?" Pilate asked.

"Yes, mostly, sir," the soldier answered. "He is teaching the Jews about their god."

"Then why are you reporting this to me?" Pilate asked slamming his fist on the table. "I do not want to hear about a Jewish teacher."

"He is stirring the people up, governor."

"How so?" Claudia asked. Pilate glared at her for speaking and she quickly turned away and stared out the window.

"The people want to make him king, governor," the centurion answered.

"Then let Herod deal with his new competition," Pilate said as he laughed.

"He also entered their temple and destroyed the vendor tables, kicking the people out, and causing an uproar amongst the people," the centurion added.

"Then let the priests deal with him. He is not *my* problem, unless...." Pilate stood to his feet and approached the centurion. "...unless he has broken Roman law." Pilate stood in front of the centurion and continued. "Has he?"

"No, commander. He has not," the centurion replied.

"When he does, deal with him swiftly," Pilate ordered as he returned to his table.

"Yes, commander," the centurion said as he waited to be dismissed.

"Until then, Herod or the priests can deal with him," Pilate replied. "Dismissed!"

"As you wish, governor," the centurion said as he saluted and left.

Claudia turned to Pilate with a concerned look and said, "Raised from the dead?"

"It's trickery of some sort," Pilate replied, brushing her question off as he did with the centurion. "No one can do that."

"But he said he was healing people, too."

Pilate laughed. "Again, trickery. Or..." Pilate laughed nervously and continued. "....or a very good doctor!" Claudia turned away to look at the mass of people once again, not saying anything, but contemplating what she had just heard as Pilate continued. "It is nothing that should concern ourselves, at least not right now. If he breaks *any* Roman law, then he will be punished swiftly and severely. That will cause his 'followers' to scatter like scared children," Pilate said as he returned to his paperwork.

Claudia stared out the window and whispered, "Who is this man?"

Pilate slapped his papers on the table, obviously irritated they were still talking about Jesus. "He is a Jewish teacher, nothing more," he said.

---****---

It was now a few days before the Passover and the religious leaders had yet to capture Jesus or Lazarus as planned at the special meeting of the Sanhedrin the day before. Caiaphas called several priests and elders of the Jewish people to his palace to discuss how to deal with Jesus and capture him. His father-in-law, Annas, was present. He was an elderly man who had been high priest in the past and was instrumental with Caiaphas's appointment many years prior. The Sanhedrin still considered him a high priest working in conjunction with Caiaphas, yet not officially holding the position. Now, because of his tenure and experience, Annas was exercising his influence on the Sanhedrin, particularly on Caiaphas, with dealing with Jesus.

"We must find a way to capture this Jesus and kill him before the whole world goes after him," Annas said.

"If we arrest him during the festival, we might spark a riot," one of the priests said.

"The people follow him like sheep," another added. "Thousands of people."

"They were laying palm branches before him and calling him 'King'," Caiaphas added. "He's no king. He will never deliver us from Rome's control. Only fools would think so."

"Many believe he was sent from God," someone said.

"Sent from God? He has said he *is* God!" Caiaphas declared.

"He is a man!" Annas shouted. "A man with trickery, or a demon. Nothing more, and we *must* kill him to show the people that he is not God Almighty, but a false prophet, a fraud before he leads our people astray and destroys our nation!"

"We must spread the word that we want to talk with him, privately," Caiaphas remarked. "Offer a reward. People will do anything for money. The more we offer, the more likely someone will turn him in. Pay it to anyone who will disclose his location that we may 'speak' with him. Then, we will be able to capture him at night and deal with him......appropriately."

"How much should we offer?" someone asked.

"Thirty pieces of silver should suffice," Annas declared.

"Very well," someone answered.

"The sooner we deal with this Jesus, the better it will be for our people," Annas said. "We must make them see he is a fraud...before it is too late."

---****---

A middle-aged man walked briskly down the dark street toward Caiaphas's palace. He was quite slender with a long unkept beard, dirty clothes and long hair. As he passed the temple, he tried to ignore a woman of the night offering him her services. "Looking for some fun?" she asked as he tried to walk briskly past her. She flashed him a big smile revealing her crooked, stained teeth.

"Leave me alone," he said as he pushed the woman out of his way and continued on his* mission.

"Hey!" she said as she stumbled backwards and fell.

He ignored her and picked up his pace, almost running as he rounded the corner to the entrance of Caiaphas's palace. He saw that the gates were closed. A young, male servant was walking toward the main building carrying a tray. "Hey! You!" he called. The servant stopped and looked back to him. "Tell Caiaphas that I ..... I know where the man is."

"What man do you mean?" the servant asked.

He hesitated for a moment and looked around to insure no one would hear him. He motioned for the servant to come closer. As he did, he leaned his face close to the bars and whispered, "Jesus of Nazareth."

Caiaphas was sitting on a balcony overlooking the temple and enjoying the warm, night air of spring with several other priests of the Sanhedrin as the servant approached and bowed. "There is a man at the gate that says he knows where Jesus of Nazareth is."

Caiaphas nearly choked on his wine as he heard the news. "Send him in. Immediately!" he ordered.

The servant left as the priests began chattering about what the new development meant. The excitement grew that they could actually apprehend Jesus under cover of night before Passover. It was a perfect way to stop him and avoid a riot at the same time.

The servant soon returned and escorted the stranger to the balcony where the priests were anxiously waiting. Caiaphas spoke first. "We hear you have news for us?" Caiaphas said with a smile. The man looked around nervously. "It's safe. No one else is here but us," Caiaphas said as he motioned to the other priests. "Who are you?"

"Judas Iscariot," the man replied. He was sweating from the combination of the warm air, brisk walk and nervousness. "I know where Jesus is."

"And how would you know such a thing?" one of the priests asked.

"I am one of his disciples," Judas replied.

"His disciple?" Caiaphas asked. "Then why would you turn your teacher in to us?"

"I saw him waste some very expensive perfume on himself," Judas said almost indignantly.

"How so?" someone asked.

"We were at a house when a woman came and poured a large vial of very expensive perfume on him. I told her to stop, but he allowed it. The perfume could have been sold for a year's wages and the money could have been used to feed the poor. But he wasted it without a thought," Judas replied.

"You see!" Caiaphas said to the other priests. "He has no concern for the poor. He is more concerned for himself than anyone," he said as he stood to his feet and approached Judas with a smile. "You are right, Judas." he said as he patted Judas on the shoulder. "We just need to speak with him about the inconsistencies with his teaching."

"I heard there was a reward. What....what will you give me if I reveal his location?" Judas asked.

Caiaphas smiled and motioned to one of the priests who pulled a small bag from his satchel and handed it to him. Caiaphas held it out to Judas, who took the bag, opened it, and poured some of the coins into his hand. "Thirty pieces of fine silver," Caiaphas replied.

Judas smiled as he saw the bright, shiny coins fall into his hands. "This will feed many," he said as he returned the coins to the satchel and closed it.

"Where is he?" one of the priests asked.

"He is at the garden of Gethsemane with the other disciples," Judas replied. "He will be there all night."

"Very well," Caiaphas said. "But how will we know who he is? There could be many people following him as there have been."

"I will greet him with a kiss. Then you will know who he is," Judas replied.

"Good," Caiaphas said as he turned and walked away from Judas, ignoring him as he whispered to the other priests. He looked back to Judas and dismissed him. "We will be at the garden soon. You may go." He turned his back to Judas as though he didn't exist.

Judas bowed and quickly left.

Caiaphas turned to the servant. "Go. Be a witness to what occurs and report back to me."

---****---

"Joseph ben Caiaphas," the soldier announced as Caiaphas walked past the guard and into the room where Pilate was seated before the soldier finished his introduction. Caiaphas was alone and had no concern for becoming defiled as he had in the past. Not this time.

"Why are you here at this hour?" Pilate asked. "It better be good."

"Mighty governor," Caiaphas began. "We know where this Jesus of Nazareth is and can arrest him without trouble."

"And why do I care about him?" Pilate asked.

"He is stirring up our people, governor with his teachings and fake miracles."

"That is of no concern to me, Caiaphas. He is your problem," Pilate replied dismissively.

"I fear if he continues, he will invoke a riot. That would not be good for either of us, governor," Caiaphas replied. "We need to get him away from the people now, especially during the Passover. Many, many of our people listen to what he says."

"So?"

"If he orders them to do something, anything, I fear they will do so, even take up arms and resist Rome," Caiaphas answered. "There are 100,000 sojourners here. We do not know if any are secret followers armed and ready to fight Rome."

Pilate stood to his feet at the thought of a possible rebellion arising. "I cannot have that," he replied. "No. Not at all. You need to keep your people under control, or I will, and you will not like my solution to your problem!"

"That is why I am asking for your assistance," Caiaphas replied with a bow and continued. "We know where he is and wish to capture him."

"And what will you do with him?" Pilate asked.

"Hold him at our palace until after the Passover. The people will leave the city and his popularity will wane when he does not make an appearance," Caiaphas replied.

"What do you need from me, then?"

"Soldiers to arrest him."

Pilate thought for a moment. "Very well. Take ten soldiers…"

Caiaphas interrupted. "I do not believe ten soldiers are enough. He has had thousands of people following him. If we take but ten, they could easily become overpowered and…."

"Stop!" Pilate ordered. "How many soldiers do you need then?"

"A cohort," Caiaphas answered.

"Cohort? Almost five hundred men to arrest one man and a few followers?" Pilate asked incredulously. Caiaphas didn't answer but just nodded. "Take a full cohort, then! Guard!" A soldier rounded the corner and saluted. "Inform the centurion of the cohort he is to escort this priest to capture this man, Jesus."

"Yes, governor," the soldier replied. He saluted and left.

"A cohort to capture one man!" Pilate added. "You must be very afraid of this Jesus."

Caiaphas bowed. "Mighty governor. If he is able to trick thousands of people into believing he is the Messiah, that he is the Son of God, then he could easily sway them into a revolt. Thus, we should both be afraid," he replied. "You should be afraid."

Pilate walked up to Caiaphas and stood in his face. "Watch what you say, or I will have your tongue cut out and fed to you!"

Caiaphas was shocked to see Pilate's anger. "Please forgive me governor for my offense," he said as he bowed, turned and started to leave when Pilate grabbed his arm and stopped him. "One more thing, Caiaphas. You make sure this man does not become a problem for Rome." The priest bowed and quickly left.

---****---

The smell of flowers filled the early morning air in the garden at Gethsemane as a large group of soldiers and priests approached. It was still dark as the smoke from their torches quickly overpowered the sweet aroma in the garden. Judas led the group up the hill to the spot where Jesus and his disciples stood, waiting. It was an unusual scene to see five hundred soldiers strung down the hill coming to arrest one unarmed man in the middle of the night.

Judas cautiously approached Jesus. "Greetings, Rabbi," he said as he kissed him on the cheek.

"Do what you came to do, friend," Jesus replied. He looked at the group standing before him and asked, "Who is it that you are looking for?"

"Jesus of Nazareth," the centurion replied.

"I am he," Jesus said. The men leading the group stumbled backwards with some falling to the ground. Then, the centurion jumped to his feet and yelled, "Seize him!"

One of Jesus's disciples drew a sword and swung it at a man standing nearby. It was Caiaphas's servant who was ordered to go as a witness to the arrest and report back to Caiaphas. The sword narrowly missed the man's head, slicing off his ear. The man screamed in pain as his ear fell to the ground.

"Put your sword back in its place...." Jesus said to him, "....for all who draw the sword will die by the sword." He stepped closer to his disciple and quietly said, "Do you think I cannot call on my Father, and He will at once put at my disposal more than twelve legions of angels? But how then would the Scriptures be fulfilled that say it must happen in this way?" The men surrounding him watched as he leaned down and picked up the servant's ear. He gently reached over, held it to the servant's bleeding head and miraculously reattached it. The crowd watched in amazement. The disciple with the sword dropped it at Jesus's feet and stepped back. The servant felt his ear in disbelief and stared at Jesus.

Jesus turned back to the centurion. "Am I leading a rebellion, that you have come out with swords and clubs to capture me? Every day I sat in the temple courts teaching, and you did not arrest me." He turned to his disciples standing nearby and said, "But this has all taken place that the writings of the prophets might be fulfilled."

"Take him," the centurion ordered. The guards hesitated. "We have our orders! Take him!" he yelled. The guards took Jesus into custody and roughly escorted him out of the garden.

All of the disciples fled in fear as Jesus was taken into custody and removed from the garden, all but one. Judas stood by the servant who looked at him with tears in his eyes. "I let you in to see Caiaphas. Why this?" he cried.

The two stood watching the torch lit procession leave the garden and weave its way down the hill toward the city.

---****---

Pilate lay in bed unable to sleep. He thought about his friend, Sejanus, who was recently executed for treason. He wondered if Tiberius would remember how he and Sejanus were friends. The fiasco with King Herod and the standards had passed and he felt safe for now, but this arrest of the man Jesus could change everything and weighed heavily on him. *What if there is a bloodbath at Gethsemane? Why would Caiaphas need so many soldiers if Jesus had no army? He must be expecting some form of resistance.*

His wife, Claudia, was restless and kept waking him during the night with her tossing and turning. His wandering thoughts combined with her restlessness afforded him little sleep. He got out of bed and walked over to the window and looked toward the Mount of Olives. The cool air felt good as he noticed a torch lit procession slowly moving down the mountain to the city. He sighed and lowered his head as he leaned on the window ledge. He feared it was going to be a long day.

---****---

The streets of Jerusalem were awakening to the sound of the entourage escorting Jesus from the Garden of Gethsemane to the house of Annas, Caiaphas's father-in-law who shared the high priest role with Caiaphas. As they approached the house, the centurion ordered most of the cohort back to their barracks, while twenty or so men continued to escort Jesus into the house.

Inside they found Annas and two other Sanhedrin priests dressed in their priestly garments waiting. The soldiers pushed Jesus into the middle of a large banquet room facing a courtyard and surrounded him, assuring he would not try to escape. Annas was sitting in a chair facing Jesus, who stood before him with his hands bound with twine. Jesus slowly looked at each person in the room, returning his gaze to Annas.

"You have stirred up much trouble with your teaching, Jesus of Nazareth," Annas began. "You are uneducated, a common man, yet you teach as though you are a scholar about God Almighty. Where did you learn this teaching?"

Jesus said nothing.

"Why do you say you will tear down the temple and rebuild it in three days? That is impossible for any man to do, yet you claim you can do so. That is a lie from the devil!"

Nothing.

Annas began to anger at Jesus's silence. He stood to his feet and approached Jesus. "You teach about heaven, yet you, a simple man, a child of fornication could not possibly know what heaven is like. Is it not true that you have been teaching such things and misleading our people?"

A rooster crowed, distracting the questioning for a moment as Jesus looked out to the courtyard where several people had gathered by the fire. He returned his gaze to Annas and said nothing.

Annas was getting angrier, as were the other two priests who also approached Jesus. "Have you not been teaching against upholding the sabbath as sacred? Answer me!" he yelled.

Jesus remained silent. He took in a deep breath and closed his eyes, smelling the fragrant blooms of the flowers wafting in from the courtyard. Annas lowered his voice and spoke to Jesus in a condescending manner. "You claim to be a Jew, yet you refuse to answer a high priest?"

Jesus opened his eyes and looked at Annas. "I have spoken openly to the world," Jesus replied, surprising Annas when he spoke. "I always taught in synagogues or at the temple, where the Jews come together. I said nothing in secret. Why question me? Ask those who heard me. Surely, they know what I said."

One of the other priests slapped Jesus across the face. "Is this the way you answer a high priest?" he asked.

Jesus recoiled and looked at the man who slapped him. "If I said something wrong, testify as to what is wrong. But, if I spoke the truth….. why did you strike me?" he asked.

"Enough of this!" Annas yelled as he threw up his arms in frustration and returned to his seat. "He is a fraud. Send him to Caiaphas and let him be tried according to our laws and customs."

The guards quickly grabbed Jesus and pushed him toward the door. Jesus stumbled and fell. One of the guards kicked him as he yelled, "Get up!" Jesus stood and continued out the door, guarded by the soldiers and followed by the priests.

---****---

Springtime in Jerusalem brings the warm air that bathes the hillsides and invites the flowers to show their vast colors, painting the landscape with hues of every color. During the day, children play while adults tend to the chores of everyday life. At night, the lingering fragrance of the roses and hyacinth fill the night air for the morning. One would think a sunrise filled with such beautiful fragrances would offer a calming sense to anyone awake so early. For Judas Iscariot, it was far from the truth.

Judas maneuvered his way through the streets toward the Hall of Hewn Stones where the Sanhedrin met. He was crying unconsolably, so hard that he couldn't see where he was walking. The prostitutes of the temple were long gone. Several people lay on the ground along the street asleep in their drunken stupor. Judas was looking behind him to see if someone was following when he stumbled into a man and tripped, falling hard on the ground. The encounter had no effect on the sleeping man. Judas got to his feet and continued working his way toward the Hall.

As Judas approached the Hall, he composed himself and wiped the tears from his face. He could see there were people standing outside the Hall peering in. He recognized Peter in the courtyard but hid himself so that he would not be seen as he slowly maneuvered his way to the back of the Hall unnoticed.

Jesus was standing on a platform in front of Caiaphas, who was seated in a chair much like a throne. Jesus's hands were bound, and his garment torn. His eye was swollen and red. Several priests were seated on each side of him. The remaining members of the Sanhedrin that were called to the special meeting were in their seats listening to the trial. Roman guards were stationed around the room.

"You refuse to answer?" Caiaphas asked. Jesus said nothing. Caiaphas motioned to two young men standing to the side of the platform. "We have more witnesses." Two men cautiously approached as Jesus watched them. "What have you heard this man declare?" Caiaphas asked.

The young men looked around at the full hall and then at Jesus. "I heard this man say, 'I am able to destroy the temple of God and rebuild it in three days...without using my hands'," one of them said. The other nodded.

"Absurd!" someone yelled. "Heresy!" another declared.

The second older man stepped forward. "I heard him say that whoever eats his flesh and drinks his blood has eternal life, and he will raise them up on the last day."

"Cannibalism!" someone yelled. "He is insane," another called out.

The witnesses quickly scurried off the platform and into the audience encircling the members of the Sanhedrin.

Caiaphas raised his hands. "Order!" he said. Judas watched as the entire room quieted. It fell completely silent as Caiaphas stood to his feet and approached Jesus, who was looking down at his feet. "You have heard these many witnesses confirm that you have said you were from Heaven, that God Almighty was your father, and that you were able to tear down and rebuild the temple in three days without the use of your hands! We have heard you ourselves teach against our sacred laws of the sabbath." Caiaphas moved closer to Jesus. "Are you not going to answer? What is this testimony that these men are bringing against you?" Jesus remained silent. Caiaphas raised his voice and said, "I charge you under oath by the living God: Tell us if you are the Messiah, the Son of God!" he ordered.

Jesus slowly raised his gaze and looked directly at Caiaphas. "I am!" Caiaphas stumbled backwards a couple of steps and just stared as Jesus continued. "You have said so," Jesus said as the crowd began to raise their objections. He looked around the room and continued in a loud voice. "But I say to all of you: From now on you will see the Son of Man at the right hand of the Mighty One and coming on the clouds of heaven!"

The assembly broke into an uproar as Caiaphas screamed and began tearing at his priestly robes. "He has spoken blasphemy," he yelled. "Why do we need any more witnesses?" He addressed the assembly. "Look, now you have heard the blasphemy!" he said as he pointed to Jesus. "What do you think?"

"He is worthy of death," one of the priests yelled as he stood and struck Jesus in the face, knocking him backwards a step. Another approached from the audience. "He is a fraud," he said as he kicked him in the legs. Another yelled, "He is a child of fornication!"

Joseph of Arimathea stepped forward to stop the assault. "Wait!" he said as he tried to make his way to the front of the assembly. "Stop! He has done nothing that deserves this! He performed many miracles of healing. We have witnessed these things. *I* have witnessed these things."

"He performed those miracles through trickery!" someone yelled.

"Or witchcraft!" another added.

"But what if it was through God's power and favor?" Nicodemus yelled from the audience.

"It wasn't!" Caiaphas replied.

Nicodemus rose and raised his hands to address the assembly. "Brothers," he yelled over the commotion gaining their attention. "What have you to do with this man? This Jesus has performed many signs and miracles that we have not seen before. If the signs he is performing is of God, then they will stand. If they are not of God, they will fail, and he will eventually vanish and his followers scatter. It will come to nothing. I say to let this man go for he is not deserving of death."

"But he has blasphemed Almighty God and our laws demand that he be punished!" Caiaphas yelled.

"He should die!" another shouted. Soon, several priests pushed Joseph and Nicodemus aside, causing Nicodemus to fall to the ground. The furious priests started hitting and kicking Jesus, who was starting to slump from the blows.

"Son of God," someone yelled as he spat on him.

"Prophecy to us!" another yelled as he hit him in the face. "Who hit you?"

"Stop!" Judas yelled from the back but was drowned out by the uproar.

Jesus fell to his knees as they continued to kick at him.

Joseph pushed his way through the mob to Jesus. "Enough!" he yelled. "Enough!" He shielded Jesus with his body as the men slowly backed away. Jesus, who was on his knees, looked at Joseph and whispered, "This must be done." He slowly struggled to his feet with Joseph's help. His face was swollen and bleeding from the blows. Joseph looked at him in amazement and slowly backed away from Jesus, who returned to his standing position in front of Caiaphas.

Caiaphas waited as the assembly quieted down and some of the priests returned to their seats. "Jesus of Nazareth. You have committed blasphemy by making yourself out to be equal to God Almighty. Your blasphemy is worthy of death. Therefore, you will be taken to Governor Pontius Pilate for judgement and execution according to Roman law." Caiaphas moved closer to Jesus. "If we had authority to execute you, I would do so right now on this spot."

Jesus said nothing.

"Take him to Pilate!" Caiaphas ordered the guards standing nearby.

Joseph and Nicodemus watched as the guards grabbed Jesus and nearly drug him from the room, continuing to hit and kick at him. The audience quickly followed them out of the hall, yelling their disbelief and indignation as they emptied the chamber. Joseph and Nicodemus quietly left through the opposite exit.

Judas approached Caiaphas as the hall was emptying. "Not death!" he cried in protest.

"What are _you_ doing here?" Caiaphas asked indignantly as he saw Judas approaching.

"Not death. You said you wanted to speak with him. You lied!" Judas said as tears started down his cheeks. "He has done nothing to deserve death!"

"He has blasphemed!" Caiaphas yelled.

"I have sinned," Judas said as he reached in his satchel, weeping. "I have betrayed innocent blood," he said as he pulled the small bag of silver from his pouch with shaking hands.

Caiaphas looked at him indignantly. "What is that to us? That is your responsibility!" He said as he turned and started to the door with the other remaining priests.

"No!" Judas yelled as he threw the money at them and ran out of the Hall, weeping.

The priests stopped and gathered the coins off the floor. "What are we to do with this money since it is blood money?" one of them asked Caiaphas. "It is against our laws to put it into the treasury," he said.

The man handed the coins to Caiaphas, who refused to accept them. "Buy the potter's field. We can use that place to bury foreigners," Caiaphas replied as he walked out of the Hall with the remaining priests.

Judas ran through the streets and past the temple. He could hear the mob yelling as they made their way to the Praetorium near Herod's Palace where Pilate stayed. He wept bitterly as he made his way through the waking city to the hills near the base of the Mount of Olives. Once alone, he fell to his knees and wept.

"What have I done?" he cried. "How could I...?" He looked around for help, but no one was nearby. "What am I going to do?" he cried. "Help me!" he yelled as he looked to the sky. He saw a large tree towering over him. The early morning sunrise filtered through the branches as the leaves gently rustled in the light, morning breeze. He slowly rose and wiped the tears from his face so he could see more clearly. A rope was tied to the base of the tree, likely left by someone who recently tied an animal to it. Judas untied the rope and made a noose. He began to weep again, making it difficult to finish the knot with his shaking hands. He stood on a rock under the tree and tossed the rope over a branch, then secured it to the base of the tree, still weeping.

"I have sinned against God," he said as he climbed back on the rock and placed the noose around his neck. He looked up at the leaves again, rustling in the breeze as he wiped the tears from his face. A dove was cooing in the distance. The air was fresh and smelled sweet from the aroma of the blossoming flowers. Judas was expressionless as he closed his eyes and stepped off the rock. After a few moments of struggling, his body went limp and quietly swayed in the morning breeze.

Chapter 12   The Trial

It was early morning the day before the Passover Celebration, called the Day of Preparation, and people were up early already preparing for the Passover meal. They came out to the streets to see Caiaphas and several priests of the Sanhedrin followed by Jesus and the Roman guards making their way from the Hall of Hewn Stones to Herod's Palace.

As the procession approached the Palace, Caiaphas ordered them to stop in the courtyard. "We must wait here and summons the governor, otherwise, we will be defiled if we enter." He motioned to the guards. "Go. Tell governor Pilate we must speak with him, immediately." One of the guards bowed and entered the compound where Pilate was staying.

Inside, Pontius Pilate sat at a table reviewing a list of prisoners to decide who he should release for the Passover. Each year, as a gesture of good faith, Pilate released one prisoner for the Jews. He was so focused on the list, and distracted by his thoughts, that the food sitting before him was now cold and tasteless. He had no appetite. He looked up as the soldier entered. "Commander," the soldier greeted as he saluted. "Caiaphas ben Joseph and other members of the Jewish Sanhedrin request your presence outside," he said.

"I was waiting for this," Pilate replied. He followed the soldier out the door to the court immediately outside the palace to see a mob of fifty or more people gathered around a man who was bleeding from the beatings. The man wore a long robe that was stained with blood and partially torn. His hands were bound. Jesus looked at Pilate as he approached. Pilate motioned for the guards to untie Jesus and said to Caiaphas, "So, this is the man you took a cohort to arrest? I could have taken him alone!"

"He is a dangerous man," Caiaphas said. "You should keep him bound."

"Dangerous?" Pilate laughed. "He is nothing. What charges are you bringing against this man?" he asked.

Caiaphas answered. "If he were not a criminal, we would not have handed him over to you."

"A criminal?" Pilate laughed again. "He doesn't look like a criminal nor dangerous. Take him yourselves and judge him by your own law," he ordered and started to walk away.

"But we have no right nor authority to execute anyone," Caiaphas replied.

Pilate stopped and turned back toward the group. "Execute?" he asked. He looked at the people surrounding Caiaphas and Jesus.

"We have found this man subverting our nation," Caiaphas explained. "He opposes payment of taxes to Caesar and claims to be Messiah, a king."

"A king?" Pilate asked. He moved closer to Jesus and asked him, "Are you the king of the Jews?"

"You have said so," Jesus replied.

Pilate looked around. There was no army, no armed rebels, nothing that would cause him concern that Jesus had any followers or that would indicate he was a problem for Rome. Just angry Jews. "A king with no army," he whispered to Jesus. "Do you hear the testimony these people are bringing against you?" Jesus said nothing. Pilate turned back and addressed the crowd. "I find no basis for a charge against this man."

One of the priests shouted, "He stirs up the people all over Judea by his teachings. He started in Galilee and has come all this way," he said.

"Galilee?" Pilate knew Galilee was under Herod's jurisdiction and that he could hand this problem off to him. "Then take him to Herod for judgment," he ordered and walked away, leaving the group standing in the courtyard outside the palace.

Herod Antipas was having breakfast on his balcony with his wife, Herodias, watching the people around the temple when he noticed a commotion in the lower courtyard. He moved closer to the railing for a better look. "What is going on there?" he asked.

"I don't know," Herodias replied. "Looks like Caiaphas leading a group with some soldiers."

"I can see that, woman," he snapped. He walked out to the steps to meet the entourage.

"King Herod," Caiaphas said as he bowed.

"What is this all about?" Herod asked.

"This is Jesus of Nazareth who has been spreading false doctrine and disrupting our people," Caiaphas replied as he pointed to Jesus.

Herod looked at Jesus with great interest. Jesus was bloody and dirty from the beatings and stood expressionless. "So, you are Jesus of Nazareth," Herod declared with a smile. "I have been waiting to meet you for a long time, Jesus."

No answer.

Herod slowly approached and closely examined Jesus from head to toe, sizing him up like he was purchasing a prime horse as he began to circle him. "I have heard you can perform great miracles."

"He uses trickery to sway the people to believe his false teachings," Caiaphas said loudly. Several in the group loudly voiced their agreement.

"Silence!" Herod ordered. He returned to inspect Jesus. "I heard that you have even raised people from the dead," Herod said with delight.

No answer.

"Can you do a miracle for me?" Herod asked gleefully. "Just a small one. Maybe something like…..like heal your bloody lip?"

No answer.

Herodias walked up and stood in the background watching. She was also curious to see who this Jesus was as Herod continued.

"Too hard?" Herod chuckled as he glanced at a plant blooming in a pot nearby. He reached over and plucked a flower from it and held it in front of Jesus's face twirling it in his fingers. "Maybe you can turn this white flower….uh…red, maybe?" he asked.

No answer.

"This is no time for tricks, King Herod," Caiaphas said.

Herod turned to Caiaphas. "Don't tell me what I should or should not do, priest," he said angrily.

"But this man has ridiculous claims," another priest said.

"Such as?" Herod asked.

"He claims he can tear down the temple and rebuild it in three days without the use of his hands," Caiaphas replied.

Herod began laughing. "And this is why he is on trial?"

"No. He is on trial for blasphemy because he has said he is the Messiah, the Son of God," Caiaphas explained.

"Ohh! The Messiah," Herod said smiling. He looked at Jesus. "So, you are the Son of God?"

No answer.

Frustrated, Herod tossed the flower to the ground and addressed Jesus. "I am so disappointed that you did not perform even one miracle for me, Jesus." He turned to Caiaphas. "Return him to Pilate," he ordered. "Let him deal with the 'king'," he said as he walked away.

Outside the palace where Pilate was staying was an area called the Stone Pavement at the Praetorium where the Seat of Judgment sat. This was the equivalent of a courtroom where trials and judgments were administered by Governor Pontius Pilate. The seat was a physical chair much like a throne elevated four feet above the pavement. It gave an air of authority as the judge was able to look down on the criminals as they were sentenced.

Each year Pilate would release a prisoner at the Stone Pavement to show his favor to the Jews. He would prefer to just imprison or execute the criminals, but he felt he needed to show some benevolence toward the Jews to continue to get their cooperation from the priests.

A crowd began to gather around the large courtyard area surrounding the Stone Pavement. It was mid-morning, and many people were arriving to hear which prisoner Pilate had chosen to be released for the Passover when Caiaphas and the mob approached with Jesus. They stopped below the seat of judgment and called a guard to summon Pilate.

Pilate walked out to the judgment seat and was surprised to see several hundred people gathered around the area waiting to hear who he might release. He looked down to see Caiaphas and several priests and guards standing before the seat with Jesus. "You brought him back?" Pilate asked surprised.

Caiaphas bowed. "King Herod ordered us to return this man to you for judgment and execution."

"For what?" Pilate asked.

"He has said he is king of the Jews," Caiaphas replied. "There is no king but Caesar."

"You are an intolerable people, Caiaphas," Pilate said. "You brought me this man as one who was inciting the people to rebellion, yet I see no army, no weapons. I have examined this man in your presence and have found no basis for your charges against him. Neither has Herod for he sent him back to me. As you can see, he has done nothing deserving of death."

"He has thousands of people following him," Caiaphas said. "He is a troublemaker and makes himself out to be our king."

"I have no charge against him deserving of death," Pilate replied as he looked at Jesus who stood silently before him.

Someone from the crowd yelled, "Free him." Pilate looked out to see several people crying. He thought for a moment that maybe the crowd would be willing to free this man. "Very well, then. I will have your people decide," Pilate said. He turned to the guards standing at the entryway. "Bring out the prisoner," he ordered as he seated himself in the judgment seat.

Four guards escorted a prisoner to the area in front of the judgment seat where Caiaphas and Jesus were standing. He was a large, middle-aged burly man with a shaggy beard. He was dirty and looked mean. The priests and guards that were standing around Jesus slowly backed away. Barabbas looked at Jesus and then to the crowd where a few people immediately started cheering, "Barabbas! Barabbas!"

Pilate raised his arms to silence them. As the crowd quieted, he looked at Caiaphas who was standing to the side, then to Jesus who stood silently before him. Pilate looked back to the crowd which continued to grow. "It is customary that each year at your Passover that I show the mercy of Rome by releasing one prisoner to you. This man Jesus Barabbas has been convicted of insurrection and murder and has been sentenced to death," Pilate yelled to the crowd as he pointed to Barabbas. "This man Jesus of Nazareth claims to be your king," he said as he pointed to Jesus. "Who shall I release?"

Several of the priests in the crowd yelled, "Free Barabbas!" Some in the crowd quickly joined in. Others called to release Jesus. Soon the volume of competing requests rose to shouts. People continued to stream into the courtyard to see what was happening.

Pilate raised his arms to silence the crowd. "Bring him to me," he ordered as he pointed to Jesus and walked to the entryway of the palace. The guards escorted Jesus to where Pilate was waiting at the entryway behind the Seat of Judgment. "Go!" he ordered the guards who saluted and left. Pilate was alone with Jesus, who stood quietly before the governor.

Caiaphas could see Jesus and Pilate talking in the entryway of the palace but could not hear what they were saying. He turned to the priests nearby and said, "We must make sure Barabbas is released and not Jesus," he said. "Go. Spread the word to release Barabbas or suffer being cast out of the synagogue." The priests left Caiaphas who walked down the stairs to the stone pavement watching Jesus and Pilate.

"Are you king of the Jews?" Pilate asked Jesus.

"Is that your own idea or did others talk to you about me?" Jesus asked.

Pilate laughed. "Am I a Jew?" he laughed again. "Your own people and chief priests handed you over to me. What is it that you have done?"

"My kingdom is not of this world. If it were, my servants would fight to prevent my arrest by the Jewish leaders," Jesus replied. "But now my kingdom is from another place."

"Oh!" Pilate exclaimed with a smile. He was amused to have a man standing before him in tattered clothes, beaten and bloodied claiming to be a king. "Then you *are* a king!"

"You say that I am a king. In fact, the reason I was born and came into the world is to testify to the truth," Jesus replied. "Everyone on the side of truth listens to me."

This piqued Pilate's curiosity as he moved closer to Jesus's face. He was fascinated that Jesus would bring up truth. Greek and Roman scholars have attempted to define truth through the ages. Socrates, Plato and other great philosophers pondered the meaning of truth. Now, he had a man, a common man standing before him claiming to know the truth. "What is truth?" he asked.

Jesus said nothing.

"You have no defense of these charges?" Pilate asked. "You refuse to answer me?" Jesus continued to remain silent.

Frustrated, Pilate roughly grabbed Jesus's arm and led him back to the platform above the crowd. "I find no basis for a charge against this man," he yelled to the crowd. He looked at Caiaphas. "Look. All of the multitude does not wish him to die," he said as he pointed to some women crying.

"May I approach, governor?" Nicodemus called from the crowd. Pilate saw that he was a priest and asked, "For what reason?"

"To advocate," Nicodemus replied. Pilate motioned for him to approach as Caiaphas tried to voice his disapproval but was silenced by Pilate. Nicodemus turned and addressed the crowd. "I said to the elders and the priests and the Levites and to all the multitude of the Jews, and the synagogue, 'What have you to do with this man? This man does many wonders and signs, which no one of men has done or can do. Let him go, and do not devise any evil against him. If the signs which he does are of God, they will stand but if a man, they will come to nothing.' I say to let this man go, for he is not deserving of death."

"Have you become one of his disciples too?" someone yelled from the crowd. "You are a traitor," someone else yelled.

Pilate stood and addressed the multitude, which was now reaching almost a thousand people. He was surprised at their reactions to what Nicodemus said. "Why are you gnashing your teeth at this man when he is speaking the truth?" as he pointed to Nicodemus.

Caiaphas glared at Nicodemus as he rejoined the crowd.

Another man quickly approached the front where Jesus stood. "Governor, may I speak?" he asked.

Pilate could see the man had been crying. "So speak."

The man briefly looked at Jesus who smiled at him, and then faced the crowd. "For 38 years I lay in infirmity in my bed and very grievous pain. And some young men had pity on me; and carrying me in my bed, laid me before Jesus. And Jesus seeing me had pity on me, and said the word to me, 'Take up your bed and walk.' And immediately …" The man began to get choked up but continued. "….I was made whole; I took up my bed and walked."

"He broke our laws by doing this on the sabbath," Caiaphas yelled as the man took Jesus's hand and kissed it before returning to the crowd.

Barabbas stood quietly and looked in amazement at Jesus and the man.

Another middle-aged man quickly approached the front and stood by Jesus. He did not ask for permission to speak. "I was born blind," he yelled to the crowd now gathering across the back of the area and along the wall. "I heard a voice and saw no man. As Jesus was passing by, I cried out with a loud voice, 'Have pity on me son of David.' And Jesus had pity upon me and laid his hands upon my eyes…." The man began to weep. "..and immediately I saw," he said as he knelt before Jesus and kissed his feet.

Jesus reached down and touched the back of the man's head. "It's all right," he whispered. The man rose and went back into the crowd which quickly quieted.

Barabbas said not a word.

Pilate watched in amazement from the judgment seat when a woman named Veronica cried out from the crowd, "I was flowing with blood for 12 years; And I touched the fringe of his garment and immediately the flowing of my blood stopped."

Jesus saw Veronica in the crowd and smiled.

"We cannot take testimony from a woman," one of the priests yelled from the crowd.

"Enough," Pilate yelled as he stood to his feet. "I find no basis to charge this man of any crime. Why do you wish to shed innocent blood?"

"He has blasphemed our God by saying he is the Son of God!" Caiaphas yelled. "He claims to be king of the Jews. We have no king but Caesar."

"You are a seditious nation," Pilate yelled. He could see the crowd continuing to grow and was concerned that a riot may soon break out. People were now standing on the stairways leading into the Praetorium. They were seated and standing along the top of the wall encircling the palace. "It is your custom for me to release to you one prisoner at your Passover. Do you want me to release 'the king of the Jews'?"

"No. Not him," someone yelled. "Release Barabbas," another yelled. "Release Jesus," another yelled. The crowd started to ramp up again.

"Silence," Pilate ordered. He pointed to Jesus and said, "I will punish this man and let him go." Pilate sat back in the judgment seat and called out, "Guard!" A soldier quickly approached Pilate and saluted. "Forty lashes," Pilate ordered.

The guard grabbed Jesus by the arm as another approached to take the other arm. They pulled Jesus off the platform and down to a second level where they pushed the crowd back exposing a single post in the middle of the Stone Pavement. Some people in the crowd saw Jesus was being taken to be flogged and began yelling, "He is not our king!" Others continued to cry and yell, "No. Have mercy!"

Caiaphas quickly went to where several other priests and elders were standing below the seat of judgment so they would not be heard. "This is not enough," he said. "We must get rid of him. He must be executed."

As Caiaphas was addressing the men they watched as the flogger tied Jesus to the post. He pulled his garment down to his waist and stepped back. The flogger looked to Pilate who nodded. Jesus let out a yell as the first lash struck. The flogger's whip had several long pieces of leather with sharp steel barbs tied on at the ends designed to inflict maximum pain. As each lash struck, pieces of flesh were torn from the body. The priests turned away from the gruesome, bloody scene as Jesus cried out with each blow.

"He may die from this lashing," one of the men said.

"And if he does not?" another asked as Jesus continued to yell in pain as the flogger counted the number of lashes out loud.

"Then we must incite the crowd to have him executed," Caiaphas replied. "We cannot have him released. Go through the crowd. Tell them that he has blasphemed Almighty God and must be crucified and if they do not agree they will risk being cast out of the synagogue."

The men split up and filtered into the crowd again spreading the word that Jesus blasphemed God and should be crucified. As they coerced the crowd, the flogger continued his assault on Jesus's body.

"I think the 'king' should be properly dressed," one of the guards said as he grabbed a purple robe from a Jew in the crowd who was watching the flogging.

Yes!" another guard agreed. "He needs his crown, too," he said with a laugh as he took some thorn branches from a bush and wove them into a makeshift crown.

"Thirty-nine," the flogger yelled and stopped. Roman law mandated that any person administering a flogging would be flogged themselves if they exceeded the number of lashes of the sentence, thus they always did one less than sentenced.

Jesus hung from the pole bleeding profusely from the lashing. Pieces of his skin were torn from his back so badly nearly all of the skin was gone. The flogger lifted Jesus's head to see if he was still alive. He nodded to Pilate, who motioned to have Jesus brought to him. As they untied him, the two guards approached with the robe and crown. They wrapped him in the robe and forced the crown on his head. Jesus yelled as the thorns ripped his scalp and brow open, causing him to bleed profusely onto his face. The guards slapped him and kicked him as they said, "Hail the king of the Jews!" Then they drug Jesus to Pilate who looked down on him lying on the ground, bleeding. Barabbas stared in disbelief at the blood covered Jesus lying on the ground next to him. He feared he would be next.

"Here is your king," Pilate yelled as he pointed to Jesus who struggled to his feet, weaving from the loss of blood and pain. Jesus's condition was such that even Barabbas was moved to help him as he slowly stood and faced the crowd. It was completely silent as the people gazed in horror at the bloodied man. Soon, someone yelled, "He is not our king." Others quickly joined in.

One of the priests yelled, "Away with him! Release Barabbas!" Most of the crowd joined in, drowning out those calling for Jesus's release.

"But what has this man done?" Pilate yelled, only to be drowned out by the crowd yelling to free Barabbas. "Then what shall I do to the man Jesus of Nazareth?" Pilate asked.

"Crucify him!" someone yelled from the crowd. Others quickly joined in. "Crucify him! Crucify him!" drowning out the others pleading not to. The crowd was quickly becoming restless and unruly.

"Guards! Front line!" Pilate ordered. Twenty guards quickly formed a line between the crowd and the judgment seat. Pilate was concerned that the division of the crowd would resort in a riot.

Caiaphas walked up to Pilate and stood before him. "We have a law, and according to that law he must die," he said as he pointed to Jesus and continued. "... because he claims to be the Son of God!"

"Son of God?" Pilate looked at Jesus standing silently near death as the crowd grew louder and louder yelling for his crucifixion. Pilate looked over the crowd as a guard approached and handed him a note. "From your wife, commander," the guard said as he bowed. "She said it was urgent." Pilate took the note and the guard left.

Don't have anything to do with that innocent man, for I have suffered a great deal today in a dream because of him.

    Pilate looked up to see Jesus looking at him. He pointed to Jesus and ordered, "Take this man to my chamber." He quickly rose and left.

    With a guard on each side, Jesus was led to the room behind the judgment seat where Pilate was waiting. Pilate motioned to the guards to leave. As they let go of Jesus, he fell to his knees and struggled to slowly stand and face Pilate.

    Pilate circled Jesus looking intently at him. He knew the crowd was growing and becoming more dangerous by the moment. If a riot occurred, many Jews would be killed, and the news of a possible revolt could get back to Tiberius who was busy purging the Roman ranks of anyone associated with Sejanus. He did not want the scrutiny of Tiberius upon him for failing to stop a revolt, much less invoking one.

    Another problem was his authority as judge. He knew he didn't have the direct authority to execute a Jew unless a Roman law was broken that demanded it. Today as judge he had to apply the law to maintain civil order and control.

    Pilate decided he would judge Jesus for sedition according to the cognito extra ordinem, a form of trial for capital punishment used in the Roman provinces and applied to non-Roman citizens that provided the Prefect with greater flexibility in handling such a case as this. Even so, he felt Jesus was innocent of any crime and didn't deserve punishment of any kind, but something had to be done to appease the mob. He had to tread carefully, or he could be called to account before Tiberius.

    Jesus stood quietly, bleeding onto the floor. Pilate stopped in front of Jesus and faced him. "Do you hear these charges they bring against you?" Jesus said nothing. Pilate moved a little closer. "Do you not have anything to say in your defense?" Jesus continued to look down at the ground ignoring Pilate. "Where do you come from?" he asked. Jesus continued to stand quietly, occasionally wincing from the pain. Pilate became irritated and leaned in closer to Jesus's face. Through clenched teeth he said, "Do you refuse to speak to me? Don't you realize I have the power to either free you or to crucify you?"

Jesus slowly raised his eyes to look at Pilate. He struggled to talk because of his facial injuries and the blood. "You …. would have no power over me ……. if it were not given to you ….. from above," Jesus replied as he slowly raised his eyes to heaven.

Power? Pilate was incredulous that Jesus would say something like that as he literally faced death. He was the absolute power and authority in the region. No one questioned his authority. No one. Now this man standing before him is challenging his authority and power yet is completely calm and confident in his speech showing no fear while facing death.

Pilate took a step back and looked at Jesus intently, who lowered his gaze and watched as he circled him. There was no crime committed punishable by death. In fact, there was no crime at all that Pilate could see. What he saw was a man, an innocent man, ready to face death for no crime, yet he was not afraid at all. Pilate moved to within inches of Jesus's face. Blood was running down Jesus's brow and onto the floor. Pilate could see the cuts and swelling from the beating Jesus received at the hand of the priests and guards, yet his eyes were open and clear, almost sparkling. Pilate leaned in close, very close and whispered, *"Who are you?"* As the two men looked intently into each other's eyes, several drops of blood fell from Jesus's face onto Pilate's hands. Pilate looked down at the blood on his hands and back to Jesus's eyes. He gasped and stepped back, shaken by what he saw, bumping into a table beside him and knocking over a statue that crashed to the floor in pieces. It didn't distract him from looking into Jesus's eyes, which were fixed on Pilate. It was as though they had a hold of him, of his very soul.

A wave of remorse fell over Pilate for a life of brutality that he had led. He instantly thought of the men he killed in battle and how he enjoyed it. The people he had crucified over the years. The man who stole bread that he crucified with a loaf in his mouth. He wanted to run and hide, to ask for forgiveness for his brutality. He didn't know why he was feeling this way and panicked. He turned away from Jesus and yelled, "Guards!"

Two guards entered the room as Pilate frantically wiped the blood from his hands. "Remove him!" he ordered. The guards grabbed Jesus and escorted him to the stone pavement next to Barabbas in front of the crowd once again. Barabbas looked at Jesus with disbelief. "Why are you doing this?" he whispered.

Jesus didn't answer.

Pilate paced around the room, alone with his thoughts. "Who is he? What was that?" he whispered out loud. He walked to the entrance and watched as Jesus stood solemnly before the crowd, who were still shouting obscenities at him and calling for his crucifixion. He looked at Barabbas, a known criminal. *What am I to do?* He continued to pace for a few minutes and then stopped. *You are a Roman commander!* He thought. *He is but a man.* Pilate was finding it difficult to focus. He knew what needed to be done to appease the mob, but he desperately wished there was another way.

Pilate noticed his hands were shaking, something they had never done before. He took a deep breath and composed himself. He walked out onto the platform in front of the judgment seat and stood between Jesus and Barabbas. He scanned the crowd now several thousand strong and saw angry, men and women calling for crucifixion mixed with those weeping and asking for mercy. He wanted to release Jesus and pointed to him. "Here is your king! He has been punished," he said hoping that would be sufficient to appease the bloodlust of the crowd and he could release him.

Many in the crowd continued to yell, "Crucify him." Pilate could see the priests filtering through the crowd whispering to people as they became more vocal. "Crucify him!"

"But I find no charges against this man," Pilate replied, almost pleading with the mob. "Shall I crucify your king?" Pilate asked as he continued to unconsciously wipe his hands against his uniform.

Caiaphas was standing nearby and approached Pilate. "We have no king but Caesar," he said. He leaned in close so Pilate could hear him and whispered, "If you let this man go, you are no friend of Caesar. Anyone who claims to be king opposes Caesar." Caiaphas turned and walked away, leaving Pilate standing before the mob calling for death.

Pilate knew Caiaphas and the elders would petition Caesar about the situation and would likely claim Pilate was negligent with his responsibilities to administer proper judgment against a person guilty of sedition. Tiberius's scrutiny of this situation could easily evolve into a death blow to him. The crowd was growing louder and louder as Pilate slowly took his place on the judgment seat. He watched as the intensity of the crowd grew. He kept looking down to his hands where Jesus's blood had fallen. He felt trapped. He closed his eyes and took a deep breath.

"Release Barabbas!" he yelled.

The crowd cheered as the guards removed the shackles from Barabbas's wrists and ankles. He raised his arms in triumph as he jumped down from the platform and joined the crowd. People patted him on the back and cheered.

Jesus stood quietly and watched. A small pool of blood was forming around his feet.

Pilate motioned to a guard to bring him a bowl of water. He washed his hands fervently, removing any trace of blood on them. "I am innocent of this man's blood," he shouted as he looked at Jesus who was looking back at him. Pilate stood and faced the crowd. "It is your responsibility," he said as he pointed to them. "*You* crucify him!"

One of the people in the crowd yelled, "His blood is on us and on our children!"

Pilate looked at Jesus who stood quietly, watching the crowd. "Centurion!" Pilate yelled. Jesus looked at Pilate one more time as a soldier approached and saluted. "Longinus. Go with the priests and observe. I want to make sure this is done properly. Report back to me."

Centurion Longinus saluted. "As you command," he said. "Guards, prepare the prisoner." Two guards came to lead Jesus away to be executed. They pulled off the purple robe tossing it to the ground and redressed him in his own garment. Many of the crowd cheered and followed Jesus off the Stone Pavement and down the walkway toward Golgotha. Some stayed behind and wept.

Pilate stood by his chair and looked at his hands again. "Why?" he whispered as he washed his hands again, glancing at the blood that had been spread across the stone pavement and into the entryway of the palace. "Guard," he yelled. "Get this cleaned up."

Claudia was sitting in her bed chamber crying when Pilate walked in. "Claudia," he started but was cut off.

"I dreamt that he was innocent. I told you that," she said getting irritated at him. Claudia looked at him with swollen eyes, red from crying. "How could you crucify him?"

"I know. I know. I... I didn't know what to do." Pilate started to pace as he continued. "If the crowd rioted, there would be bloodshed. I feared Caiaphas would petition Tiberius who...."

"Feared?" Claudia interrupted. "Your fear of Tiberius has consumed you and clouded your judgment. You have never shown fear, ever."

"I had no choice!" Pilate yelled and walked out to the balcony.

Claudia followed him, still weeping. "You can do as you please," she said.

"No, I cannot!" he yelled as he turned to her. He saw the anguish on her face. "I had to appease the bloodlust of the Jews," he said. "They were going to riot. I had to control the situation," he explained. He took Claudia by the shoulders and looked at her eyes, red and swollen. "They demanded he be executed for breaking their laws, so I turned him over to them to do as they please," he said.

"Semantics," Claudia replied. "*You* executed him."

"I did not!" Pilate yelled as he shook Claudia, who broke free. She stepped backwards and looked at him in fear. It was the first time she had ever seen that in him towards her. "Claudia," he said softly. "Wait," he pleaded. "I saw something in him that I have never seen before," he said.

"What....what do you mean?" she asked.

Pilate moved closer to Claudia and continued. "I don't know. I.. I saw an innocent man who... who knew he was going to die ... for no crime, yet never resisted or stated a defense. He was.... completely calm. It was as though he wanted this to happen."

"Marcus, he was a *holy* man." She moved close and comforted him.

"What else could I do? The people were becoming a mob ready to riot."

"But the people who testified of his miracles! How could you ignore that?" she asked.

"Because I had to satisfy the blood lust of the people," Pilate replied.

"Hah!" Claudia said as she turned and walked to the balcony. "The people! You mean the blood lust of the Jewish priests!" She turned back to Pilate. "I saw them instigating the people to murder him," she said. "They were going through the crowd telling them what to say under threat of being put out of the synagogue."

"As did I," Pilate confirmed. "But I could not stop them. The crowd was growing out of control. There were thousands watching."

"Still, is that a reason to kill an innocent, holy man?" Claudia asked.

"I didn't kill him," Pilate retorted. "*They* killed him!"

"But you allowed it!"

"I had no choice!" Pilate yelled.

Claudia stood firm, looking intently at Pilate. "You always have a choice."

"And risk a riot that would cause scrutiny from Caesar?"

Claudia walked up to Pilate and stood boldly in front of him. "Marcus. Better Caesar than crucifying a god," she said.

"And you believe he was a god?" Pilate asked.

"It does not matter what I believe," she replied. "It is what *you* believe that matters," she said as she ran out of the room, leaving Pilate standing alone on the balcony. He looked to the horizon and saw the three crosses holding the three men perched on top of the hill just outside the city wall. A line of people were slowly walking past the crosses. He could relent and stop the execution, but his reputation and authority would be severely compromised. Word would undoubtedly get back to Rome if he did. He felt trapped and knew he had to let the execution stand. He lowered his head and sighed.

Chapter 13   The Crucifixion

Caiaphas waited for Pilate outside the palace with three other priests. He wanted to make sure their meeting was discreet and that no one saw him there so soon after the trial of Jesus of Nazareth.

"What do you want now, priest?" Pilate asked in disgust. "Haven't you caused me enough grief already?"

"You had a sign made for Jesus of Nazareth saying, 'This is the King of the Jews'. That is wrong!" Caiaphas exclaimed. "Do not write that he is the King of the Jews, but that he *claims* to be the king!"

Pilate's anger started to grow. "What I have written, I have written," he yelled. "Now get out of here before you join him!"

Caiaphas and the priests quickly left the room.

It was nearing the sixth hour[72] and the sky was beginning to darken. Pilate stood by the window and watched the dark clouds forming. They looked angry to him. He looked at the three crosses on the hill where two criminals, Gistas and Dysmas, hung on each side with Jesus in the middle. Pilate could see the line of people slowly moving past the crosses. He was deep in thought as Claudia walked up from behind and touched his shoulder, causing him to jump.

"Oh, Marcus," she said. "I'm sorry."

"It has been a difficult day," he said.

Claudia placed her arm around Pilate and leaned her head against his shoulder. "I feel so lost."

Pilate patted her hand. "Look how the clouds are forming," he said. The clouds were black and growing rapidly as they watched. "I've never seen anything like that."

---

[72] Sixth hour - noon

It was near the ninth hour[73] in the afternoon when Caiaphas and several priests went to see Pilate once again. They bowed as they entered the banquet hall where Pilate and Claudia were seated. The table was covered with food and drink, yet their plates were empty. They had not eaten, nor were they going to. Both were too distraught. The banquet hall was void of Roman symbols, so they needed not be concerned with becoming defiled as they had in other locations.

Pilate stood to his feet when he saw Caiaphas enter the room. "What is it now, Caiaphas?" he asked showing his irritation. "Have I not done enough already?" He walked around the table to meet them.

"Mighty governor," Caiaphas said as he and the men with him bowed low. "I know we have asked much of you, and you have been gracious to accommodate our requests, but we have one last item that we must address."

Pilate glared at Caiaphas. "Go on."

"Tomorrow is the sabbath, and we cannot have Jews being executed on the sabbath," Caiaphas said. "It is against our laws."

"Your laws, again?" Pilate said raising his voice.

"We ask that you break the legs of the criminals so that their death may be expediated," Caiaphas said.

Claudia gasped as she heard Caiaphas's request. "No!" she yelled.

"Guard!" Pilate yelled never taking his eyes off Caiaphas. A guard entered and saluted. "Tell centurion Longinus to quicken the criminals' death. Break their legs as this 'merciful' priest has asked," he ordered. The guard saluted and left. Pilate continued to glare at Caiaphas. "Do not come back here today, I warn you."

The priests bowed and left.

"Must you do that?" Claudia asked.

---

[73] Ninth hour - Jewish hours were measured from 6 am to 6 pm with 12 hours of daylight. Thus, ninth hour would be nine hours after 6 am, or 3 pm.

Pilate walked over to Claudia and sat next to her. "It is better this way," he said calmly. "Crucifixion is a painful death, and the men will not suffer as long," he assured her.

Claudia laid her head on his shoulder. "Marcus, I wished this day had never happened."

Pilate sighed. "As do I."

Less than fifteen minutes passed as Pilate stood on the balcony watching a growing storm combine with an eclipse to blacken the sky to the point it looked like night outside in the middle of the day, creating a frightening spectacle. Suddenly, the ground started to shake from an earthquake. Manlius yelled from inside the palace as the quake intensified, knocking statues and vases onto the floor. He jumped as a flash of lightening followed by a deafening clap of thunder surprised him. "What is happening?" Manlius yelled.

Pilate held onto the railing as the quake continued. "I don't know," he said. "A tremor of some type." He looked out at the hill where the crosses were. He saw people running from the hill as several more flashes of lightening followed by thunder coincided with the continuing quake. In a matter of minutes, it was over.

Manlius ran to the balcony and stood next to Pilate. "But the lightening?" he asked.

"It was just a coincidence," Pilate replied. "It's over now." They both looked out to the hill and saw the clouds beginning to part revealing the waning eclipse. "I've never seen anything like that," Pilate said.

"Neither have I," confirmed Manlius.

They both stared in disbelief toward the hill where Jesus was crucified.

Joseph of Arimathea and Nicodemus stood patiently waiting for Pontius Pilate to arrive. They were instructed by the guard to wait in the courtyard because of the damage and mess in the palace caused by the earthquake. They had requested a brief meeting with Pilate regarding Jesus. They bowed as they saw the governor approach.

"Honorable Governor. I am Joseph of Arimathea, and this is Nicodemus."

"You are priests, are you not?" Pilate asked.

"We are," Joseph replied.

Pilate looked at Nicodemus. "I heard you advocate for Jesus at the trial. What is it?"

"Governor, we would like your permission to take the body of Jesus of Nazareth and bury him," Joseph replied. It was customary for an executed criminal to be buried in an unmarked grave outside the city and Joseph wanted to prevent that from occurring.

Pilate turned back in surprise. "He's dead?" he asked.

"Yes," Nicodemus answered.

"Guard!" Pilate yelled. The guard entered and saluted. "Is the centurion from the execution back?" he asked.

"He is commander."

"Bring him here, immediately," Pilate ordered.

"I have a tomb outside the city wall, governor," Joseph said. "I would like to bury him there."

"Why?" Pilate asked. "He is an executed criminal. No one from the family has claimed him, so he should be buried in an unmarked grave, not a tomb."

"I am compelled, mighty governor, to offer my personal tomb for him because....because...." Joseph stopped.

"Because why?" Pilate asked.

"It is the right thing to do. He is a Jew who healed many people," Nicodemus replied. "We would like to prepare his body and bury him properly according to our customs and before the sabbath."

The centurion entered as Nicodemus was talking and saluted.

"Longinus. Is the man, Jesus of Nazareth, dead?" Pilate asked.

"He is commander."

"Are you sure?" Pilate asked again.

"Yes, commander," Longinus replied.

"Then breaking his legs helped to expedite his death," Pilate said, almost remorseful.

"We did not have to break his legs, commander," Longinus replied. "It was necessary for the other two criminals, but not Jesus."

"How then do you know he was dead and did not require his legs to be broken?" Pilate asked.

"Commander, I pierced him with my spear to assure he was dead. Water and blood spilled onto the ground from the wound," the centurion reported.

"Very well," Pilate replied. "Is there anything more that you wish to add?"

The centurion hesitated. "Yes, commander. He died …. at the same time the earthquake occurred," he replied. Pilate was shocked to hear he had died so quickly and, even more troubling, during the earthquake and thunderstorm.

"Very well, Longinus," Pilate replied.

Joseph and Nicodemus looked at each other and back to Pilate. "If I may, governor. May we remove his body and bury it?" Joseph asked.

"Yes. Go ahead. Remove the body," he ordered.

"Thank you, mighty governor," Nicodemus and Joseph said as they bowed and left Pilate alone with the centurion.

"Commander. I…." The centurion paused.

"What is it, Longinus?" Pilate asked.

"Jesus said something when he was on the cross that….that I cannot shake, commander," the centurion said uneasily.

"What did he say that troubles you so?"

"'Father. Forgive them for they know not what they do'."

"Forgive them?" Pilate asked. "How can a man, an innocent man no less, ask for forgiveness against those who hate him so? Or kill him?"

"I do not know, commander, but when he died, he shouted something," the centurion added.

Pilate looked at the centurion in disbelief. "He shouted? How is that even possible? He would have no air in his lungs at the point of death." Pilate observed enough crucifixions to know suffocation was the cause of death. No one would have any breath to even whimper, much less yell just before they died. "What did he say?" he asked as he moved closer to the centurion.

"'It is finished!'"

Pilate stared at the centurion. "Finished?"

"Commander. The way he died; I believe he was… a righteous man. The Son of God, as he claimed."

Pilate froze. He could see the fear in Longinus's eyes. Pilate had known this centurion for many years before they came to Judea and knew him to be a man of courage and strength. Now, the centurion confirmed, without provocation, what Pilate had been thinking. "Dismissed," he whispered.

The centurion saluted and left Pilate alone with his thoughts looking toward Golgotha.

---****---

People watched as Joseph and Nicodemus walked briskly through the campsites that lined the path through the outskirts of the city toward Golgotha. Joseph stopped to buy a long piece of linen from a vendor on the side of the path. As they approached Golgotha, they could see the poles that held the victims still standing on the hilltop, vacant of the executed criminals and Jesus. They saw several soldiers with the garments of the criminals leaving. There were two remaining soldiers preparing to place the body of Jesus on a cart where Gistas and Dysmas lay when Joseph stopped them.

"We've been granted permission from the governor to remove and bury that man," he said as he pointed to Jesus's lifeless body lying on the ground under the pole that held him.

Longinus walked up right behind the priests and called to the guards. "Leave him be and go, bury those two," he said as he pointed to the two men on the cart nearby.

The soldiers saluted and left Jesus's body on the ground, naked, bloody, and dirty. Joseph unfurled the linen and covered Jesus's body as several people standing to the side approached the two men at the base of the cross where Jesus lay. People hugged and wept. A man with a small cart walked up the path to where the group was standing. "Here," he said to Joseph. "You may use this cart."

They gently lifted Jesus onto the cart, careful to cover every part of his mutilated body. Nicodemus saw the crown of thorns laying nearby and cautiously picked it up and placed it on top of Jesus's body lying on the cart.

Joseph and Nicodemus led the procession of a handful of people with Jesus's body through the camps surrounding Jerusalem. There were more than 100,000 people camped around Jerusalem in anticipation of celebrating the Passover, which was tomorrow. Many people were preparing their evening meal outside and watched as the procession weaved its way down the hill on the narrow path through the camps. It was a short distance from the place where Jesus was crucified at Golgotha to Joseph's tomb just outside the inner wall of the city near the Praetorium. People stopped what they were doing and stared at the bloody, linen wrapped body of Jesus lying on the cart with the crown of thorns on top. Many whispered that this was the man who claimed he was the Messiah. They stared and gawked as the cart made its way to the tombs nearby. Many said nothing and just watched.

When they arrived at the tomb, several people helped lift Jesus off the cart and carried him into the cave. It was a large tomb cut into the hillside of stone. The entrance was about five feet high and several feet wide. There was a large, round shaped stone leaning against the wall near the entrance. They gently laid Jesus's body inside on a stone slab.

Nicodemus carried about thirty-five kilos[74] of a mixture of myrrh and aloe into the cave and laid them on the ground as Joseph and one of the women pulled the linen back to start

---

[74] 35 kilos – 77 pounds

cleaning the body. The woman gasped in horror and began to cry. The body was covered with blood and dirt from the assault. Jesus's face was disfigured from the blows he received. She started to clean the body but was so distraught she turned away and wept.

"Stop," Joseph said quietly as he placed his hand on her shoulder. "Not now."

"We must go, Joseph," Nicodemus said as he placed a linen napkin over Jesus's face. "The sabbath is beginning."

Joseph pulled the blood-stained linen back over Jesus's mutilated body. "Very well," he said.

The people exited the tomb and called to two other men to help them move the stone back in place. The four of them struggled greatly to push and roll the stone to the entrance and shove it into the opening of the tomb. The stone was hand hewn to make a tight seal around the entrance of the tomb. "There," Joseph said. "We will finish this after the sabbath."

The group left the sealed tomb where Jesus lay. They desperately wanted to see Israel delivered from the Romans and believed Jesus was the Savior, yet he lay inside the tomb. Their hopes for a deliverer were dashed and despair filled the void.

---****---

Pilate walked through the corridors of Herod's palace to the main banquet hall where he expected Herod Antipas would be entertaining guests or watching dancers in his debauchery. Instead, as he rounded the corner and past the guards, he saw Herod sitting in a chair near the archway looking out toward the temple. He was alone and unaware Pilate was nearby, lost in his thoughts.

"Herod," Pilate called, startling the tetrarch.

Herod turned to see Pilate standing opposite the archway looking at him. "Did you see the eclipse?" he asked.

"I saw more than that," Pilate replied as he approached the Jewish king. "And felt the earthquake beneath my feet as Jesus died on that cross," he said as he pointed toward Golgotha where the poles holding the crosses were still visible.

"As did I," Herod whispered as he looked toward Golgotha.

"Why did you send him back to me?" Pilate asked. "Were you so cowardice as to not have him condemned?"

Herod laughed. "Said the man who also refused to condemn him." Herod stood to face Pilate. "He was …. different. He never said a word in his defense when he was here."

Pilate looked at Herod and, for the first time, realized they had more in common than not because of the trial of Jesus. Pilate turned away and walked out into the courtyard followed closely by Herod. "He had no fear. In fact, he was completely at peace, even calm, though he was facing condemnation and death and offered no defense," Pilate said. "I've never seen anything like that."

"Nor have I," Herod added. "He had so many followers, I fear my people will revolt because of his execution. If that happens, we will lose our nation to Rome."

Pilate turned to face Herod. "Though I despise most everything about you, we have one thing in common."

"And what is that, pray tell?"

"To keep your people under control," Pilate replied. "If you hear anything that would cause you concern that an army is being raised, or a revolt is imminent, I expect you will let me know so…. so that *we* can stop it before your nation is lost."

Herod nodded. "Agreed."

---****---

It was early Passover morning, well before sunrise, when Caiaphas and several elders went to see Pilate about another problem they had. They were waiting patiently in the courtyard of the palace when Pilate approached from the hall. "Why are you here, Caiaphas?" Pilate asked. "What is it now?" he said as he stood glaring at the men.

"Sir," Caiaphas began. "We remember that while Jesus was still alive that deceiver said, 'After three days I will rise again.' So please give the order for the tomb to be made secure until the third day. Otherwise, his disciples may come and steal the body and tell people that he has been raised from the dead."

"I thought I was done with this man," Pilate said. "Haven't I done enough for you by allowing you to crucify him?"

Another elder spoke. "If this occurs, then the last deception will be worse than the first."

Pilate thought for a moment. "Very well. Take a guard and go make the tomb as secure as you know how."

Caiaphas nodded. "We will need to post guards continually to keep watch over the tomb."

Pilate moved closer to Caiaphas. "Take another cohort then. I don't care. Do what you must to secure the tomb so that I can be done with this man, and with you," he said angrily. "Guard!" A soldier entered and saluted. "Tell Centurion Longinus to go with these men with as many guards as they need to secure the tomb."

"Yes, commander," the soldier said and saluted.

"Now go!" he shouted as he pointed to the door.

Caiaphas and the men bowed and quickly left.

The sun was peaking over the horizon as centurion Longinus and twenty-four guards followed Caiaphas and two other priests the short distance from the palace to Joseph's tomb where Jesus was laid. Caiaphas preferred to ask Joseph to show them the tomb but was relieved when another priest knew where it was. Caiaphas feared if they asked Joseph, Jesus's disciples would hear of their plan and remove the body before they arrived.

"This is it," one of the priests said as he pointed to the large stone sealing the entrance. "Joseph showed me his tomb earlier this year."

"Open it!" Longinus ordered.

Four soldiers rolled and pushed the stone away from the entrance, leaned it against the wall and stepped back. The odor of the spices that were left by Nicodemus covered the smell inside the tomb. Longinus lit a torch and stooped down to peer in. He entered, followed by Caiaphas and the two priests. They saw the body lying on the slab covered by the blood-stained linen. The crown of thorns lay on the ground beside it.

"Is this necessary, Caiaphas?" one of the priests asked.

Caiaphas looked at the man in disbelief. "Do you not understand what is at stake here?" he answered. "If we do not verify that this is Jesus, then they have already taken the body and replaced him with someone else, and our very nation and our beliefs will be in peril!"

Caiaphas walked over and pulled the linen back from the face of the body. He reached down and lifted the linen napkin to reveal the swollen disfigured face with deep gashes on the forehead and scalp cause by the crown of thorns. The priests gasped at the sight. Caiaphas pulled the linen down further and saw the body covered with dried blood and dirt. There was a gaping hole in the side of the body where Longinus pierced it with a spear when Jesus was on the cross to insure he was dead.

"That's him," Caiaphas said as he turned to leave the tomb.

"It is," Longinus confirmed quietly.

One of the other priests carefully placed the linen napkin back over the face and pulled the linen shroud over the body. The men exited the tomb, followed by Longinus. "Seal it!" he ordered.

With great effort the men moved the huge stone back into place and placed a large strap of leather across the front containing a circular brass Roman seal in the center. They secured it by hammering a nail through the ends of the leather strap and into the rock on each side. Then they melted wax over the nails and leather careful to make a complete seal around the spikes.

"I want eight guards here at all times, two at the entrance, three at the flank, three at the road, relived every two hours until further notice," the centurion ordered. "You eight take first duty," he said as he pointed to eight men. The men immediately double timed to their stations as ordered, two in front of the tomb, three at the flank and three on the road. The guards were careful to insure they were within each other's sight.

"Now they can't deceive us. We saw he was dead and have sealed the tomb." Caiaphas said as the priests and remaining guards left the cemetery with Longinus.

Chapter 14   The Resurrection

The Passover was a day when the Jewish people celebrated their exodus from slavery in Egypt. It was a quiet day with no events or unrest of any type. Claudia avoided Pilate for most of the day. He was fine with that. He already met with Caiaphas earlier that morning and wanted nothing more to do with the Jews. It was a day that he was able to reflect on the events of the day prior and be hopeful that nothing was surfacing today. He needed rest, so he went to bed early and collapsed from exhaustion.

That night, Pilate was sleeping when a small earthquake awakened him. "What is that?" he asked as he looked around. After but a few moments, the quake stopped. He glanced over to Claudia, who was still asleep. "I must have been dreaming," he said as he laid back down pondering the events of the past two days. After an hour of restlessness, he finally rose and walked to the balcony. He looked at the twinkling stars and sighed.

---****---

It was very early Sunday morning, well before sunrise. It was the day after Passover when many people would be preparing to leave Jerusalem and return home. Caiaphas was already awake pondering the past two days that weighed heavily on him. He was looking forward to a more peaceful day when several guards pushed his servant out of the way and entered his palace without notice. Caiaphas heard the commotion and quickly grabbed a robe and went to the outer chamber to see eight guards confronting his servants.

"What are you doing here at this hour?" Caiaphas asked. He thought they may have come to arrest him for something, but then noticed something odd about them; they looked afraid.

"Caiaphas," one the guards started. "Something happened at the tomb we were guarding."

"Did someone come and take the body?" he asked.

"No. We don't know," the guard said excitedly. "There was an earthquake and a tremendous light, and a man appeared from nowhere and moved the stone from the entrance of the tomb!"

"What?" Caiaphas asked. "What do you mean 'appeared'?"

"He just appeared," the guard answered. "We were at our posts and...."

Another guard interrupted. "He was dressed in white, bright clothing. It was blinding."

"I think he was an angel," another said.

"Stop!" Caiaphas yelled. "Stop!" He walked away from the guards and started to pace. "An angel?" he said as he turned back to them.

"Yes," the first guard answered.

"What did this angel do?" Caiaphas asked.

"He...he opened the tomb and sat on of the stone that covered the entrance," another guard answered.

"Impossible!" Caiaphas yelled. "One man cannot remove that stone."

"He did," the first guard answered. "He said Jesus was not there, that he has risen."

"Enough!" Caiaphas yelled. The guards watched Caiaphas pace around the room. He turned to them and said, "Do you realize your failure to perform your duty could result in your execution?"

The first guard stepped forward. "I feared that angel more than any Roman court, Caiaphas."

Caiaphas could see the men were scared. Roman soldiers were never scared, even when faced with death. These men, however, saw something that could not be explained. "Come with me," he ordered.

"Where are you taking us?" the first guard asked.

"To meet with some other priests and.....and figure out what we must do," Caiaphas answered. "We must contain this now, before news of this spreads."

"That's impossible!" one of the priests yelled.

"Absurd," said another.

"Wait!" Caiaphas ordered. "Listen to me. Do you think these men would make up such a story if their failure to guard the seal would result in their execution?" The priests relented and listened as the eight soldiers watched.

"I suppose not, but this is difficult to hear," one of the priests replied.

"Would it not be easier to say they were overpowered by men, than... than by an angel?" Caiaphas asked.

"Of course," a priest answered.

"What are we to do?" another priest asked.

"This happened just over an hour ago. Their reliefs have not yet reported to duty," Caiaphas turned to the soldiers. "You go back to your post and tell your reliefs you were overpowered by men who took the body."

"But Governor Pilate will execute us," one guard said.

"Not if we intervene on your behalf," Caiaphas answered. "You may be punished, but not executed."

"Is there not another way?" one of the guards asked.

"I see no other way," Caiaphas answered. "The tomb is open, and the body gone, and all we have is what you say occurred. Pilate will not believe you."

"We will pay you well if you cooperate with us," one of the priests said.

"What good is money to a man who is dead?" a guard asked.

"Listen!" Caiaphas said sternly. "Pilate will not execute you if we stand with you. You must not say it was an angel, but his disciples, who came during the night and overpowered you. *They* took the body."

The guards looked at each other. "We have no choice," one of them said. "We did not protect the seal and stand to suffer greatly, unless we have someone to advocate for us."

"Then we must hurry and go to Pilate now before your reliefs report for duty," Caiaphas said. "Pilate must hear this from you, not your reliefs."

Pilate had not eaten for the entire day before because of his distress and now could not find peace to sleep. He was standing on his balcony breathing the fresh air and looking toward Golgotha. The poles still stood on the hill void of their victims. He thought about his interaction with Jesus. The words the man said were deeply troubling. *How could an innocent man allow himself to suffer so? It was as if he wanted to die*, he thought. He heard footsteps approaching the courtyard and saw Caiaphas and several priests followed by eight Roman soldiers enter the courtyard. He went inside and quickly dressed.

The guard at the palace told the men to wait while he announced them. Within minutes, Pilate appeared through the archway fully dressed in uniform.

"Now what, Caiaphas?" Pilate asked.

Caiaphas stepped forward. "We have some troubling news, governor," he began.

"Every time you have come to see me, Caiaphas, it has been troubling," Pilate retorted. "What is it now?"

The lead guard stepped forward and saluted. "Commander. The disciples of the man, Jesus of Nazareth, came during the night and …. overpowered us and took the body."

"What?" Pilate yelled. He could feel his heart race and his blood pressure immediately rise. "Some Jews overpowered eight armed Roman soldiers?"

"Commander. It was very late, and they surprised us," one of the guards said.

"It happened so fast we had no time to react," another added.

"Stop!" Pilate ordered. The men were silent. Pilate looked at them sternly. "It was your responsibility to be prepared at all times. Do you realize you failed to protect the Roman seal on the tomb?"

"We do, commander," one of the soldiers replied, still standing at attention.

"And the punishment for such failure is death?" Pilate added.

"We do, commander," the lead soldier replied. "We are at your mercy," he said as he kneeled before Pilate who looked down on him with disdain.

Caiaphas fully expected Pilate to draw his sword and behead him on the spot. "Mighty Governor, if I may say something?" he interrupted.

Pilate looked at Caiaphas with contempt. "What could *you* possibly say that would help in this situation, priest?"

"Your men confirmed our suspicion; that this Jesus's disciples would come and steal the body and proclaim he was raised from the dead," Caiaphas said.

Pilate glared at the priest. "Go ahead."

"Now that we know their deception, the issue is over," Caiaphas added. "Your guards will testify to that fact …. if they are alive."

Pilate thought for a moment. He looked at the guards with contempt. According to Roman law, they should be executed. However, Caiaphas raised a valid concern. Pilate wanted this to be over. He did not want word to spread about this Jesus, resulting in some revolt that would eventually get to Tiberius.

"The eight of you are to be punished for your failure to perform your duty," Pilate said. "But not executed."

"Thank you, Governor," Caiaphas replied and bowed and started to leave when Pilate stopped him.

"Not yet, Caiaphas," Pilate barked. "I am leaving tomorrow for Caesarea Maritima. I do not want to see you again," he said as he glared at him. Caiaphas bowed and stepped back.

"And as for you," he said to the soldiers. "I will decide your punishment later. Guard. Secure them until further notice," he ordered. "Go!"

The soldiers saluted and were led out by two guards. The priests bowed and followed them. Pilate watched the group scurry across the courtyard and out of sight.

"Will this never end?" Pilate whispered.

----***----

It was two days after Passover and Pilate was preparing to return to Caesarea Maritima with Claudia. He was anxious to leave Jerusalem and get back to a place where he felt secure and in control. The past week had shown him, if anything, how quickly one can lose control of a situation involving these Jews. To him, they were an obstinate, evil, vicious group of people led by a dogma of rules that would even go so far as kill an innocent man. Now, some of the Jews even tried to convince their people that Jesus had risen from the dead when, in fact, he believed they just came and stole the body.

Yet, the events of the death of Jesus, the way he died, the words he spoke before his execution, the calmness and confidence he displayed was something Pilate had never seen before nor ever heard of. All people when faced with eminent execution usually show some level of fear, apprehension, regret. Jesus displayed a peace about him that Pilate could not explain. It was unnerving, perplexing and deeply troubling.

The words Jesus said as he was dying on the cross were just as troubling if not more so. *What did he mean by 'it was finished?' How could he forgive them for executing him?* The questions repeated themselves in Pilate's head over and over with no answer, making him anxious and unsettled.

The caravan was lined up outside the main wall in Jerusalem ready to depart. Claudia had gathered her last few personal belongings and approached the carpentum where Pilate was standing to greet her. "Are you ready to go?" he asked politely. Claudia ignored him and boarded the wagon. Pilate, disgustedly, started to follow when Manlius stopped him.

"Governor," he said. "There is a report that I believe you should hear before we depart," he said as he looked around.

"What report would that be?"

Manlius leaned in to whisper so the nearby guards could not hear. "There is a report that…. an angel appeared at the ninth hour[75] early yesterday morning and raised the Nazarene from the dead."

Pilate scoffed. "I know. It was his disciples that removed the body during the night. Not an angel," he replied and again started to board the wagon.

"But Pontius. Others have said the Nazarene appeared to them that morning," Manlius added.

Pilate froze. "Appeared?"

"Yes. The word is spreading that this Jesus has been raised from the dead, just as he promised he would, and many people claim they have seen him," Manlius replied.

"Manlius. It is a deception orchestrated by his followers," Pilate replied. "The guards told me what happened. They were overpowered by the Nazarene's disciples who removed the body."

"Overpowered?" Manlius asked. "How many guards, governor?"

"Eight."

Manlius stepped back. "Eight armed Roman soldiers overpowered by some Jews?" he asked in disbelief. "Was there a battle? How many of the Jews were killed?"

Pilate hesitated. "None."

"How many soldiers were injured?" Manlius asked.

Pilate paused as he stepped closer to Manlius. "Bring the guards to the Praetorium immediately."

"Yes, commander," Manlius replied as he bowed and left.

Claudia watched as Manlius left. "Marcus," she whispered.

"Wait here. This will not take long," he said ignoring her.

Pilate was in the courtyard as Manlius, four guards, and the eight prisoners approached. "Leave them!" Pilate ordered as the guards left the prisoners standing in front of the governor and Manlius.

"Should I stay, governor?" Manlius asked.

"Yes. I want a witness to their testimony before I cut off their heads," he replied in anger. He turned to the prisoners. "You

---

[75] Ninth hour – 3 am.

told me the Nazarene's disciples came and overpowered you during the night. Is that correct?"

"Commander," one of the soldiers began but was quickly cut off by Pilate.

"Stop!" Pilate ordered. "Before you say another word, you had best choose your words carefully and be sure to be truthful, for nothing other than the truth will deliver you from my wrath. Now, speak!"

The lead soldier fell to his knees and bowed before Pilate. He looked up to Pilate and began. "We saw an angel of God come and move the stone from the entrance," he said, weeping.

"What?" Manlius asked.

Another soldier fell to his knees, as did the others. "There was a bright light, like that of the sun. Brighter than any I have ever seen."

"It blinded us!" Another said.

"And the earth shook as the angel rolled the stone away from the tomb," said another.

"Stop!" Pilate ordered, but they continued.

"The angel said Jesus had risen, that he was not there," said the lead soldier.

"Silence, or I will cut your tongues out right now to silence you," Pilate yelled as he drew his dagger.

"I cannot be silent, my lord," the lead soldier said as he bowed low. "I have seen God!"

With dagger in hand, Pilate grabbed the soldier by the hair and pulled his head back, exposing his neck and face. His cheeks were wet with tears, yet his countenance was calm. The soldier looked at Pilate with the same look Jesus had, complete peace. The soldier closed his eyes, opened his mouth and slowly extended his tongue. Pilate froze for a second, then quickly released the man and stepped back in horror. Once composed, he continued. "Guard. These men and their families will accompany me to Caesarea Maritima."

"Yes, commander," The guard replied as he and his fellow guards escorted the prisoners out of the room.

"Pontius. I have never heard of such a thing," Manlius replied.

"Nor have I."

"What are we to do?" Manlius asked.

"I do not know. For now, we must remove them from here so that they do not add to the rumors with their testimony," Pilate replied. "I will decide their fate later."

---****---

The streets were lined with people watching Pontius Pilate's procession leaving Jerusalem. Many of the camps had been torn down and packed. People were walking along the same roadway as the procession, often blocking the road with their animals and carts. They would quickly move to the side to allow the procession to pass. Others stood watching from their makeshift camps. Children waved as though it was a parade. It was an intimidating sight to see more than 1,000 soldiers and the supply wagons leaving the city led by the Roman standards and followed by Pilate and his commanders. Rome's power on display.

At the end of the procession was the wagon carrying the eight soldiers accused of dereliction of duty and failure to protect the Roman seal at the tomb. They were subdued as they passed Golgotha where the poles that held the crosses still stood. Following the imprisoned soldiers were their families, pulling carts with children in tow.

Claudia was quiet as Pilate looked out the window at the people. They looked like normal peasants with children playing hopscotch along the roadside while adults packed the camps and loaded their carts, donkeys or backs. He looked at them but didn't see them because he was deep in thought. *Could he have risen? Was he the Son of God? He was so calm during the trial. Why would the soldiers be willing to die proclaiming they were afraid of an angel rather than have honor in trying to defend their posts? Yet, there were no injuries, no dead enemies. How could that soldier be so willing for me to cut out his tongue?*

"Marcus," Claudia said, interrupting his thought. He turned to look at her. "I overheard Manlius."

"And what do you think of what he said?" Pilate asked.

"Honestly?" she asked.

"Always."

"I believe him. I believe they saw an angel open the tomb," she said.

"And do you also believe he came back to life? A dead man with a hole in his side?"

Claudia leaned close and whispered, "Yes, I do."

"How can you? It is difficult to believe such a tale," Pilate replied.

"As difficult as seeing an innocent man completely at peace and allow himself to be brutalized and executed…. for no reason with no defense?" she asked. "Or the miracles he performed that many have attested to?"

Pilate looked back out the window. "The miracles have been verified," he replied.

"Yes," Claudia added. "Verified by many people."

He turned back to Claudia. "And some soldiers as well. They followed him for many months and confirmed many of the miracles. That was why I never stopped his teachings. He posed no threat and was doing good."

"The priests even confirmed the miracles, Marcus, even raising someone from the dead but were angry that they occurred on their sabbath," Claudia added. "Is it, then, so difficult to believe that an angel appeared and he was raised from the dead?"

Pilate turned back to the window. "It is unless I see it…see him myself."

After a few moments of silence, Claudia spoke. "What are you going to do with the guards?" she asked.

"I do not know. I will decide later," he said as he continued to stare out the window.

"Please don't execute them, Marcus. I beg you," Claudia pleaded.

Pilate didn't reply but continued to look out the window as they passed the three poles on the hill of Golgotha.

---****---

The midday sun shone brightly onto the flowered courtyards as eighteen armed soldiers with the eight prisoners marched through them and into the hallways leading to the large arena across from the palace at Caesarea Maritima. Being soldiers themselves and having been confined to their prison cells for nearly three months, several knew that this could very well be their last walk. They hoped for leniency but expected none. The public arenas were sites of games of competition and exhibition as well as venues of administering judgment on convicted criminals, often capital punishment. The prisoners had resigned themselves to expect the latter.

The men looked at the colorful flowers as they passed by, smelled the fresh sea air blowing in from the Mediterranean, and watched as hawks circled high above on the updrafts. Everything was alive, vibrant. It was as though their senses were heightened as they approached the entrance. None of them appeared to be anxious or afraid though they expected the worst. They marched like soldiers, in step and formed as a unit.

The group entered the arena through the main gate and crossed to the opposite side where the governor's balcony was situated draped in white linen lined with roses. On the balcony sat Pontius Pilate and his wife, Claudia Procula, watching them approach. The prisoners were surrounded by eighteen soldiers, six on each of three sides, and directed to the area below the governor's balcony.

"Halt!" came the command from the centurion leading the prisoners into the arena. "Regroup right!" The eighteen soldiers turned and marched into a formation to the right of the criminals, then marched out of the arena, leaving the men facing the governor's balcony alone.

"Please, don't do this," Claudia pleaded. She started to rise when Pilate grabbed her arm.

"Trust me," he said. "You need to be here." Claudia looked at him curiously and returned to her seat. She had no idea what Pilate was up to or why she had to be there, but she had no other choice than to obey.

Pilate turned to face the men standing before him. "You have been charged with dereliction of duty and failing to protect the Roman seal on the tomb of Jesus of Nazareth in Jerusalem," he yelled. The men looked at him expressionless. "How plead you?"

"Guilty," one of them immediately said. "Guilty," came another and then another until they all admitted their guilt, without hesitation.

Pilate looked down on them and saw eight men standing before an authority who could execute them on the spot, yet none showed any signs of fear. He watched as two doves flew by. The white clouds billowed against the deep blue sky. The air smelled so good.

"I have pondered your testimony of that night for many weeks now and have wrestled with the idea of an angel appearing to you. You are Roman soldiers. As such, you should obey no man except your commander!" he yelled. "Failure to do so is a capital crime." The men said nothing.

Claudia started to rise when a soldier gently pushed her back into her seat and whispered, "I have been ordered to keep you here."

"I am your commander. Yet, I am but a man," Pilate said. The men looked at each other curiously and back to Pilate who continued. "I expect any man in your position would do the very same thing. I would do the same. We must obey our gods before we obey a man."

"What?" one of the men whispered.

Pilate lowered his voice and moved closer to the balcony railing. "You have suffered enough," he said. "You are to be released into the region of Germania......" Pilate motioned to the guards across the arena to open the gate and continued. "…. With your families." A stream of men, women and children, all young and old, walked into the arena and looked around. The men before Pilate turned to see their families enter the arena. Several children saw their fathers across the arena and ran to them, yelling and crying. Soon, the two groups ran toward each other and embraced and wept. Several soldiers grabbed their children, hefted them into their arms and walked back to stand before Pilate where they once were followed by their families.

Claudia rose to her feet and smiled broadly. She walked over to stand next to Pilate as he continued to address the group.

"Men, I have no other recourse that would be acceptable to me or God. You did not fail Rome through your actions. No," Pilate said. "You honored your humanity. We are but mere men. Who are we to obey man if we dishonor God? Therefore, you will be relocated to Germania to finish your service to Rome."

The men cheered as Pilate announced sentencing. Claudia wept.

Pilate raised his arms to quiet them. "My mercy is conditional." The men quieted down so Pilate could continue. "My command, albeit a request, is that you are not to discuss this with anyone until after my death."

The lead soldier stepped forward with his four-year-old daughter in his arms and saluted. "Long live Pontius Pilate!" he yelled. Soon, the entire group was saluting and, in unison, saying, "Long live Pontius Pilate!"

Chapter 15   **The Letters**
32 AD

It had been six months since Jesus was executed. Many people swore they had seen Jesus alive after his execution, causing the news of his resurrection to spread rapidly through Judea and beyond. Hundreds and hundreds of people said they saw him. Even more said they saw him taken into heaven by a cloud that enveloped him. All of them believed he was the Son of God.

    Reports from the tribune in Jerusalem indicated many people were being converted to a new form of religion called 'Christianity.' They were followers of Jesus of Nazareth who believed he was the Christ, the Messiah of the Jewish people whose appearance was foretold in the ancient scriptures of the Jews. The Romans tended to think the new religion was just a faction of the old Jewish religion and not a threat to Rome militarily in any way. They were just people creating squabbles and skirmishes that were annoying to Pilate, sometimes requiring him to intervene with force to break them up.

    The guards at the tomb swore they saw an angel roll the stone away during the night. Rather than execute them, as Roman law would require for failure to protect the seal on the tomb, Pilate chose to imprison them in isolation for several months to maintain their silence. At the request of Claudia, with his own conviction, he decided to release them into the region of Germania. He told them his mercy was given in exchange for them to maintain their silence, but he knew they would not. The news was spreading too quickly. He could not pull himself to punish them for what they truly believed happen and were willing to die for rather than change their story to appease their commander and live. It was 'truth' to them.

    Something changed in Pilate after his encounter with Jesus. He couldn't explain it, but it was becoming difficult for him to administer any punishment, particularly a harsh punishment, on criminals. He knew it was his duty, his Roman duty as a commander, but he was beginning to despise his responsibility.

The Jewish leaders continued to downplay the reports of Jesus's resurrection as being false or sensationalized. Some of the leaders, however, were also being converted to this new religion, creating a division amongst the council. There were even reports of Jewish leaders in the Sanhedrin, specifically Joseph of Arimathea, who said he saw Jesus personally.

Jesus's disciples were adding fuel to the religious fire as they reported their personal interactions with Jesus and expounded on his teachings. They were teaching a religion of forgiveness and mercy. They claimed that anyone who believed that Jesus was the Son of God and that he was raised from the dead would be 'saved from their sin[76]' enabling them to have everlasting life with God Almighty. At one meeting, more than 5,000 men converted to Christianity in one day. They said that Jesus was the sacrificial lamb that was attested to during the Passover celebration. The disciples spoke with authority and an absence of fear from the Jewish leaders and the Romans. Their boldness was even greater than that of Jesus. They were also performing miracles and astounding people. There were so many believers now, the priests could do nothing to stop them, and Pilate didn't care.

Religion was a major factor in the life of every Roman so the message of salvation from a god who showed mercy and grace was not too outrageous for them. Shrines to various gods were erected inside homes, military units, and in public spaces. One of the many gods they worshipped or acknowledged was Clementia: the goddess of mercy and grace. Some Romans believed Jesus may have been her brother.

The Romans had established many religious practices that were endemic to their culture. They believed that their success as a

---

[76] Saved from their sin – Jewish belief is sin causes a person to be separated from God, therefore removal or elimination of a person's sin is only accomplished through a blood sacrifice. Christians believe Jesus accomplished this on our behalf through his death and resurrection.

world power was attributed to their collective religious piety that resulted in good relations with their gods and enabled them to conquer inferior peoples. Many Romans believed some people could become a god, such as Augustus, who was confirmed by the senate to become a god after his death. Acknowledging that Jesus could have been a god on earth, or even the Son of God, was not too far-fetched for the Romans to accept. The idea that they had him executed was appalling to them.

The events of the past few months had to be reported to Caesar Tiberius, though Pilate exceedingly disliked the idea of doing so. He knew Caesar Tiberius had spent two years purging Rome of anyone affiliated with Lucius Sejanus, the prefect of the Praetorian Guard and his friend. He did not want Tiberius to remember his prior associations with Sejanus and preferred to remain in power quietly until Tiberius died. However, the crucifixion and now resurrection of Jesus resulting in this new religion spreading throughout Israel and beyond had to be reported to Caesar.

---****---

A special session of the Roman senate was called to discuss a letter from the governor of Judea, Marcus Pontius Pilate, addressed to Caesar Tiberius regarding a certain man in Jerusalem who was being purported to be a god yet executed by crucifixion. No one had ever heard of such a thing occurring in history. The Roman culture was rift with gods of all types, and even several leaders of the Roman Republic, such as Caesar Augustus, were made gods by the decree of the senate. In fact, Roman law stated that a person could not be considered a god unless the senate confirmed them.

Tiberius was ailing in his latter years from a malady of health issues, one of which was dementia. His escapades on the island of Capris were well known and many thought he could only do such things if he was truly mad. It was a topic no one would bring to bear, particularly since Tiberius had the admiration and support of his grandson, Caligula, who would likely become the next Caesar. The friendship between Caligula and the commander of the Praetorian Guard, Naevius Sutorius Macro, kept many in fear of reprisal should they voice their concern of Tiberius's mental capacity to rule.

Since the execution of Sejanus two years prior, many opponents of Tiberius and Caligula were removed and either executed or exiled. Tiberius returned to Rome on several occasions to regain administration of the affairs of state and show he was still in power. One such affair was this issue of making Jesus of Nazareth a god. Tiberius would often have Caligula join him on these ventures to expose him to being an emperor. This time, however, Caligula was 'too busy' with overseeing the activities at Capris and refused to join his grandfather to present a petition to the senate to have Jesus of Nazareth confirmed as a god..

"I hold in my hand a letter from the prefect of Judea informing me of a man in Jerusalem that he believes was a god," Tiberius began. The members of the senate began murmuring about such an issue.

"Silence!" commander Macro ordered. The chamber immediately quieted down. When Macro spoke, people listened and obeyed for fear of punishment.

Tiberius motioned to Senator Bracchus to step forward and handed him the letter to read to the senate. Senator Bracchus stood by the throne in the middle of the platform of the curia and began to read.

To the most mighty, venerable divine Caesar Tiberius

I, Marcus Pontius Pilate, governor of the east sends greetings. I have, most mighty Caesar, a narrative to give you on account of which I am apprehensive for in this government of mine of which one of the cities is called Jerusalem developed a situation that was unusual. The leaders of the Jews and all the people of the city have delivered to me a man named Jesus bringing many charges against him which they were not able to convict him of by the consistency of their evidence. One of the heresies they had against him was that Jesus said that their Sabbath should not be a day of leisure and should not be observed, being in blasphemous violation of their beliefs. For he performed many cures on that day: he made the blind receive their sight: he healed paralytics that were not at all able to make any movement of body or to keep a nerve steady, but who had only speech and the modulation of their voice.

    Some of the senators began to whisper their amazement as Senator Bracchus continued.

And he gave them the power of walking and running and removed their illness with the power of a single word, which is strange even with our gods. He even raised a man dead four days by summoning him with a single word though the dead man had his blood corrupted in his body.

    "Raised someone from the dead?" a senator shouted.
    "How is that possible?" another asked.
    "Silence," Macro ordered. When the senators quieted, Senator Bracchus continued.

*   Jesus, seeing him lying in the tomb, ordered him to walk. These are the things which I had in mind to report which Jesus accomplished on the Sabbath and other signs greater than these he did so that I have perceived that the wonderful works done by him, or even greater than these, can be done by the gods whom we worship.*

And the Jewish leaders and Jewish king along with all the people delivered him to me making a great uproar against me that I should try him. I therefore ordered him to be handed over to them to be done with as they pleased thus having him crucified, but first having him scourged, yet having found against him no cause of evil accusations or deeds.

    The senators began to talk again as Macro raised his hands for silence.

At the time he was crucified there was darkness over all the world with the sun being darkened at midday. At that time there was also a tremendous earthquake which remained from the 6th hour of the preparation. It has since been reported to me that there was a sound out of heaven at the third hour of the night and that the heaven became enlightened sevenfold more than all the days. The sun was seemed brighter than it had ever shown before lighting up all of heaven. People have reported that the Jesus that was crucified is risen.

"How is that possible? A dead man coming back to life?" someone yelled. The volume of the senators increased as Macro quieted them one more time, showing his frustration with their outbursts.

Many others have testified that they have seen the appearing of Jesus in the vicinity but that he soon thereafter disappeared into the heavens. Being in perplexity and seized with apprehension, I have written what I have seen and heard and have reported to my majesty.

Marcus Pontius Pilate
Prefect of Judea

The curia erupted with shouts from the senators overlapping. Senator Bracchus handed the letter back to Tiberius and returned to his seat across from Tiberius.
"Senators!" Tiberius yelled. "Senators! We must address this remarkable event," he yelled. The senators quieted down as Tiberius continued. "These occurrences can only be attributed to a god, not a man," he said.
"Or some sort of trickery or witchcraft," Senator Cassius called out.
"Senator Cassius. How can a man doing good be the result of evil intentions from witchcraft?" Tiberius asked. "Senators, I

believe this man, Jesus of Nazareth, is a god and should be confirmed as such."

"But would a god be killed by a man?" someone asked.

"*Could* a god even be killed by a man?" another asked.

"His death may have been what made him a god. We do not know why or how," Tiberius said. "His miracles attest to his divine nature and, as such, should be installed as one of our gods."

"Great Caesar Tiberius," Senator Bracchus said as he stood. "Our law requires that a person cannot become a god unless the senate unanimously agrees to such. Since none of us have been privy to witness these events, nor able to meet this god, then how can we possibly confer divinity upon him?"

"Here, here," someone yelled.

"He should have been sent to Rome to meet with us rather than be executed for breaking Jewish rules," another shouted.

"The governor said he was innocent, yet he executed him unnecessarily!" another yelled.

"Senators," Tiberius said as he raised his hands to quiet them. "I agree he should not have been executed. If he is not a god, then he should have been treated as a physician for his healing powers. To execute him needlessly angers me greatly!"

The senators began discussing amongst themselves this catastrophe when one of them stood and raised his hands for silence.

"Speak, senator Disymus," Macro said.

"Senators. We cannot confer divinity upon this man," Disymus began. "We have not seen the man nor any of his miracles and have heard from no witnesses directly. We have no other evidence than the testimony of this letter. Therefore, we cannot, by Roman law, confer divinity on such a person." The senator took his seat as others agreed with his conclusion.

"Very well," Tiberius said. "I will respond to the governor's letter. However, we should not chastise anyone who believes this has happened or that he is a god because, if he is a god, we do not want his wrath upon us or our nation for his execution."

"Here, here," someone shouted.

"And, if he is not a god, then this issue will die along with him," another yelled.

"So be it!" Tiberius declared as he handed the letter to Macro and walked off the platform, followed by Macro.

---****---

The meeting of the senate failed to confirm Jesus of Nazareth as a god, primarily because they had no physical witnesses or evidence that would compel them to do so. Caesar Tiberius was furious that they had not, but more so, he was angry with Pilate for executing someone who could have possibly healed him of his infirmities. The Roman physicians had done their best to treat the ailing seventy-four-year-old emperor of his many ailments but were unsuccessful. The best they could do was to continue to administer pain killers, which dulled his mind and exacerbated his dementia.

Tiberius was preparing to write to Pilate regarding his first letter and to voice his dissatisfaction with the execution of, not only a possible god, but a proven physician when a guard entered his chamber and saluted.

"From the governor of Judea, mighty Caesar," the guard said as he handed the scroll to Tiberius and quickly left the room. Caesar considered calling Caligula in to read with him, but these days Caligula spent much of his time entertaining his friends and participating in nefarious acts of debauchery. Tiberius had enough of those escapades as he aged, so he let Caligula run rampant around the palace.

Tiberius unfurled the scroll and began.

From Pontius Pilate Governor of Judea
To Caesar Tiberius emperor of Rome

Greetings upon Jesus Christ, whose case I had clearly set forth to you in my last letter, at length by the will of the people a bitter punishment has been inflicted, myself being in a sort unwilling and rather afraid. A man, by Hercules, so pious and strict, no age has ever seen nor will have. But wonderful were the efforts of the people themselves, and the unanimity of all the scribes and chief men and elders, to crucify this ambassador of truth, notwithstanding that their own prophets, and after our manner these symbols, warned them against it; and supernatural signs appeared while he was hanging, and the opinion of philosophers, threatened destruction to the whole world. His disciples are flourishing, in their work and the regulation of their lives not belying there master; yea, in his name most beneficent. Had I not been concerned of the rising of a sedition among the people, who are just on the point of breaking out, perhaps this man would still have been alive to us; although urged more by fidelity to that dignity than induced by my own wishes, I did not according to my strength resist that innocent blood free from the whole charge brought against it, but unjustly, through the malignity of men, should be sold and suffer, yet, as the scriptures signify, to their own destruction.

Tiberius threw the scroll to the floor in anger. "Guard!" he yelled. A guard entered and saluted. "Bring me my secretary!" The guard left and soon after a man entered and saluted.
"You called, mighty Caesar?" he asked.
"I need to send a letter to the governor of Judea," he said. The man took a seat at the table and, with quill pen in hand and parchment before him, sat ready.

*To Marcus Pontius Pilate Governor of Judea
from Caesar Tiberius of Rome*

Because you condemned Jesus of Nazareth to a violent death that was completely unjust, and before condemning him to death you handed him over to the insatiably furious Jews, and you showed no sympathy for this righteous man, but dipping your pin you delivered a disastrous judicial decision. And having him flogged you handed him over to be crucified without cause, condemning him to death, sympathizing with him with what you said but, in your heart, handing him over to the lawless Jews. For all this you will be brought to me as a prisoner to defend yourself and render to me at account of what you have done on behalf of this one whom you handed over to death without cause. Oh, your shamelessness and hardness! When I heard about this in a report I was moved in my soul and cut to the core. I have heard personal testimony that this one performed great healings; he made the blind see, the lame walk and the deaf hear. He cleansed lepers and, to put this simply, he performed these healings by a word alone. How could you permit him to be crucified without cause even if you did not receive him as a god? At least you should have sympathized with him as a physician but even from your own treacherous writing that has come to me you have pronounced your penalty since you write that he is greater even than the gods that we worship. How could you deliver him to death? But just as you condemn this one unjustly and delivered him to death, I in turn will deliver you to punishment.

When the secretary finished, he laid his pen on the table and waited for the ink to dry. He handed the finished scroll to Tiberius, who read the letter. After a few moments, he melted some wax and sealed the scroll. He handed the sealed scroll back to the secretary. "Have this delivered right away," Tiberius ordered.

"Very well," the secretary replied as he took the scroll and left.

Tiberius returned to his seat unaware that he neglected to issue the order to apprehend Pilate and bring him back to Rome for trial.

Chapter 16   Transfer of Power
AD 34

Pontius Pilate received the letter from Tiberius more than a year ago and expected he would be arrested and sent to Rome for trial. But the arrest never occurred. He suspected Tiberius may have died and the news of his death had yet to reach him. It sometimes took months for correspondence to pass from Rome to Judea even though a sophisticated courier system was created for communications. Factions, skirmishes and opposition groups caused disruption throughout the courier system. Or possibly Tiberius's mental faculties were such that he forgot. Rumors of his lack of capacity spread throughout the empire, some attributing it to syphilis or some other form of venereal disease. Regardless, Pilate and Claudia lived each day expecting the worst. It was terrible pressure to be under, considering the new religion continued to grow across the region casting the Judean province into the limelight throughout the empire.

    Pilate was not concerned about this new religion being a threat to Roman rule. No one associated to this new sect proposed a danger or military threat against Rome. The Jews continued to complain of Rome's oppressive rule, but the new sect was peaceful and, if anything, different. They challenged the Jewish authorities and regularly encountered opposition from the Sanhedrin and Jewish leaders but did nothing to threaten Rome militarily. The greatest concern Pilate had was trying to administer justice under Roman law as his position required because he had lost his passion to be judge.

---****---

Pilate was with Manlius discussing building a new aqueduct for the eastern edge of the city of Caesarea Maritima when a guard interrupted them and saluted. "Commander. A report from

Jerusalem," he said as he handed him a scroll and waited. Manlius and the soldier watched as Pilate read the letter.

"What is it?" Manlius asked.

Pilate closed the scroll and turned to the guard. "Dismissed," he ordered. The guard saluted and left the two men in the room to discuss the letter. "Apparently, the Jews have stoned a man to death....for blasphemy," he said disgustedly as he tossed the scroll onto the table.

"How can any people be that foolish?" Manlius asked. "Was this another god?"

Pilate began to pace. "It does not say, but I doubt there would be anyone like Jesus of Nazareth again," he added.

"Blasphemy," Manlius said. "Again, it is their religious laws that cause these problems."

"Problems for me," Pilate said. "They are administering capital punishment without authority."

"What do you plan to do?" Manlius asked.

Pilate walked over to the archway looking out toward the city. He could see the hustle and bustle of people living their lives in security and safety. Children were running down the streets. Vendors were selling their wares by shouting prices and quantities.

"Nothing," Pilate replied.

Manlius was perplexed. "Nothing?"

Pilate walked back to Manlius and looked him in the eyes. "Let's see if this develops into anything more than a mob of angry Jews killing a man for disobeying their religious laws. Send a cohort to the tribune there and, if they need additional troops, send them. Otherwise..... we wait."

"Very well," Manlius said as he exited the room.

---****---

Since the trial of Jesus of Nazareth, Pontius Pilate was having an extremely difficult time sentencing criminals to severe punishments for their crimes. Some were deserving. Many not. Roman law was absolute and demanding for certain crimes yet leaned toward leniency for others. Times past he would have no difficulty pronouncing a sentence for a criminal that would make a statement to the local population and instill fear of him. Now, he struggled with most all sentencings. The interaction with Jesus of Nazareth had a profound impact on him and Claudia. He had to do something.

As governor, he was expected to tour the region and occasionally appear in various locales to show Roman strength and administer law. It had been more than a year since he left Caesarea Maritima to tour the province, becoming more of a recluse each day. To continue the appearance of an active prefect and exercising Roman control over the province, Pilate decided to delegate the judicial reviews to his tribunes in the regions. One tribune would oversee the north and another the south. This would provide him the greatest oversight of the province without having to directly sentence criminals in the region.

A tribune entered the chamber and saluted Pilate. "Yes, governor," he said.

Pilate looked up from his notes and saw a man about thirty, ambitious and ready to serve. It reminded him of when he was younger and eager. A time past when he would compete against the best soldiers in the military at the ludi in Rome. He wished for those times again.

"The administration of justice in this province is a daunting task, tribune. The unruly Jews are constantly creating situations that require me to travel more than I desire at present," Pilate said as he stood and approached the man standing at attention. "You have shown yourself to be attentive, dedicated to the causes of Rome, and a formidable leader of your men."

"Thank you, sir," the tribune said.

"Therefore," Pilate continued, "I am conferring upon you the authority to administer justice on my behalf in the province of Judea." Pilate handed him a scroll. "This gives you the authority in this province to sentence any prisoner under Roman law to a just punishment under my authority. I caution you, tribune, do so with honor, justice and, when appropriate, mercy." The tribune looked at him curiously. "Manlius will provide you the guidelines for all crimes and subsequent punishments."

"Yes, commander," the tribune replied.

Pilate leaned in close to the young man. "Do not dishonor Rome, or you will have me to deal with, tribune. Do you understand?"

"Yes, commander."

"Good. Your first assignment is to travel to Jerusalem and meet with the Jewish leaders regarding their recent stoning and execution of a certain Jew named Stephen for breaking their religious laws."

"Jerusalem?"

"Yes, Jerusalem." Pilate looked at the man sternly. "Is there a problem tribune?"

"No, commander. Just wondering why they would kill their own for breaking religious rules?"

Pilate walked across the room toward the balcony as he replied, "Because they are an obstinate, stubborn, dogmatic people full of evil and treachery." Pilate looked back at the tribune to see him staring at him. "You will see, tribune. I expect you will set them straight about their authority."

"Yes, commander."

"More importantly, I want you to watch them closely to assure nothing more comes of this," Pilate ordered. "You are to remain there for six months; at which time I expect a full report of any developments in the region. Take two cohorts with you."

The tribune looked surprised. "Yes, commander. Six months."

"If anything is worthy of a sooner notice, I expect you will not hesitate to do so."

"Yes, commander."

"You are doing this for Rome, tribune."

"For Rome, commander," the tribune replied.

"For Rome," Pilate replied. "Dismissed."

The tribune saluted, turned and left the room.

Pilate walked to the balcony and watched the tribune walk across the courtyard and out of the palace. He had no desire to ever see Caiaphas or the Jewish leaders of Jerusalem again. With the tribune assigned to Jerusalem, he prayed he never would.

Chapter 17   Mount Gerizim
36 AD

About seventy-five kilometers[77] to the southwest of Caesarea Maritima stands a mountain considered one of the holiest places on earth: Mount Gerizim. The 880 meter[78] high mountain has a steep slope on the north facing side and gentle slopes elsewhere sparsely covered with trees. This is the mountain where Moses led the Jewish nation out of Egypt and into the 'promised land', where Noah landed the ark upon dry land after the flood, where Abraham nearly sacrificed his son Isaac to his god, and where Jesus met the Samaritan woman at the well. The mountain is replete with Jewish history with the Samaritan people.

    Samaritans are a sect of people evolved from a split of the Jewish nation during the time of Moses. The nation of Israel was divided with some staying in Babylonia and intermarrying with non-believing people called gentiles. The resulting mix of ½ Jewish and ½ gentile people became Samaritans and were rejected by the Jewish nation. They were looked down upon by the Jews and ridiculed as being impure. If a Jew spoke with a Samaritan, they were considered to be defiled and required a cleansing ritual to become 'pure' again.

    At the base of the mountain sat a small village called Tirathana. Mud and straw houses lined the streets of the village leading to the village square at the center of town. It was the heart of the village where residents would socialize while shopping at the many vendors that lined the square selling their wares. In the cool of the summer mornings people would gather at the square to share stories, walk along the paths to the gardens nearby, share a meal or watch the children play. It was also the place where a person could address nearly the entire village by standing on a platform erected in the middle of the square.

---

[77] 75 kilometers – 46 miles
[78] 880 meters – approximately 2,900 feet

An older man of strong stature stood on the platform and pointed to Mount Gerizim with a large staff that he carried. He wore a long robe and had a lengthy, gray beard. "On that mountain lies some sacred artifacts of Moses," he yelled as he pointed to Mount Gerizim.

"How can you be so sure?" someone asked from the crowd that was quickly gathering.

Dositheus did not hesitate to answer. "God has shown me in a vision where they are buried," he replied.

Several people gasped. They had heard through stories passed down from generations that Moses buried certain artifacts on the mountain. They believed Dositheus because he was well reputed and known for his spiritual leadership. He had been with John the Baptist near Jerusalem and taught several of their leaders including Simon. He had many followers and was adding more each day.

"We must ascend the mountain and retrieve the artifacts before the Romans come and desecrate this holy place," he yelled. The crowd was now several hundred people strong and growing as he spoke. "We are a holy people before God. Our history lies on top of that mountain and must be retrieved and protected," he shouted. "God has commanded that I lead you to the top of the mountain to gather unto us the sacred relics that Moses buried there. Once we have the artifacts, we will be a powerful people unto God," he yelled as he raised his hands in victory. They believed the artifacts were akin to those in the Arc of The Covenant[79].

People began to cheer and shout their agreement as the crowd continued to quickly grow. Several Roman soldiers stationed in the area stood at the back of the group dressed in tunics so they would not be discovered. They listened as Dositheus continued.

"We will meet tomorrow at the third hour[80] and ascend this holy mountain together, as one body, honoring our God,"

---

[79] Arc of the Covenant – the most sacred of Israeli relics that is said to contain the ten commandments of Moses and more. It is believed the entity in possession of the arc will receive great power.

Dositheus yelled to the satisfaction of the crowd, now more than five hundred men strong. Some men in the group carried swords and raised them high, shouting in agreement with their leader.

The soldiers watched the crowd becoming more animated as the speech went on. When they saw the swords, they considered this could be an uprising of some sort. "We must inform the governor right away of this unrest developing," one of the soldiers said.

"You weigh less than I. You go," the other soldier ordered. "I will stay and observe."

It was nearing the ninth hour[81] when the soldier rode his horse into the courtyard at Pilate's palace in Caesarea Maritima. He quickly dismounted and ran to the entrance where two guards stopped him because he was not in uniform. He saluted the guards. "I am from the post in Tirathana and have an urgent report for the governor," he said. The guards saluted and let him pass.

Pilate was in the second courtyard with Manlius when the guard entered. "Who are you?" Manlius asked, obviously confused since the man was wearing a simple tunic.

The soldier saluted. "I am from the post in Tirathana," he replied. "I have a report of an uprising, commander," he said as he stood at attention.

Pilate moved closer to the soldier. "Report."

"A Samaritan leader named Dositheus is gathering the people to a rebellion on Mount Gerizim," he said. "We watched him stirring the people this morning to ascend the mountain with arms."

"Arms? For what reason?" Pilate asked.

"To remove ancient artifacts that they believe will give them godly power, governor."

"How many people?" Pilate asked.

"I estimate – 400 to 500 men," the soldier replied.

---

[80] Third hour – 9 AM
[81] Ninth hour – 3 PM

"When?" Pilate asked.

"Tomorrow at the third hour[82]."

"We cannot allow armed men to obtain anything that they believe will give them power. We need to squash this before it starts," Manlius said.

Pilate thought for a moment. He was calculating the distance and time he would need to arrive and stop the revolt. "Very well, get some food and drink for you and your steed. Dismissed," he ordered. The guard saluted and left the two men to discuss the situation.

"Send 200 of our cavalry to intercept them before they ascend the mountain," he ordered. 'They should be able to arrive well before they attempt their ascent."

"Very well, commander," Manlius replied. "I will send Praefectus Equitatus[83] Janus Mitius."

Pilate moved closer to Manlius. "They are only to stop their ascent. I do not want them to engage in battle until I arrive," he said sternly.

"What if the Samaritans engage our troops?" Manlius asked.

"I suspect once they see the force of Rome standing between them and the mountain, they will withdraw," Pilate replied. "However, if they engage us, return with like force," he ordered.

"Very well," Manlius replied as he left the room.

"Guard," Pilate called. A soldier entered and saluted. "Send in centurion Dionysius," he ordered.

The centurion stood at attention before Pilate holding his vine staff. "Yes, commander."

"We must go to the village of Tirathana tomorrow morning at the ninth hour[84] of the night. I have advanced the cavalry to

---

[82] Third hour – 9 am
[83] Praefectus Equitatus – Cavalry commander
[84] Ninth hour of the night – 3 am

meet us there. Have 50 more cavalry ready to depart with me," he ordered.

"Yes, commander," the centurion said as he saluted and left.

Pilate walked out onto the balcony and watched the twinkling stars. It was going to be a short night and a long day. He felt he was getting too old for this. He needed to get something to eat and a little rest before he left for Tirathana in the morning.

A large dust cloud followed the 200 soldiers of the Roman cavalry that was advancing toward Mount Gerizim at a fast pace led by soldiers carrying the Roman standards and Praefectus Janus Mitius. They rode at a fast gallop as they passed between Mount Gerizim and Mount Ebal toward the village of Tirathana. It was sunrise and the mountain was revealing its landscape to the soldiers. Janus could see smoke rising from some campfires burning in the village below about four kilometers[85] away as they summited the pass. He led the soldiers into a large clearing concealed from the village by a small grove of trees. "Halt!" he ordered as he brought his horse to a stop.

A soldier rode up to Janus and saluted. "Commander. We have scouted the area and discovered a spring to the east over that rise," he said as he pointed.

"Very well. Take the troops to water their horses," Janus ordered. "Make it quick."

The soldier saluted and barked orders for the men to follow in formation over the ridge close by. Janus stayed with six other soldiers to survey the landscape in the morning light. He could see the contour of the mountain and pathways leading out of the village toward the summit. He determined which route was the most likely for the Samaritans to take from the village to start their climb.

"I want one half of the men stationed in a line across that southern slope," he said as he pointed to an area about two

---

[85] 4 kilometers = 1.8 miles

kilometers[86] below them. "That will block their ascent. They will be forced to go up this route and meet our blockade. Then, they will either flee or engage," he said.

"Yes, commander," one of the soldiers said as he and another galloped toward the spring to water their horses and assemble their men.

"Place the remaining troops on the flanks, evenly divided, blocking their escape," he said as he pointed to the flanking hillsides. "Once they realize they are trapped, they will have no recourse but to return to the village."

"Very well, commander," another soldier said as he and a second soldier followed the previous two soldiers toward the spring.

Janus climbed down off his horse and walked to the edge of the clearing where a large boulder sat. He climbed on top and looked down on the village. A crowd of people were gathering in the center of the village. Janus estimated there could be five hundred or more men in the crowd and growing. "Let's get these horses watered and ready for battle," he said as he walked back to his horse and remounted

"But commander. We were ordered to not engage," one of the soldiers replied.

Janus turned and looked at him sternly. "We were ordered to stop their ascent! I doubt five hundred men will allow us to push them back into the village without a fight," he replied. He turned his horse and galloped toward the spring with the two other soldiers closely following.

---****---

The sun was rising as the soldiers took their positions on the hillside. As Janus had predicted, the mass of men, women and children started to slowly move up the mountain toward them. He watched from a secluded position in the trees with two other

---

[86] 2 kilometers = 1.20 miles

soldiers as the Samaritans inched closer. "Advance at a walk," he ordered. The two soldiers spilt off with each going to the flanks and ordered their troops to advance. Janus led his troops out of the trees and into the open.

Dositheus looked up the mountain to see a wall of horses approaching toward them. He turned to face his people and saw two other lines of horses advancing from the sides to hem them in. He raised his hand for his followers to stop. "Do not be afraid, for our God is with us," he yelled.

The cavalry advanced and stopped when they met the Samaritans part way up the mountain. Dositheus stood before Praefectus Janus who was sitting on his horse.

"Turn around and go back to your homes, people," Janus yelled to the crowd. "You will not pass."

"We are a peaceful people ascending this holy mountain," Dositheus replied. "We seek no conflict."

"If you do not turn around now and disband, you will have conflict," Janus replied.

"Why?" Dositheus asked. "We have done nothing to provoke you."

"My orders are to have you disband and leave this place," Janus replied. "You need to leave now or face the consequences."

"But this is *our* holy mountain, not Rome's," one of the men near Dositheus replied defiantly. "We will not leave!"

Janus jumped off his horse, angry that he was challenged in front of his men by the Samaritan's refusal to obey when they were obviously overpowered. He reached down and grabbed a handful of dirt as he approached the man who spoke. "*Your* mountain?" he yelled. "He grabbed the man by the back of his neck and shoved the dirt into this mouth. "Here is *your* mountain!"

In an instant, a man standing near Dositheus drew a sword and swung it, cutting off Janus's right hand that was in the man's face. Janus let out a scream and fell to his knees as some soldiers near him drew their swords and slayed the man attacking Janus.

"Stop!" Dositheus yelled as he raised his staff.

Two other men near Dositheus pulled their swords to defend their comrade but were knocked down and slain as the troops quickly advanced their horses into the crowd with soldiers wielding their swords. The Romans believed the entire crowd was armed, but they were not. Only the three men near Dositheus had weapons to protect their leader. The remaining crowd was unarmed and was no threat to the mighty cavalry.

As the cavalry advanced, Dositheus was pushed to the side near a boulder and fell, hitting his head. People at the front of the crowd began screaming and tried to retreat but were stopped by the people behind them. The troops to the sides and behind Janus did not know what was happening. They heard the screams and saw a commotion developing with some soldiers wielding their swords. "Attack," came the order and the cavalry advanced from all sides. The people at the back of the crowd saw the commotion and heard the screams and yelling and began to flee in all directions. Chaos erupted. Death followed. Men, women and children were trampled and slain. The unarmed mob was no match for the well-armed Roman cavalry. Within minutes, hundreds of Samaritans lay along the pathway back to the village. Janus lay near his severed hand bleeding to death.

"Commander," a soldier yelled as he stopped at the summit of the mountains and pointed toward the village below. Pilate rode up next to him and stopped. He could see the Roman soldiers walking through the mass of bodies looking for anything they could take as their spoils of war.

"What have they done?" Pilate asked. He took off at a gallop followed by his men. As he approached the flashpoint of the battle, he saw a soldier holding Janus in his arms. Another soldier was trying to stop the bleeding from the severed arm by applying a tourniquet. Janus was still alive, barely. Pilate dismounted.

"What happened here?" Pilate asked.

One of the soldiers stood to attention and saluted. "They attacked, governor," he said.

Pilate looked at Janus lying with a severed arm. He looked around and saw three swords nearby and no other weapons, just bodies. "Why?" he asked. "Could they not see they were overpowered?" Pilate dismounted and walked up to Janus. He looked at his severed arm with the tourniquet and the pool of blood around him. "Who provoked the attack?" Pilate asked.

The soldier standing at attention started to speak when Janus stopped him. "Help me up," he ordered. The soldier attending him helped Janus to his feet. Janus weaved from weakness and leaned on the soldier. "They did, commander."

Dositheus moaned and coughed as he came to from the blow to his head. A soldier nearby drew his sword and started toward him. "Stop!" Pilate ordered. The soldier sheathed his sword and stood at attention as Pilate walked past him to where Dositheus lay. "Who are you?" Pilate asked.

Dositheus sat up and continued to cough and held his bleeding head. "I am Dositheus," he replied. "The leader of the Samaritans," he said as he wiped some dirt and blood from his face.

"Are you not afraid that I will slay you?" Pilate asked as Dositheus looked around to see the bodies of his slain people. He leaned on the boulder and slowly stood. "No, I am not. Do what you believe you must," he said as he hung his head.

"Tell me, Dositheus. What happened here?" Pilate asked.

Dositheus looked at Pilate puzzled. "We were ascending our holy mountain when your troops blocked our path. When one of my men said this mountain is our holy mountain, your commander forced a handful of dirt into his mouth. One of my men drew his sword and struck your commander, thus severing his hand. From there, I remember nothing."

"Then, your men were armed?" Pilate asked.

Dositheus coughed. "Only my bodyguards. Three of them." He winced as he reached behind his head to feel a gash. "They reacted wrongfully with emotions, not wisdom, commander," he said as he looked at the three bodyguards laying lifeless on the ground nearby and continued, "...and paid the ultimate price."

"Three of them?" Pilate asked as he stood and retuned to Janus who had sat back on the ground from weakness. He was leaning against a tree trunk as Pilate squatted down next to him. "Janus, as a commander, you should first know the strength of your enemy before you engage. They had three swords against a cavalry of 200 armed Roman soldiers."

"But commander, they attacked," Janus pled as he licked his parched lips.

"Attacked?" Pilate asked as he stood and walked to his horse to retrieve a pouch of water. He returned to Janus and continued. "No. They defended *your* assault. Here," he said as he squatted next to him and poured some water into his mouth. Janus took a few swallows and coughed. "It is a dishonor for a Roman commander to slay unarmed, innocent people," Pilate said looking at Janus.

Janus looked at Pilate curiously. "Did you not crucify an innocent Jew?" Janus asked.

Pilate froze. News of him and Jesus had spread throughout the ranks very quickly. "The Jews crucified him, not I," Pilate replied.

"But you...."

"I am not on trial here, praefectus," Pilate barked. "Do not provoke me."

"I relent, commander," Janus said as he leaned his head back against the tree. "Are you to believe a Samaritan over your praefectus?" Janus asked.

Pilate looked at him intently. "There is no purpose for him to lie. There is for you to do so, however," he said as he turned and walked back to his horse and returned the pouch of water.

"Commander," Janus called. "I....I may have erred in my assessment of the enemy."

"Enemy?" Pilate asked rhetorically. He squatted next to Janus again and spoke in a very low, calm voice. "Praefectus Janus Mitius. You will be charged with dereliction of duty and disobeying an order because *you*, as commander of this assault, will be held responsible for killing unarmed people."

"I understand, commander," Janus replied, weak and tired from the loss of blood.

"Janus. You can still have honor… in death," Pilate said as he touched the tourniquet on Janus's arm.

Janus looked down to his bloody stump wrapped in the tourniquet, then looked back at Pilate, who stood and remounted his horse. From atop his horse, Pilate watched as Janus slowly unwrapped his tourniquet and lay it next to him. The blood began flowing from the severed stump onto the ground, quickly forming a pool beside him. "For Rome," the young praefectus said as he closed his eyes.

"For Rome," Pilate replied as he turned and left the soldier by the tree.

Pilate thought about what Janus had said about killing an innocent man as he made his way along the path to the village looking from his perch on horseback at the twisted bodies strewn about. The remains of a battlefield, be it civil or military, is gruesome. He felt a wave of sadness come over him as he looked at the men, women and children who had been trampled by the horses or slain by the sword. He thought of the times he walked a battlefield after killing many men without a second thought. That was a time when he no regard for the sanctity of life. Things were different now. Pilate was ashamed of what his men had done. He realized he was no better than the Jewish king who slaughtered little boys. He could hear Claudia saying it was terrible that Herod killed 'defenseless little children.' Pilate realized he had become what he despised.

As he slowly walked past the bodies, he heard a whimper. He looked around to see a little girl about four years old laying on her back with her eyes open following his movement. She was motionless, paralyzed from the assault. She moaned again, trying to breathe. Pilate dismounted and squatted next to the child. He looked into her blues eyes.

"Mommy," the girl said as she closed her eyes. Pilate lifted her into his arms and held her close to his chest. Her arms and legs hung like a ragdoll. He could feel her faint breaths for a few moments, then she stopped.

The soldiers nearby watched their commander curiously as he held her in his arms and quietly wept.

---****---

Lucius Vitellius was a middle aged Roman from an influential family of Rome well connected to Roman politicians. He was the younger of four sons who all became involved in Roman politics. He was close friends with Tiberius Claudius Caesar Augustus Germanicus, also known as Claudius, and his wife Valeria Messalina. They were the aunt and uncle to Caligula and wielded influence among the senate. Vitellius's connections ran through various levels of the Julian family and politics, including some prominent senators. Those connections are what enabled him to be appointed as the legate of Syria overseeing several provinces to the west including Judea.

News of the bloody slaughter spread quickly through the region. More than two hundred unarmed men, women and children were slain by the Roman cavalry in less than an hour. It was a dishonor to the Roman empire and a black mark for Pilate. Pilate explained to Claudia what had happened, but it was of little consolation to either of them. Pilate suspected he would be called to account for this disaster.

Dositheus and several leaders of the surviving Samaritans sent a petition to Lucius Vitellius complaining of the brutal assault against his unarmed people and demanding Pilate be held to account. Pilate was ordered to Syria to be deposed by the legate regarding the slaughter.

Vitellius was seated at a table reviewing documents and discussing the ensuing meeting with Governor Pontius Pilate with his secretary when a guard entered and saluted. "Prefect Marcus Pontius Pilate," the guard said.

Pilate entered the room and stood at attention. "Dismissed," Vitellius said to the guard. "Please, be seated," he directed Pilate.

Pilate pulled the chair from the table and sat quietly. He looked around the room at the statues of Caesar, the vases, and the exquisite décor. He glanced to the secretary who was seated next to him with pen and parchment ready to take notes. Vitellius sat across from Pilate still looking at documents.

"I was petitioned by Dositheus and his council of Samaritans to investigate the occurrence at Mount Gerizim," he said without looking up. "They reported your men slew more than two hundred unarmed people." Vitellius lowered the papers and looked at Pilate. "Unarmed men, women and children," he said slowly and sternly.

Pilate said nothing.

Vitellius looked back to the papers. "We will be taking your deposition today regarding the events."

"Understood," Pilate replied.

"Very well. Did your men engage a group of Samaritans at Mount Gerizim?" Vitellius asked.

"They did."

"Did they do so under your orders?"

Pilate hesitated. "My orders were to stop the Samaritans from ascending the mountain and to use 'like force' if engaged," Pilate replied.

"Were you not present at the battle?"

Pilate shifted in his seat. "I was not. I dispatched Praefectus Janus Mitius, my cavalry commander, to intercept the Samaritans as they tried to ascend the mountain from the village. He arrived three hours before me. He was to wait unless he was engaged by the enemy," Pilate replied.

Vitellius looked at Pilate intently. "Enemy?"

Pilate shifted again. "We did not know what to expect. Our scouts reported they saw armed Samaritans at a meeting the night before. We prepared for a possible battle. That was why I dispatched 200 cavalry with Mitius."

"You said they were to use like force if engaged. Is killing more than two hundred unarmed people like force when you suffered only one casualty?" Vitellius asked.

"No. It is not," Pilate replied.

"Then why did they engage the Samaritans?"

"Sir. Praefectus Mitius placed the troops across the pathways to the mountain and ordered the Samaritans to return to the village. The Samaritan leader, Dositheus, refused to comply. Mitius dismounted and approached Dositheus. A physical altercation ensued."

"Why?" Vitellius asked.

"Why what?"

Vitellius, frustrated, asked again. "Why the physical altercation?"

Pilate cleared his throat and shifted, obviously uncomfortable at answering the question. However, he was a Roman commander and had to tell the truth to his superior or face the consequences. "Praefectus Mitius was angered about their noncompliance and shoved some dirt in the face of a man."

Vitellius looked down at the documents on his table. "You confirmed what the petition states," he said.

Pilate was relieved that he told the truth. Had he not, he would have been severely disciplined for lying in a deposition and having his future responses dismissed.

"Why the engagement with weapons then?" Vitellius asked.

"A bodyguard near Dositheus drew his sword and cut the forearm off of Praefectus Mitius."

The secretary stopped momentarily and gasped at the thought of such an action. Vitellius glared at him, and he resumed taking notes.

"Then, they were armed?" Vitellius asked.

"My men thought so. Two others drew swords and started battling my men nearby. According to Praefectus Mitius, my men thought many of the Samaritans were armed, thus the ensuing conflict," Pilate replied.

Vitellius stood and started to pace. The secretary and Pilate watched him walk to the window. Without turning around he asked, "Did your men think the women and children were armed?"

"No, sir. The Horses became unruly during the initial battle, trampling many of the victims," Pilate replied.

Vitellius turned back to Pilate. "Two hundred as collateral damage, commander?"

Pilate lowered his head. "No, sir. They should have stopped."

"And why did they not stop?"

Pilate sighed. "Because there was no one in immediate command of that regiment of troops after praefectus Mitius fell, sir."

Vitellius walked up to Pilate and looked down on him. "And why was that?"

Pilate didn't want to answer, but he had to. "I wasn't there. I arrived soon after the battle."

"Where were your other commanders?"

"One on each flank of the path with Praefectus Mitius on the ground bleeding, sir."

"Where is Praefectus Mitius now, governor?" Vitellius asked.

"Dead, sir. He was our only casualty."

"Did you or your men not provide aid?"

"We did. He refused it and chose to bleed to death rather than face the dishonor of his actions, sir." Pilate replied.

Vitellius stood and paced around the room for a few seconds, then returned to his seat. "No more questions," he said. Pilate started to rise when Vitellius said, "Don't leave just yet." Pilate sat back down as Vitellius continued. "It is clear that command was absent resulting in the dishonor you brought upon Rome and the name of Caesar. I am removing you from your position as governor of Judea and ordering you to stand before Caesar to be accountable for your actions and the dishonor you have brought upon the empire and his great name."

Pilate showed no expression, no remorse, no concern. He sat stoic listening to the legate.

"You will be required to accept and prepare your replacement in Caesarea Maritima for three months, at which time you will travel to Rome to stand before the senate and Caesar."

"Yes, sir," Pilate replied.

Vitellius leaned forward. "Marcus Pontius Pilate. I consider you a disgrace to Rome and her honor. You crucified an innocent man in Jerusalem and now you have slaughtered innocent Samaritans in Tirathana. If I could, I would slay you myself, here and now."

Pilate felt a lump in his throat as he remembered the face of Jesus when he looked into his eyes and the blood fell onto his hands. He remembered the little girl trying to breathe and then calling for her mother as she died in his arms. He said nothing.

"Dismissed," Vitellius ordered.

Pilate stood, saluted and left.

---****---

Pilate walked into the hall where Manlius and Claudia were patiently waiting his arrival and got right to the point. "I have been removed as governor of Judea and ordered to go to Rome to meet with the emperor and the senate regarding Mount Gerizim," Pilate said as he sat next to Claudia and laid his dagger on a side table. "Ten years of dealing with these obstinate people has come to this."

"I will go with you, Marcus" Claudia said as she approached Pilate.

"You do not need to," Pilate replied.

"I want to," Claudia responded. "I will always be by your side," she said as she held his arm close.

"I do not know what to say, governor," Manlius said quietly.

"Manlius. You need not say anything. You have been a faithful companion," Pilate replied.

Pilate pulled away from Claudia and sat at the table where the dagger laid. He fiddled with it as he spoke. "My worst dream would be to bring dishonor to Rome," he said quietly. "I believe this is best for me… for us." He looked up to Claudia. "I am tired and wish no more to be governor of this wretched place," he said. "I want to go home… to Rome."

"I shall leave you two alone," Manlius said as he bowed and left the room.

Claudia moved to stand behind Pilate and placed her arms around his shoulders. She said nothing as she hugged him.

"You realize they will punish me over this," Pilate said quietly.

"I do," Claudia replied.

"Tiberius is an unforgiving emperor and is quick to administer capital punishment." Pilate stood and faced Claudia. "He may remember my association with Sejanus and decide……"

"Stop," Claudia said as she placed her hand on Pilate's lips. "No need to say anything more."

Pilate slowly pulled her hand away from his mouth. "You do not need to come with me, Claudia," he said. "Your death would be senseless for you are innocent." Pilate paused. "As was the death of Jesus of Nazareth," he whispered.

"Marcus. You have done nothing wrong. I have nothing else in my life to live for other than you," she replied. "I am not scared to die. I have lived a good life."

Pilate was quiet as they embraced, thinking of the trial of Jesus and his calmness facing death though he was innocent. He could see that same calmness in Claudia. He wished he could have a portion as well.

Chapter 18   Pilate Held to Account
37 AD

The bedroom chamber was dark and cold where Tiberius lay in bed, weak and breathing shallow. Caligula and Naevius Sutorius Macro, commander of the Praetorian Guard, stood quietly by the bed watching the 78 year-old emperor struggle for each breath. It was March 16, 37 AD: 81 years and a day after Julius Caesar was assassinated.

"Yesterday was the ides of March," Caligula said as he looked at his dying grandfather. "He should have died yesterday," he said with a chuckle. "Would that not have been appropriate, Macro?"

Macro smiled. "Yes, it would Caesar," he replied.

A servant came in to wipe the brow of the ailing emperor. "Call me if anything develops," Caligula instructed the servant as he and Macro left the room to meet with several senators outside the chamber.

"Senator Bracchus," Caligula said as he greeted one of the leading senators of the senate.

"Gaius Caesar Augustus Germanicus," he said as he bowed. Caligula liked it when people called him by his formal name, rather than the nickname he received when he was a child. "How is your grandfather?" Senator Bracchus asked.

Caligula played the role of a bereaved grandson well and developed a downcast look, causing Macro to turn away rather than start laughing. "Not well, I fear," Caligula replied.

"He has no successor appointed. It would seem you would be the next viable successor, with the approval of the senate," Bracchus commented.

Caligula leaned close to Bracchus as Macro turned to look at them. "Do I have your support, senator?" Caligula asked.

"Most certainly," Bracchus replied, knowing to not do so could result in a future death penalty should Caligula decide to exercise his authority and control over the Praetorian Guard with Macro, a longtime friend, by his side. "My full support, Caesar."

"And of the senate?" Caligula continued.

"Yes, I believe so," Bracchus replied and bowed.

"Very well," Caligula said. "We should hold a session of the senate to discuss this issue since my dear grandfather is doing poorly," Caligula said. "Should we not be prepared for the worst?"

"Yes, Caesar. We most certainly should," Bracchus replied. "I will call a meeting of the senate tonight to discuss succession to the...."

Bracchus was interrupted when the servant attending to Tiberius came running out and bowed before Caligula. "Mighty Caesar," he said, never lifting his head. "Caesar Tiberius, the mighty and venerable, has passed to the Fields of Elysium."

Caligula turned away from senator Bracchus and gave a faint smile at Macro. He quickly replaced the smile with a downcast look and turned back to senator Bracchus. "My poor grandfather shall suffer no more," he said.

Bracchus knelt before Caligula. "Hail Caesar Gaius," he said.

Macro and Caligula entered the bedroom chamber to view the body of Tiberius. The emperor lay motionless on the bed with a servant standing next to him. "Leave us alone to mourn for him," Caligula ordered. The servant bowed and quickly left.

"He looks so peaceful," Macro said.

"Death is peaceful, Macro," Caligula replied. "No one in death has ever raised an objection about it," he said with a snicker.

Caligula walked slowly around the bed looking at his dead grandfather. "Caesar. Emperor. I like the sound of that," he said.

"As do I, Caesar," Macro said and knelt. "I am your servant unto death."

"I know you are," Caligula confirmed. "I have trusted you my entire life. You have never disappointed me, Macro. I will make you..."

Suddenly, Caligula's mini speech was interrupted by a gasp from Tiberius. He opened his eyes to see the two men standing at the front of the bed. "Food," he said as he struggled to sit up.

Caligula and Macro looked in disbelief. "Why you old goat!" Caligula said angrily. Macro grabbed some bedding and began smothering the old man. Tiberius struggled greatly, flailing his arms and legs trying to escape the suffocation. Caligula helped Macro smother Tiberius ignoring the muffled screams of the emperor.

"Die, Caesar," Caligula said through clenched teeth. "Just die!"

The struggle lasted less than a minute and the muffled screams dissipated. Tiberius quickly went limp. Macro held the bedding on Tiberius's face for another few seconds, then removed it when he was sure the emperor was dead. He checked for a pulse, then looked at Caligula who was staring at him. Macro fell to his knee and bowed again.

"Mighty Caesar," he said. "I humble myself before you."

Caligula smiled. At last, he was the emperor of Rome.

---****---

The carpentum rattled down the street past several children playing hopscotch on the side of the road. They stopped to wave at the carriage as the horses passed by snorting and prancing. The driver smiled and waved back. He soon pulled up to the front of the palace at Caesarea Maritima and stopped to unload his passenger: Linus Marcellus, the new prefect of Judea.

Marcellus was only forty years old and a bit pudgy. His years of working as a politician showed around his belly from eating well and exercising little. He was excused from mandatory military service after serving only five years. His father, a prominent senator in Rome, was able to convince Tiberius to excuse his son from service and, instead, assign him to various positions in the provinces. People were seldom excused from such service unless they were wealthy and well connected. Marcellus was both.

The driver helped Marcellus out of the cramped carriage. "Thank you," he said as he stretched and looked around. The children playing hopscotch watched as the driver then helped Marcellus's wife and two children out of the wagon. The children stopped their game of hopscotch and ran to meet the newcomers who were eight and ten years old, boy and girl respectively.

A soldier approached the wagon and saluted. "Governor Marcellus?" he asked. Marcellus smiled and saluted. "This way, if you please," the soldier said as he motioned toward the palace.

"Please tend to the children and our belongings," Marcellus directed the driver as he followed the soldier.

They ascended the steps of the palace and into the main courtyard where Pontius Pilate and Claudia were seated at a table filled with food and drink. They were beginning their midday meal as the trio approached. The soldier saluted and announced the new governor. "Governor Linus Marcellus," the soldier said.

The man bowed. "This is my wife, Cere."

Claudia rose and quickly greeted the younger woman. "Hello. I am Claudia," she said with a broad smile. "Please, join us."

Pilate rose and greeted Marcellus.

The couple chatted for a few moments during their introductions when they were interrupted by the giggling children the soldier brought into the courtyard.

"Oh!" Claudia exclaimed. "You have children!"

The kids ran up to their mother's side and stood quietly. "Yes," Cere said. "This is Cato and Priscilla."

Claudia was immediately drawn to Priscilla. She leaned down to greet the ten-year-old at her level. The little girl had long, brown hair and a bright smile. "What a beautiful name," she said. "And you, Cato," she said as she turned her attention to the boy. "What a strong young man." The children giggled and bowed. "Good manners, too. Come, we have food for you."

The group chatted over small talk of the weather, various sights nearby, and their history. Marcellus was a longtime friend of Lucius Vitellius, the legate of Syria, and was honored to have been asked to step in and fill the vacancy that would be left when

Pontius Pilate was removed as governor of the province. He had his hesitations of meeting with Pilate before his exit but was ordered by Vitellius to do so.

When they finished their meal, Pilate rose and addressed them. "If you will excuse us, we need to discuss some affairs of the province," he said as he directed Marcellus to join him in the nearby chamber.

When they were alone, Marcellus began. "I must begin by saying I had reservations meeting with you, Pilate."

"Why so?" Pilate asked.

"Your reputation of being…. excuse me for being direct but being a butcher caused me concern."

Pilate looked at Marcellus intently. "A butcher?"

"I wish not to anger you, but the events at Mount Gerizim and the execution of Jesus of Nazareth are well known in the empire," Marcellus replied. "They do not speak well of you."

"I suppose not," Pilate said with a sigh. "There were mitigating circumstances that were…. beyond my control even as governor."

"Care to explain?" Marcellus asked.

"For what reason?" Pilate asked.

"For my education, if you will," Marcellus replied. "Should I be confronted with similar circumstances, your experiences could prove valuable."

"Very well. I shall be brief," Pilate said as he stood and began to pace as he spoke. "Mount Gerizim was a tragedy caused by my late arrival. I received reports from scouts that there was an armed group of several hundred Samaritans attempting to ascend a nearby mountain to obtain some artifacts that they believed would give them power. I sent troops ahead to stop the uprising. They were ordered to not engage the Samaritans but to delay them until I arrived. When my praefectus assaulted the leader of the Samaritans, he was attacked. He then exercised poor judgment instead of restraint, resulting in the massacre."

"I see. Quite unfortunate that you were not present to stop the onslaught." Marcellus took a sip of wine and asked, "And this Jesus of Nazareth?"

Pilate reclaimed his seat across from Marcellus. "That was most unusual, and I doubt will ever happen again."

"How so?" Marcellus asked leaning forward.

"He infuriated the Jewish leaders who demanded he be executed for breaking their religious laws."

"A religious law and not a Roman law?" Marcellus asked.

"Yes. I was concerned that a riot would follow the trial, so I handed him to the Jewish leaders for them to decide appropriate punishment based on their laws and to administer that punishment. It was better than invoking a riot."

"I see. So, again, you abdicated your authority."

"I did not!" Pilate shouted surprising Marcellus. He rose and walked to the window. "I made a decision that I believed was in the best interest of the empire by allowing them to execute one man," Pilate said as he turned and returned to his seat. "One man, Marcellus."

"Have they not settled down and behaved themselves since?" he asked.

"To some degree. They are an evil, obstinate, contentious people, Marcellus," Pilate said. "You will have difficulty with them, no doubt." Pilate paused for a moment while the words sunk in. "They recently stoned a prophet to death without consultation with me."

"So, it continues," Marcellus said as Pilate nodded. "And your punishment to them was….?"

"Nothing," Pilate replied.

"Nothing?" Marcellus asked, incredulously.

Pilate rose again and began to pace. "Yes. Nothing. I felt it was best to allow this death rather than engage with these people again because of their dogmatic rules and beliefs." He turned back to Marcellus. "They were no military threat to Rome."

"Just one more man," Marcellus said as he poured another glass of wine. The drink was giving him courage to voice his opinion to the commander. "It certainly appears that you abdicated your responsibility to govern these people."

"No! I did not!" Pilate retorted.

Marcellus looked at him curiously as he continued. "Did you not do so to both the Jew and Mount Gerizim?" Marcellus asked.

"You will see, Marcellus, that these people are intolerable. Discerning a military threat from civil unrest is most difficult."

"I see."

"No. You do not see, Marcellus, but I assure you, you will in time," Pilate said as he reseated himself.

Marcellus laughed. "Pilate. I tend to agree with you that allowing the Jews to govern themselves more and having Rome govern less is a good approach as long as they are not a military threat to Rome." Marcellus took another sip and smacked his lips and held up his goblet. "I would prefer to enjoy the fruits of the land rather than spill the blood of the Jews unless..." He paused.

"Unless what, Marcellus?"

"Unless I am provoked to do so," he said as he placed the goblet back on the table.

"I see," Pilate replied. "Let us hope, then, that they not provoke you," Pilate replied as he lifted his goblet and took a sip of wine. Pilate really didn't care how Marcellus would rule. He was done and wanted to leave this vile province that had branded him as a butcher and ineffective leader. He wanted to return to Rome.

"I can see you long to leave this place," Marcellus said.

"Yes. I long to see Rome again."

"It has changed since Tiberius died," Marcellus said matter of factly.

"What?"

"Oh. You did not know. Tiberius died almost two months ago."

"Old age?" Pilate asked.

"Yes. He just stopped breathing. He went peacefully."

"Who is his successor?"

"There was some confusion about that since Tiberius designated his successors as joint Caesars."

"What?" Pilate asked in surprise.

"Yes. The old goat named his adopted grandson, Caligula along with his true grandson, Tiberius Gemellus as joint successors."

"That must have created confusion of the senate's confirmation of the appointed Caesar."

"It did. However, Caligula has the support of Naevius Macro, commander of the Praetorian Guard."

Pilate thought back about the power Sejanus wielded as the commander of the Praetorian Guard and knew that any person with their support would likely be conferred as emperor. "That is significant, Marcellus."

"It is. In fact, many people have already accepted Caligula as emperor and celebrated his appointment, though he has not been confirmed by the senate as sole emperor." Marcellus thought for a moment. "The people are receiving Caligula well. He has endeared them to him because he was Germanicus's son," Marcellus explained. "They even call him 'our baby.'"

"And that does not anger him?" Pilate asked.

"It appears not."

"One does not want to invoke the anger of a Caesar. Tiberius is evidence of that," Pilate said.

"Yes, he was. Caligula is different."

"How so?"

"He has forgiven those who may have opposed Tiberius and welcomed them back into the empire," Marcellus said as he took another sip.

Marcellus's statement as part of a casual conversation had significant ramifications for Pilate. He no longer would need to be concerned about Tiberius's wrath against him as a friend of Sejanus. It had been many years ago that the purge started, and he believed Tiberius may have forgotten due to his dementia. Regardless, now he knew he would not need to fear standing before Tiberius for the charges against him. "That is good to hear," he said without showing his relief. "Forgiveness is a powerful tool to endear people to you."

"And our new emperor apparently has figured that out. The people have sacrificed more than 160,000 animals over the past two months to celebrate his ascension, though the senate has yet to ratify it," Marcellus added. "They should do so soon."

"I am sure they will," Pilate added. "Sounds like Rome is truly different."

"Commander," Marcellus began. "I can see that you were in very difficult situations. In one, you directed your troops to act a certain way and they did not. In another you were considering the death of one man for the appeasement of a nation. Though it does not excuse your abdication of authority, which I still believe existed, it does show you were thinking of what was best for Rome."

"I was," Pilate replied, surprised to hear Marcellus say such things.

"Therefore, I would like to show my support for you by drafting a recommendation to Senator Bracchus requesting leniency toward you for these charges."

"Senator Bracchus?" he asked. Pilate could not believe what he was hearing that Marcellus had the ear of the senior senator in Rome and would petition for leniency on his behalf.

"Yes. Senator Bracchus," Marcellus confirmed.

Pilate stood. "I am humbled that you would even consider such actions, governor," he said as he extended his arm to grasp Marcellus's.

The two men could hear the laughter of the children and women in the courtyard as they continued to discuss the affairs and administration of the province. All the while, Pilate could feel a tremendous wave of relief pour over him. He was anxious to go home. Rome was calling.

"They were a pleasant couple, Claudia said as she and Pilate entered their private chamber. "The children were so….."

"Claudia," Pilate interrupted. "Tiberius is dead."

Claudia looked at him in disbelief. "Who is emperor?"

"Caligula, and he has stopped Tiberius's purge and allowed the exiles to return to Rome."

Claudia smiled broadly. "Then, that means…"

"Yes. We no longer need to be concerned of his wrath toward me for Sejanus," Pilate said with a smile. Claudia hugged him as he continued. "I still have to account for the fiasco at Mount Gerizim, but I believe I might have a chance to avoid serious penalty because Marcellus is advocating for me." He handed the scroll to Claudia who opened it and read. She finished with a broad smile.

"This will most certainly help, Marcus," she said as she handed the scroll back to him. "I never thought we would ever look forward to returning to Rome."

"Nor I," Pilate said as he hugged his wife and smiled.

---***---

Senator Bracchus stood in front of the senate chamber in the curia and faced the senators. Caligula and Gemellus were seated to the side. "The issue before us is the appointment as princeps[87] according to the wishes of our late emperor, Tiberius Caesar Augustus."

"Here, here," someone called.

"Of most unusual designation, our emperor has appointed as his successor both Gaius Caesar Augustus Germanicus and Tiberius Gemellus as joint princeps to the empire," senator Bracchus declared. Members of the senate began mumbling amongst themselves until Bracchus raised his hands for silence. "As such, the senate is to confirm their appointment to princeps."

The senators immediately left their seats and advanced to the platform where Caligula and Tiberius Gemellus sat. All of the senators rose and surrounded the two men, showing their favor, and affirming their appointment.

"Very well," senator Bracchus said. He turned to the two men sitting on the platform and bowed. "All hail Caesars," he said.

---

[87] Princeps – Latin meaning 'first of order'. It was used to name the emperor instead of the word king or dictator.

The senators clapped as they returned to their seats to continue the meeting.

"The next order…." Bracchus began but was quickly interrupted by Caligula.

"Senators," Caligula said as he rose from his seat. Macro walked over to stand next to him, showing his support of the one Caesar. "We must be unified in all things. Though my grandfather desired to have joint appointment as his successor…" The senators began to whisper while Gemellus watched perplexed as Caligula continued. "…my first order of business as princep is to void my grandfather's will and declare my appointment as his sole successor."

The curia erupted in shouts and confusion. "How can this be?" someone yelled. "You cannot do this!" another yelled.

Gemellus started to rise as Macro nodded to two guards by the door to secure him. They pushed him back into his seat. He knew there was nothing he could do since Caligula had the full support of the Praetorian Guard.

Caligula raised his hands for silence, but the senators ignored his request.

"Guards!" Macro yelled. Twenty guards double timed into the curia and stood between the men on the platform and the senators, who immediately quieted.

"I can see you are disappointed with my first action as princep," Caligula said sternly. "I have spent many years with my grandfather on Capris and I know what his wishes were." The senators continued to quiet down. "Would it not make sense for me, his close grandson, to continue on his path?" No one answered. "I am the son of general Germanicus. I assure you, as emperor, I will bring honor to our empire and our people and lead in the same way my father led his troops; with honor and courage suitable to a Roman."

Several of the senators began to clap and were soon joined in by most of the remaining senators in the curia. They realized, too, that with Macro at his side, it was best to acquiesce to

Caligula's sole appointment rather than face his wrath, which was well known from his experiences on Capris.

Gemellus hung his head knowing that he would likely be imprisoned or executed.

---****---

After Caesar Caligula manipulated the senate into confirming him as the new sole emperor, the first few months of his reign could be described as almost blissful. He was a young, admired leader from the line of beloved Germanicus, a successful and honored general of Rome. Caligula's youthful nature and appearance endeared the Roman citizens to hailing him as their 'baby' or their 'star.' The people loved to see him prancing through the streets on his beloved white horse; Incitatus. Caligula was generous to the military and the Praetorian Guard giving them raises and bonuses in exchange for continued support. Naevius Macro remained as the prefect of the Praetorian Guard and a close associate and ally of the new emperor.

The new Christian religion was viewed as another extension of the established Jewish religion, except that a god appeared on earth who promoted salvation and eternal life based on just believing in him. Caligula was annoyed to think becoming a god could be so easily obtained by a Jew. He believed a Roman had a better likelihood of becoming divine since they were a more elite society. He had aspirations for his own divinity. Thus, the Christian belief annoyed the new emperor with its simplicity.

Tiberius Gemellus had a difficult time accepting Caligula as emperor. He believed his cousin robbed him of his right to hold the position considering he was older and a true grandson of Caesar Tiberius, not an adopted fraud like Caligula. He was also concerned that Caligula might choose to eliminate him someday as a competing factor for the rule of the empire. Caligula showed no animosity toward him but would often ignore him in public gatherings. The bitterness Gemellus held against his cousin grew each day until finally he decided to do something about it.

The banquet hall at the palace was filled with guests who were invited by Caligula to celebrate the completion of his stable for his horse Incitatus. The stable sported such luxuries as a marble stall and ivory manger. Many thought Caligula's infatuation with the animal was too bizarre to believe and their curiosity compelled them to attend. They were surprised to see how correct they were when they saw the horse attending the celebration by having his own stall at the end of the banquet hall. Others believed if they refused the invitation, the wrath of the young emperor would fall upon them because of their disrespect to him and the steed. Both were correct. The result was a hall filled with a variety of guests praising the animal and celebrating the completion of the stable and the beauty of Incitatus.

"It would appear your celebration is well attended," Macro said as he surveyed the guests around the room. He reached across the table to pour another glass of wine as a woman walked up and put her arms around him and kissed his neck.

"It looks like you have an admirer," Caligula said with a laugh as he raised his wine goblet in salutation.

"Not now," Macro said as he pushed the woman away. She looked at him disappointedly and walked to another man a few seats away and put her arms around him. He did not reject her advance and, instead, invited it.

"There," Caligula said as he pointed to the woman. "You see? She found someone who wants to be her friend," he said with a laugh. He took a large bite of chicken and chased it down with wine.

A servant walked up to him and handed him a bowl of fresh fruit. "Oh. Yes," Caligula said as he eyed the sweet treats. "I prefer the grapes," he said as he took a large cluster from the top of the bowl and began picking at them. Another servant followed behind with a pitcher of wine. She filled his goblet and smiled enticingly to him. Caligula reached out to pull her close. She handed the pitcher to the one with the fruit while she embraced her emperor. No one noticed that the other servant bowed and left the room with the remaining fruit and wine without offering them to anyone else.

As the celebration wore on, Caligula began to feel woozy. "I suspect I may have partaken of too much wine this evening," he said as he lowered his head onto the shoulder of the female servant sitting next to him.

"Should I call a physician?" Macro asked.

"No. No. I.. I just need to go to bed," Caligula said. He looked at the female servant and added, "Alone," with a weak laugh. He started to rise but lost his balance and fell onto the table, spilling the wine and food all over Macro and other guests. The female servant gasped and left the table. Macro jumped to his feet as other guests laughed and pointed. Caligula lay unconscious on the table with his face in the food.

The commotion caused Caligula's horse, Incitatus, to jump and neigh. He knocked over a stand with a bust of Caesar Tiberius on top breaking off its nose. People ran in from the side hall to render aid to their emperor. Tiberius Gemellus knelt down to check Caligula. "We should take him to his chamber," he said to Macro. "He does not need to be seen like this drunk and face down in his meal."

Macro agreed and directed two guards to help him and Gemellus lift the emperor and carry him to his bed chamber. As they carried him, Caligula urinated. Drunken guests pointed and laughed as the emperor left a stream as he was carried away. Another servant untied the horse and walked him out of the room. The remaining guests continued to eat and drink as though the disruption was part of the entertainment.

"I do not know why he has not responded," the old man said as he examined the ailing emperor lying in his bed. The physician had been examining Caligula every few hours and administering various potions to try and cure the young man from his unknown ailments.

"What shall we do?" Macro asked.

"Continue to administer this potion every hour. Just a few sips," he said as he handed the vial to Caligula's sister, Julia Drusilla. "You may need to pour it in gently if he is still unconscious being careful that he not choke."

"Do you think my beloved cousin will recover?" Gemellus asked.

"It is difficult to say," the physician replied. "His condition does not appear to be worsening, so that is a good sign. He is strong and young. We can only hope the gods will have mercy on him and allow him to heal."

The physician left the room with Macro, Julia and Gemellus looking down on the young emperor. Julia was crying softly.

---****---

Though Pilate wanted to return to Rome right away, it took four months to wrap up the affairs of the transfer of leadership from Pilate to Marcellus instead of three as ordered. He didn't care. Pilate wanted to make sure Marcellus had the full support of his troops, so he and Marcellus traveled through the province to meet with various commanders and Jewish leaders. Their meeting with both Herod Antipas and Caiaphas in Jerusalem was tenuous at best. No one discussed the crucifixion of Jesus nor the stoning of Stephen. They all agreed that the Jewish leaders and king would work together with the new governor to assure control over the Jews. With that in place, Pilate was free to leave Judea and return home to Rome.

"Hoist the main sail," the captain shouted from the helm as he looked up to the flag of Rome flying atop the main mast. Four men, two on the port[88] and two starboard[89], strained against the ropes hoisting the large sail into position to catch the wind.

---

[88] Port – left side of a ship looking forward
[89] Starboard – right side of a ship looking forward

"The time has come," Pilate said as he pulled Claudia close to him and looked out across the water toward Caesarea Maritime. The city was slowly sinking into the horizon as the ship sailed further and further from shore.

"Do you remember how beautiful it looked when we first arrived?" Claudia asked.

"Yes, I do," Pilate replied. He took a deep breath, taking in the fresh salt air. "It looks even more beautiful now that we are leaving."

"Marcus. I am so looking forward to going home," Claudia sighed as she leaned her head against his shoulder.

"I never thought that I would say that I do too. With Tiberius gone and Caligula calling Tiberius's treason trials a thing of the past and recalling those sent into exile, it appears we will be able to live out our days at home free of reprisals against me," he said. "I believe the senate will hear my testimony about Mount Gerizim with reason and consider Marcellus's advocacy for me."

"As do I," Claudia added.

"It is good to be alive and leaving this wretched place," Pilate said as he hugged Claudia.

The couple stood and watched as the city slowly sank into the horizon until it was gone. The sun was rising in the October sky and quickly warming the morning, so they decided to retire to their quarters in the ship, leaving the captain on deck barking orders to his men.

---****---

It had been a week since Caligula fell ill. The young emperor was recovering and sitting up in bed talking with Macro as his sister, Julia, walked in with some soup. "You look well, brother," she said as she handed Caligula the bowl.

Caligula took the bowl of soup and looked inside. He handed it back to his sister. "You take a sip, first," he said with a scowl.

Julia took the bowl and looked at Caligula with concern. "But why?" she asked.

"I believe someone tried to poison me," he said quietly.

"If that is so, I will find out who and deal with them swiftly," Macro replied.

"*I* will deal with them!" Caligula barked. He looked back to Julia. "Please, dear sister," he said with a smile. "Partake."

Julia stared at her brother and, without breaking her gaze, took a large sip of the soup and swallowed. She handed the bowl back to him, turned, and started to walk out.

"No! Stay!" Caligula ordered.

Julia turned back and stood staring at him. Caligula waited to see if she would become ill. After a few uncomfortable minutes passed, Julia broke the silence. "Your soup is getting cold, dear brother."

Caligula took a sip of the broth. "Thank you, sister," he replied. Julia turned and left the room.

Caligula looked at Macro with contempt in his eyes. "I will find out who it is and, regardless of who they are, will deal with them harshly and swiftly."

Macro was shocked to see this in his emperor and friend. "You look to me as a suspect, great Caesar," he said. "I have been faithful to you unto death," he said as he bowed low.

"Then find out who poisoned me that I may have their head," Caligula replied through clenched teeth.

"I will," Macro committed as he bowed and left the room.

Caligula took another sip of the broth and held it in his hands as he stared out the window.

Two weeks ago, Caligula was lying face first in his food at a banquet celebration. Today, he was fully recovered, but changed. The reality of his mortality and the thought that someone wanted to kill him weighed heavily on him. He could trust no one. Roman history was replete with conspiracies and family murders of those who would kill to ascend to power. The next viable candidate to become Caesar should Caligula die was Tiberius Gemellus, his cousin. Caligula's first order of business was to have the head of Gemellus. From there, it was open season on everyone Caligula believed would oppose him or attempt to overthrow him. Caligula poisoned his grandmother, executed his brother-in-law and father-in-law, and had his two sisters exiled after he personally defiled them. Caligula considered disposing of his uncle Claudius, but he decided to keep him around as a bumbling fool and make a mockery of him, demonstrating that he was a powerful emperor and the best choice for the people. Better than his disabled uncle.

Many believed Caligula had gone insane after his illness. He petitioned the senate to make his horse a consul knowing that this would infuriate the senators that a horse could hold a higher, more prestigious position than they.

One role the new emperor now relished was the sentencing and administration of justice. It reminded him of his time on Capris with his grandfather when they would torture or execute people for the sheer excitement of doing so. Over the years he developed many methods of killing a person or inflicting great pain. Now he was able to administer those methods without reproach. No one would challenge him. No one.

"Marcus Pontius Pilate?!" Caligula shouted. "When?"
"We expect he will arrive in two days, Caesar," Marco replied.
Caligula smiled as he returned to brushing his horse. "Pilate. The 'javelin man'," he said. He stopped brushing the horse and turned to Macro. "I remember him well. Why is he here?"
"He was removed as the prefect of Judea and ordered by the legate of Syria to stand before Tiberius regarding an incident with the Jews at a place called Mount Gerizim."
"Judea?" Caligula paused.
"Yes," Macro replied. "That was where he executed that god, Jesus. Jesus of Nazareth."
"Ah. Yes. And Mount whatever?" Caligula asked.
"Mount Gerizim, Caesar."
"I don't care what the place is called you fool!" Caligula yelled as he threw his brush down. "What happened?"

Macro bowed again. He had seen a significant change in Caligula since his illness and was now cautious with every interaction with the emperor. "My apologies, Caesar."

"Continue."

Macro took a deep breath. "He killed more than two hundred unarmed Samaritans in a battle there."

Caligula laughed. "A battle?" Caligula laughed again. "What an evil man," he said sinisterly. Macro said nothing as he watched Caligula walk around admiring his horse. "And now he must stand before me. How wonderful our gods are, Macro!" Caligula exclaimed as he picked up his brush and returned to brushing his horse.

"I don't understand."

"And you need not!" Caligula barked. Macro immediately bowed as Caligula continued. "Prepare a room for him at the Tullianum," he said. "I'd like to welcome our guest appropriately."

Macro didn't question the order. There was a time when he would have, but no longer. "Yes, Caesar. And of his wife?"

Caligula stopped brushing again. "His wife?"

"Yes, Caesar. She has accompanied him on his return."

"This just gets better," Caligula said with a smile. "She should be afforded the same honor as our esteemed governor."

"Very well," Macro said as he saluted and quickly left.

"Incitatus," Caligula said to his horse as he carefully brushed him. "I get to see my old friend, Marcus Pontius Pilate," he said with a chuckle as the horse neighed.

---****---

"Land ho!"

"We must be near," Claudia said excitedly as she was finishing getting dressed. She and Pilate were in their cabin at the stern of the ship preparing for the day. The captain informed them yesterday that they should make port in the morning, so she was relieved to finally be over their three-week voyage from Caesarea Maritima to Portus, the main port of the city of Rome. Normally, the trip would only take two weeks, but the prevailing north winds and high seas were contrary to them, making the trip much longer than expected and Claudia's stomach much more upset than anticipated. They were both relieved that the ship did not have to make port along the way where they would have been required to transfer to land travel to complete the journey. They were able to reach Portus before mare clausum[90] which ran from November to March.

The couple hurried up to the deck to watch the entry to the port. "Stand aside," the captain commanded them without hesitation. On a ship, any ship, the captain was absolute authority regardless of rank, position, social class, or strength. Failure to obey any of the captain's rules would be dealt with severely because failure to do so could result in the loss of all souls on board, of which the captain was ultimately responsible. Pilate and Claudia quickly moved to the railing and stood fast.

"Lower the main sail," the captain ordered. The sail flapped and rustled as it was lowered and rolled into a secure position at the bottom of the main mast.

"To the oars," he yelled as ten oars on each side of the ship were extended through the ports and held horizontally until further notice. Each oar was manned by a slave seated in the hull of the vessel.

"Cadence three to port," the captain called to the first mate.

"Aye, sir. Cadence three to port," he confirmed as he vanished through the floor of the main deck on some steps leading to the galley where the slaves sat. Pilate and Claudia could hear the water splash as the oars were lowered into the water. Soon, they heard the steady beat of a drum as the oars stroked together at a slow pace. The captain stood next to the helmsman who steered the ship from the open sea toward the wide port opening that was inviting them.

---

[90] Mare clausum – Latin navigational term for 'closed sea' still used today

Portus was an engineering masterpiece by any measure. The shoreline was a seawall twelve feet high that buffeted the waves attacking the harbor. It was formidable enough to repel any weather and waves of any size. The wall provided a second benefit by having a full-size road on top where carts and wagons could easily shuttle their cargo between inner ports and docks. It had taken years to design and construct this engineering marvel. Two smaller vessels powered by six oarsmen each, three to a side, maneuvered their vessels alongside the Sors[91] and cast two ropes to her bow. Two sailors on each side grabbed the ropes and secured them to tethers on the bow. They waved to their captain that the task was complete.

Port Augusti

"Return oars," the captain ordered. The drumming soon stopped, and the oars were lifted out of the water and withdrawn back into the hull of the ship in unison like a bird folding her wings. The helmsman steered the vessel as it was towed through the port entry and into the harbor of the Port Augusti.

"There," Pilate said as he pointed to a giant statue of Augustus standing on the point of the mouth of the port. "Statue Colossale[92]."

---

[91] Sors – god of luck

"Hard to starboard," the captain yelled to the helmsman. "Hard to starboard," the helmsman confirmed. The ship turned to the right and entered past the statue and into the large Port Augusti harbor.

"This is beautiful," Claudia proclaimed as the vessel maneuvered through the large port lined with walls and buildings and toward the canal at the opposite end. "What an engineering marvel."

"It is quite impressive," Pilate added as the vessel entered a canal and proceeded into the inner Port de Trajan.

The Romans mastered port construction as was evident by the Port de Trajan located four kilometers[93] inland. It was a manmade hexagon lake that opened on one side to the canal that linked it to the massive Port Augusti. The remaining five sides of the port were protected from the weather and sea enabling ships to safely unload their cargos at piers located throughout. Buildings, roads, and lifts were located at all of the piers around the port. Ships waiting for their turn at a pier were anchored in the middle of the harbor. Though there were many ships anchored in the port because it was nearing the end of the shipping season, the Sors was allowed direct entry to a pier, likely because of the precious cargo they carried: linen, papyrus, rope and gold from Egypt and Pontius Pilate from Judea.

"Secure portside," the captain yelled.

"Aye," a sailor called as four large ropes were tossed from the ship to the pier and secured to giant tethers.

"Drop anchor," the captain yelled.

"Aye," a sailor yelled as the clanging of the chain reverberated throughout the ship as the anchor splashed into the water.

"Prepare to disembark," the captain yelled. He turned to the couple still standing at the rail, smiled and said, "Welcome home."

---

[92] Colossale – Latin for colossal.
[93] Four kilometers – 2.6 miles

The gangway to the ship was old and rickety. Pilate held Claudia's hand to steady her, though she thought he was being courteous and showing his affection toward her. Regardless the reason, she smiled and hugged his arm as they walked toward the pier where several soldiers stood to meet them. Pilate noticed the prison wagons along the pier and surmised they were for some prisoners from other vessels or, quite possibly, for some slaves that were going to merchants to be sold.

"Marcus Pontius Pilate?" the centurion asked, standing at attention holding his vine staff in his right hand. His breastplate was made of woven metal with small emblems of various gods encircling Caesar Caligula in the middle. His helmet had a large, red half-moon shaped fan made of horsehair and looked remarkedly like a sideways mohawk. His dagger was to his right side and his sword sheathed and to his left. He was resting his hand on his sword and failed to salute the commander, which Pilate though was most unusual.

"Yes?" Pilate replied.

"Seize him!" the centurion ordered to Pilate's surprise.

"What? What is the meaning of this?" Pilate protested as two soldiers quickly grabbed his arms.

"Stop," Claudia yelled as she tried to pull Pilate from their grasp, only to meet the backside of the centurion's hand, knocking her backwards where she stumbled and fell hard to the pier.

Pilate immediately put up a fierce struggle protesting the unprovoked assault. "Stop this," he ordered to deaf ears.

The centurion struck him twice with his vine staff knocking him to his knees. "Silence!" he ordered.

Pilate knew he was defeated. He had no recourse but submit. Kneeling and bleeding from the blows to his forehead, he looked to Claudia who was partially sitting up, dazed. "Claudia," he whispered.

"I said silence," the centurion yelled as he struck him again, this time into unconsciousness.

"Ohhhh," Pilate moaned as he awakened inside a wagon rattling toward Rome. The thirty-kilometer[94] trip from the port to the city center passed by vineyards and pomegranate groves full of workers picking the ripened fruits before the cold temperatures of November blanketed the foothills. "Where am I?" Pilate asked as he tried to sit up.

"No," Claudia said gently. "Be still," she said as she easily pushed his head back onto her lap, which was covered with his blood. "Just rest, Marcus."

"The pier... Are you....?"

"Shhhh. It's ok," she assured him. "I'm fine." Pilate saw her swollen lip and before he could ask, she said, "They struck me, but it was nothing. I'm ok."

Pilate relented and eased his head further into her lap. The pain was very present as he tried to focus his eyes on her. "Where are they taking us?" he asked.

Claudia calmly answered, "Tullianum."

Pilate's eyes opened wider as he forced himself to sit up. He looked out the window ignoring the throbbing headache as he felt the side of his head where it had been bleeding. Claudia used a bloody cloth to apply pressure on the wound. Pilate took her hand and looked her in the eyes. "Tullianum?"

"Yes. I heard the guards say to take us there."

"You too?" Pilate asked. "Why are they...."

Claudia stopped him. "Marcus. It doesn't matter........."

"It does!" he said forcefully, wincing at the exertion. "It does. You have no part in what I do or what happens to me as a soldier." He realized Claudia was calm and expressed no fear. "I'm sorry that this is happening."

"Marcus. I love you and have no regrets for anything," she said. "I trust we are in God's hands."

"God's hands?" he asked. "Which god are you referring to? What do you mean......."

---

[94] Thirty kilometers = twenty miles

"Marcus," she said as she interrupted him. "Jesus. I believe he was the son of God almighty. That god."

Pilate looked at her intently. He could see the same confidence and calmness Jesus showed as He was preparing for execution. He turned and looked out the window as the wagon neared the outskirts of Rome. He could see some crosses on the sides of the road, about twelve, lined up across from each other in staggered order. Men and women were being crucified and their crimes were being displayed with small signs hanging above their heads for all who entered Rome to see. It was a common method of deterrence that Romans used when they punished their criminals.

Theft
Murder
Sedition
Christian

"Christian," he whispered. "They are crucifying Christians." Pilate and Claudia knew the followers of Jesus were being called Christians because they believed Jesus was the Christ of the Jews, the Messiah, who came to save his people from their sins by being a blood sacrifice to God on their behalf.

Claudia looked out the window with Pilate as they passed the Christian who struggled to raise himself on the cross to get a breath. "I believe in Jesus," he said loudly enough to be heard over the rattling wagon, then slumped back down and continued his struggle to breathe.

"Oh, Marcus," Claudia said as she laid her head on Pilate's shoulder. "They are executing him for his belief."

Pilate winced and moaned as he slumped over to the side and closed his eyes. He fell back into unconsciousness hearing his wife calling his name as he blacked out.

"Ohhh." Pilate moaned as he weakly opened his eyes to look around. The room was dark and smelled of urine and feces. His head was throbbing from the blows he had taken from the centurion at the pier. 'What...?" He tried to focus his eyes, but they were still blurry from the assault. He smacked his lips and tasted his blood that had trickled down his face and onto his lips. "Claudia?" he called.

No answer.

Slowly the darkness seeped away as his eyes adjusted to the dim light. He saw something glitter on the floor and scooted toward it. As it came into focus, he could see it was a dagger. He picked it up and felt the smooth blade that extended from the grip. The moonlight reflected off the shiny metal. He knew why it was there. It was left as an honorable way for him to exit this world, suicide. It was customary for Roman soldiers who had disgraced the empire to voluntarily resign their position by suicide. His thoughts of dispatching himself were quickly interrupted.

"Ow!" he yelled and scooted sideways as a rat nipped at his bare leg. He kicked at the rat, who backed away a few feet and stared at him. It was not going to leave though it was challenged. Pilate began beating wildly at the rat with the dagger, forcing it into a corner where he slew it. He looked around the room in the dim light to see if any more rodents lay in wait, but saw nothing except filth, a pot and a pile of straw. He knew where he was. The Tullianum. He had visited prisoners there in the past and knew its reputation, but had no idea how the conditions of such a horrible place would leave any prisoner feeling hopeless.

"Claudia?" he yelled louder.

A guard walked up to the bars and yelled, "Silence, or I *will* silence you!" Pilate just looked at him as the guard smiled. "I see you've found our present," he said as he motioned to the dagger Pilate held. Blood from the rat was running onto Pilate's hand from the dagger. "You have until morning," the guard said as he turned and left Pilate in the dark cell with his head throbbing holding the bloody blade.

Pilate knew there was nothing he could do. He didn't fully understand why he would be thrown into prison for the events at Mount Gerizim. The advocation sent by Marcellus should provide some consideration for a lighter punishment. It was the only hope he could grasp. Why he was in prison was beyond him. Pilate reached into his pocket and retrieved the scroll and examined it briefly before returning it to his pocket. He leaned back against a wall, looked at a small window near the ceiling and sighed. It allowed just enough light and air in so he could breathe and not be totally blind in the dark.

Thoughts began to run wild through his head. He thought of the little girl he held at Mount Gerizim and the senseless slaughter. He thought of his wife and wondered if she was alive and hoped she wasn't suffering. His stomach growled from hunger though he had no appetite. His head throbbed. He thought of Jesus standing before him showing no fear. He could picture him clean and smiling, then bloodied from the assault, blood running down his face from the crown of thorns perched on top of his head digging into his brow. He could see his eyes again, clearly. He thought of the Christian hanging on the cross on the road into Rome confessing his belief about Jesus as the Son of God.

Pilate looked around the cell for a possible escape knowing it would be futile because he would be met by armed guards willing to dispatch him quickly rather than tend to him. Even with the dagger, he would be no match for them. Still, he had to assess his situation with an end goal of escape. There was none. He scooted across the floor and leaned his back against the wall once again. The dead rat in the corner looked back at him with dead eyes.

"Jesus," he whispered. "Why me? What have you done to me?" Suddenly a gust of wind blew through the bars of the window. Pilate looked up to see the moonbeams filtering into the cell. He looked at the dagger in his hand, shiny and sleek with blood on the blade. He turned it so that blade was resting against his chest in the center of his left rib cage, ready to penetrate into his heart. It was the noble thing to do. He curiously looked at the wrist guards on either side of the bloody blade forming a cross. He pictured Jesus on the cross, suffering, asking God his father to forgive those who were punishing and executing him and then declaring 'It is finished'." *What does that mean?* He remembered

Jesus telling him he had no authority to do anything unless it was given to him by God, his father. The earthquake, the guards and their testimony, the lightning and eclipse, the news of his resurrection; all of it rushed through his mind like a river flooding him with emotions and regret. Suddenly, a dove landed on the window ledge and cooed. Pilate looked up as the dove looked directly at him and then flew off.

The dagger clanked as it fell to the floor. Pilate slumped onto his knees, hung his head and wept.

---****---

The throne room where Caligula sat to administer justice was opulently decorated. It had to be because Caligula thought of himself as a god, and gods should only have the best of everything. It was an easy way for him to deny his mortality and face each day of uncertainty and the fear that someone may try and dispose of him that day in their quest for power. The young emperor was quick to dispatch anyone he believed was of such ambition and display their punishment by either crucifying them on the main road or displaying their severed head on a pole at the palace entrance. The gruesome displays revolted many of the citizens, but none dare speak against it.

Four guards led by a centurion rounded the corner into the great hall escorting a dirty, bloodied man in chains. He wore a Roman uniform absent the breastplate, helmet, and weapons. His uniform was dirty and smelled terribly. The side of his head had dried blood that crusted into his hair. "Marcus Pontius Pilate," the centurion announced as he saluted and handed Caesar the dagger.

Caligula smiled as he rose from his seat and gave a weak, almost nonexistent salute as though he was doing so out of obligation. "Pontius Pilate," he said as he approached the bound prisoner with dagger in hand. Pilate stood stoically as Caligula circled him, looking at the beaten man. It was the same manner in which Pilate inspected Jesus under questioning. "I see you chose the coward's way out," Caligula said as he tossed the dagger onto a table. "You smell terrible," Caligula said. "Clean him up!" he ordered as he returned to his seat.

A servant ran into the chamber with a pitcher of water and some cloths and began wiping the blood off Pilate's head and arms. Within a few minutes, the servant left with a bowl full of red water and bloody rags. Caligula slipped Pilate's dagger into his waistband and watched as they cleaned him up.

"So, we meet again," Caligula said with a smile as he picked at some grapes lying in a bowl on a table nearby. "Oh, my manners," he chuckled. "Are you hungry?" he asked as he held up a large grape. Pilate made no reply. "No?" Caligula popped the grape into his mouth and smiled. "Maybe some wine will freshen you up," he said with a full mouth as he held a goblet of wine out toward Pilate.

Nothing.

Caligula took a gulp to wash down the grape and sat the goblet on the table. "I am pleased to see our guards are taking good care of you since you wish for no food or wine," he said facetiously with a chuckle. Caligula looked to him for a response.

"Mighty Caesar," Pilate said breaking his silence. "Where is my wife?"

Caligula stood to his feet and approached Pilate. "So, he speaks." He motioned to the centurion, who saluted and left with two guards. "She is well taken care of, I assure you."

"Why am I here?"

Caligula struck him causing his nose to bleed. Pilate recoiled and bowed. "May I ask why I am here, great and powerful Caesar?"

"Well, you have been a bad boy, Pilate," Caligula said as though he was concerned. He loved how he was able to control every aspect of the conversation and the prisoner. He felt powerful. "You killed a lot of innocent people in Judea during your tenure."

"The rebellion at Mount Gerizim was unfortunate."

"Unfortunate?" Caligula laughed. "Two hundred slain, unarmed, innocent people and you say it is unfortunate?"

"They attacked my praefectus."

"Oh, the agony! They attacked *one* man and you slew them all?" Caligula paced across the room still speaking. "Oh, how I wish I could have been there to see that. To feel the blade as it pierced their flesh."

"I have a letter to senator Bracchus that I wish to deliver," Pilate said as he slowly reached into his pocket and withdrew the scroll.

"Senator Bracchus," Caligula said as he spun and saw the scroll. "Guard!" A guard approached and saluted. "Take this letter to senator Bracchus right away," he ordered. The guard saluted and Pilate handed him the letter. As the guard started to leave, Caligula called out.

"Wait! Maybe I should read this letter before senator Bracchus." He took the letter from the guard, unfurled the scroll and began to read outloud.

To: The esteemed and venerable senator Lucius Bracchus
From Linus Marcellus, overseer of Judea

Caligula lowered the letter. "So, Vitellius made Marcellus 'overseer' until I appoint a new prefect. Interesting," he said as he continued.

May the goddess of Pomona[95] fill your life to overflowing. The years that we have been acquainted have resided with me like a strong cedar. It is with great concern for justice that I send this request to you written from my own hand knowing that our quest for truth and justice reigns supreme. Before you stands one Marcus Pontius Pilate, governor of Judea, who has been summoned to stand before the senate by Lucius Vitellius, legate of Syria, for an unfortunate event involving many Samaritans and the Roman cavalry of Judea. The adjudication of the event must be borne by the senate knowing that the circumstances are unusual at best. After a lengthy conversation with Pilate and considerable reflection,

---

[95] Pomona – goddess of fruitful abundance

I ask that our trust and respect with each other may be borne through the leniency and mercy you show toward him when deciding the appropriate consequences to administer. Consider his lengthy service to Rome through his military career and leadership for a lifetime, not just the recent events in question and under scrutiny, when determining your proposal for remediation.

It is with all respect and diligence that I write this letter signed by my own hand. May the gods be with you.

Linus Marcellus

"That is a very touching advocation, Pilate," Caligula said as he rolled the scroll up and tossed it nonchalantly over his shoulder. The scroll clanged as it hit the floor and rolled. "I am certain senator Bracchus will appreciate the sincerity of the author when he reads it."

Pilate's heart sank. He knew there was not going to be a hearing before the senate, nor would justice be administered by them. For whatever reason, Caligula, and Caligula alone, was going to decide his fate.

"What I find interesting is that Marcellus did not allude to your decision to execute a god," Caligula said as returned to sit on his throne. "Why did you kill the Jew, Jesus?"

Pilate looked at Caligula, then lowered his eyes refusing to answer.

"Oh. So, you don't want to talk about killing a god?"

Pilate said nothing.

"Well, I have ways to make you talk," Caligula said as he motioned to the guard by the doorway. Within a few seconds, the centurion entered followed by two guards escorting Claudia.

"Claudia," Pilate called. The guard next to Pilate poked him in the stomach with the butt end of his sword causing Pilate to double over and fall to his knees gasping for air.

"Bowing will not help you now," Caligula said with a laugh.

Claudia was quiet as the guards positioned her next to her fallen husband. Her hands were tied in front of her, so she reached over to help Pilate stand. "I'm OK," she whispered.

Pilate struggled to regain his breath and stand. "Did they...?"

"Silence," Caligula barked. "You can chat later after you answer a few of my pressing questions," he said.

Pilate looked at the emperor curiously trying to focus his eyes. His head was still throbbing from the blows he received earlier. Everything seemed surreal, moving in slow motion. It was getting more difficult to speak. His mouth was dry. His legs weak.

"How did it feel to crucify this god, Jesus?" Caligula asked.

"Feel?" Pilate asked.

"Yes. Did he say he was a god?" Caligula asked with great interest.

Pilate looked at the emperor and remained silent.

"Oh. So, you still won't talk." Caligula stood next to Claudia who followed him with her eyes. "I have ways to make you talk, Pilate, of which I am certain you will not want to see," he said as he stroked her long, straggly hair.

"Stop!" Pilate pleaded.

Caligula looked at him waiting.

"Yes. He said he was the Son of God." Caligula walked behind the couple preparing for his next question when Pilate looked at Claudia with tears in his eyes and mouthed, "I'm sorry."

"I will also become a god someday," Caligula said matter of factly as he paced around the couple. "I heard he came back to life after a few days. Did he really?" Caligula asked.

"Yes," Pilate said without hesitation.

"How can a man who is dead return back to life?"

Pilate took a deep breath. "Through the power of Almighty God."

"Then, you believe this Jesus was a god who died and came back to life?"

Pilate looked deep into Caligula's eyes. "I do." He felt complete calmness flood through his body, as if he had just walked through a warm, cleansing waterfall. He remembered the look in

Jesus's face just before he was taken away to be crucified. He could picture the blood running along the thorns and dripping onto his hands. He looked down to see his own blood dripping from his nose onto his bound hands.

Caligula leaned in close to Pilate. His yellow, crooked teeth and bad breath were revolting to the prisoner, but he didn't move. "So, are you a Chris-ti-an then?" Caligula asked slowly, carefully pronouncing every syllable.

Pilate looked up and saw deep into Caligula's eyes. They were dark and empty. It was death staring him in the face. "I am," Pilate said without breaking his gaze.

"I have waited years for this meeting, 'javelin man'," Caligula said as he pulled Pilate's dagger from his tunic and thrust it into Pilate, entering under his left rib and piercing his lung. Pilate let out a moan and opened his eyes wide never breaking his gaze with the emperor who held fast. The centurion standing by them drew his sword and stood ready to slay Pilate should he decide to fight the emperor.

"Marcus," Claudia yelled as she tried to break free from the guard.

"You should have never embarrassed me by calling me 'little soldier boots' in front of my grandfather," Caligula said as he twisted the knife severing an artery.

"No!" Claudia yelled.

"Unnggh," Pilate moaned as he started to slump. Caligula withdrew the dagger and slumped with Pilate as he watched the blood pour out of the wound. Pilate fell to his knees and looked to Claudia. "I love you," he whispered, weaving on his knees.

"I love you," Claudia mouthed and closed her eyes.

Caligula fell to his knees with Pilate and leaned in close. "Any last words, 'javelin man'?" he whispered as he looked into his eyes.

Pilate looked at him, eyes barely open, "Jesus, forgive him," he said as his eyes rolled back into his head, and he fell sideways and died.

Caligula scooted backwards in surprise. "Forgive me?" He looked at his hand holding the blood covered dagger, then back to the dead man lying before him. He threw the dagger aside and wiped the blood onto his white tunic as the guard released Claudia who flung herself onto her husband, crying.

"Marcus," she said softly. Suddenly, she started to choke and grabbed at her chest. Her eyes grew wide as she lost consciousness and slumped onto her husband, dead from a heart attack.

Caligula sat before the dead couple, staring in disbelief as the centurion sheathed his sword.

Epilogue

There is no record of how Pontius Pilate died. Some scholars believe he was called to Rome for the event at Mount Gerizim and was offered a dagger to commit suicide in prison rather than face a trial before Caligula and subsequent humiliation. Others believe he faced the emperor and confessed his belief where he was executed by Caligula.

There is no record of Pontius Pilate becoming a Christian. The Orthodox church bestowed a sainthood upon Pilate believing he became a Christian before he died. I choose to agree.

Caligula continued to be an evil emperor of Rome. He continued to execute anyone that he believed could be a threat to his rule. In 40 AD Caligula decided he was going to move to Alexandria Egypt where he expected he could be worshipped as a living god. The thought of the emperor leaving Rome with no political leadership infuriated many of the senators who conspired to assassinate Caligula. On January 24, 41 AD Cassius Chaerea, a Tribune in the Praetorian Guard, led a group of Guard members and senators to assassinate the emperor by stabbing him 30 times. An interesting note is that Elder Gaius Julius Caesar (Julius Caesar) and Younger Gaius Julius Caesar (Caligula) both had the same name, were both assassinated by a conspirator named Cassius (Cassius Longinus and Cassius Chaerea) and both died of stab wounds. The irony is that the Praetorian Guard was established to protect the emperor, yet they were the instrument in his death.

Joseph Ben Caiaphas is believed to have moved to Crete where he lived out his life until 66 AD. Some scholars believe he was sorrowful about Jesus's death and repented becoming a Christian. He lived to see the burning of Rome in 64 AD and the beginning of the Jewish wars in 66 AD.

Christianity spread rapidly throughout the Mediterranean and beyond. Nero Claudius Caesar Augustus Germanicus became emperor in 54 AD following Claudius, the bumbling 'fool' that Caligula allowed to live through his reign of terror. Emperor Nero is believed to have burned Rome in 64 AD to 'clean it up' and blamed it on the Christians. He mercilessly crucified and executed thousands of Christians. In 66 AD Nero took temple funds from the Jews for Rome to use, which resulted in a revolt and the following Jewish wars in which more than one million Jews and Christians were killed.

Pontius Pilate will forever be known as the man who conducted the trial of Jesus of Nazareth. Hopefully, this novel has opened your eyes to the possibility of how that occurred, why, and what happened to the judge; Marcus Pontius Pilate – the Javelin Man.

Author's Comments

Writing a book that involves researching the Bible and accurately representing it was a daunting task. I am not a theologian nor claim to be. I tried to make sure I did not misrepresent what was in the Bible while creating the flow of the storyline. This novel is a fiction based on research with an emphasis to accurately represent Bible content. The gospels often complement each other with similar references from different perspectives sometimes covering different timeframes. Luke was a doctor. Peter a fisherman. Mark a man of action. Mathew a tax collector

One of the major issues I came across was in Mathew 27:62

"The _next_ day, the one after Preparation Day, the Chief Priests and the Pharisees went to Pilate."

Mathew was a tax collector and, as such, would have been educated, detailed, organized and meticulous with his recordkeeping. Otherwise, he could be punished by the Romans for not collecting taxes properly. He was one who would pay attention to detail and likely document some of his observations. Mathew states it was the _next_ day, or the day of Passover, when the Chief Priests and Pharisees went to Pilate to secure the tomb. The group would have included either Caiaphas or Annas as the Chief Priests.

Mathew is the only book that contains this reference in scripture. No one else recorded the events this way. According to Mathew there were several hours from the afternoon of the Passover (about six PM) to the early morning when no one would have been at the tomb. There is a reference that Mary stayed after Jesus was laid there, but we have no idea for how long. That would leave a window of several hours where the disciples could have come and stolen away the body before Caiaphas and the Roman guards secured the tomb.

It seemed reasonable to me that Caiaphas would take Longinus, the Roman centurion in charge of the crucifixion, to the tomb to secure it and to verify that Jesus was still buried there. Think about it; Caiaphas believed that the teachings of Jesus were so significant they would destroy the Jewish nation and beliefs. One of the priests with him even said,

"Sir," they said, "we remember that while he was still alive that deceiver said, 'After three days I will rise again.' [64] So give the order for the tomb to be made secure until the third day. Otherwise, his disciples may come and steal the body and tell the people that he has been raised from the dead. This last deception will be worse than the first."   Mathew 27:63-64

Does it not make sense that Caiaphas would have the tomb inspected before it was sealed? He would have to make sure Jesus was still there, otherwise the 'deception' would have already taken place, and he would be a fool to allow it to happen.

The Jews would have become defiled if they entered the tomb on the Sabbath. That would require them to go through a cleansing process afterwards. Nothing is recorded about that. I doubt that Caiaphas was concerned with becoming defiled considering the significance of the situation. The verification of Jesus in the tomb would have superseded any other law or requirement, in my opinion, because if he was not there, the entire Jewish nation was in peril, according to Caiaphas's belief as recorded in the gospels.

It seems reasonable that Longinus would go considering he could identify Jesus. He would also be responsible for securing the tomb and assuring the body was not removed. Thus, I believe he also would have entered the tomb and personally verified Jesus was still there before it was sealed. His life depended on it.

The posting of the guard would be such that no one would be able to obtain access to the tomb. My research of Roman military strategies revealed multiple guards would have been posted in redundant positions on the approach to the tomb from any angle with each guard able to see the others and respond to any threat in unison. Their response would have been to fight to the death because allowing anyone to break the seal would result in capital punishment to the soldiers who failed their mission.

I've talked with several friends, missionaries and pastors and was surprised to see that no one noticed the request to secure the tomb was 'the next day.' I never noticed it before after reading Mathew many times during my life. A small verse that is easily overlooked yet has significant implications.

This is but one example of my dilemma putting this story together. The difficulty of filling in the gaps where the story made sense was real. I did not want to add or detract to the Gospels, yet I needed to fill in where needed. Thus, a fictional novel.

The letters that were presented between Pilate and Tiberius were factual. The deposition contrived. The letter of recommendation to Senator Bracchus from Marcellus was contrived yet helped to paint the picture of Pilate's relief when he returned to Rome to face charges regarding Mount Gerizim, which is factual.

The Roman culture was entrenched with gods, so the idea of Jesus being a god was not far-fetched at all. In fact, it was almost welcomed. Another god to add to their list. The senate hearing to make him a god is recorded history. The dialogue contrived.

The scenes where persons interacted were fictional based on fact. For example, the scene between Sejanus and Drusus was fictional, but the animosity and interaction where Drusus slapped Sejanus was recorded history. How it happened and what was said was fictional. The end result was the fall out between the two, which is recorded history.

The trial of Jesus is well recorded, yet the gospels have little to say about anyone advocating for Jesus at the trial. The Apocrypha and other historical documents indicate many advocated for Jesus. The book of Nicodemus in the Apocrypha is a good example where people advocated for Jesus's release, thus the examples I used in the book.

Javelin-Man was a challenging work to pull together while keeping the integrity of the biblical account. I loved the research and just thinking, "What would that look like?" The visual of the feeding of the thousands was a wonderful adventure for me, as was the meeting between Claudia and Pilate and many, many other scenes.

I hope you enjoyed the story and, most of all, hope it spoke to your heart.

Jerry

Gerald Rainey   Javelin Man

References

Cover photo is IStock photo #1365194726

Roman Standards — Page 9 —
https://etc.usf.edu/clipart/1900/1915/romanstandards_1_lg.gif

Jerusalem — Page 71 & 136
https://cdn.dribbble.com/users/211211/screenshots/3056638/jerusalem clr.jpg?compress=1&resize=400x300

Villa Jovis — Page 80
Villa Jovis of Emperor Tiberius on the Island of Capri, AD 27 — Archaeology Illustrated License

https://en.wikipedia.org/wiki/Pontius_Pilate

https://en.wikipedia.org/wiki/Sejanus

https://en.wikipedia.org/wiki/Princeps

https://bible.org/article/roman-military-new-testament

https://www.britannica.com/biography/Herod-Antipas

https://en.wikipedia.org/wiki/Caligula

https://en.wikipedia.org/wiki/Sanhedrin_trial_of_Jesus

https://www.britannica.com/biography/Pontius-Pilate

https://en.wikipedia.org/wiki/Lucius_Seius_Strabo

https://www.thefamouspeople.com/profiles/pontius-pilate-5073.php

https://www.thoughtco.com/roman-army-of-the-roman-republic-120904

https://en.wikipedia.org/wiki/Imperial_Roman_army

https://en.wikipedia.org/wiki/Lorica_segmentata

https://en.wikipedia.org/wiki/Ludi_Romani#:~:text=The%20Ludi%20Romani%20(%22Roman%20Games,September%205%20to%20September%2019.

http://www.novaroma.org/ludi/html/history.html

https://roman-empire.net/society/games/

https://en.wikipedia.org/wiki/Pilum

https://en.wikipedia.org/wiki/Bellum_Batonianum

https://en.wikipedia.org/wiki/Mount_Gerizim

https://en.wikipedia.org/wiki/Julius_Caesar

https://en.wikipedia.org/wiki/Roman_Republic

https://en.wikipedia.org/wiki/Augustus

https://en.wikipedia.org/wiki/Senate_of_the_Roman_Republic#:~:text=The%20Senate%20was%20the%20governing,and%20later%20by%20the%20censors.&text=Originally%20the%20chief%2Dmagistrates%2C%20the,consuls%2C%20appointed%20all%20new%20senators.

https://en.wikipedia.org/wiki/Curia_of_Pompey

https://en.wikipedia.org/wiki/Mark_Antony

https://en.wikipedia.org/wiki/Tillius_Cimber

https://en.wikipedia.org/wiki/List_of_Roman_wars_and_battles

https://military-history.fandom.com/wiki/Tiberius

https://www.warhistoryonline.com/ancient-history/12-ranks-roman-military-officers.html?chrome=1

https://en.wikipedia.org/wiki/Roman_salute

https://en.wikipedia.org/wiki/Pilum#:~:text=The%20pilum%20(Latin%3A%20%5B%CB%88pi%CB%90%C9%AB%CA%8A%CC%83,long%20with%20a%20pyramidal%20head.

https://en.wikipedia.org/wiki/Herod_Antipas

https://en.wikipedia.org/wiki/Tiberius

https://en.wikipedia.org/wiki/Claudius

https://en.wikipedia.org/wiki/Weddings_in_ancient_Rome

https://www.shutterstock.com/search/roman+wedding

https://medium.com/lessons-from-history/tiberius-5578a9b24453

https://warspot.net/384-the-praetorians-the-emperors-guard

https://en.wikipedia.org/wiki/Agrippina_the_Elder

https://en.wikipedia.org/wiki/Pilate%27s_court

https://imperiumromanum.pl/en/roman-geography/transport-and-travel-in-ancient-rome/

https://en.wikipedia.org/wiki/Caesarea_Maritima

https://www.laurinburgexchange.com/opinion/35422/jerusalem-in-the-days-of-christ#:~:text=In%20Jesus'%20day%2C%20Jerusalem's%20population,allowing%20people%20to%20pass%20through.

https://en.wikipedia.org/wiki/Nero_Julius_Caesar

https://itsgila.com/highlightscaesarea.htm

https://en.wikipedia.org/wiki/Barabbas

http://www.biblecharts.org/biblelandnotes/Distances%20From%20Jerusalem.pdf

https://blog.adw.org/wp-content/uploads/2018/03/37-Miracles-of-Jesus-in-Chronological-Order.pdf

https://www.gotquestions.org/Jairus-in-the-Bible.html

https://en.wikipedia.org/wiki/Ballista

https://en.wikipedia.org/wiki/Germanicus

https://historycooperative.org/the-roman-standards/

https://en.wikipedia.org/wiki/Villa_Jovis

https://en.wikipedia.org/wiki/Caiaphas

http://www.imperium-romana.org/roman-weapons.html

http://bibleprobe.com/antipas.htm

https://en.wikipedia.org/wiki/Pallas_(freedman)

https://en.wikipedia.org/wiki/List_of_Roman_deities

https://en.wikipedia.org/wiki/Antonia_Minor

https://en.wikipedia.org/wiki/Naevius_Sutorius_Macro

https://en.wikipedia.org/wiki/Hall_of_Hewn_Stones

https://en.wikipedia.org/wiki/Sanhedrin

https://en.wikipedia.org/wiki/Roman_consul

https://www.lifeandland.org/2009/02/the-feedings-of-the-multitudes-when-where-and-why/

https://www.gotquestions.org/Nicodemus-in-the-Bible.html

https://en.wikipedia.org/wiki/Pharisees

https://en.wikipedia.org/wiki/Nicodemus

https://hermeneutics.stackexchange.com/questions/20781/when-does-the-cleansing-of-the-temple-happen-at-the-beginning-of-jesuss-minist

https://en.wikipedia.org/wiki/Joseph_of_Arimathea

https://en.wikipedia.org/wiki/Demographic_history_of_Jerusalem

https://en.wikipedia.org/wiki/Passover

https://bible-history.com/sketches/palace-of-caiaphas

https://i2.wp.com/www.israelhebrew.com/wp-content/uploads/map-of-ancient-jerusalem.jpg

http://www.thenazareneway.com/sabbath/39_prohib_sabbath.htm

https://www.biblicalarchaeology.org/daily/archaeology-today/biblical-archaeology-topics/how-was-jesus-tomb-sealed/

https://en.wikipedia.org/wiki/Saint_Stephen

https://oll-resources.s3.us-east-2.amazonaws.com/oll3/store/titles/1975/1333.08_Bk.pdf

https://ia800303.us.archive.org/5/items/actapilatiimport00slut/actapilatiimport00slut.pdf

https://en.wikipedia.org/wiki/Gabbatha

https://en.wikipedia.org/wiki/Religion_in_ancient_Rome

https://greekgodsandgoddesses.net/roman/

https://www.biblicalarchaeology.org/daily/biblical-topics/crucifixion/roman-crucifixion-methods-reveal-the-history-of-crucifixion/

https://lampuntomyfeetministries.church/wp-content/uploads/2021/06/Letter-of-Tiberius-to-Pilate.pdf

https://ibuzzle.com/roman-army-ranks-in-order

https://world-religions.info/dositheus/

https://en.wikipedia.org/wiki/Mamertine_Prison

https://en.wikipedia.org/wiki/Marcellus_(prefect_of_Judea)

https://en.wikipedia.org/wiki/Lucius_Vitellius_(consul_34)

https://www.julianspriggs.co.uk/Pages/Pilate

https://www.vita-romae.com/roman-carriages.html

https://en.wikipedia.org/wiki/Hopscotch

https://en.wikipedia.org/wiki/Tiberius_Gemellus

https://www.history.com/news/did-caligula-really-make-his-horse-a-consul

https://www.worldhistory.org/article/1028/roman-shipbuilding--navigation/

https://i.pinimg.com/originals/f1/df/c1/f1dfc1c386c21cabe62b43305e3dc10c.jpg

https://www.vita-romae.com/roman-ships.html

https://www.romanports.org/en/articles/ports-in-focus/181-portus-rome-s-imperial-port.html

https://eldredgrove.com/comprehensive-list-of-ancient-roman-male-names/

https://imperiumromanum.pl/en/roman-society/population-of-roman-empire/

Gerald Rainey   Javelin Man

https://en.wikipedia.org/wiki/Ludi

https://dribbble.com/shots/3056638-Ancient-Jerusalem

Made in United States
North Haven, CT
17 April 2024